RESCUE ME

FORGET THE PAST
BOOK 1

LAUREN CONNOLLY

RESCUE ME

When the universe screws you over, adopt a dog.

Paige Herbert doesn't know how she lost control of her life. Friday morning, she had her future planned. Sunday night, she's jobless and staring at her half-naked fiancé and a woman wearing her green robe. Taking refuge in her childhood home, Paige decides this time around her life partner will have four legs instead of two. But her newly rescued pit bull is in bad need of obedience training … and the perfect guy for the job has Paige forgetting the past.

Dash Lamont doesn't want to go back to jail. Out on parole and working at an animal shelter, he's focused on living life by the rules. And number one on the list: avoid temptation. Unfortunately, Paige parks in the middle of Dash's well-ordered life, demanding his attention with her offbeat conversation and sinful curves. Despite his decision to keep his distance, he somehow finds himself agreeing to her plea for help.

Awkward attempts at flirting, late-night dancing to jazz music, and a chance taken at a Halloween party lure the hesitant pair down a sensual road.

But when sins of the past work against the newly budding romance, Dash will need to decide whether to take his chance on love or stay in his safe lane, watching as Paige drives off without him.

Sign up for my newsletter for book news and freebies! All subscribers get a FREE copy of LOVE AND THE LIBRARY.

Get my free book:
https://www.laurenconnollyromance.com/free-book

ISBN-13: 978-1-949794-37-3

CONTENT WARNING

This book contains scenes with cheating (not committed by either of the main characters). This book discusses a vehicular accident, incarceration, and animal mistreatment.

CHAPTER 1

PAIGE

One of these houses is mine. I'm just not exactly sure *which* one.

A sigh pushes out, weighty and exhausted, from deep in my chest. The sun set hours ago, back when I was still on the highway. Trying to read the tiny print on each of these mailboxes isn't easy after staring out the windshield for the past two days. My eyes practically crackle, begging me to close them.

Sleep. Just go to sleep.

"That one! I…I think."

I pull up alongside the curb, letting the heavy engine rumble on as I flip through photos on my phone. Martin sent me a picture two weeks ago, a selfie of him with a large tan house behind him that looks like the one I've stopped in front of. Unfortunately, the homes on either side of it are mirror reflections.

Normally, Martin's preference for uniformity doesn't bother me. Tonight though, I wish he had picked a weird bungalow with daisies painted on the siding and a turquoise front door. Just so I know, without a hint of a doubt, that I am parking in front of *my* house.

And I am definitely parking because I need to pick one of these clone homes before I drive myself mad, puttering around this neighborhood all night.

As I shut down the engine, the whole car settles as if she's ready to sleep for the night.

"Enjoy your rest, Penelope," I mutter to the steering wheel.

I need a bed bad. A pounding started in my temples way before I even crossed the Louisiana/Mississippi border. The headache comes courtesy of long hours in the car, paired with my hair being pulled up into a high, messy bun. I'd let the heavy mass down if I wasn't terrified of its condition. Two days' worth of greasiness has built up. I doubt removing my hairband would even do anything. The hair would likely continue sitting on top of my head, permanently reshaped.

My priorities have changed; before bed, I need a shower. The vision of scrubbing a thick lather of shampoo into my scalp plays in my brain like a porno. I can imagine the transformation of the knotted mess into its normal, smooth cascade.

"Butter on bread," my mom always says when she affectionately tugs on a strand.

Not sure I approve of being compared to a boring slice of white bread, but I take comfort in the fact that she's simply referring to my complexion and hair color rather than my personality.

When I push the car door open, the heavy New Orleans air embraces me. It is almost as warm and wet as an actual shower, but nowhere near as refreshing. The humidity sits on my skin, weighing me down as I trudge up the front walk of a house that I hope is mine.

The easy solution would've been to just call Martin on Friday night when I decided to change my travel plans. That way, my fiancé would be waiting out on the porch, ready to wave me down.

Instead, I chose the surprise method. I'd like to convince myself that this is a romantic gesture.

I just couldn't stay away from you for two more weeks!

In reality, my silence arises from shame. Whenever I let my thumb hover over his number, I couldn't even imagine how the conversation would go.

"Hey, honey! Guess what. I lost my job!" I whisper under my

breath and pause with my foot on the bottom step leading up to the elevated porch.

Well, I guess I *could* say that.

Now that I'm here, potentially a few steps away from Martin, the words don't seem so inadequate. Depressing? Yeah, sure. But I can clearly envision his face, how his blond brows will dip in the middle as he scowls. Not *at* me, but *with* me. I can taste the glass of red wine he'll have poured for me as he rages over the unfair treatment.

That's when I realize why the need for surprise. I don't actually want to *talk* about how I got fired from my dream job. All I want is to see my anger reflected in the face of my partner. To feel connected to him in a way I haven't in a while.

With the moving plans, and Martin preparing to start his residency down here, and me trying to finish up all my large projects before going remote, we've barely talked. I can't even remember the last time I looked him in the eyes during a conversation. We usually just shout to each other from opposite rooms.

And sex? Well…it's been some time.

As I knock on the mystery door I hope is mine, I make a resolution. Whether I find Martin in this clone house or the one next door or the next street over, when I finally locate my fiancé, the first thing I'm going to do is stare deep into his eyes. I'll hold his gaze until our connection is firmly reestablished. Then—after a shower—I'm going to jump his bones.

Light spills into the dark night from around the edges of the curtains. At least that means whoever lives here, hopefully Martin, is still awake. After the polite taps of my knock ring out, the steady pad of footsteps sound behind the door. I brace myself, ready to stare my fiancé down.

Only Martin doesn't open the door.

A small, slim woman dressed in a robe stands before me. She is adorably petite. I could practically fit her in my pocket. Her bare feet peek out from under the floor-length robe, and her long brown hair lays in a damp mass over her shoulders.

Envy spikes hard through me. Clearly, this woman has just taken a shower. My greasy strands weep in envy.

Also, her appearance makes it clear my navigation skills have failed me. I am no closer to my own glorious shower, having no idea which one of these houses Martin bought for the two of us to live in.

"Sorry. I thought this might be my house. Do you know a blond man? About so tall?" I hold my hand a few inches above my head like the sleep-drunk idiot I am.

I'm ready to continue describing my fiancé out of pure desperation when I notice the woman's face. With a stranger knocking on her door at midnight, I would expect confusion or annoyance. But if I had to guess, her slack-jawed, wide-eyed stare is closer to horror.

Apparently, my need for a shower is even direr than I knew.

"I told you I'd get it…" The familiar rusty voice drifts from behind the stranger as my fiancé trots down a set of stairs visible just over her shoulder.

The showered girl shuffles back, so I have a clear view of Martin, clad in only a pair of gym shorts, his hair just as gloriously damp from a recent cleaning as the woman in front of me.

Our eyes meet. His top half stops, but his bottom half doesn't get the memo. Instead, one of his bare feet slips on the wooden step, and he lands hard on his ass, shocked gaze never leaving mine.

So, this *is* the right house.

It's just everything else in the world that is wrong.

Whatever way I might want to interpret this situation is made impossible when I flick my eyes back to the stranger, who I now realize is wearing *my* green cotton robe. Red splotches scorch along the tops of her cheekbones, and guilty tears pool on her lashes.

Something dark and sickening rolls in my stomach, but I flash-freeze it. After one last look at the boy I've loved since my senior year of high school, I turn to the girl he chose to hurt me for.

"You can keep the robe." Reaching out, I clasp the doorknob. "And the man." I wrench the door closed on the most devastating scene of my life and sprint back to my sleeping car.

Penelope revs to life, more dependable than any man could ever be.

I shift into first gear and tear down the street, not caring who I wake up. With the roar of my sweet girl's engine, I can't hear Martin shouting.

But I can see him. In my rearview mirror, he sprints down the street after me. I skid around a corner and lose sight of him.

And he loses me.

I drive in an emotional fog, unable to dislodge the frozen ball of grief in my chest. The devastation sticks to the inside of my skull, blocking my ability to think.

It's only when I almost run a red light that I realize I shouldn't be driving.

Pulling into the next parking lot, I somehow end up in the drive-through lane of a fast-food joint. Functioning on autopilot, I roll down my window when I reach the speaker.

"What do you want?" the woman asks with the complete disinterest that can only be achieved by someone employed for the night shift at a drive-through.

The question hits me hard. Acting as a chisel, it splits the ice in my chest apart.

Grief flows free.

"What do I want?" I laugh, high-pitched and manic. "Oh, I don't know. How about a job? Or a home? Maybe my dignity?"

And now, I'm crying.

"Um…we serve chicken."

I've gone insane. Martin's betrayal has turned me into a raving loon who drives around New Orleans in the middle of the night, scaring fast-food workers.

This isn't me. I'm not this *type of weird.*

"Oh. Right. Of course." Swiping away the tears blurring my vision and pulling in a few choking breaths, I attempt to read the glowing menu. "I guess a family meal then."

"Eight, twelve, or sixteen pieces?"

The cracked ice in my chest has given way to a massive, aching hole.

"Better make it sixteen."

"You want it with sides?"

I'm not going to be able to manage many more of these questions without the unhinged laughing/crying returning.

"Yeah, whatever sides are popular. And biscuits, please. I'm gonna need a whole lot of biscuits." A sob makes the last word come out choked.

She rattles off the total, and I pull around to the window to pay. A short woman wearing a goofy chicken hat gives me a kinder smile than I was expecting after my breakdown.

"I slipped an extra biscuit in there," she whispers while passing me the armload of fried comfort.

"Thank you," I mutter, keeping my eyes to myself and hoping I never run into this lovely woman again.

For a moment, I park and consider consuming the entire order myself.

The idea is tempting.

But I still need a shower and a bed.

Penelope's engine purrs like a comforting embrace as I pull back out on the road. The headlights point toward my childhood home.

My parents are about to get a late-night visitor, bearing fried chicken and a broken heart.

CHAPTER 2

DASH

TWO WEEKS LATER

"You smell like piss."

Cole glares at me and doesn't bother to take a step back. He invades my office with his presence and pungent scent.

"That's what happens when three different cats use you as a litter box." He crosses his arms, smirking down at me. "You saying I should take the rest of the day off to go wash my clothes?"

I snort, which is a mistake because it just drags in more of the urine smell. We both know he can't afford to take any time off. Every cent of his paycheck counts.

Which is apparently why he's in my space.

"Remember, the rent's due by Friday. It'd be better if I could get your half before then."

"Yeah, yeah. I'll get it to you."

Cole is always on my case about rent. The guy gets antsy about money. I can't complain though. He's just trying to keep us on track.

Not that I'm not, but I have a few more debts to deal with than he does.

"And you might want to go help Kim out." He throws a thumb over his shoulder.

"Kim?"

"The new front-desk worker. She's got an intense customer, and I don't think she's handling it well."

Crap.

The last thing I need is for our newest hire to quit during her first shift because of some random customer yelling at her. I shut off my computer screen and slide past Cole, holding my breath until I'm a good ten feet away from my roommate.

As I jog toward the front of the shelter, the sound of barking echoes through the walls to my right. A door opens, and out walks Mandy, one of our regular volunteers. Her gray hair tumbles in a riot of curls, and her face has turned cherry red with exertion. The cause of her disheveled state comes in the form of a black pit bull, straining at the end of his leash. Mandy handles him like a pro, keeping a firm grip, biceps bulging, causing me to wonder if I'll be in as good of shape as her when I'm sixty.

"How's it going, Mandy?"

"Oh, you know, Bourbon here is just happy for his turn outside."

The dog's nose points straight for the door that leads to the grassy area at the back of our facilities.

"Hey, Bourbon. You gonna go easy on Mandy?"

The dog disregards me until I pull a biscuit out of my pocket. I hold the treat in my fist and command him to sit. He hesitates a second before his butt hits the tiles. I push the treat out between my knuckles, letting him have the biscuit while making sure he doesn't take any fingers in the process.

I nod at Mandy before continuing toward the front, glad to know we've got people showing up today. If the volunteers don't take the dogs for their walks, it falls on the staff.

Not that I mind spending time with the animals, but that, plus a shit ton of paperwork I've got to deal with, would mean a late night.

"I'm sorry, ma'am, but I don't know what dog you're talking about." An apologetic voice sounds from around the corner.

"She's here. She has to be. This is where they told me they were taking her. Just go look. Please. She's got the sweetest brown eyes you'd ever want, and her fur is Halloween tie-dye," a huskier yet still feminine voice responds.

Halloween tie-dye?

"I don't know what that means." The first speaker sounds uncomfortable, and when I turn the corner, I recognize the curvy redhead my manager introduced me to last week.

Panic is clear in her eyes as she glances over at me. She looks ready to duck under the desk for escape.

I stifle my sigh. If someone being weird is throwing the new hire for this much of a loop, I'm not sure how long she's going to stick around. New Orleans is full of oddballs, and a bunch of them want to adopt animals.

Remembering the name Cole gave me, I approach with what I hope is a reassuring smile. "Hey, Kim. There a problem?"

When I reach the counter, the owner of the second voice comes into view, her hazel eyes flicking to mine. In their depths, I detect frustration.

Stepping up to the high counter, I use my much taller body to draw all of the customer's attention, hoping to give Kim a break so she won't flee.

The customer is a young woman, far from the most intimidating of people we've had wander in here. She tilts her chin up, but doesn't have to crane her head as much as most girls do to meet my gaze. The stranger is pretty, in the classic blonde American-pie kind of way. Her skin doesn't have a single freckle marking its smooth paleness, and her delicate lips sit pretty and pink under a cute nose.

Sweet. The thought pops, unbidden, into my mind.

She's the embodiment of the word. Like a pink lollipop.

A sense of familiarity spikes in the back of my brain, but I don't understand it.

There's only one crack in her perfect candy form, and that's a delicate slash through her slim eyebrow. That scar, small as it is, makes her seem more approachable. If only slightly.

"Um, this woman thinks we have her dog." Kim glances down at the computer screen, then to the flyers on the desk in front of her, then up to me, as if in one of these three places she'll find the answer to the problem.

"I don't think it. I *know* it." The woman may look sweet, but she sounds like an angry hornet stuck in a Coke can.

Again, I have to suppress another sigh. Running the front desk hasn't been my job for eight months, but it looks like, today, I need to take the reins.

"How exactly do you know we have your dog? Was it removed from your care? Did you abandon it here?"

The lollipop gasps, clearly offended.

"No! I would *never* abandon her. The officer who picked her up said this is where I should come to get her."

"So, she was removed? If the court ordered—"

"No one took her from me! I'm the one who called the cops!" The young woman snaps her mouth shut, eyes going wide, clearly surprised by her outburst. Her gaze drops, and a frustrated breath ruffles a few blonde strands of hair that came loose from her ponytail.

Kim and I share a baffled look.

"Ma'am, I don't understand—"

"I'm not a *ma'am*. Ma'ams have their shit together." She lets out a soft growl, and I try not to think about how cute the sound is. "Sorry, sorry. I'm messing this up." Her voice lowers, almost as if she's talking to herself. "Get ahold of yourself."

I don't know what to make of this woman. For some reason, I feel the urge to circle around the counter and rub a reassuring hand over her back.

Since when did I become the comforting type?

Instead, I keep my voice level and firm, the way I would with a stressed animal. "Why don't you start at the beginning?"

The pretty customer blinks, raising her gaze enough to meet mine again. In the bright fluorescent light, I catch a hint of green just around her pupils.

"The beginning. Okay. Like a story. I can do that." She breathes in deep, as if settling herself, then starts the tale, almost rapid-fire with her words. "Yesterday, I was running. I've been doing that more lately because…well, that's not important. So, I was running. And I heard this sound. I don't wear headphones when I run. It's not safe. You should always be aware of your surroundings." She makes a wide gesture with her arms as if Kim and I are students in a self-defense class and she's the instructor. "The noise made me stop. Then, I heard it again. Like a whining. It was coming from a side street, so I walked toward it. The alley was filthy. Mud everywhere. But, you know, it's New Orleans. Everything is wet all the time. And New York wasn't pristine by any means. So, dirty street, no big deal, right? Then, I saw her."

The woman pauses, gaze distracted, as if she's replaying the memory, not seeing me or the shelter's waiting room anymore.

"Saw who?" Apparently, the story has Kim captivated because the redhead leans forward, voice hushed as she asks the question.

The woman blinks, coming back to us. "My dog. Well, I guess she's not technically *mine*. Yet. In a legal sense." The blonde places a piece of paper she's been clutching on the counter, smoothing it flat.

An adoption form.

"But she's mine in a *soulful* sense. I know she is. I found her. Or she found me." The customer worries her bottom lip. "She was in bad shape. Which is why I called 911. Because I didn't know what else to do. How to help her. But I know now. I want to take her home with me."

As I pick up the application, my eyes seek out the first line for some vital information.

Paige Herbert.

"Paige?"

She nods and gifts me with half a smile. The curve of those perfectly shaped lips sends a warning shot through me. Suddenly, I realize why she seems familiar.

I doubt I've ever met this particular girl before, but I've met her type. Dealt with them all through grade school. The Paige Herberts of the world—pale, blonde, pretty—are used to getting their way.

Teachers give them A's for showing up and smiling. Boys trip over themselves to carry their lunch trays. Everyone jockeys to sit next to them on the bus, and in class, and at the lunch table.

The rare times those girls took notice of me, their noses wrinkled, and their mouths sneered. They'd whisper behind their hands to friends and giggle as their mascara-lashed eyes flicked my way.

When I was a kid, the spoiled rich guys did their best to break me down physically, but it was the pampered blonde girls that messed with my psyche.

As an adult, I've done a good job avoiding Paige Herbert's kind.

It's in my best interest to get things figured out and send her on her way.

"What did the dog look like?" As far as I know, three dogs were picked up yesterday. My guess is, she's looking for the Pomeranian. After a bath, the thing was pretty cute, but those small dogs come with huge attitudes.

"Like I was saying, she's got these huge brown eyes that just carve out your heart. And she's this wonderful Halloween tie-dye color." The woman, Paige, stares at me with expectation, as if what she just said makes any sort of sense.

"So...pretty fluffy? About this big?" I use my hands to indicate something the size of a basketball.

Paige's light eyebrows dip down as her mouth pinches. "What? No. Her hair is short. And she's at least this tall." When she steps back from the counter, her hand hovers at mid-thigh.

I wish she hadn't done that.

Our counters are tall, about chest high on most people, to keep dogs that get loose from jumping over them. Now that Paige stands far enough away to indicate the size of the dog, I get a full view of her body.

She's wearing those stretchy exercise clothes that cling to every curve. And, hell, does she have some nice curves.

Before I can linger too long on the peaks and valleys of her luscious hips and chest, I tear my eyes away and pretend to read over her application while forcing my mind back to dogs.

The only one that came in yesterday that even remotely fits her description is a pit bull, which is not what I would've guessed. That dog was pretty beat up. Cuts and scratches littered its brindle coat...

That's when it clicks.

Brindle, aka a combination of black and burnt orange. Halloween tie-dye.

She definitely means the pit bull.

My shoulders sag just a bit.

"Okay, yeah. I know the dog you're talking about."

"You do?" Paige steps forward to grip the edge of the counter, excitement clear in her voice.

I don't want to have to look at her joyous smile, knowing the sight will just unsettle me, so I keep my eyes averted.

"Yeah. Pit bull. Brought in around ten in the morning. Found chained up with a duct-tape muzzle. Probably used as a bait dog."

"That's her." Her response is less enthusiastic but still eager. "Can I take her home?"

With the trouble we have adopting out pit bulls, I should be overjoyed to have someone here, asking for one. Problem is, I'm not sold on Paige. She shows up to the shelter in the middle of a weekday when most people are at their full-time jobs, dressed like she's on her way to a yoga class. My guess is, she's a bored housewife, looking for a charity project, and I don't like the idea of her adopting a dog on a whim, only to find she can't handle the responsibility.

Luckily, I have a completely valid excuse for turning her away.

"The dog is still getting checked out by the vet. Stitching cuts is quick, but she might have infections that take longer to treat. Then, after that, she needs to go through different socialization and behavioral tests before we can make her available for adoption." Tired of talking to a piece of paper, but not wanting to meet her pleading eyes, I instead focus on the imperfect scar. "You're looking at anywhere from a couple of weeks to a couple of months."

"So then, I just come back every day to check in? Does she have an ID number assigned to her so there's no confusion in the future?"

Paige tilts her head to the side just enough to catch my eye, and I find myself stumbling over a response. Her unwavering commitment to the animal is making me doubt my initial assumption, and my skeptical heart has to admit there might be a slight chance she follows through.

I'm tempted to tell her that, yes, she does need to come back to the shelter every day. Partly to find out if she actually would, but also a little bit because I wouldn't mind listening to her weird rambling a few more times.

I shouldn't want anything to do with her, I remind myself.

"We can take down your name and phone number and give you a call when she's available. But there's only a twenty-four-hour hold, and then she's up for anyone interested." I say that like there's real competition. The general public's fear of pit bulls means they tend to stick around longer than other breeds.

"That won't happen. You call me, I'll be here"—she leans over the counter, squinting her eyes at my chest—"Dash."

I flinch in surprise, not expecting to hear my name in her husky, sweet voice. The sound puts me in a temporary daze, until I realize I'm wearing a name tag.

"Well"—I clear my throat—"we have your contact info here." I hand the application form to Kim, who's been watching the entire exchange with the fascination of a person trying to learn her new job.

Paige nods and steps back, affording me another view of her full, fit body. I shove my clenched hands into my pockets and move to retreat to my office.

"Dash." The pleading tone she uses tightens my skin in a delicious way. As hazel eyes stare me down, I meet her intense gaze, knowing all the while that I shouldn't. "Tell her that I'm coming back for her. She's mine, and I'm hers. Tell her that."

The request is so odd that I can't do anything other than nod.

A hesitant smile curves at the corners of Paige Herbert's mouth before she turns abruptly, her neon-green sneakers squeaking on the linoleum tiles as she strolls out of the front entrance.

Kim and I share baffled looks.

"So, does that happen a lot?" she asks.

I swallow past the blockage in my throat caused by Paige's half smile.

"No. That...that was new."

CHAPTER 3

PAIGE

I t's official; I'm cutting chocolate out of my diet.

If a dog consumes chocolate, it's the same as eating poison.

And it's not just chocolate. There's a whole list of human food that can kill dogs.

"Poor puppies," I mutter to myself as I scroll through the article on my computer screen.

As I contemplate bringing my dog home, I can't help cringing when I recall my behavior.

Last week, when I went to the shelter to pick up my new life partner, I may have gotten a little pissy with the guy at the front desk. It was a couple of things. First off, there was how he looked.

My apartment back in NYC had a big, beautiful bedroom window, but since we lived in a city full of skyscrapers, I couldn't use the same descriptors for the view. At least at first.

Whenever the curtains were open, it was hard to focus anywhere other than the giant ad space just across the street. For the first few months, Martin and I looked out at the movie posters for the latest blockbuster hits. I didn't mind. It was nice to be reminded of what was playing.

Then, there was the era of beer ads. The same cheap lager greeted me each morning when I opened the blinds.

But I longed for the six-pack when we entered the year of diet campaigns. Every day, I had to see an uber-fit woman telling me I could be as slim as her if only I bought whatever product I adamantly refused to learn the name of.

Then, one morning, I went to let some sunshine into our tiny abode, expecting to find the same guilt trip taunting me. Instead, I discovered that finally, the ad had changed.

And the new image was mesmerizing.

A male model stared at me, his hooded eyes piercing as he stroked a finger across his full bottom lip. The gesture put an expensive-looking watch on display, the timepiece hugging a corded forearm, revealed only because his shirtsleeves were rolled up.

The ad was erotic. At least, to me, it was. The man seemed to watch me move around my bedroom, and I was seconds away from pulling out my vibrator when I realized Martin was still home.

My fiancé hated the new view. When he came out of the shower and saw it, he grumbled and scowled, ranting that our apartment was shitty if we had to look at that.

Martin was always complaining about our living space. He hated how we only had one bedroom and one bathroom and not enough square footage for a full dining table. One more reason he jumped on the chance to relocate to New Orleans, where we could afford an actual house.

I liked the small space. And I liked the new view.

After a day or so of pretending only mild interest, I finally broke down and googled the advertising campaign. Turned out the model was some well-known actor in Taiwan, who had started to appear in American movies. He'd recently become the face of this high-end watchmaker. Which meant that I got to enjoy his face outside my bedroom window.

Sometimes, at night, when Martin worked late, I would crack the blinds just enough to stare into that set of dark, hypnotizing eyes. My imagination would run away with me as I let my hands explore my body, and I would find a release with more pleasure than my partner had given me in years.

My happy little fantasy lasted for about two months. Then, I opened my curtains and found a cow telling me I should eat more chicken. When Martin asked why I'd let out a pained moan, I blamed it on a stubbed toe.

Eventually, I convinced myself it was better not to be lusting after some celebrity I'd never meet.

Then, I walk into the dog shelter and find a guy who's my watch model's doppelgänger. Only this man exists in the real world, looking like the actor stepped out of the ad, stopped shaving his beard for a few days, and decided to start rescuing helpless animals.

So, that mythical sexiness, combined with the fact that he wasn't immediately handing over my dog, put me in a bad mood. Just a few weeks out from Martin's betrayal, I'm not in any type of headspace to deal with attractive men telling me what to do.

But now, I'm thinking that holding off for a little while on adopting my doggo might have been a good move. If all of my research has taught me anything, it's that I am not prepared to be a dog owner.

Yet.

"Don't worry, baby girl. I'll figure it out," I whisper my reassurance to the empty air, hoping that, somehow, my words will reach that poor, pitiful puppy I found abandoned in a dirty alley.

After a week of bingeing on fried chicken to smother my depression, I realized I needed to either start working out or purchase a new wardrobe in larger sizes. Going up a couple of numbers doesn't bother me, but shopping does. I hate sorting through endless racks of clothes, then stripping down in front of those floor-to-ceiling mirrors in randomly lit dressing rooms.

I'd rather run.

So, a week after discovering a beautiful pixie woman in my house and my robe, I decided to funnel my rage into jogging rather than food.

Well, more like jogging *and* food.

Life needs balance.

It was on one of those outings that I heard the whining and discovered the new, most horrifying scene of my life. Tied up to a chain-link fence was a skeleton of a dog. Each one of her rib bones stood out, clear enough for me to count, even ten feet away. Open wounds were crusted with dried blood, and a thick swatch of duct tape held her large jaw clamped shut. But even through the makeshift muzzle, little heartbreaking cries filtered out.

When I took a step closer, she curled in on herself, shakes racking her emaciated body. Not wanting to scare her, I sat down, making myself smaller, and pulled out my phone to dial the police.

While the two of us waited for someone who knew what the hell they were doing, I hummed to her, using up only half of my arsenal of Disney songs before a police van pulled up.

Once the officer freed her and loaded her into his vehicle, my mind was made up. Whether it was fate or chance, I was the one who had found that dog, and I would be the one to make her whole again. The issues I have going on suck, but they're nothing compared to being beaten and left tied up to die.

The roar of a heavy engine sounds from downstairs.

Mom must be working.

I sigh and shut down my computer, standing up with a spine-cracking stretch. The chair at my childhood desk lacks proper lumbar support. I glance around the bedroom I hadn't slept in for eight years until three weeks ago. At some point, Mom took down my posters and pictures, repainting the walls a warm, dark brown. But the furniture is still the same. White dresser, white desk, white bed frame with a plush queen-size mattress. It's not a bad room.

The major flaw is that it's in my parents' house. A place I vowed never to live again.

An insistent buzzing from my cell phone puts a pause on my descent into self-pity. At least, it does until I read the name of the caller.

The bastard whose fault it is that I'm back in my childhood home in the first place.

Martin.

"Fuck you." I glare at my phone as I mutter the curse, but I don't toss the device away like I've been doing ever since the night I arrived to find him shacked up with someone he hadn't committed to spending the rest of his life with.

Ignoring him isn't a long-term solution. I should probably talk to him. Or scream at him. I still haven't decided which when I click to accept the call.

"Hey, douchebag. What do you want?"

"Paige! You answered!"

I roll my eyes. "You have limited time. Your choice if you want to spend it stating the obvious."

"Baby. Sweetheart. I'm sorry. I'm so sorry. Nothing happened, I swear."

Liar. Maybe I would've believed him if I hadn't gotten a call from an unknown number a few weeks ago. Turned out it was the mystery pixie woman, calling to apologize for acting as the home-wrecker. Apparently, she's a resident at the same hospital as Martin, and they were just sleeping together for stress relief. The affair was supposed to end before I ever got to town.

Guess I ruined their well-laid plans.

Her call was shocking and scraped away the scant bit of hope that what I had seen was just one giant misunderstanding. But in a weird way, I'm grateful for both her sleeping with Martin and then telling me about it. Now, I know what type of person he truly is.

"If nothing happened, then why are you sorry?"

That gets him to stumble, and I almost smile as he stutters over his words. "I-I, well, just…I mean, I'm sorry you felt hurt, by me. But I didn't…of course I wouldn't—"

"Just stop, Martin," I cut him off, sighing heavily and pressing the pads of my fingers into my eyelids to try staving off the headache threatening.

Why did I pick up the phone?

"Please, Paige. I want to talk to you. Face-to-face. I know you hate phone conversations."

He's right about that. But after dating for eight years, there's not much this man doesn't know about me. Too bad that didn't keep him from hurting me.

"I don't know." *What would we even say to each other?*

"Come on, Paige. This can't be how it ends. Just have lunch with me. Next week."

I try to imagine it. Never having experienced a post-breakup meal, I don't even know how to approach the situation. As I pace around the room, a sparkle on the bedside table catches my eye. The little shimmer comes from the diamond in my engagement ring.

The first night I slept here, I chucked the ring across the room. The next day, after I accidentally stepped on it and cursed the universe for the physical pain to pair with my emotional turmoil, I picked the jewelry up and placed it where the sharp stone couldn't do any more harm.

From then on, the ring has been mocking me.

Lunch would be a good time to give it back. Get that physical representation of our relationship out of my eyeline.

And as much as it rankles to admit, I kind of agree with Martin. After eight years together, I think I need more closure than just storming out on him.

"Okay. Lunch. When?"

His sigh sounds almost happy, and for the life of me, I can't fathom why.

"Tuesday at noon. Angelo's. You remember it? We went before prom. That silky dress you had on—"

"Yeah. Got it."

I hang up, done with his familiar voice and his manipulative trick. Dragging me down memory lane won't erase the fact that his dick was in another woman.

Unfortunately, I won't have the option to hang up on him at lunch.

CHAPTER 4

DASH

"That weird girl is back." Kim leans her head into my office, an excited smile on her face.

Unexpectedly, I catch myself grinning in return.

I didn't think Paige would come back.

When I arrived at work this morning, there was a note on my desk, saying the brindle pit bull had a clean bill of health and passed all behavioral evaluations. She's ready to be adopted.

After closing the door to my office, I pulled the wrinkled application out of the filing cabinet and spread it out before me, trying not to wonder why I was making such a big production about this call. It was only when I got an automated voice mail that I realized I'd been eager to hear Paige's voice again. But all I got was the slightly distracted way she stated her name for the voice mail. After leaving a message, I pushed thoughts of her far away.

Until now.

I follow Kim up to the front lobby, and there she is. Paige has her wavy blonde hair pulled up in a ponytail again and is wearing another set of those tight athletic pants, all black, paired with a loose T-shirt with big letters that read NYU across her chest. This time, my eyes stray to her left hand. I don't spot a ring.

Okay, so maybe not a bored housewife.

I don't let my mind linger on the other benefits of her not having a ring.

"She's still here, right? You didn't give my dog away?" Paige's questions come out panicked as she rushes forward the moment I open the waiting room door. She stands close, staring up at me with hope and worry creasing shallow lines in her face.

At this proximity, I pick up more details. Though her skin is smooth and clean, the area under her eyes is shadowed, almost bruised. As far as I can tell, she doesn't have any makeup on, which leaves her eyelashes pale golden, like her hair.

She's beautiful. And tired.

Again, I get the strange urge to draw her into my arms and run my hands down her spine in a comforting gesture. I'd pull her close, pressing our bodies together, and whisper nonsense in her ear until all the tension that was radiating off her melted away and she relaxed into me.

Stop it. She's not for you.

Focusing on my job, I keep a distant, reassuring smile on my face. "Don't worry. She's still here. Why don't you come back to our meeting room, and I'll bring her to you?"

Paige nods eagerly and follows close behind me. I leave her in a room with a low wooden bench and boxes full of a variety of toys. I check the whiteboard to see which kennel the dog is in before grabbing a leash and a handful of treats.

When I approach the enclosure, the brindle pit bull spins in excited circles before jumping at the chain-link door.

"Hey, baby girl. How you doing? Think I might be able to send you home today." I keep my voice low and soothing as I unlatch the door and maneuver my arm inside with the slip leash dangling wide. She's jumping around so much; it's difficult to get the rope around her neck, so I keep up my calming murmurs. "I think you already know this girl. She's the one who found you. You liked her, right? Real pretty girl.

She's already calling you her dog." The angle works out, and I slip the leash over her head, pulling it tight.

Once the dog is secure, I wrap the thick rope around my hand a couple of times before opening the door wider. She's a strong one and does her best to drag me around, but I'm a pro at this by now. Keeping her bracketed between my legs, I direct both of us back to the adoption meeting room.

The moment we push through the door, Paige's face lights up brighter than the night sky on the Fourth of July.

"Oh, sweetheart! Look at you!"

She's on her knees in an instant. Too trusting for her own good. But the dog rushes up to her, sniffing and licking, its whole body wriggling in unbridled joy.

I let the two of them get reacquainted, enjoying the happiness both of them radiate. After the dog calms down enough to go sniff in the box of toys, Paige straightens up from her crouch and turns an ecstatic, piercing stare on me.

"So, can I take her home now?"

"Just need you to fill out some paperwork and pay the adoption fee. You sure you're ready to take her home today?"

She nods eagerly. "Yes. Definitely. I've been researching."

I'm tempted to ask what she means by that, but I don't want it to come off like I'm trying to talk her out of the adoption. With a nod of acceptance, I slip out of the room to retrieve a clipboard with the forms she needs to fill out.

Returning, I encounter a vigorous game of tug-of-war.

Paige lets the dog win and settles next to me on the bench, accepting the clipboard. Only after we've worked our way through most of the paperwork do I remember an important detail I wish I could've hidden.

But Paige spots the note before I can snatch the clipboard away.

"You named her after me?"

"I...um...yes." The truth stutters out before I can think of a plausible excuse.

Paige wrinkles her nose. "Well, we can't both be Paige. I don't want everyone to think I'm conceited. And imagine the confusion. I'd never know if someone is talking to me or my dog!"

Dog Paige lets out a bark as if in agreement.

"It's not set in stone. We can change it. What do you want to name her?" I cross out where I carefully filled in a name for the dog.

Her hazel eyes go wide, flitting between the dog, the form on the clipboard, and back to my face. "Way to put me on the spot, Dash! This is like going to the hospital for stomach pain and finding out I'm nine months pregnant! And then having to tell them what the baby's name is!"

I fight a smile, her absurd analogy completely ridiculous in a way that makes me want to bark out a laugh. "Sorry. We can leave it blank."

"Leave it blank?" Her voice has gone breathy with affront, and she clutches at her chest like she's searching for a string of pearls to clasp. "She deserves a name! Her *own* name." Paige stands and starts to pace, tugging at her earlobe distractedly. "Give me a minute."

I lean back on my hands, losing the battle against my grin as Dog Paige follows Human Paige around the room. They make a cute pair. Human Paige's ponytail swings in almost the same motion as Dog Paige's tail. I bet when they go on walks, eyes will turn in their direction. Men will probably want to approach Human Paige because of her tempting curves and sweet lips, but I bet they'll think twice when they spot Dog Paige's powerful jaw and muscular build.

Those men don't deserve either one of them.

Abruptly, Human Paige drops to a crouch, startling both me and Dog Paige. She cups the puppy's massive head in her pale hands and meets the dog's gaze squarely.

"What's your name?"

As if the question means something to the animal, Dog Paige huffs out a breath, gives a full-body shake, then trots over to the toy bin. Human Paige appears lost for a moment, but she starts to smile when the dog returns, carrying a plush pumpkin. With a few flexes of her jaw, the dog makes the toy let out a series of high-pitched squeaks, then drops it in front of her new owner.

Human Paige snatches the pumpkin up with a triumphant laugh.

"We've got it, Dash!"

Each time she says my name, a spark of awareness shoots down my spine. It's like getting gently bitten in the middle of sex—surprising, welcome, and with a slight twinge of pain.

Human Paige tosses the toy across the room, and Dog Paige chases it in a flurry of muscular motion. Distracted by the dog's mad scrambling, I realize with a jolt that the enticing woman has come to stand directly in front of me.

Paige leans down, giving me a wonderful view of the valley between her cleavage. Her soft hands brush against mine as she slides the clipboard and pen from my grip. With her bending over me, I'm not only treated to a mind-melting view down her loose neckline; I also get hit with a wave of her scent.

Just from glancing at her sweet face and pale skin, I would've guessed a sugary or flowery perfume. But when I breathe in deep, I don't pick up bubblegum or roses.

Paige smells like coffee.

The dark notes drift in the air around me, making me drowsy and my mouth water, just like every morning when I stand at the coffeepot, waiting for that magical elixir to finish brewing and provide me energy for the day.

Would pressing my lips against hers be like taking that first sip? Would she wake me up? Warm me from the inside out?

Moving a step back while she scribbles away, Paige takes her delicious aroma with her.

I can't stop myself. Under the pretense of reading what she's writing, I stand up and hover just beside her. The coffee scent is back, clinging to her in some mysterious way.

Does coffee perfume exist?

"Here." She tilts the clipboard my way and beams up at me.

Again, I make an inaccurate prediction. I expect her handwriting to be big and bubbly, but instead, she's written one word in small, clear script.

Pumpkin

"Pumpkin. Paige and Pumpkin." I try out their names together, enjoying the pop of the p's on my lips.

Her smile widens. "I'm a fan of alliteration. Besides, with that coloring, she's practically demanding a Halloween-themed name."

Paige hands the clipboard back to me and gets into another bout of tug-of-war.

Watching them together, I realize one more thing I was wrong about.

Paige isn't backing out of this. That dog, Pumpkin, is hers.

She was right that first day.

We wrap up the rest of the paperwork, including Paige filling out a check for the adoption fee. Normally, once everything is approved and paid for, I let the adopter go on their way and head back to my office. But this time, I decide to walk Paige and Pumpkin out.

I try to reason that I just want to make sure Paige is comfortable handling the big dog. The lie doesn't even work on me.

The minute we step away from the building, I realize breaking my normal routine was a mistake.

In the bright afternoon sunlight, all the cars in the parking lot give off a shine, but none more so than a gorgeous classic Chevy. The beautiful machine has a wicked candy-apple-green paint job, and the shape of the body immediately brings to mind muscle cars from the '60s.

When Paige saunters up to the vehicle and sticks a key in the door, I feel my dick twitch.

This woman is bad news.

I should turn around. Right now. Go back inside, where it's safe and my life is simple.

My feet disregard the rational directions, walking me closer to the gorgeous girl and her wet dream of a car.

Paige pulls open the back door, and I see multiple thick dog beds on the seat, along with a pile of plush toys. Pumpkin ignores them in favor of her namesake, which she's still carrying around and squeaking. The dog hops up into the back seat, pretty as you please.

My eyes can't seem to decide where to settle. The fantasy of a car or the fantasy of a woman. When Paige turns to me with a bone-melting smile, the choice becomes easier, though not necessarily healthier.

"I think we're all set. Thank you, Dash. For making sure Pumpkin and I ended up back together." She clasps her hands in front of her. "We're going to be good for each other. I'm sure of it."

The sight of the over-the-top preparation connects with some of Paige's earlier comments in my mind, clicking into place to form a sudden realization.

"Paige?"

She moved to slide off Pumpkin's leash but turns back to me. "Yeah?"

"Have you ever owned a dog before?"

She grimaces, and my stomach clenches in worry.

"Is it that obvious?" Her hand presses on her collarbone as she gives me a pleading look. "I know it's all new to me, but I can figure it out. I swear."

"It's more than just buying the right supplies, Paige. Even though Pumpkin passed the behavior tests, she's still going to need some obedience training." I run my hand through my hair as worries start to pop up in my mind. So many things could go wrong.

"Okay. I can do that. I'll get a trainer. I promise." Paige blinks up at me, a question in her hazel eyes. "Do you have any recommendations?"

Some of the tension eases from my chest. "I've got a list somewhere in my office. I can email it to you."

Paige opens her mouth to respond, but whatever she was about to say gets cut off by an excited bark behind her. We turn simultaneously to watch Pumpkin launch herself out of the back seat, making a beeline for one of the feral cats that often wanders the rescue's property.

Working on pure instinct, I let out an eardrum-piercing whistle. By some stroke of luck, it gets Pumpkin to pause and glance back at me.

Maintaining eye contact and pitching my voice low, I speak one firm word. "Sit."

Thank the universe, she actually does. Not realizing Paige moved, I'm surprised to find her already beside the dog, looping the leash around the animal's thick neck.

When the two of them get back to the car, I notice Paige's hands have a slight quiver to them. I'm about to point out that this is exactly why training is so necessary when she cuts me off.

"I want you."

I almost swallow my tongue. I cough to get it out of my throat before responding, "You want me?"

Paige directs Pumpkin into the back seat of the car and closes the door firmly before giving me back her attention.

"Yes! Don't bother sending me that list. I want *you*. Besides, Pumpkin already likes you. I don't know how she'd be with a stranger."

The true meaning of her words dawns on me, and I silently berate myself for letting even a little bit of excitement filter into my brain.

"You want me to be your dog trainer."

"Yes. Exactly." Paige nods as she reaches through the cracked window to scratch behind Pumpkin's ears. "When can you start?"

"I don't train dogs." That's not technically true. I used to train them all the time, and I tend to help out with the dogs in the shelter whenever we're short-staffed, which is a lot of the time.

Still, I know any further association with Paige Herbert is sure to tilt my world off its precarious axis. Better she leaves today and I never interact with her again.

"But you know how, don't you? I mean, what you just did, that was, like, a dog-whisperer-level display. You have puppy magic." She wiggles her hand in front of Pumpkin's nose as if casting a spell.

I'm not sure I've ever seen anything more adorable.

"Please, Dash."

Refusing Paige would be so much easier if she wasn't looking up at me like I was some kind of hero.

Would it really be that bad? To help her out?

I could show her how to handle a dog like Pumpkin. I could spend some more time around her. Get to hear her strange ramblings a couple of more times. Maybe I could move in close enough to smell her earthy coffee scent or even reach out to stroke her temptingly soft skin.

Shit. Bad idea.

"There are better dog trainers in this city. Trust me. You'll be better off with one of them."

"But I want *you*."

Hell. Could she please stop saying that?

An idea for how to get out of the situation dawns on me. A solution that will wipe away all that worship and eliminate any inkling of want she might have. Paige is too sweet, too innocent, to be comfortable around the real me.

All I need to do is be honest.

"Look. It's not a good idea. You don't want to be around someone like me. I'm on parole."

There it is. I've dropped the hammer. Now, it's time to watch her get uncomfortable, throw out a lame excuse, then make a quick escape in her glorious car, leaving behind only enough of a memory for me to think about tonight when I'm in my bed.

"Okay. What were you in for?"

This woman has a knack for robbing me of words. For a moment, I just stare down at her curious face, my mouth bobbing open as I attempt to figure out what to say next.

"What was I in for?" Apparently, my brain still isn't working right.

"Yeah. Did you kill someone? Murder or manslaughter?"

"What? No!"

"Okay. That's good. Did you assault someone?"

"No! Paige, that's not…" I trail off, trying to figure out how best to relate my degenerate status.

"Cross that one off then. Did you—"

"I stole cars!" I had to cut her off before she continued running down a list of possible crimes. We could've been standing around all day till she made it to the right one.

"Oh." Paige's face goes blank, and I'm impressed with how well she's hiding her discomfort.

I take a step back, making her escape easier.

Only she doesn't hurry around to the driver's side of her tempting vehicle. Instead, Paige shoves her hands into her pockets and resumes her pleading look.

"So, would thirty dollars an hour work? Or am I lowballing you? How much do people normally charge for lessons?"

Shit. Now, she's brought money into it. And for some reason, Paige doesn't seem uncomfortable with the fact that she's standing next to an ex-con. This girl makes no sense.

"I'm a criminal, Paige. You should hire someone on the up-and-up."

She frowns, and the expression puckers her lips enticingly. "No, you're not. You're on parole. You served your time."

My hair flops on my forehead as I shake my head, and I can't stifle my exasperated sigh. "You're too trusting."

———

PAIGE

"Yeah. I guess that's true."

Dash's words hit me harder than he probably meant them to. How could he know I just had my trust demolished by the guy I'd planned on spending the rest of my life with? Somehow, I'm able to keep from wincing.

Maybe Dash is right. Maybe I should go with a professional trainer.

Problem is, I don't want to sort through random people and potentially risk calling in someone I know nothing about. I've only interacted with Dash a couple of times, but there's this familiarity, a sense of comfort, that overwhelms me when I'm around him.

I swear it's not because he's hotness on a stick, coated in sexiness and deep-fried in butter.

Maybe I like the fact that he hasn't pointed out how weird I am—yet. People seem to do that a lot as if it's a compliment to clarify I'm awkward.

I get it. I'm always tempted to snap. *No need to broadcast my social ineptitude to the world and any passerby who may be listening.*

And if I want to be completely honest with myself, I need to acknowledge that I don't let a lot of people into my life. Somehow, it seems like Dash has already found himself a spot.

So, why bother with anyone else?

When it comes to his past mistakes, I have no room to point fingers. His parole status barely registers on my radar.

Then, there's his open honesty to take into account. I could use more people being straight with me. I've had enough lying.

Glancing up at Dash, I pick up on the discomfort and indecision on his face. My urge is to keep pushing for what I want. My brain wants to babble at him until he gives in and says yes.

But that way, I might end up doing more harm than good. Time to treat him like one of my reluctant writers. When I'm editing a manuscript, some authors just need me to lay out my argument, then take a step back. That way, they can come to a conclusion on their own terms and be happier with the end result.

Time to give Dash the room he needs to make his own decision.

"Here's the deal, Dash. I want you. Pumpkin wants you. I'll pay you for each lesson, and you can tell me how much." I pull open my passenger door and push aside the overflow of dog toys. Pumpkin stretches her head in between the seats to watch my movements, and I pause long enough to press a kiss to her giant block head.

After a moment, I locate the book I finished reading this morning. I use a green pen from my glove compartment to scribble a quick note inside the front cover. Then, I turn and offer the book to Dash. "There's my cell number. If you decide you're up for lessons, text me."

His long fingers reach out hesitantly as if he thinks the pages will bite him.

"You're giving me a book?" He sounds incredulous.

"I'm giving you my number. In a book. So, technically, yes."

His dark eyes flick between me and the cover, which has a woman in a Regency era fuchsia dress.

Doing my best to interpret his hesitation, I reassure him, "Don't worry. I've already read it."

Dash's eyebrows still sit high on his forehead.

I've done something weird.

What's new?

"Why didn't you just use a scrap piece of paper?"

I shrug. "I don't have any. I just have the book. It's really good. Even if you don't call me, you should think about reading it."

His dark eyes trace the woman in the hot-pink historical gown, and then he slowly drags his sultry gaze back up to mine.

Excited tingles shiver down my spine. To cover the reaction, I give him my biggest, most reassuring grin. "I swear. It's fantastic. Think about it. And think about me." Blood flushes hot in my cheeks, and I fight the urge to smack my forehead. One of these days, I hope to have an acceptable string of words come out of my mouth. "I mean, Pumpkin and me. Think about the two of us. Helping us out. Because we need you."

Oh no. I am quickly approaching a babbling cliff and am in great danger of slipping right off. Better head out before I say or do something to permanently put Dash off.

"Well. I'll…just go now." I walk backward around the hood of my car until I reach the driver's-side door.

Dash watches my retreat, an unreadable expression on his face.

Only once I'm pulling out of the parking lot do I risk a glance in the rearview mirror. He's still standing where I left him, clutching a paperback romance novel with my phone number written in the front cover.

The last man I saw like this, I never wanted to look at again. But this time, I find myself throwing out a silent wish that this won't be my last sight of the handsome dog whisperer.

CHAPTER 5

DASH

I stare at the pile of T-shirts on my bed, wondering when exactly I lost it. Choosing what to wear when I'm just going to train a dog shouldn't be difficult. I shouldn't even have to think about it. But for some reason, I've tried on half the shirts I own and discarded all of them.

I should cancel.

When I gave in and texted Paige yesterday, I decided to up the price and then back out if she tried to haggle with me. Problem is, she agreed right away.

Now, I'm stuck.

"What's up with you?" My roommate's voice startles me, and I whip around to find Cole leaning on the doorway between my bedroom and the kitchen.

In our shotgun-style house, he has to use my room as a go-between to get to his, unless he wants to walk out the back door and circle around to the front. Not the best layout when I'm trying to brood in seclusion.

"Nothing. What's wrong with you?" My deflection is pathetic.

"Nothing." Cole smirks as he munches on dry Cheerios. The guy hates milk for some unknown reason. "I'm not the one glaring at my clothes."

With a sigh, I ruffle my hair and avoid his gaze. "Just trying to find something clean." I hesitate, then decide to be honest. "I've got a job."

He stops picking at his cereal. "What do you mean, *a job*?"

"Just something to make some extra cash." I grab a red tank top with no visible holes and pull it over my head.

"Fuck, Dash. You driving again? We agreed. None of that shit anymore." Cole's voice goes low and angry, and I wince when I realize what my hedging must've sounded like.

"No, man. I swear. I'm not driving. Nothing illegal. Just…this woman adopted a dog the other day and asked if I'd help out with obedience training." I make sure to meet his eyes, so he knows I'm not lying.

Cole and I met while serving out our sentences. We were both in a program where convicts worked with rescued animals. The idea was to give us some responsibility. Something to care for. Also, it gave us life skills once we got out. The director of the program, Charlene, liked both of us. Apparently, she thought we weren't lost causes. She told us to get in touch with her when we got out, promising to find us full-time work. Charlene came through for us, and we decided to keep each other in check.

Cole's anger is completely valid if he thinks I've fallen back into old habits. He watches me, his insanely blue eyes tripping over my face until his glare finally fades.

"Okay. Obedience, huh? You sure you're up for that? Been a while since you worked directly with the dogs."

"You're just jealous that I was always better than you."

He smirks, flipping me off before digging back into his bowl. "Which dog?"

"A brindle pit bull. Brought in a few weeks ago."

"Paige?" I flinch when he says her name, then realize he's talking about the dog.

"Uh, no. The dog's name is Pumpkin now. Paige is her new owner."

Cole studies me again, probably seeing too much. I busy myself by slipping my wallet into the pocket of my basketball shorts and searching for my phone in the pile of clothes on my bed.

"That's a hell of a coincidence."

I shrug. "Not really. She's the one who found the dog. Came in, wanting to adopt it the next day. I told her she'd have to wait. The dog needed a name, and I suggested Paige, not expecting the girl to show back up. I was wrong. End of story."

"And now, you're going over to her house? To *help* her?" The way Cole says it adds an extra layer to the question.

Luckily, my phone starts ringing, giving me the perfect excuse to cut this conversation off before he digs any deeper.

"Yeah. Later." I open my beat-up, out-of-date flip phone as I head to the front door, not sparing my roommate another glance, even though I can distinctly feel his smirk burning against my back. "Hello?" The front screen of my device cracked a few months back, meaning whenever someone calls, it's always a mystery.

"Hey, Dash. How's my favorite ex-con doing?" The sultry voice caresses the question, as if the label is a compliment. Knowing Teresa, she probably thinks it is.

"Hey. What's up?" I reach my shabby white Saturn and brace the phone against my ear with my shoulder, needing both hands to wrench open the door. A metallic screech from the rusted machine drowns out her response. "Sorry. Say that again."

"Come over. I wanna have some fun."

I stick the key in the ignition, mouth a silent prayer, and smile in grim satisfaction when the engine sputters to life. After turning the radio down, I consider her offer.

Teresa's version of fun is hot, sweaty, and doesn't involve clothes. Exactly what I was looking for after getting out of jail. I had this almost unquenchable thirst for a body in my arms.

The problem is, after more than a year, that thirst is still there. Teresa hasn't been filling the void the way I hoped she would. And now, as I think about canceling on Paige and driving over to Teresa's house, my gut reaction is to shake my head.

Because fucking Teresa isn't worth the loss of revenue.

At least, that's what I tell myself.

"Sorry, Tea. I've gotta work."

"But you have Sundays off." I can hear her pout through the phone.

"Got another job. Heading there now. See you around."

Her annoyed sigh gets cut off when I flip my phone shut. I drop it in the cupholder and back out of the driveway.

Thoughts of my hookup slide away on the warm breeze drifting through my open windows. Instead, an image of Paige bending over my lap as she reaches for my clipboard fills my thoughts.

It's about the money. This is all about the money.

But even in my mind, the words don't sound convincing.

CHAPTER 6

PAIGE

"I'm just not sure about this, sweetheart."

I tap my fingers on the granite island and breathe deeply through my nose. "Not sure about what, Mother?"

"Oh God. Don't call me Mother. It makes me feel like I'm some 1950s housewife." My mom glares at me from the other side of the kitchen, where she's washing her hands in the big farmhouse sink.

I fight a smile. Good to know I haven't lost my ability to ruffle her feathers. "Okay. Not sure about what, ma'am?"

"That's even worse!" She flicks water at me before reaching for a dish towel.

I dodge the droplets, still attempting to keep a curious, innocent expression. "Well, I don't know what you want. I'm running out of options here. How about matron? Dowager? Biddy?"

"That's it!" She lunges back for the sink, slams the faucet on, pulls out the hose, and aims it at me.

Cold water shoots across the room, soaking the entire front of my shirt. I gasp and try to run but end up slamming into a solid object. When I glare up at the obstruction, I realize it's my dad.

He shakes his head at the two of us. "Ginny, are you abusing our daughter?"

"She called me ma'am!" My mom's attempt at indignation is ruined by her giggling. You'd think a woman over fifty would have a bit more gravitas.

"Thank heavens you're here, Dad. She's gone mad!" I wave at the giant water stain down my front. Not that I need to, seeing as how our collision ended up transferring a good deal of the water to his polo shirt.

"Now, we're going to be late. I have to go change."

Someone unacquainted with my dad might interpret his dry tone as anger, but my mom and I can see the amused sparkle in his eye. Dad loves Mom's childish antics.

"Oh, don't bother. It's just water. We'll open the car windows, and you'll be dry by the time we arrive."

The two of them have plans for an afternoon of sailing on a family friend's boat. I was invited.

I said no.

Sailing might've been fun, but the idea of dealing with pity stares turns my stomach worse than seasickness could. I'm not ready to be the center of everyone's gossip.

Besides, I have an important appointment. One that I was hoping my mom would let be. That was too much to ask for.

"Richard, could you please back me up here?"

"Don't back her! Back me, Dad!"

He glances between the two of us. "I'm going to need some more information."

My mom huffs in frustration, and I scowl at her, knowing I'm not going to like what she's about to say.

"We're talking about *the dog*."

"She has a name!"

My mom rolls her eyes but concedes the point. "Fine. We're discussing Pumpkin."

"No, actually, we're *not* discussing her. Because this is not a democracy. My life is a dictatorship. I am the supreme leader. What I say goes, and I say that Pumpkin is a permanent fixture. She's not going anywhere." Gone is the joking atmosphere of moments before. I cross my arms and glare at both of them.

"But, honey, she's a"—Mom lowers her voice to a whisper—"pit bull."

Silence descends on the kitchen after her quiet warning.

The tension is broken by a loud, incessant squeaking. The three of us glance over to the corner of the kitchen, where I've placed one of the multitudes of dog beds I purchased. Pumpkin lies sprawled on the thing, her namesake toy clutched in her mouth. She wags her tail and flexes her jaw, simply reveling in the high-pitched noise it emits.

"Really, Mom. I never would've thought you'd be prejudice."

She sputters at my accusation. "I—well, I—that's just..." Her words trail off as she watches my dog.

"Pit bulls can be rough, Paige. We're just worried you've signed up for more than you can handle." My dad's comment is gentle and stabs me straight in the gut.

This is exactly why I didn't want to move home. Not because I don't love my parents or because I have any doubt that they love me. I just didn't want to stay under their roof for any length of time because I knew sooner or later, they'd get around to pointing out how helpless I was. Immature. Little better than a child.

But then again, why wouldn't the two of them doubt my ability to take care of a dog? I haven't even proven I can take care of myself.

Still, whether my parents believe it or not, I'm sure I can get this right. Pumpkin is meant to be mine, and I'm meant to be hers. We'll figure out things together.

With a fortifying breath, I square my shoulders and face the pair of them.

"I know pit bulls have a bad reputation, but if you do any kind of thorough research, you'll see that they can be very sweet dogs. And I'm taking precautions. Hence the obedience training today." I move to crouch next to Pumpkin, scratching her exposed belly. "Trust me. I can do this. We'll be fine."

My mom still looks worried, but my dad gives me a resigned smile and wraps his arm around his wife's shoulders.

"All right, Paige. We'll leave you to it. Call us if you need anything."

When the front door closes behind them, a pressure eases off my shoulders. Then, a twinge of guilt pinches under my rib cage. Plenty of people in the world would kill for a set of loving parents like mine. They aren't bad people—exactly the opposite. But I can't seem to go a day without getting into some type of snit with them. Especially my mom.

Living together is not working out. I should've stuck to eighteen-year-old me's declaration that I'd never live under their roof again. Of course, eighteen-year-old me was madly in love with a faithful Martin. At least, I thought he was faithful. Who knows how long he's been running around with other girls behind my back?

"Nope. Not dwelling on that." I stand up abruptly and walk toward the back door, snatching up a pair of sunglasses on my way. "Come on, Pumpkin. I need some air."

My faithful companion scrambles from her bed in an awkward mess of limbs before loping after me.

When I pull open the glass doors leading to the backyard, hot, heavy air practically smacks me in the face. Early October in New Orleans is a hell of a lot different than in New York City. In the northeast, the leaves are probably already changing color while, here, all the vegetation is a continuous thick mass of green. Like a never-ending mossy cushion.

Pumpkin shoves past me to barrel around the perimeter of the yard. Luckily, Mom and Dad already had an eight-foot privacy fence, so my pup had immediate access to space to run. But I read online that even dogs with yards benefit from daily walks, so Pumpkin and I have made a few passes through the neighborhood.

Maybe Dash will be able to help figure out how to keep her from wrenching my arm from my socket at every passing squirrel.

While my dog sniffs and pees on each corner of my parents' property, I jog over to the gate to make sure that even though it's latched, it's unlocked.

After typing out a quick text, I set my phone on the patio table and step back onto the grass, reaching for two squeaky tennis balls.

"Hey, Pumpkin!" I squeak one of the toys. "Wanna play—"

My words are cut off by her attack.

————

Paige: *Come around back when you get here. Fence is unlocked.*

DASH

I stare down at her text for a moment before glancing back up at the house I'm parked in front of. If I had any hope that Paige might be in my league, those dreams are thoroughly dead now.

She lives in a fucking mansion.

Okay, maybe the place isn't a full-on mansion, but the house is larger and nicer than any I've ever been in. This whole street consists of a spacious row of homes I could never dream of affording, even if I stole a whole showroom floor of Ferraris.

"Stop measuring things in terms of what you can steal," I mutter to myself.

On the other hand, it's probably a good idea to take my criminal past into account as I consider following Paige's instructions.

I reach over to the passenger seat for my handwritten directions. Without a smartphone or GPS, I had to stop by the library and use one of their computers to look up the address Paige had given me, copying down the unfamiliar streets needed to get here. I grew up in New Orleans, but not this part of town.

This looks like the right place, but being wrong could land me in some pretty deep shit. Don't want someone calling the cops on me for looking like I'm trying to break into their house.

So, the conflict is, text Paige to come outside and collect me, making me look like an idiot, or potentially violate my parole.

Pride versus prison.

Should be an easy choice.

My groan comes out low and frustrated. After shutting off my car engine, I use my foot to help push the rusted old door open. Hell, I might not even need to approach the house to inspire a 911 call.

Anyone who looks out their window and sees this piece of shit parked on the street is going to know someone is here who doesn't belong.

I fiddle with my phone, on the verge of texting her when a female shout filters from behind the house I'm hoping is Paige's.

"Pumpkin! You beast!"

Looks like I got the right place.

But it sounds like things might not be going so smoothly between the girl and her dog.

An aggravated sigh pushes out from my chest as I jog up the front path before circling around the red-brick exterior. I thought Paige meant it when she said she wanted this dog. Today is going to be shitty if I end up having to stop into work because the rich girl got in over her head and opted to surrender Pumpkin back to our care.

The wooden fence blocks any view I might have of what's going on, but barking fills the thick, humid air. I grab the wrought iron handle and tug, ready for an unpleasant sight.

Instead, I pause, taking in the ridiculous scene.

Pumpkin has her front half low to the ground with her butt high in the air, tail wagging madly as a thick rope toy dangles from her mouth. Paige crouches in the same position, minus the tail and the toy. In addition to the strange standoff, the woman's whole left half is smeared with mud, and a good portion of her golden hair spills out of a haphazard ponytail.

The dog huffs a teasing woof, which comes out muffled by the toy, before dodging to the side and racing off around the yard.

"Not so fast!" Paige is up almost as fast, sprinting after the pit bull.

The dog and her girl play chase before Paige catches one end of the rope. Then, things devolve into a round of tug-of-war.

"Give it up! You'll never win!" she shouts dramatically.

Pumpkin play growls all the while, whipping her heavy head from side to side. Paige gets jostled with each movement yet still maintains an impressive hold.

"You may have teeth, but I have opposable thumbs! Better work your way further up the evolutionary ladder if you wanna—"

Neither Pumpkin nor I get to hear the end of Paige's taunting speech, as her foot lands on a stray tennis ball. Hands fly out for balance as her foot rolls to the side, but the sudden lack of tension in her arms sends her toppling backward.

The sound of Paige hitting the ground reminds me of a skin-splitting belly flop off the high dive at the community pool. I wince in sympathy, quickly making sure the gate is latched before jogging over to where she lies prone on the ground, Pumpkin attacking her face with sloppy, wet dog kisses.

"Here, go fetch." I toss the tennis ball across the yard, and the dog sprints after it, enabling me to get a good look at her disheveled owner. "Paige? You okay?" I crouch beside her, searching for any reason why she's not getting back up.

Sunglasses hide her hazel eyes as her mouth bobs open with short, shallow gasps. "Br-breath…"

"Got the wind knocked out of you?"

Paige manages a nod before rolling onto her side and coughing in a few deeper gasps. For the third time since meeting her, I'm overwhelmed with the urge to stroke her back in comfort. This time, I finally give in.

As Paige lies in the grass, facing me, trying to recover her breath, I gently place my palm on the top of her spine and smooth some reassuring circles, keeping my touch friendly.

Eventually, she pushes herself into a seated position. I retract my hand while cementing the memory of her heat against my palm.

"Did you hurt your ankle?"

When she stepped on the ball, her foot bent at a dramatic angle.

Paige holds her foot off the ground and gives it a few experimental rolls before shaking her head.

"Do you think I'm a weird mess?"

Her question surprises me into sitting back on the ground. The thick grass is as soft as a cushion.

"Why would I think that?"

Even with the aviator-style sunglasses, I can still see her pale eyebrows, one with its charming scar, lift high on her forehead.

"Because you walked in on me having a debate with my dog about genetic advantages. Plus, I look like I'm halfway through my transition into a swamp monster." She pinches the material of a tank top that likely used to be gray, but now has a heavy coat of mud and dirt along one side and all over the lower half of the back.

Paige tries to wipe some of the mess off, but only succeeds in covering her hands in the muck.

Even though I bite my bottom lip hard, the chuckles escape out my nose. She frowns at me, but one corner of her mouth twitches. Then the other. Soon, she's smiling, and I'm letting my laughter flow free.

And, hell, it feels good. So good that I lie back in the damp grass and let the hilarity infuse every inch of my body. It's like at the end of a long day, one where I've spent hours hunched over my desk, I finally get to stand up, stretch my arms over my head, and crack every vertebra in my spine.

Reinvigorating.

When my outburst runs its course, I push myself back up. Then immediately choke on my tongue.

Paige stands in front of me. Shirtless.

At some point while I was distracted, she removed the soiled tank top and is currently using the only untouched section of it to wipe her hands clean. That done, she tosses the shirt to the side and reaches up to pull out her hairband while strolling to the other side of the yard, where her dog happily chews on a stick. A colorful sports bra criss-crosses over her shoulder blades, and a set of loose sweatpants sits happily on her luscious hips.

In reality, Paige has only revealed a stretch of her back and a glimpse of her stomach. Way less than I'd get to see if she were to put on a bathing suit. But there's something about the fact that all she has on is a bra.

Luckily, with the heat of the day, I can blame the sudden increase in my body temperature on the weather.

Paige jogs back over, Pumpkin following close behind, trying to grab at the tennis ball her owner holds just out of reach.

"Thank you for agreeing to do this. I swear we'll be good students. What do you want me to do?"

There are a lot of answers I have to that question. Only none of them have anything to do with dog training.

CHAPTER 7

PAIGE

"**P**umpkin, please sit."

Pumpkin does not sit. Instead, she stares up at me, happy doggy grin on her face, whip-tail wagging enthusiastically.

"No, I told you, short, firm commands. Pumpkin." Dash snaps his fingers to get my dog's attention on him. "Sit."

Her colorful butt plops down in the grass, not one ounce of hesitation.

"It seems rude. To be so curt with her. Why can't I just let her frolic around and be happy? Hasn't she had a hard enough time already?" My voice comes out grumbly as I shove my hands into my pockets and fiddle with the kibble bits Dash gave me at the beginning of the lesson. Every time Pumpkin follows my command, I'm supposed to feed her one, like Dash is doing now.

His pockets are almost empty while mine remain full.

"You're not being mean to her, Paige. You're keeping her safe."

Dash kneels next to Pumpkin and uses his long fingers to scratch behind her ears. My dog wiggles in ecstasy. Her tail pounds against the ground, and she closes her eyes as she leans into his touch.

The sweat trickling down the back of my neck from the heat of the day is starting up an itch of my own, and I suddenly find I'm jealous of Pumpkin.

If I sit on command, will Dash offer to massage my scalp?

I try to focus on his words, not wanting him to somehow read my inappropriate thoughts and back out on our lessons.

"Safe? What do you mean?"

Dash sighs before standing up, towering over my dog. Pumpkin still faces me, but she lifts her chin high, trying to peer at the man behind her. She's so adorable; I can't help melting at the sight. It helps that the backdrop is next-level handsome.

"When you look at Pumpkin, what do you see?" Dash's voice has gone low and intense. He stares at me.

The question seems like a trick one, but I don't know what answer he's going for, so I pick the easy one even though I'm sure it's wrong.

"An adorable puppy."

His expression softens slightly, but his mouth keeps to a grim line. "Well, that's not what the general public sees. To them, she's a vicious animal, always one second away from killing something or someone."

As if to disprove his point, Pumpkin lies down between us, flipping onto her back and rolling around in oblivious bliss.

"That's ridiculous." I glare over the fence surrounding my parents' backyard as if that'll change the world's mind.

"You're telling me in all that research you did, you never came across any anti-pit-bull rhetoric?"

One of Dash's thick eyebrows crests high in disbelief. His right eyebrow. It has a beautiful shape all on its own, but when he moves it around like that, I'm practically hypnotized. I want to stroke it.

"Paige?"

Shoot. Was I just mesmerized by a single eyebrow?

"Um…yeah. I saw a few articles. But I hoped they were overexaggerating."

"I doubt they were." Dash stands relaxed, thankfully oblivious to my attraction. "There are some shitty people in this world, and they train pit bulls to do bad things. Those are the dogs the news reports on, and people start thinking all pit bulls are inherently violent." He crosses his arms over his chest, causing his biceps to bulge nicely. The red of his shirt contrasts enticingly with his golden skin. "So, imagine if Pumpkin sees some kids that she wants to meet and goes running toward them. People are going to think she's attacking."

I glance down at my sweet dog, who's sprawled in the grass, panting and being a good girl, waiting nicely for us to finish our conversation.

"Paige." Dash's insistent voice has me meeting his eyes again. "She needs to listen to you. Or else she might do something that scares someone, and they'll hurt her or call animal control on you, saying you have a dangerous dog. If she behaves—sits when you tell her to, comes when you call her—then you can keep her safe."

It's not fair, but he makes a good point. Really, the same point I was making to my parents earlier.

"Okay. Yes. I want her to be safe. I'll try harder."

Dash smiles, small but sincere. "Good. Now, try *sit* again. Use a firm voice. You can be kind, even when you're being firm. And"—Dash reaches out and wraps his fingers around my wrist, tugging my hand from my pocket—"use hand motions too. A lot of dogs respond better to hand signals. There may be a time you need to give Pumpkin a command when there's a lot of noise, and she might not hear you."

He spreads my palm out flat, positioning it so it faces toward the ground. I'm baffled as to why he didn't just demonstrate the gesture with his hand, but I'm not complaining about the physical instruction.

Paired with the heat of the day, his touch is scalding against mine. More sweat beads on my skin as my heart rate picks up. The pads of his fingers are rough from use, covered in calluses.

What would those hands feel like, dragging all over my body?

My soft places want to be teased and tormented with his rough touch.

Stop it, Paige! I scold myself.

"Paige?" Hell, even his voice holds edges that catch and abrade my psyche.

I nod and retract my hand, hoping to regain some of my mental faculties. "Got it. Be direct. Firm. And use my hands."

A half-choked noise comes from Dash, and I glance up fast, in time to catch him running his fingers through the shaggy black hair that falls across his forehead. His cheeks tinge with redness that also creeps down his neck.

The heat of the day is probably getting to him too. NOLA weather, even in the fall, is no joke. Today has already reached the upper eighties. I'd better start getting this right, so we don't have to sweat our asses off out here much longer.

The three of us work for another twenty minutes until Pumpkin and I have mastered the basics—sit, stay, and come.

"We don't want to do more than that today. When Pumpkin stops having fun, she'll stop listening." Dash's words are supported by my dog trotting away from the both of us, heading back toward the house.

"Looks like someone misses the AC. Come inside. Is cash okay? Do you like sweet tea?"

I want to offer him more than just a beverage. Dash is in good shape, but he seems on the thin side to me. Like he needs a few extra meals to fill him out.

Is it weird that I want to sit him down and fix him a plate of food?

He looks like he could do with some caretaking.

That's not my job, I remind myself.

I hop up the stairs and pull open the back door to let Pumpkin in, then cringe when I realize she's tracking muddy paw prints all over the tiled floor.

"Oh crap. Take off your shoes, Dash! We're a fucking mess!" I yell this over my shoulder as I toe my sneakers off and sprint after my dog.

In the kitchen, she's drinking deeply from her water bowl. I pull a dish towel from one of the drawers and work on wiping her paws off, then crawl across the floor to clean up each puppy footprint.

"You need help with that?"

I glance up to find myself kneeling directly in front of Dash. In his right hand, he's dangling his dirty sneakers, and as he stares down at me, his beautiful, floppy hair falls over his forehead.

"I got it." My voice comes out in a higher octave than I was aiming for. Quickly, I move to stand, my position introducing too many naughty thoughts into my wandering mind.

Why do I have to find him so attractive?

Why do I have to find any *men attractive?*

My life can be amazing with just Pumpkin and me. Men are annoying and complicated. And they break things. Like hearts.

With this reminder ringing heavy in my chest, I force all thoughts to business, with just a dash of Southern hospitality my mother drilled into the core of my being.

"So, sweet tea. Would you like a glass?" I lead the way back into the kitchen.

"That would be great, Paige."

Damn. He shouldn't be allowed to say my name. Not in that husky voice of his.

"Are you sure you didn't hurt your ankle?"

His question has me pausing, and that's when I realize I must've been limping. The exercise should've helped with the stiffness, but it always creeps back in.

"I'm fine. That's nothing new. Hurt my leg when I was younger, and it cramps up sometimes." Avoiding what I'm sure is a curious gaze, I busy myself, pulling out a pitcher of the almost-syrupy, thick drink from the fridge and rummaging through the cupboards for a glass.

"You run a coffee shop from your house or something?" Dash's question has me glancing over my shoulder, confused until I realize he's examining the large brass espresso machine that takes up more than its fair share of the kitchen counter.

He shoots me a half smile, and I end up spilling sweet tea over my hand and onto the floor.

"Crap," I mutter, reaching for yet another dish towel to wipe myself off, and then push Pumpkin away from the puddle so I can clean it up.

"You need help with anything?"

If I look at him, I'll just end up messing something else up. "Nope. I'm good. Just clumsy today." With the utmost care, I pass him his glass of tea. "And, yeah, the espresso machine is a bit much. But I'm a sucker for fancy coffee. Get that from my mom. That used to be my grandfather's. He had it set up in his dealership and would serve his customers fresh cappuccino. Said that the showroom always smelled like coffee and that meant more customers." The memory of my grandfather brings on a warm, sad tingle in my chest. He was a gruff, sweet man, and the heart attack that took him away from us two years ago came out of nowhere.

"So, is that what you do? Sell cars? Must be pretty good at it to afford a place like this." Something in Dash's voice has changed. The words he says sound like small talk, but there's a coldness to the statements.

He sets down his glass without drinking any of the tea.

"What? No." I struggle over what exactly to say, not enjoying how pathetic the truth makes me seem. Still, Dash was honest about his ex-con status. I can at least be as straightforward. "This is my parents' house. My dad is a judge, and my mom refurbishes classic cars. Chevys from the '60s, like my grandpa used to sell. So, yeah, they make good money. I, unfortunately, lost my job a few weeks ago. I worked for a publishing company as an editor, but now, I'm a free agent, trying to figure out my next move."

There. That sounds better than *I've been wandering around my childhood home, sleepless, for weeks, too lost and depressed to apply for new jobs, and I can most often be found sprawled on the couch, watching episodes of* The Great British Baking Show *while eating fried chicken.*

No wonder my parents don't take me seriously.

"Your father…is a judge. And…your mother…works on cars." Dash's words start and stop as if he has to give deep thought to each one.

"Yeah. They're both good at their jobs. Do you not like the tea?" He hasn't even tried it, but maybe he just agreed to a glass to be polite. "I could make you a coffee instead. A cappuccino? Or a latte? I brew one for myself every morning."

Dash meets my eyes and smiles at me, but it doesn't shoot off sparks in my chest. Probably because, despite the upward curve of his mouth, it doesn't feel like a smile. More like an obligatory positive mouth movement.

"No. That's okay. I just realized I need to head out."

"Right. Just a second." I jog to the hall closet and pull my wallet out of my purse to grab the cash I owe him. Dash doesn't look me in the eye as I offer him the bills. "Thank you. For today. I swear we'll practice."

He nods, giving me another one of his not smiles before heading for the front door.

As he leaves, I relive the happy moments I had out in the backyard with Dash and Pumpkin just a few minutes ago. The warm bubbles that filled my chest at each accomplishment.

Because I'm excited to be a good dog owner.

Not because I want to impress the cute rescue worker.

CHAPTER 8

PAIGE

"You are a strong, independent woman, and he's an idiot for losing you. He fucked up. Not you." I glare into my own eyes in the rearview mirror.

I've parallel parked a short way from the restaurant. This place has valet parking, but dark thoughts in the back of my mind urged me to maintain my ability to make a quick getaway.

In case things go like the last time I saw my fiancé.

Ex-fiancé, I remind myself.

Haven't gotten used to that yet. But I will.

My sigh is so deep and drawn out that I imagine the air from my lungs filling the car. If only there was enough hot air in here for me to float away.

Different scenarios for how this meeting will go play through my mind.

Will I curl up in the fetal position at his feet as I sob out my heartache? Will I run into his open arms, shouting that I forgive him for all the world to hear? Will I punch him in the testicles?

Only one way to find out.

Finally, I climb out of my car, making sure my long skirt has cleared the door before shutting it. With the warmth of the day, I decided to go sleeveless, but I still made sure to cover my legs, like always.

Angelo's is in a gorgeous, old building in the French Quarter. Ferns hang in baskets from the second-floor balconies, swaying in the gentle breeze of the day. Tourists pause outside, posing for selfies with the classic New Orleans architecture acting as the perfect backdrop.

After stepping inside and passing the hostess stand, I reluctantly scan the restaurant, almost wishing that Martin decided to be as unfaithful to our lunch date as he had been to me so I can turn right around and leave.

No such luck.

At a table by the windows, Martin stands from his chair and raises a hand to catch my eye. My hesitant step turns into a stumbling stop when I realize that he isn't the only one seated at the table.

Obviously picking up on my disbelief, Martin whispers a word to his companion, then leaves her to weave his way over to me.

"Paige. You're here. I—I"—his words trip together as he grins down at me—"I'm so glad to see you."

When Martin clasps my upper arms, I go stiff at the touch. Either not noticing my discomfort or disregarding it, he leans forward to press a kiss to my forehead.

I wish it were a slimy kiss or overly dry with chapped lips. I want to breathe in a heavy odor of cooked broccoli or wet garbage. Instead, his familiar caress is warm and soft, and I pick up a subtle hint of his favorite cologne. The same one I bought him a bottle of with my Christmas bonus.

Damn Martin for not being an accurate embodiment of my betrayal.

"What is *she* doing here?"

My ex doesn't even have the grace to grimace or apologize.

"She wanted to see you."

He strokes down my arm, running his fingers over my slack palm. I realize his intent in time to pull away and cross my arms over my chest, balling my fingers into fists.

No way am I holding hands with the man who obliterated my trust.

Martin frowns, but simply moves to cup my lower back. At the light pressure, I move toward the table, so used to following his directions. When I pick up my pace, trying to get away from his touch, he keeps in step with me.

Arriving at the table, I stare down at the woman, at a complete loss for what to say to her.

"Paige! My dear girl. It has been far too long."

"Mrs. Blanche. Good to see you," I mumble, just one step above an irritated mutter. Not that I'm angry with *her*.

"Oh, now, we can't keep doing this whole Mrs. Blanche nonsense. Not when we're going to be family. Hopefully soon now that you're both home." Martin's mom stands from her chair and encircles me in a tight hug.

All the while, I stare, flabbergasted, at her son.

Family? She still thinks we're going to be family?

Martin wears a broad smile, even as he refuses to meet my eyes. Instead, he moves to pull back the third chair at the table.

I let Mrs. Blanche guide me to sit in it as I struggle to figure out where the miscommunication occurred.

Then, Martin leans over to press another one of his unfortunately pleasant kisses on my cheek, and clarity crashes into me with the force of a tree branch knocked loose in a hurricane.

He hasn't told her.

It's been a month, and he hasn't told his parents—at least not his mom—that he shit on any possibility of the two of us spending the rest of our lives together.

How has he kept it to himself?

My parents found out the night it happened. My dad, normally an even-tempered man, was only kept from accosting Martin by my mother hiding all the car keys. The feat was difficult, due to the large number of cars at our house, but she did it, all the while raging about stupid, selfish boys.

And yet Martin has gone all these weeks without letting on?

I can't fathom how he managed the feat until I start paying attention to Mrs. Blanche's energetic chatter.

"I think it is so sweet how the two of you have decided to live apart until the wedding. You know how Martin's father and I felt about the pair of you living together in New York. But we kept it to ourselves because who wants to be the villain in a love story as romantic as yours?" Her blue eyes, the same robin's-egg shade as her son's, go liquid with adoration.

It's all I can do not to grab the fork next to my plate and plunge it into the thigh of the true villain—the man sitting beside me, pretending as if everything is right in the world.

And I curse myself because I should have seen something like this coming.

You don't spend eight years with a man and not learn how his mind works. This is typical Martin. He's not the kind of guy to explore all sides of an issue. He's not one for debate and discussion. Martin is intelligent and therefore trusts his decisions and views to be the right ones. Then, he just makes following his preferred course of action the easiest road for everyone around him.

On nights we planned to eat takeout, he'd pick up the meals on his way home from work before I even suggested a restaurant.

When I brought up using my vacation time to visit my friend Charlie at his new place in Germany, Martin informed me he had already booked us a trip to Hawaii that would use up the rest of my days off.

I wasn't sure if I wanted to buy or rent a place when we moved back to NOLA. He wanted to buy, so he did.

All of these decisions frustrated me, but it was hard to justify my anger when he was purchasing things for me. So, I got used to it.

That was Martin. The man I loved.

But now, he's Martin, the man who decided to sleep with another woman. And now, he's trying to make staying with him, marrying him, the path of least resistance.

His conflict resolution tactics have never instilled this level of rage in me before.

He knows exactly how I feel about his mother. She's a little old-fashioned and can be formal at times, but I still love the woman.

Now, I have to make a choice.

Do I keep my mouth shut and keep that lovely smile on her face, or do I break her heart?

Damn him.

I still haven't made up my mind when our waitress comes to take our orders. The idea of food is repulsive at the moment, and I read off the first item on the menu without even comprehending the words coming out of my mouth.

"We'll have to set up a time for you and your mother to come over to my house, and we can talk wedding planning. Of course, I know you have ideas of your own. I would just really love to help."

At the same time Mrs. Blanche smiles at me, the heavy weight of a hand settles on my knee under the table. A familiar hand. A hand I've known and loved for eight years. A hand that contains twenty-seven individual bones I want to break.

And it's too much.

"No!" The plates on the table rattle as I stand abruptly.

"Oh, Paige, dear, I'm sorry. I did not mean to overstep." Mrs. Blanche stares up at me, hurt clouding her eyes, and I'm tempted to retract my outburst.

But despite Martin's attempt to steamroll me back into a relationship with him, there is an end date on us; we passed it the moment I arrived at the house I'd never wanted to buy in the first place.

Lying to Mrs. Blanche might bring back her happy smile, but it wouldn't be right.

"You can be kind, even when you're being firm."

Dash's direction whispers through the back of my mind, and I realize how apt his advice is for my current situation.

"No, Mrs. Blanche. I'm sorry."

Martin's worried expression clears at my statement. He shouldn't relax just yet though.

"I would love to plan a wedding with you. The problem is, Martin and I are not getting married."

Mother and son gape at me, wide-eyed—one confused, one terrified.

"I-I don't understand." Her perfectly lined lips quiver.

In a spurt of hurt anger, I'm tempted to relate exactly why our relationship is over. Lay out all the details, give her a clear view of the man her son has become.

But another part of me decides that there's no point in outing Martin's dirty secrets. We're done either way.

"I regret not being able to be your daughter-in-law. However, your son and I have different ideas of what being in a relationship means. Please give Mr. Blanche my best."

I reach into my purse and place a couple of bills on the table to pay for the meal I can see the waitress carrying toward our table now.

Whatever I thought this lunch might be, it definitely is not, and I see no point in staying. Without glancing at my ex-fiancé, I practically sprint to the exit, glad I planned for a quick escape and angry that I need one.

I'm halfway to my car when I hear my name.

Just like that night last month, Martin chases after me. This time, I pause to let him catch up. I need this to be over.

Maybe then it'll stop hurting so much.

"Paige!" He halts in front of me, reaching for my hands, but I cross my arms again. "Don't do this."

"Don't do what? Leave you? I've already done it, Martin. Just because I'm here doesn't mean I'm not already gone."

Across the way, a man with a trumpet begins playing, the happy rhythm of his song almost mocking. People pause to listen to the musician, and I wish desperately I were one of them, stopped on the sidewalk for an impromptu show rather than a showdown with my cheating ex.

"But you don't have to go," he says, as if I never considered that I could simply stay with him. That I *should*.

My temper snaps.

"Of course I do. Don't you see? I'm just following the natural arc of our story." I trace a curve in the empty space between us as if teaching a lesson.

"Girl meets boy. Girl dates boy. Girl falls in love with boy. Boy asks girl to marry him. Girl says yes. Girl moves across the country for boy. Boy cheats on girl. Girl breaks up with boy." I pause to take a deep breath, using the moment to push back tears threatening behind my eyes. "It's you who's attempting to throw in random chapters, like *girl sits awkwardly with boy's mom and tries to decide whether to lie or not about how big of an asshole boy is.*"

I glare at Martin, and he ignores what I said in favor of a hopeful smile.

"But you showed up, Paige. You came here. There's a chance for us. Couples go through rough patches, and they fix things."

I shake my head in disbelief and denial. Maybe someone else wouldn't think cheating is a deal-breaker. But that's not me.

"That's not why I'm here. I came to give you this." From the bottom of my purse, I pull out a velvet box he presented to me on that Hawaii trip we went on last year.

I wish I had gone to Germany to see Charlie instead.

"No. We're not over." Martin scowls at the jewelry box as if I'm handing him dog shit.

And suddenly, I'm exhausted.

"Yes, Martin, we are."

My ex-fiancé keeps his hands shoved firmly in his pockets, refusing to accept the ring.

So, I bend down, placing the box on the sidewalk between us before standing and walking to the driver's-side door of my car. I half expect him to sprawl across the hood of the car, refusing to let me leave. For a moment, I wish he would. Just so I can call the police on him.

But he stays on the sidewalk, staring down at the velvet box.

As I press my foot on the clutch, an ache starts deep in my leg. Maybe if I go for a run, it'll help with the combined physical and emotional pain of this day.

I pull into traffic, not looking back to see if he's picked up the ring.

CHAPTER 9

DASH

Every time I press the brake pedal, my car shakes ominously. Probably low on fluid, but I can't be sure until I get it up on blocks and check underneath. I pray I don't need to replace any parts because I don't have the money for that right now.

Today is already turning out to be shitty. A dog was returned halfway through my shift. The family had adopted it when it was just a puppy, and their reasoning for giving it back was that the dog "got too big, too fast."

What kind of ridiculous excuse is that? Did they think puppies stayed puppies forever? And who in their right mind wouldn't still find the full-grown Lab-mix adorable?

So, now, we have a dog that grew attached to people and has no idea why they decided to abandon him. Probably doesn't even realize he's been abandoned. He's just sitting in his kennel, waiting for the family he loves to come pick him back up.

Poor sucker. I know just how terrifying that wait can be. And just how devastating it is when no one comes.

Now, all I want is to get home, shower, and veg out in front of Cole's TV.

I turn onto a street full of potholes and slow my car even more to make sure nothing important falls off as it bumps over the uneven pavement.

An attractive figure catches my eye. On the sidewalk, which is in little better shape than the road, a woman jogs just ahead. Even as her round curves bounce with each step, her movements are smooth, arms pumping and legs stretching long. The bright neon-green sneakers grip the cement and propel her forward in strong, ground-devouring strides.

I home in on the shoes for a moment, their style and color memorable, before giving the runner a more thorough inspection. The shape of the body could be right, and the sunflower-yellow ponytail poking out from the Saints baseball hat is a familiar shade.

But it can't be her. This is not the area she would be running in.

New Orleans is like any big city with streets safe for tourists to walk without worries and then places where you need to keep a sharp eye on every passerby if you want to keep your valuables and your life. This street, while not the worst that could be found, is closer to the dangerous end of the spectrum.

The moment I roll past the jogger, she turns her head to examine my car, as if realizing the importance of being aware of her surroundings.

Through my window, I meet Paige Herbert's eyes.

Her steps stutter, but she keeps up her pace, smiling wide and giving me a friendly wave. Like she thinks this is a casual run-in and I'm not feeling a sudden onslaught of panic about her safety.

As quickly as I can, my car shuttering in protest, I pull to a stop against the curb. Afraid she'll jog straight past, I tug my keys from the ignition and hop out of my vehicle, pushing aside the shame of having Paige see me drive such a huge piece of shit.

"Hey, Dash!" Paige pauses, bending over to brace her hands on her knees as she works to catch her breath.

"Paige, what're you doing here?" I move to stand on the sidewalk in front of her, as if I can block her from continuing her ill-advised exercise.

She wipes strands of sweat-soaked hair off her forehead, staring at me with amused eyes. "Running."

"Yeah, I can see that. By why are you running *here*?" I wave at the neighborhood around us that is clearly last on the list for post-hurricane restoration. Doesn't matter that it's been over a decade since Katrina blew through. Half the houses here are just rotting bones, abandoned because the owners likely weren't well off enough to rebuild after the natural disaster. Crappy houses don't guarantee crime, but in this neighborhood's case, there's definitely a correlation.

"I've been increasing the amount I run each day, so here's where I ended up. Why are you here?"

"Just because this is a good distance from your house doesn't mean you should be running on this street. This area isn't safe for a woman on her own."

I expect Paige to either laugh off my concern like a spoiled rich girl who's never had anything bad happen to her and therefore thinks nothing bad will ever happen to her or that she'll realize the truth in my words, apologize, and ask me to drive her back to a safer part of town.

She chooses none of the above.

"I know."

For a moment, we stare at each other—me struggling to comprehend her simple statement, her waiting…for what, I don't know.

"If you know this area isn't safe, why are you running here?" I shove my hands into my pockets to keep from reaching out toward her. If I get my hands on her damp, salty skin, I'm not sure what I'll do. Maybe try to shake some sense into her. Maybe toss her in my car and drag her out of this neighborhood. Maybe pull her close enough to see if she still smells like a concoction from that over-the-top cappuccino machine in her parents' kitchen.

The conversation in her house had me resolute that we were never going to see each other again. The Herbert family is the embodiment of everything I need to avoid to keep my life on track. Her father is the law, her mother is expensive cars, and Paige is…

Paige is temptation.

Even now, when I should just leave her here, drive out of her life, I find myself stepping in closer to watch the beads of sweat trace down her collarbone to be absorbed in the dark gray tank top plastered to her chest.

"This is where I found Pumpkin."

Paige's answer drags me out of my inner turmoil to focus back on the issue at hand.

"This is where you found Pumpkin?" I glance around the dirty street, trying to remember everything I learned about the brindle pit bull's pickup from the rescue officer that brought her in.

"Well, not *here* exactly. A few streets over. But this general area." Paige props her hands on her hips, still staring up at me.

"So, what does that have to do with running here?"

Paige shrugs. "If I'm going to be running anyway, why not do it in an area where I might find abandoned animals? Then, I can call it in to the rescue. Just imagine if I hadn't been running here the day I found Pumpkin. Who's to say she would've been found at all? I don't even want to think about it." She bites her bottom lip and blinks rapidly.

Hell, that's not something I can argue with. I mean, my whole job revolves around saving animals. But I can still point out the flaws in her method. "Paige, there are rescue officers that patrol the city, looking for animals. You don't have to do that. Besides, you already admitted that this area isn't safe for you to be alone in. You shouldn't be putting yourself in danger on the off chance you might find another dog."

She's shaking her head before I've even finished. "I conceded that this area isn't safe for an average female on her own. I am not average."

Frustration has me growling, "People here won't give a shit that your daddy is a judge."

Paige snorts. "Well, duh. It's not like my sole defense mechanism is yelling out my father's occupation." She shifts from foot to foot and glances over my shoulder. "I've still got two miles to go. It was good seeing you, Dash. I'll text you about next week's lesson, okay?"

She doesn't wait for my answer, choosing to dodge around me, faster than I expected, and continuing her run down the street.

"Paige!" I curse when her only response is to raise her hand in a wave. Worried about what might happen to her if left on her own, I jump back into my car, mutter a fervent, "Thank you," when it doesn't hesitate to start, and hurry to catch up.

For the next mile, I follow her, keeping my car to the same speed as her running. It takes only a moment or two for her to realize what I'm doing. She glances over her shoulder, meeting my eyes through the windshield. Paige gives me a dramatic wave, indicating I should pass her by. I make sure my head shake is firm and unyielding.

When I don't follow her command, she throws her arms up but keeps on jogging. From that point on, Paige doesn't acknowledge me in the slightest. Occasionally, she passes a person on the sidewalk, and I notice them giving my car a curious stare. I realize how suspect what I'm doing must look, but I figure keeping Paige from getting mugged is more important than avoiding looking like an ass.

After maybe a mile, her route takes her into a more gentrified area frequented by tourists. Likely realizing this at the same moment as me, Paige turns to jog backward for a few steps, giving me a thumbs-up and a wink before facing forward and sprinting into a crowd of people.

I sigh, realizing how tense my shoulders have been.

My original plan was to tell Paige I couldn't be her trainer anymore and text her the number for a few other options in the area. But now, I'm resolute that I need to see her at least one more time in person. We're going to talk about her self-destructive choice, and I'm not walking out of her life until I know her running won't take her to my end of NOLA anymore.

And when I'm sure she's safe, I'll leave her alone.

Really, I will.

CHAPTER 10

PAIGE

"Please, if you just meet her, she's so sweet. Not a mean bone in her body."

"I'm sorry, ma'am. It's our policy."

"But policies can be changed! I swear, she's better behaved than most dogs you'd meet. Breed doesn't factor into that; it's all about how the dog is treated. Mean people make mean dogs. And I'm really nice!" A fact that should be clear from the way I restrain myself from snapping at yet another person calling me ma'am.

"We are not changing our policy. But if you would like to find another home for the dog and move into our apartment complex without a pit bull, we would be happy to review your application."

"Find another home? You want me to give up Pumpkin?"

"Pumpkins are allowed on our property. Many tenants have placed them out for Halloween."

"I'm not talking about gourds! I'm talking about my life partner!"

"We are an inclusive property. We do not discriminate against any sexual orientations."

I scoff. "Of course not. Just adorable dogs who want to live a happy life free from abuse. Never mind. This was a waste of my time."

I hang up my phone, pressing on the screen with an angry flourish. I miss the days of my childhood when we had a landline, when I could slam down the receiver dramatically to emphasize my anger. Now, it's just smartphones with sensitive screens.

A loud, incessant squeaking has me peering down at my innocent puppy. She's sprawled on her dog bed while I sit at the kitchen island, my laptop in front of me. Today, she's chosen a fuzzy pink pig toy to chew on, having finally ripped the fluff and squeaker out of her favorite pumpkin toy. I was worried she'd come to regret the destruction, but apparently, my dog has a fickle nature.

Staring down at Pumpkin as she calmly enjoys her new life of luxury, I can't help comparing her to the wounded animal I originally found. Other than some pink scars, there's no trace of the wounds she was covered in. The consistent diet of quality dog food has filled her out and helped bring a beautiful shine to her coat.

I did this. She's healthy because of me, and a balloon of pride and affection inflates underneath my rib cage.

How could that woman think for even a moment that I'd choose to give up my dog just so I could live in her boring apartment complex?

"If they don't want us, then we don't want them."

Pumpkin ignores me, too focused on her pig to pay me any mind.

I return to my apartment search without much enthusiasm, scrolling through the list of properties, but not getting any sense of excitement as I read about way too many that have breed restrictions.

But dog prejudices aren't the only problem.

Living under my parents' roof began to chafe almost immediately, so it makes sense I would be searching for a place to move into. However, while I do have a comfortable number in my savings account, that'll run out fast without a regular means of income. The solution seems pretty obvious—find a new job. But that's not as easy as it sounds. Mainly because I haven't decided where I want to work. New Orleans? Or some other random part of the country?

When I was a senior in high school, everything seemed so clear-cut.

Martin wanted to go to New York. I wanted to leave NOLA far behind and be with the boy I loved, so NYC sounded great to me. And I adored living in New York. The food, the culture, the massive number of bookshops. The only downside was having to put Penelope away in storage. Owning a car in that city was not a practical choice. Sometimes, on weekends, I'd break her out and escape the city, giving her engine a chance to show off.

Still, New York felt like a place I could spend the rest of my life.

Then, Martin's dad pulled some strings and got his son a great residency back here in Louisiana when he graduated med school. The idea of returning to my hometown was not appealing, but I figured that people made sacrifices for their partners. I also reasoned I would have a greater sense of freedom than when I had been younger because I was a grown woman and I would be living in my own place.

Look how well that worked out.

And now, nothing is tying me here. I could search for a job in New York if I wanted.

But do I want that?

Getting fired from my job feels like more than just a loss of employment. It's almost as if the city itself rejected me.

So, maybe not New York.

But where then?

The question flips over and over in my mind. For once, my life and my future choices are fully my own.

Why is that so terrifying?

My phone rings, and I snatch for it, thankful for the distraction. A grin plumps my cheeks when I see the FaceTime request.

"Chili Dog!" I pull out my childhood nickname for my best friend, Charlie, suddenly needing some nostalgia.

"Pancake!" he responds in kind, showing off his straight white teeth in a blinding smile. The effect is even more stunning against his maple-brown skin.

I've missed his face.

"It's good to see you. It has to be pretty late for you." I glance at the clock on the oven. "What is it, like ten p.m.?"

"Eleven. Remember, New Orleans is an hour behind New York."

"Oh yeah. Duh." I find it funny that Charlie has my time zones down better than I do. I'm pretty sure he knows the time in every major city across the globe. Probably from all the traveling he did with his parents when he was younger.

Charlie Keller grew up two houses down from me and has been my best friend in the world since before I can remember. His mom has a beautifully soulful singing voice that she makes a living off of. Her tours take her around the world, and she always made sure to bring her little family with her. Sadly, that meant there were large chunks of time where my best friend was missing from my life, but he always came back in the end.

Now a sales representative for a fabrics company, Charlie has lived on multiple continents. For the past two years, his home base has been Germany.

"I feel like it's been forever since we last talked. Catch me up." I carry my phone into the living room and get cozy in one of Mom's favorite lounge chairs.

As Charlie regales me with stories of his wild German adventures, Pumpkin saunters into the room. First, she lays her head on the armrest, giving me wide, pleading eyes. I try to ignore her, but she doesn't give up. Ever so carefully, she climbs up onto the chair and overtakes my lap.

"You experiencing an earthquake there or something?" Charlie's voice floats out of the phone as I try to settle my arms around my dog while still holding the screen so I can see his face.

"Sorry. I have a pushy companion. You remember that dog I told you I found when I was running?"

Charlie raises one eyebrow, and the gesture has me thinking of Dash. I resolutely push the sexy dog trainer out of my mind, focusing back on my best friend.

"Yeah, I remember."

"Well..." I tilt the camera until my grinning face appears next to Pumpkin's square head.

"Holy shit. You actually adopted it?"

"Not *it*. Her. Say hello to Pumpkin."

"You're wild, Pancake. But in a good way."

Charlie's approval of my adoption of Pumpkin eases an ache in my chest I didn't realize was there. I guess I was more worried about my decision than I realized.

"I love her so much. She's my new life partner."

"Much better than your old one. You heard from that piece of shit?"

I grimace and relate the story of the disastrous lunch. When I get to the end, Charlie is somehow melding both muttered curses and laughter.

"That's just...fuck...I can't even comprehend how his brain works."

"See, I'm the exact opposite. After eight years, I know *exactly* how his brain works. Problem is, after all this time, I'm not sure he knows me." I suck in a breath. "I'm not sure I know me."

Charlie scoffs, and I decide to focus on a different topic, not ready to delve into my lost psyche.

"How long do you think is a healthy time to wait before I start lusting after someone new?"

"Five minutes. Really, you should've gone straight out to a bar and slept with the first halfway attractive guy you saw."

"Charlie!"

My friend chuckles in a deep way that made all the girls at our high school sigh with longing. His rumbly voice and smoky eyes never affected me the way they did the rest of my gender. For a couple of weeks of sophomore year, we tried dating. But that first kiss, I might as well have been locking lips with a relative. Charlie is more like a brother than anything. I think with both of us being only children, we decided to adopt each other.

"So, who are you lusting after?"

Suddenly, I'm embarrassed. This topic is so foreign to me. I've been with the same guy since senior year of high school, which means any crushes I've had over the years got pushed so far to the back of my brain that they eventually fizzled out and died from lack of sunshine. The only love life Charlie and I discuss is his.

I don't know how to do this.

"It's ridiculous. No reason to even think about it. I just latched on to the first hot guy I saw. I'll get over it soon."

"I disagree. Why get over him when you can get under him?"

Charlie wiggles his eyebrows with such a devious skill level that I can't help giggling.

Pumpkin grumbles and shifts on my chest, obviously not a fan of the vibration.

The laughter leaves me feeling lightheaded and lighthearted with only my longing weighing me down. "I miss you. When is your next trip back to the States?"

Charlie's award-winning smile reappears. "Not sure, but I think I can make some time before the end of the year. You still going to be in NOLA?"

"I don't know." I frown past my phone, focused on my current living situation again. "I hope I'm out of this house at least. But I need to figure out what my life is, sans Martin."

Charlie nods, and we talk about our parents for a bit before he starts yawning too much to keep up with the conversation.

"Go to bed, sleepyhead."

"Okay. But we should make these video chats a more regular thing. I miss your face."

Despite his sweet words, I grimace. "You know I don't like talking on the phone."

Charlie rolls his eyes. "Really? So, you've just been in misery for this last hour?"

A quick glance at the clock proves his time-telling correct. Funny, with Charlie, everything seems easier.

Can't let him know that though. He'll get a big head.

"Okay. Okay. I'll think about it."

After we end the call, I consider getting up and making something for dinner for my parents and me. Only I have no idea when the two of them will be home. Mom is off delivering a car, and the work of a judge can sometimes lead to late hours.

Besides, I have a heavy, warm puppy on my lap that I don't have the fortitude to move.

Instead, I settle back in the chair and open up my text messages.

Paige: *Dog training Sunday still a go?*

I've almost drifted off to sleep when my phone buzzes with a response.

Dash: *Yes. We'll work on walking.*

Oh good. The ache in my shoulders grows worse each day as I get a thorough workout, holding on to Pumpkin during our morning walks.

I sigh in contentment, the idea of seeing Dash again bringing about a warm tingling in my toes.

Or maybe I'm just losing circulation in my legs from having an eighty-pound dog on my lap.

CHAPTER 11

DASH

"Good. Make sure her nose doesn't go past your thigh!" I call out to Paige as she and Pumpkin walk around the edge of their backyard.

It took some time to get the dog to understand what we wanted from her, but that pit bull is a people pleaser. Now that she knows the rules of the game, she's happy to play.

After our first lesson, I had myself convinced I wouldn't be coming back here again. But finding Paige running through that shitty neighborhood started up this nagging in the back of my brain. A need to check up on her.

For some reason, this girl thinks she's invincible.

How can I convince her that what she did was reckless?

I'm not leaving here until I get her promise to stay in the safer areas of NOLA. Places she belongs.

Not on the rough edges of society that I call home.

"This is working so well! Hopefully, we do as well out on the street." Paige and Pumpkin come to a stop in front of me. "Oh, and watch!" The girl turns to her dog, and without a word, she makes a firm downward movement with her hand stretched flat.

Pumpkin sits.

"We've been practicing!" Paige grins up at me, and all I want to do is step in closer to absorb every ounce of her joy.

Instead, I stuff my hands into my pockets and give her a stiff nod.

Some of the happiness drifts away from her eyes, but she keeps on smiling. "I think, once we get better at walking together, I'd like to take her on a run with me. Do you think that's something she'd do well at?"

"Probably. And at least, that way, you wouldn't be so vulnerable, wandering through those shitty neighborhoods."

Paige's mouth twists as she returns her gaze to me. "I told you, I can take care of myself."

I snort.

That was a mistake because the next moment, I'm tilting to the side, my right leg having been swiped out from under me. The only thing that helps me keep me balanced and upright is Paige's surprisingly strong arm wrapped around my waist.

Pumpkin dances around us, yapping and excited at the new game her owner is playing.

"You would be on your ass right now if I wanted you to be." Paige gives me a smug smile from her place at my side.

I'm torn between chagrin, curiosity, and excitement.

"Surprise attack. That was just a lucky shot."

"You're probably right." The last word is barely out of her mouth before her hip hits the outside of my thigh hard.

Only this time, I'm ready for her. When she tries to pull me backward, I roll with the movement, catching her around the waist and carrying her with me to the ground. We land side by side. I expect us to share a laugh.

But Paige isn't done.

She launches on top of me, pinning my arms to the ground with her knees. For a moment, it seems like she's won. But I buck my body enough to free one arm and shove off the ground, flipping us until I'm on top.

As we pant, our chests brush against each other. I brace for her next attack, but it doesn't come. Instead, Paige wraps one hand lightly around my neck, her thumb trailing over my pounding pulse.

Blood roars through my ears as I stare down at the blonde-haired goddess beneath me. What started as a grappling match has now ended with her legs wrapped tightly around my torso and our faces hovering only inches apart. The smell of coffee mixes with the light, salty scent of sweat.

Her hazel eyes seem to flicker green as she gazes up at me.

Then, she raises her head off the ground, closing the distance between us. I hold my breath, unwilling to stop what is no doubt going to be a heavenly experience.

In my fantasies, I've imagined I might be able to catch a taste of Paige. But here she is, preparing to kiss me.

At least, that's what I think she is planning on doing, until a gentle bite presses on my nose. For a second, she pinches the appendage between her teeth before releasing me, letting her head fall back into the grass. Paige gazes up at me, wearing a silly grin.

"If this were a real fight, you wouldn't have a nose anymore. Point to me."

My mouth bobs open and closed for a moment as I comprehend her attack. "You would bite my nose off?" I sputter, lifting my head farther away from her dangerous teeth in case she decides on a more literal demonstration.

Paige's goofy smile fades away, and I miss it immediately. Then, with a powerful wrench of her thighs, I find myself in the bottom position again.

This girl is hiding some major strength.

She stares down at me, face drawn tight, eyes serious.

"If someone attacks me, I'll use every weapon at my disposal. Teeth. Elbows. Knees. Nails. I'll gouge a man's eyes out with my thumbs if he gives me a reason to." To emphasize the point, she cups the side of my face and brushes her thumbs along the curve of my eyebrows. The gesture is a strange combination of tenderness and threat.

I hope she doesn't notice how aroused I am.

As Paige hovers above me, straddling my chest, I see her as something more than an awkward, rich girl with a soft spot for animals.

I see a weapon.

"Who taught you how to do all that?"

The secret ninja pushes off me, and I immediately regret the loss of her body against mine. With the day so hot, I shouldn't want to press myself against her warm softness. But I do.

"My parents had me take a bunch of self-defense classes, growing up. And boxing. And sparring. I was also on the boys' wrestling team my freshman and sophomore years of high school."

Trying to come to terms with this new version of Paige, I ask the first question that pops into my mind. "Why'd you stop?"

Paige tosses a ball across the yard, and Pumpkin sprints after it. "I'm not that competitive, and the dieting to make weight was miserable. I figured I could grapple with people at a gym and not worry so much about the medals."

"So, your parents are into you fighting or something?"

Paige settles on the patio steps, and I move to join her. We both stretch our legs out—hers in baggy sweatpants again and mine in shorts. Now that I think about it, every time I've seen Paige, she's been wearing pants despite the high temperatures. I wonder if it's a modesty thing. Or maybe her body runs cold. The second option doesn't seem likely after experiencing the heat rolling off her when we were tangled together moments ago.

"I told you my dad is a judge."

When Paige glances at me for confirmation, I nod and try not to grimace. I don't like being reminded about all the different reasons she's off-limits to me.

"He's overseen some big cases throughout the years. Every so often, my parents would get death threats, mainly aimed at me. Freaked them out. Whenever it happened, there'd be some kind of protection detail, like a marshal. But they thought it would be a good idea if I also knew how to protect myself, just in case."

"Wow. That's pretty heavy to put on a kid."

"Oh, I didn't know about it until high school. For most of my life, I thought they were nuts. I never understood why they were so much more protective of me than other parents were with my friends. Other kids got to ride their bikes to different neighborhoods. Other kids got to hang out after school with their friends. Other kids got to go to weekend parties. Other kids got to go on dates." She snorts after that last one. "Not that a lot of guys were asking out the only girl on the wrestling team, but still. I felt so suffocated. And sometimes, I lashed out.

"I would do dangerous things that were technically within their rules. Like if they said I couldn't leave the house, I'd climb out onto the roof." She points up to the steeply angled tiles two stories above us. "One time, when they refused to let me go to a party, I broke into my dad's liquor cabinet and drank half a bottle of whiskey. Spent that night bent over a toilet." Her smile is rueful.

"So, what? They told you only to run in the safe areas and you decided to do the opposite?"

The stories from her childhood are interesting, but they just annoy me in the end. Teenagers behaving immature is no big news, but she's a grown woman now. She should know better.

Paige stands up from her seat, glaring down at me, fists on her hips. The pose is fierce and adorable. "No. I'm not running in less reputable parts of town to stick it to my parents. I learned my lesson. I know how shitty things can turn out when I make my decisions out of spite."

I bet that whiskey burned pretty bad on its way back up. I can see how it would make a lasting impression.

"So, why then?"

"I already told you! I'm keeping an eye out for other dogs like Pumpkin."

"But why were you running there in the first place? Before you found her? You looking for a real mugger to practice your skills on? Because let me dissuade you of that fantasy now. No matter how good you are in a gym or a ring, real life is different. There's no referee. There's no tapping out. And when you get hit for real, it comes out of nowhere."

At some point, I stood up, too, and now, I'm the one glaring down at Paige. I'm torn between reaching out to shake some sense into her and pulling her to my chest to hold her so tightly that she won't ever run off again.

Paige huffs out a frustrated breath. "I wasn't looking for a fight! I'm not an idiot. Half the reason I run so much is because I'd like to err on the side of flight over fight if the choice ever came up."

"Well then, why were you there?"

"I got lost!" She throws her hands up in defeat and stalks away from me.

I follow after her. "Lost?"

"Yes. Lost. One minute, I knew where I was; the next, I didn't. So, I kept going. Then, I found Pumpkin. When the police officer came to pick her up, he gave me directions back toward my house." She turns on me, eyes guarded. "I didn't know where I was. Honestly, I don't know where most things are in this city."

"Didn't you grow up here?"

She rolls her eyes. "Yeah, but I just told you, my parents, while loving, kept me pretty close to home. I never explored much. I didn't have a car until college, and college was up in New York. I've been back here only a handful of times since I moved away, and those were all short visits. I may be a New Orleans native, but this city is kind of foreign to me."

"That's…" I search for the right word. I'm also a NOLA native, but where Paige's parents were restrictive, mine were pretty much negligent. My whole childhood was freedom, in an unhealthy way, seeing as how I ended up in the back of a police car. But at least I got to know my city. "Sad."

Paige avoids my eyes, choosing to kneel on the ground and rub Pumpkin's exposed belly. "Yeah, well, it's not like I had a bad life. Just kind of sheltered."

"So, you've never gone out? Experienced the bars and the nightlife?"

Her shoulders grow stiff. "I've gone out! I'm not some weird hermit that locked herself away in her apartment. I went out all the time in New York."

"But that's New York going out." I shake my head, tugging my fingers through my hair. "Not New Orleans going out."

She shrugs. "Is it that big of a difference?"

I can't help but sputter. "You can't be serious! People fly here from around the country, from around the *world*, to get a taste of what this city has to offer. Of course it's different."

Paige's doubtful expression raises my blood pressure, and I have an intense urge to prove to her what she's been missing.

"What are you doing tomorrow night?"

Paige's eyes blink open wide, and her hand falls away from Pumpkin. "Why?"

"Because you need to give this city—*your* city—a chance."

"What does that mean?"

I crouch down in front of her, bringing our gazes level. "That means, Paige Herbert, I'm taking you out."

CHAPTER 12

I hesitate outside the door to the bar, trying to hold on to this moment where I am in complete control of my faculties. Because who knows what will happen the minute I see Dash?

Only yesterday, I decided to use him as a self-defense dummy, and I still get the occasional tingle along my abdomen as I recall how it felt to have his warm chest pressed against mine. Intoxicating.

Then, this morning was the metaphorical hangover from hell.

How could I attack him like that?

I can't manhandle someone just to prove a point. No matter how much I wanted to run my hands over his biceps. And his chest. And his face.

Ugh, now, I'm thinking about touching his face like I've suddenly lost my sight or something. I have eyes. I can stare at him. But I shouldn't.

I'm going to fuck this up. I don't know how I haven't already.

Still, Dash was the one who asked *me* out.

Or, at least, he asked if I wanted to get to know my city better.

I'm still torn between whether or not I want this to be a date. On the one hand, Dash is hot, and sweet, and smells like sheets fresh from the dryer. On the other hand, I'm still sporting a broken heart and haven't figured out if I'm able to trust someone with a penis.

He probably didn't mean for this to be a date.

More likely, Dash thinks I don't have any friends, felt pity for me, and reluctantly invited me for a weeknight get-together in hopes that I won't get too depressed and do something dramatic. Like shave my head.

"You coming in or what?"

The gruff voice knocks me out of my inner musings, and I realize the doorman has been watching me chew my lip and debate with myself for a good five minutes.

"Yes. Sorry. Just thinking…about hair," I finish lamely.

He stares at me for a moment before shrugging and holding his hand out. "ID."

After the bouncer checks my age and stamps my hand, I slide past him into the dark interior of the bar. With Halloween a couple of weeks away, the bars have started decorating for the occasion. Skull-shaped lights dangle from the ceiling all around the room, pairing well with glittery spiderwebs and painted pumpkins. The place smells like damp wood and beer. Jazz music plays from hidden speakers, but in the back of the bar, I catch sight of a band setting up their instruments.

It's been months since I've heard live music.

For a Monday night, the place still has a decent crowd. But that's New Orleans. A never-ending party, especially with a holiday approaching. Of course, Halloween has nothing on Mardi Gras.

In early February, New Orleans explodes like a purple, yellow, and green piñata. Every street becomes a celebration for weeks. When I was a kid, Mom and Dad eased up on their strict *stay inside after dark* rules to take me down to the parades. Each day we'd pick a spot, setting up chairs and a stepladder for me to stand on. Back then, I wasn't so tall and needed the help to see over the heads of the drunk partiers. We came home with bags full of goodies tossed from the floats —masks, purses, coins, stuffed animals, flowers, and of course, beads. I wore so many strings by the end of the night that my neck ached from the weight. I'm lucky I didn't strangle myself.

The memory of my dad attempting to carry me with the added weight of my plastic jewelry has me smiling.

I wonder if I'll still be in town for the wildness this year.

Would Mom and Dad want to go out? Could I convince my taciturn father to raise his hands in the air, begging the float riders to toss him a prize?

The image has me chuckling to myself.

But almost as fast as the bubbly feeling comes, my humor fades away to a sense of sad loss. Chances are, I won't be here. By that time, I should be employed, most likely in a city far from New Orleans. Somewhere I can start my life fresh. On my own. Without relying on my parents to support me every time I stumble.

I'm supposed to be an adult. My days of being carried home by my dad are long gone.

And that is why, tonight, I shouldn't even be hoping that this is a date. No reason to get attached to a guy when I'm going to be leaving soon. Maybe Dash can just be my friend for the moment. Someone to show me the parts of New Orleans I missed out on when I was younger.

Tomorrow, I'll stop putting off the inevitable. I'll update my résumé and send it out. Anyplace that sounds even slightly appealing, I'll throw my hat into the ring.

I'll be the responsible, capable adult I've always wanted my parents to see me as.

And when I get hired, I'll leave New Orleans behind again.

This time for good.

———

DASH

The guy sitting next to me at the bar scowls my way. That's when I realize I've been rapping my knuckles on the wood in a light, nervous rhythm. I stop and turn my back on him.

Excitement rattles through my nerves, and I'm so twitchy that people probably think I'm jonesing for a hit.

Only if they consider a woman to be addictive.

This adrenaline, the fast fluttering in my veins, the distinct pound of my heart pulsing under my rib cage, is familiar. It's the same reaction I had moments before I jimmied the lock on some poor bastard's Toyota. My body would vibrate, but my hands would stay steady as I reached under the dashboard to hot-wire the car. Then, I'd revel in the growl of the engine, grip the steering wheel tight, and press the gas pedal down to make a quick getaway that earned me my nickname.

All the warning signs are here.

I ignore them.

Even fate seemed to be against me making this date. My crap car refused to start, no matter how many times I turned the key in the ignition. After popping the hood, I realized it wouldn't be a quick fix.

I could've canceled.

I should've canceled.

Instead, I gritted my teeth and dealt with the expense of calling a cab. Without a smartphone, I couldn't even take advantage of the cheaper rideshare services.

Now, I'm here, nursing a glass of water, waiting for a girl that affects my body in dangerous ways.

If only I could take a drink to calm my nerves, I might not be so annoying to sit around. But that's a bad idea. Against my parole. I shouldn't even be in a bar. But how can I show Paige the NOLA nightlife, everything she's been missing, without bringing her to a place where people are drinking?

I take another swallow of water and glance at the entrance again, waiting for her.

And like my wanting summoned her, she appears through the crowd.

Good thing I already swallowed my drink because the sight of Paige causes my throat to constrict.

So far, I've mainly seen her in baggy sweatpants and tank tops. Of course, there was that amazing time when she took her shirt off in front of me. The image is firmly saved in the back of my brain.

Tonight though, Paige isn't dressed for running or dog training.

A dark pair of jeans hugs her legs tight, revealing a round ass and toned thighs. The pants would probably take some time to peel off her, but I'd be up for the challenge.

She has on a flowing white top that's short enough to show flashes of her smooth stomach. The sleeves hang off her shoulders. For the life of me, I have no idea how the thing even stays up on her. I wonder if I give the bottom a light tug, would the fabric slide low enough for her nipples to pop free?

I can imagine gripping her waist, pressing her back against the bar, and leaning down to feast on them. Would they be light pink? Or maybe slightly purple, like a plum. I bet if I sucked on them long enough, they'd turn as red as strawberries.

And if I did it right, I might get to hear her sexy noises.

Would she gasp? Moan? Whisper dirty things in my ear?

"Do you think this place has nachos?"

Apparently, our minds are on different tracks.

Paige asks her question as she slides onto the stool next to me.

"Hello to you too." I suppress my inappropriate thoughts and fight the smile that threatens as her eyes go wide. A blush chases over her cheeks.

"Hell. That was rude. Sometimes, when I'm hungry, I forget proper social conventions." Paige's lips twist before she sighs. "That's not true. I struggle with proper social conventions, even on a full stomach. So, um…" She glances at me, clearly uncertain, then stands back up from her stool.

When Paige leans forward to wrap me in a light hug, I sit frozen. She's soft and smells of coffee, and she retreats too soon.

"Hi, Dash. Good to see you again. Thank you for inviting me out." Her greeting comes out stiff, and even though I'm still absorbing the fucking amazing sensation of her body pressed against mine, I have to admit, I liked her nacho opening better.

It was more honest. More Paige. Something she'd say to a friend.

"You're welcome. I don't know about the nachos. We can ask. You want anything to drink?"

After I flag down the bartender, we find out they do have a menu, and it does include nachos. Paige orders an Abita on tap, and I watch her drink the amber liquid with envy. Both because I miss the taste of beer, but also because I'm jealous of the glass for getting a chance to kiss her mouth.

"You don't drink?" She reaches over to flick my water glass.

"Parole."

I brace myself for her reaction, guessing she's found a way to temporarily forget my criminal past to spend time with me.

Instead, Paige only nods before gripping my arm in excitement and changing the subject.

"I took Pumpkin running with me this morning! She did so well! Except for this one incident with a squirrel, but those fuzzy little critters practically beg to get chased, so I can't blame her for it."

Dogs are safe talking territory. I latch on to the subject.

By the time the nachos arrive, I've gotten Paige to tell me everything she wants Pumpkin to learn to do. It all sounds relatively basic. Material that could be covered in a handful of lessons. Not something that would keep me around long-term.

"Have you considered agility training?" I throw out.

"Agility?"

"Yeah. It's like an obstacle course for dogs. But you guide them through it. There are competitions, but a lot of people do it for fun. And it's good for the dog. Teaches them better discipline. Gets their minds thinking about complex tasks. I could teach you and Pumpkin."

"Yes. I want that. We will do that, and Pumpkin will dominate because she is fucking amazing." Paige emphasizes her point by chomping down on a chip covered in melted cheese, jalapeños, and all the other variety of fixings her nachos are overflowing with.

I watch her chew, enjoying the way she attacks the food with gusto.

"Eat." She pushes the plate across the bar toward me.

"I don't want to take your food." I play the gentleman and hope she doesn't hear the way my stomach growls over the music. The peanut butter sandwich I made myself earlier is not filling me up the way I wish it would.

"Dash, if you don't help me with these nachos, I will eat all of them. Not because I'm that hungry, but because they are sitting in front of me. *Tempting* me." Paige nudges the appetizer even closer until I can smell the cilantro and green onions sprinkled across the top. "So, please, for the sake of my ever-fluctuating waistline, eat some. Sharing is caring."

I give in. The first tortilla chip hits my tongue in a glorious combination of salt and spice. I try to restrain myself from chewing like a maniac and swallowing quicker than a vacuum cleaner. To save some extra cash, I've been cutting back on my groceries. Hunger has become a constant companion that I do my best to ignore.

Paige gifts me with a sweet curl of her lips as she picks up the little cup of sour cream and places it closer to me. I dip the next chip and enjoy the cool freshness, paired with the heat from the peppers.

A little happy hum emanates from Paige's throat as she goes back to eating her food.

"You said you're looking for a job, right? What did you say you do again?" My brain kind of short-circuited the first time she told me, too focused on her parents' professions. I've promised myself to stay far away from beautiful cars and trouble with the law.

Paige traces her finger through a puddle of condensation on the bar top. "I was a book editor at a publishing house in New York. I still want to do that. I just need to figure out where."

A book editor. Now, the way she originally gave me her cell number seems less odd. But only slightly.

"What exactly does a book editor do?"

"Oh, it's great. For the most part, you get to work with authors and their babies!" She clutches her hands to her chest, eyes shining with excitement.

"Their babies?"

"Books. Their books. Which are like their babies. And you get to see them at all levels of their developmental stages. It really is like kids going to school. Some of them send in chapters, and they're basically asking, *Is my kindergartner ready to go to college?* And you have to figure out how to tell them no. But gently, so they don't spiral into a pit of devastation. Authors do that a lot. Good editors know how to avoid it."

"And you're one of those good editors?"

Paige smiles and rests her chin in her hand, staring at me as she talks. "In the beginning? Not really. I've gotten better. And how you handle each author is different. Some need a light touch, and others need blatant honesty. You just have to figure out the person you're working with. Some of my authors..." The happy expression on her face fades, leaving behind a wistful frown. "Well, they aren't mine anymore. I guess they've been reassigned to other people on the team."

"What happened? With your job?"

Paige gazes out over the crowd of people gathering closer to the back of the bar.

"I asked my boss if I could work remotely when I decided to move here. He agreed, but then a few weeks before I was set to leave, he told me that wasn't an option anymore. I either had to stay and keep my job or leave and lose it."

"That sucks."

Paige grimaces, then downs her beer.

I'm about to ask why she was so set on moving back to New Orleans when the band lets out the first few notes of a rumbling song. My companion squeals and reaches out to clutch my arm.

"I love live music. Have you heard these guys play before? Are they any good?"

I nod as I restrain myself from eating any more nachos, having already devoured close to half the plate. "They're popular around here."

Paige finishes the last swallow of her beer and flags down the bartender to ask for another. The alcohol brings a ruddy flush to her cheeks and neck. I bet if I leaned in close, heat would radiate off her skin.

The sound of a trombone brings a jazzy edge to the guitar and drums blaring from the back of the room. People all around us cheer and start dancing. A new kind of life pulses through the bar. A beat of enthusiasm and barely restrained insanity. Everyone laughs louder, and the lights shine brighter.

This is a taste of the real New Orleans.

Paige has fully turned around in her seat, leaning back against the bar as she sips her beer and watches the musicians enchant the room. She's as enthralled as everyone else. Her eyelids sink slightly as her head nods and sways with the rhythm.

While everyone else is focused on the entertainment, I can't look away from the woman next to me. If someone were to simply glance at Paige, they might make the same mistake I did on first meeting her. They'd see the pretty face, blonde hair, nice clothes, simple makeup, and conclude she's an average beautiful girl, who probably fits nicely into a cookie-cutter mold.

But spend a few minutes with her, and you realize she's more than surface level.

Paige is odd but in an amusing, intriguing way. She's capable of passion and compassion. Plus, she can probably kick the ass of most people in this bar. And I get the sense she's holding secrets, past hurts, under the surface of her guileless hazel eyes.

"Do you dance?" She doesn't look at me when she asks, her gaze skittering around to all the people swaying and moving along with the music.

Again, I err on the side of honesty. "Not usually."

This earns me her stare. Paige watches me over the rim of her glass, smoothly swallowing the last bit of her second beer. She sets the empty cup down and slides off her stool, coming to stand practically in between my spread knees.

"Is tonight a usual night?"

If she were any other girl, I'd swear that line was meant to be flirtatious. But with Paige, I can't tell. She simply sounds curious.

And maybe it's the fact that I *want* her to be flirting with me that I give in so easily.

"I guess not."

That was the right answer. Paige's face radiates joy, and she grabs my hand to pull me after her into the crowd. She settles on a tiny chunk of free dance floor, turning to face me. Letting go of my hand, she begins to move.

Watching Paige dance is like observing a pile of tinder catch fire.

Slow, then all of a sudden, the whole of it is up in flames. Paige starts with her shoulders, simply tilting them back and forth. Then, the movement spreads to her hips, which sway and dip. When her arms rise in the air, all tension leaves her body, and she's simply moving. As untamed as an open flame.

Even though I'm here with her on the floor, Paige is dancing for no one but herself. Her moves match the music's beat, but not in some seductive display. There are lots of girls around us who move with more skill and sensuality as their eyes skip between men in the room. They know what they want, and they're actively looking for it.

Paige just wants to dance. I'm convinced that even if I'd turned her down, she would've come out here by herself. She's not even looking at me. Instead, my partner has her eyes closed, one arm stretched high above her head, the other hand tangled in her hair, as she rocks and bounces to the music.

Like a moth, I'm drawn to her light, stepping in close enough to act as a reflection to her movements, but not so close that I restrict them. I let her have her space and make sure that everyone else does the same.

A blare of the trombone has Paige's eyelashes fluttering open. Seeing me directly in front of her, she wrinkles her nose in a grin. Both her hands reach out to clutch mine, our fingers twining, and then we're moving together. First, it's just a little game of push-pull, until I spin her like we're swing dancing, and she laughs so light and joyful that I find myself grinning right along with her.

The songs begin to blend into each other, and I only notice the passage of time from the growing heat gathering under my skin and from how much closer Paige and I work our way together. The first brush of her chest against mine lasts less than a second. So quick that I doubt if it even occurred. But the next lasts longer, maybe three seconds, before Paige dances away. This happens over and over. A quick press of her body against mine in time with the beat of the music, then gone almost as fast. She never gets too close. Just enough to let me know she's there.

I think the teasing feel of her is going to drive me crazy.

The next time it happens, I don't let her retreat. Instead, I free one of my hands so I can wrap my arm around her lower back. Holding her flush against me, I execute a low dip as an excuse for my sudden possession of her body.

Paige laughs with joy and lets her head fall back. The smooth expanse of her throat is the color of whipped cream, and I fight the urge to lick the hollow at the base of her collarbone.

To do away with the temptation, I stand us both upright.

But I don't let her go.

One hand holding hers, the other pressing into her spine to keep every curve of her lush body pressed against me, I keep us dancing.

Paige settles her free arm around the back of my neck, and I shiver at the caress of her hot breath dipping under the collar of my shirt. She leans in closer, practically burying her nose in my shoulder.

The top of her golden head sits level with my mouth, and I have the strange urge to tilt my chin down and press my lips into the silky mass. I hold back, barely, choosing to rest my cheek against her like she's a pillow. The gesture still gives me a strong sense of intimacy, but it could be interpreted as friendly.

The more we move together, the hotter my skin becomes, until I'm worried I must be burning her. But Paige holds on to me just as tightly as I do her. The salty tang of sweat mixes with her coffee scent, and I want to drink her in.

Does she feel this need to consume me too?

It's better if she doesn't.

At the moment I'm sure I'm about to release her waist, Paige tilts her head up to meet my eyes.

"You're an amazing dancer!"

Her goofy smile breaks down what little resolve I had to separate us. Instead, I find myself leaning in closer.

Before I can decide whether I should answer her or kiss her, the band lets out a blast of a note meant to signal the end of a set. In the sudden lack of noise, I peer around in a daze, resurfacing from the drug-like state caused by dancing and the proximity to Paige.

I don't know why this woman is hitting me so hard. New Orleans is full of beautiful women, a lot of them looking for quick flings. That's who I should be dancing with—some girl who just wants fun for the night, and we can part ways the next day. No need to even exchange names.

Instead, I'm still holding Paige Herbert, someone who's better suited for a relationship. Paige doesn't seem the type to hook up, then not call the next day.

No, Paige is the type of woman you take on dates. Someone you sit down at a restaurant with and have actual conversations. She's fun, and sweet, and deserves someone a lot better than me.

I'm one step above trash. And that's me being generous with myself.

I let my arms drop and walk back toward the bar, unsure if Paige will follow me or not. Even though the band has taken a break, more music spills out of the speakers.

"Dash!"

At first, I think that Paige shouted my name, but when I turn around to look at her, she's peering off to the side. That's when I realize the voice, while familiar, didn't send pleasure goose bumps racing over my skin. I search around the dance floor until I find the speaker.

And try not to frown.

Teresa weaves her way through the crowd, charcoal eyes locked on me, red lips tilted in a sultry smile. When she reaches me, her hand snakes around my neck and drags me down so she can press a kiss on my cheek.

"I haven't seen you around lately. Where've you been?"

"Working." I shrug and shift to the side.

Teresa stands directly in between me and Paige, who's watching the two of us with an unreadable expression.

"Look at you. Professional man. I like that. Maybe next time we—"

"This is my friend Paige," I cut Teresa off before she can get to whatever comment she was about to make. Knowing her as I do, it probably would've been extremely suggestive and left no doubt in Paige's mind that we've hooked up in the past.

For some reason, I'm desperate for her to remain in the dark about that.

Teresa turns to get a look at my companion. With her back to me, I have no idea what expression is on her face, but Paige offers a hesitant smile and a half wave.

"Hello."

"Well, hello, Miss Paige. I'm Teresa. And how do you know my good friend Dash?" Teresa's voice gives nothing of her inner thoughts away, which starts me sweating. If she wants, Tea could destroy whatever slightly decent image Paige has of me in her mind.

Maybe I should let her. It would probably be better for the innocent girl to get away from me.

But apparently, I'm being selfish tonight because I take a step toward Paige, ready to hustle her away from Bomb Teresa.

"Dash helped me find my life partner. Well, actually, I found her. He just gave her back to me once he was sure she was ready to go." Paige stumbles over her explanation, laying out our meeting in the most awkward wording imaginable.

I turn to glance at Teresa's face, wondering if I'll find jealousy or confusion.

Instead, her eyes have homed in on Paige in distinct interest.

"Your life partner, huh? Surprised she let you out with a scoundrel like Dash." Teresa says my name in an almost-affectionate manner.

"Oh, Pumpkin loves Dash. Maybe even more than me." Paige grins up into my face, her voice coming out steadier.

"Pumpkin? That's a sweet little pet name." Teresa moves in closer. I expect her to step toward me, but instead, she saunters into Paige's space. "So, you, Pumpkin, and Dash are close?" She flicks her eyes to me, a smoldering in their depths.

And suddenly, I realize her angle. I'm torn between laughing hysterically and bundling Paige under my arm to sprint out of the bar with her.

Teresa and I have hooked up a few times, just the two of us, but I'm not unaware of her reputation. She likes to experiment with multiple partners. At once. I shouldn't be surprised that Paige, who I've been panting over since she walked into the bar, would strike Tea's interest.

For a moment, I imagine it—me, Paige, and Teresa. Should be any guy's fantasy. But when I get another look at the predatory nature of Teresa's stare, I realize that I don't want to share Paige with her.

I want the curvy, innocent book editor all to myself.

"Pumpkin is a dog!" My words come out louder than I expected them to.

Both girls turn to stare at me—Paige wide-eyed in confusion, Teresa with offense.

"I doubt that, Dash. I'm sure Paige's Pumpkin is beautiful. Isn't that right, sweetie?" Teresa strokes a hand up Paige's bare arm, and the blonde girl smiles.

"Yes. She's gorgeous."

I sigh, slightly amused at the hole Paige is unknowingly digging herself further into.

"I meant, she's an actual dog. Paige adopted her from the rescue where I work."

Teresa's lips pinch in momentary disappointment, and I jump on the opportunity to escape.

"Good to see you, Tea. But we were just heading out. I'll see you around." My arm wraps in tight possession around Paige's waist, and I guide her toward the door before she can protest.

"Nice to meet you!" Paige calls out sweetly, glancing over her shoulder to wave at the pouting Teresa.

Stepping out into the night air that has cooled slightly with the setting of the sun, I feel almost as if we've escaped a hazardous situation.

"Did I embarrass you in front of your friend? I'm sorry. Sometimes, I think I'm doing just fine, but then I realize I've fucked it all up. Martin could never—" Paige shuts her mouth quickly with a grimace and glares off into the night, leaving me wondering who Martin is and what he did to bring such a dissatisfied expression to Paige's face.

"No. You're good."

How she could be so unaware baffles me. Wasn't it obvious how Teresa was one step away from propositioning her? I wonder what kind of bars Paige went to in New York if she can't even tell when she's getting hit on.

"Okay. So, thanks for dancing with me. And showing me some more of the city."

Paige turns to leave, but my hand reflexively reaches out to stop her.

"Wait." This night can't be over already. I need more time with her. I scramble for something to keep her with me. "Are you hungry?"

I'm about to cringe at the ridiculous question, seeing as how we just shared some nachos, when Paige nods.

"I could eat."

CHAPTER 13

PAIGE

"Oh my gosh. Where have you been all my life?" I moan, my mouth full.

Dash stares at me as if he thinks I'm insane. "You've got to be kidding me, Paige. I know you said you didn't get out much as a kid, but how could you live in New Orleans for eighteen years and never have had a po'boy?"

I swallow before smirking at him. "I've had them plenty of times. But never after a night of drinking and dancing. That just adds a new layer of deliciousness."

We're sitting side by side on a bench, eating classic NOLA fare. We decided to share a fried catfish po'boy, and the sandwich is fulfilling all my food fantasies. Fried food usually does that.

My arm pressed against Dash's is bringing back some of the happy, warm tingles that got snuffed out when I watched Teresa claim him so blatantly in the middle of that bar's dance floor. Not like I have any right to be jealous. Dash and I are just friends. Plus, Teresa seemed nice.

Still, that smear of red lipstick on Dash's cheek serves as a reminder that I'm obviously not his type. And I shouldn't even be letting the idea of going out with a hot guy enter my mind. I need to focus on finding a job, not improving my dating life.

I'll find someone to lust after in whatever new city I settle in.

"I'm sorry about Teresa. She can be a bit much."

Dash's comment shocks me out of my musings, and I try to figure out what he means.

"A bit much what?"

He raises one of his sharp eyebrows as he peers over at me. "She comes on strong. Been that way since high school."

I shrug, still not sure why he's apologizing. "Someone being friendly is nothing to complain about. If anything, I envy her." *Shit, why did I say that?* Now, he's going to think I'm mooning over him. Wanting what Teresa so clearly has. "Because I don't talk to people. Well…I mean…I do talk to people. I just always seem to mess up what I'm trying to say."

The way he smiles does strange things to my insides, like my heart is an engine and he's slowly pressing the gas pedal. I'm inconveniently revving to life.

"That ever give you trouble at your job? Aren't you supposed to make sure people's writing makes sense?"

A fair question, and something I've pondered myself. I suck on my bottom lip for a minute as I attempt to figure out how to articulate my conclusion. When I think I've got it, I meet Dash's eyes, only to find him focused on my mouth. There's a strange intensity in his dark irises that matches the expression I noticed in Teresa's earlier.

Curious.

I choose to ignore the mystery and power on.

"Words on a page? I can pick them apart, study them, apply rules to them, and test them out. They just work better that way. For me. And a lot of times, the authors I work with enjoy writing in strange, interesting ways that don't follow normal social conventions. My favorite author"—I glance around as if I might see one of the other writers I work with glaring at me from across the room in affront at finding out I have a favorite—"she crafts her stories in the most creative ways. If someone talked like she writes, you'd look at them like they were an odd ball. But for her and her work, it is perfect."

I shake my head, realizing I've been using the present tense during my explanation when that is all in my past now. The memory of my author friend, Marianna Tweep, makes my heart ache. She's a gorgeous woman, who always reminded me of Morticia Addams, but with a dash of Marilyn Monroe. I miss sitting with her in the dark speakeasy-themed bar she preferred, reviewing my editing suggestions for her latest memoir. Over the past few weeks, I've considered contacting her, just to check in.

But I held back. I try to convince myself that my hesitancy is because I don't want to cause strain between her and her publisher.

Really, I'm just a coward.

What if she only liked me for my edits? What if she stopped even liking those and was happy to hear I'd been canned?

I'm not sure I could take the mortification of discovering Marianna no longer wanted to associate with me.

"Sounds like you miss it." Dash watches my face, and I wonder what he's looking for.

"I do. It's all I've ever wanted to do, once I figured out you could earn a salary helping authors develop their books." I think about the job applications I finally started to fill out. All of the positions were technically for editorial work, but none of the job descriptions sounded anywhere near as interesting as my old position.

But beggars can't be choosers.

I take the final bite of my sandwich and wipe any trace of mayo from my lips. Even though this isn't a date, it's exactly what I would want to do on one if a man I liked asked me out.

Drinks, dancing, delicious food…and Dash.

Damn it. The realization that I'd like to end my night with a healthy dose of the guy sitting next to me has me berating myself.

This is not the time to lust after a man. This is the time to take a romance hiatus.

"Thank you. For offering to come out with me. You were right about New Orleans. I'll have to spend more time exploring while I'm still here."

He freezes in the act of wiping his hands. "You're leaving?"

I shrug. "I'll have to go wherever I find a job."

Dash gives a curt nod before gathering our trash and dumping it in a nearby bin. I watch him. The guy is tall with ropy muscles that shift with each of his smooth movements. Why can't he walk around like a dorky scarecrow? There's nothing about him that detracts from his handsomeness. Even erring on the thin side just makes me want to take him out to dinner and watch him eat. Earlier, I had a silent celebration for every nacho chip he ate.

If only I could cook for him. The idea of creating a meal from scratch, placing it on a table in front of him, and getting to admire his long, callous fingers carry my creation to his lips…

Who knew fantasizing about feeding a man could make me so hot?

I stand up and subtly try to fan a little cool air under my loose shirt to keep myself from sweating.

"I'll walk you to your car." Dash stands in front of me, hands shoved deep in his pockets, staring down into my eyes.

For a moment, I'm stuck, feet adhered to the sidewalk, gaze latched on tight to the striking black of his eyes. Only they're not black. This close, I realize the color is a deep brown. Like a piece of dark chocolate without an ounce of milk to dilute the cocoa.

"Paige?"

My name on his lips is sinful. I want to lean forward, press my mouth against his, and have him whisper it again so I can swallow the sound. A slight pressure on my chin feels an awful lot like his rough fingers.

My eyelids flutter, wanting to close as I memorize the contact, but also stay open to keep mapping his angular face.

"Are you too tipsy to drive? Should I call you a cab?"

His questions pierce my infatuation fog, and the heat of embarrassment slams hard into my cheeks. I take a quick step back, away from Dash and all his distracting handsomeness.

"No. I'm a good driver." I fiddle with the edge of my shirt. "I mean, I had two beers, and it's been more than two hours, and I was just lost in thought for a moment there, and my blood alcohol level is most definitely below the legal limit."

If anything is high, it's my blood pressure. I doubt most girls would consider it a compliment when the guy they're crushing on looks deeply into her eyes and then concludes that she's wasted.

My ego pretty much no longer exists.

"Do you remember where you parked?" He still sounds doubtful of my ability to act as a sober human being.

I barely keep from moaning in mortification.

I don't want him to walk me to my car anymore. I want him to leave me alone, so I can curl into a ball and hibernate until I become a fully functioning adult.

"I doubt we're parked near each other. We can part ways here."

And then because, apparently, I want to put a cherry on top of my idiot cake, I reach up and pat him on the head.

Like a dog.

This is how my brain chooses to show Dash that I'm sober.

"Did you jus—"

"No!" I turn and power-walk in the direction I parked earlier, praying to every deity I've ever read about that Dash goes in the opposite direction.

It seems that the gods and goddesses know deep down that I'm not normally so devout because I've only taken a few steps before a hot hand presses against my back.

"I'm walking you to your car, Paige."

"That's silly. You should go to your car, and I'll go to my car, and then we will be at the proper cars."

And maybe I'll stop talking like a robot.

Dash snorts. "I didn't drive here, so no need to worry about that."

I peer up at him as we pause, waiting to cross an intersection. "You took a cab? Why? You didn't even drink."

The side of his face I can see grimaces. "Car trouble."

"Oh." I hesitate for a moment, weighing the pros and cons, before realizing I don't care what the cons are. "I can give you a ride home."

Dash's hand drops away from my back as we dodge around a loud group of men that are either a fraternity or bachelor party with the loud, drunken way they're carrying on. Once we're side by side again, he shakes his head.

"Don't worry about it. I'll just call a cab."

Down the street, I see the beautiful emerald shine of my '68 Chevy Impala. She's sitting happy and calm, just where I left her.

"That doesn't make any sense. Why pay money for a ride when I'm offering a free one?"

"I'm out of your way."

"So what? It's not like I have a job to get to tomorrow morning."

"A cab will be fine."

I don't know why he's being so weird about this. Unless…

"Dash. Look at me."

We pause about ten feet from my parking spot, and he turns his head to the side to meet my eyes. The move seems reluctant.

"I swear I'm not drunk. Look."

To prove I'm telling the truth, I walk a straight line, heel to toe, while alternately touching my pointer fingers to the tip of my nose. Once I make it the distance to my car, I turn with a flourish.

"See. Functioning at full capacity. Now, get in and tell me your address."

He stands still, staring at me for a good moment. Long enough that I'm almost certain he's going to turn around and walk away.

Finally, Dash's shoulders drop, and he slouches to the passenger side.

I thought I would feel a sense of triumph. Instead, there's a tingle of embarrassment that he's so obviously opposed to riding with me.

Is the idea of being stuck in a small, tight space with me so unappealing?

Once we're both buckled in, I unlock my phone, open a GPS app, and hand it to him. "Type in where we're going, please."

Again, he hesitates, but then plugs in his address and places my phone on the mount attached to my dashboard.

Just because I drive an old car doesn't mean I didn't ask my mom to include a few upgrades.

"Copilot picks the music." I reach out an olive branch, trying to figure out how I can ease the stiffness in Dash's posture and bring back the easy friendliness from earlier in the night.

One of his tantalizing eyebrows notches up, but he reaches for the radio dial after I turn the key in the ignition. My engine growls, sending vibrations through the seat. With Dash beside me, the sensation is somehow naughtier than I ever considered it could be.

I doubt he notices.

Instead of watching his long fingers press my buttons, I focus on shifting into the right gear as I pull out of the parking spot, following the directions presented by my GPS in a sexy Australian accent. Out of the corner of my eye, I think I catch a slight twitch of Dash's mouth, but I'm not sure.

He settles on a hip-hop station. I don't know the song, but attempting to listen to the words while also listening to the GPS and traversing New Orleans late-night traffic gives my mind enough distraction, so I don't have to focus on the guy next to me or the weird happy-sad flutters he sets off in my chest. It's like my stomach is full of manic, unmedicated butterflies.

But another more insistent sensation makes itself known as we get farther into our drive. A pressure that refuses to be ignored.

I need to pee.

I try my best not to squirm as I break at a stoplight. Dash was right; his house is out of my way. Normally, I would not mind in the slightest, but with every block we travel, I add another minute onto when I'll have access to a toilet.

Damn beer. Damn me for not realizing the alcohol and water would eventually convene in my bladder.

By the time the GPS announces we're a minute from our destination, I'm bordering on agony. The pain has turned sharp, and I'm not sure I even have the strength to make it to a gas station.

When I pull up to a curb in front of a tall shotgun-style house, I turn to Dash before fully putting the car in park.

"I'm sorry, Dash. I know you're just looking to go inside and go to bed and be done with me, but I need to use your bathroom, and I wouldn't impose on your privacy if it wasn't an emergency, and I swear I'm not trying to sneak into your place to ravish you." My pleading spills out in one long tumble of words. This time, I most definitely fell off the babbling cliff.

He stares at me, wide-eyed, for a moment, then glances out the window and back at me. "You want to come inside?"

"I need to use a bathroom. Please, can I use yours? I promise I'll be quick." Now, I am squirming, a pathetic dance that does nothing to release the pressure, just somehow temporarily convinces my body to hold off on wetting myself for another minute or two.

Dash must realize I'm not joking because he nods before climbing out of my car.

I would have sagged in relief if I wasn't terrified that'd give my bladder the go-ahead to unload. Instead, I hop out after him, following close, but not too close.

"It's not that nice," he mutters.

I'm too focused on not peeing my pants to figure out what his tone means.

Instead of going in the front door, Dash walks us around back, and we head up a handful of rickety wooden stairs.

"As long as it has a bathroom, it's at least nicer than my car."

Dash grunts as he unlocks the back door and holds it open for me. We're in a kitchen. I'd love to have the brain capacity to take in my surroundings, but I'm five seconds away from bursting.

"Through the bedroom, there's a hallway; bathroom door is on the left."

"Thank you, you wonderful man," I murmur feverishly as I sprint through the doorway he points to.

I pass a room, barely seeing more than a bed before reaching a hallway with a door open just a crack. Through that small opening, I spot a glorious porcelain throne.

Door closed and locked, pants pulled to my ankles, butt on a chilly seat. Never can I remember having such a satisfying pee. The fact that the bathroom is barely bigger than a closet doesn't matter to me in the least. The toilet is so close to a washer/dryer set that I have to keep my elbows tucked to my sides. A half-empty bottle of laundry detergent sits eye level. I'm tempted to reach over, unscrew the cap, and take a whiff on the chance that the liquid is what gives Dash his tantalizing fresh scent.

But then I remember that I'm supposed to be a sane adult.

After I finish my business, I wash my hands thoroughly, but quickly. When I was on the verge of bursting, the pain of my predicament pushed aside any embarrassment. Now, I watch a flush steal over my cheeks as I look at myself in the mirror.

Might as well say a final goodbye to Dash because after this display, I doubt he'll want to even continue dog-training lessons with me.

I sigh and dry my hands before pushing the door open.

And then I stand still for a moment, trying to remember which direction I came from.

The sprint to the bathroom was so frantic; I can't recall if I came from the right or the left. The hall is short, and there's an equal distance to both cracked open doorways. Should I call out for Dash or just try one?

I decide to turn left and hope I've got it right.

My choice does bring me to a bedroom, only I'm not sure if this is the one I sprinted through a moment ago. The curious thing about it is, there's a man sprawled across the bed with a notebook propped on his knee and a pen skittering across the page. The pen halts when he notices me.

Was there a man in the bedroom on my way to the bathroom?

I'm not sure I would've seen him if there was.

"Who are you?" His voice hits whip-fast, and it's all I can do not to flinch at it.

"Paige," I answer because it's the only thing I can think to say.

We stare at each other for a moment. I'm not sure what he sees, but I get the impression of danger. Or at least anger. The guy lounges, a scowl on his face, dark, twisting ink covering his arms and chest. That's when I realize he's shirtless, wearing only a pair of black sweatpants. Silver studs glint in his ears, and a little loop pierces his eyebrow.

"Are you fucking Dash?"

His question has me rocking back on my heels, and I glance down at my pants, which are fully zipped and buttoned.

No dick currently in there—that's for sure.

"At this very moment? No. If you meant to use past tense—as in, *Did you fuck Dash?*—then again, the answer is no. If you meant to say, *Are you going to fuck Dash?* referring to either tonight or at some point in the future, then I can't give a definitive answer. I have no psychic skills. However, I'd say the answer is still likely to be no, seeing as how I doubt your roommate is interested in me that way."

Damn, I'm babbling again.

"You're here," he says in a way that leads me to believe the presence of a girl in their house normally equates to them being fucked by Dash. Interesting. And also disheartening.

"Well, we were hanging out, like friends do, and I practically had to beg to use y'all's bathroom. So, yeah. Sex is unlikely." Wanting to change the subject from my complete lack of sexual appeal, I nod toward his notebook. "What are you writing?"

He stares at me, unblinking for a long time. The guy brings to mind a python deciding whether or not it wants to bother with devouring a passing warthog. Me being said warthog.

Eventually, he smirks, the expression full of disdain. "A torrid sex scene between a warrior werewolf and his succubus mate."

If this dude was trying to scare me off, he failed royally. I practically trip over myself to move in closer, sitting cross-legged next to his bed.

"Really? He's a warrior? Who is he fighting? Is this urban fantasy or set in another realm? Does she want to be his mate, or is he seducing her? Or is she seducing him?"

The guy's eyes widen at my sudden approach, then narrow as he stares down at me. Once again, he takes a moment before answering, but when he does, the words sound like a gift.

"I'm Cole."

DASH

How long does it take a girl to pee?

Maybe Paige was so embarrassed when she saw my house that she decided to climb out the window rather than face me. I bet her parents' basement is nicer than this place.

I don't exactly live in poverty. More like poverty adjacent.

Cole and I share half of this ancient shotgun-style house. The owner, a crotchety old man, lives in the other half. He only puts up with us because we're quiet and we get the rent in on time.

Not that there's a lot of competition for this place. We're in a crappy area of town, where a shiny green Chevy Impala really shouldn't be left unattended. The house itself is well past its prime, if it ever had one. The kitchen appliances are older than I am, and they come in an unappetizing pea green. Scorch marks mar the tattered wallpaper above the oven, and the vinyl flooring, which probably started as white, has long ago stained itself yellow.

We keep the space clean, but there's only so much lipstick you can put on a pig.

Dreading that Paige has gone for the window, I leave the kitchen and cringe when I realize the state of my bedroom. Never expecting to bring her back here, I didn't bother to clean up the clothes I'd discarded after work or the ones I decided not to wear tonight. The random shirts and pants strewn about are some of the few decorations in my bare room. Here, at least, there's wooden flooring, better than the shit in the kitchen. But I've done nothing to cover the dingy white walls. My furnishings consist of a mattress on a simple bed frame, a dresser, and a chair in the corner.

Not much different than my cell.

Hell, she probably thinks I lied about stealing cars and that I'm some kind of psycho murderer.

I push the door leading to the hall open far enough to realize the bathroom light is off and the little room is vacant.

That's when I hear the voices.

"So, if they're at war with the succubi, how do his warriors feel about the mating?"

Shit. Cole is going to be pissed. He hates being bothered while he's writing.

I jog the few steps it takes to get to his room, only to stumble in shock when I hear his response.

"They don't know. Not at first. She's a hostage." Cole's voice comes out dry, but after living with him for over a year, I can tell he's not mad.

"Ooh. I love it!"

When I walk into the room, the scene throws me for a loop. Paige sits on the floor beside Cole's bed like an eager child at story time, and my roommate is giving her what could almost be categorized as a smile. At least when it comes to Cole.

"Hey." It's all I can think of to say when, really, I want to walk over, scoop Paige up in my arms, and carry her to my room.

Paige jumps up and turns to face me with a guilty expression.

"Sorry! I made a wrong turn and found Cole. But don't worry. I made it clear we are definitely not fucking."

My roommate grins like a demented demon behind her back. "Yeah, Dash. Paige set me straight. No past, present, or future fucking."

I keep my face expressionless as I walk over to place a hand on Paige's lower back, guiding her away from the jackass and making sure she doesn't see the scathing glare I throw him over my shoulder.

We're almost clear of him when Paige halts abruptly. She turns back, and I barely stop myself from stepping in between the two.

If I can't have her, why should he?

"Cole, before I go and never see you again, I wanted to tell you…" She hesitates, and I think Paige is trying to figure out how to speak without her trademark awkwardness. I want to tell her it's okay. Neither Cole nor I have any room to judge.

"Yeah, babe?"

Oh, fuck no.

I do my best to burn an angry hole in my roommate's forehead for using a pet name with my girl.

He smirks, and I realize he can do whatever the hell he wants. Because she's not my girl.

His mocking smile helps Paige clarify her thoughts because she powers on. "You are doing something fantastic. Writing a book. Some people talk about it, but you're actually doing it, and that's amazing. I think you're amazing."

Her words hit Cole like a slap, knocking all the mockery off of his face and leaving a lost, stunned look in his eyes. I've never seen him like this before, and I suddenly feel self-conscious for him. I shouldn't be here. Not when Paige is peeling back his protective layers.

"And it might get hard. You'll probably get frustrated or feel blocked at some point. Or maybe you won't. The words might come easy to you. But if you ever want to talk to someone about your writing, there are writers' groups all over the city. Check online or at the local libraries. Just don't give up. Because I want to read your book. Okay?" Paige stares across the room, waiting for Cole to respond.

After a moment, he gives a jerky nod of his head, eyes glued to her.

I need to get Paige out of this room before my roommate falls in love with her.

"Let's go. Leave him to write that book." I slide my hand into hers, needing to lay some type of claim to her.

She whips her head around to glance at our twined fingers before staring up at me with a confused smile.

"Okay. Bye, Cole." Paige waves over her shoulder as she wanders out of the room, me trailing close behind.

In the hall, I move into the lead, dragging her fast through my house so she doesn't have a chance to absorb too much of the decay.

Back beside her car, I let go of some of the tension in my shoulders, but the street still puts on display how crappy my living situation is.

"Thank you. For letting me use your bathroom. I'm sorry I shoved my way into your house. And tell Cole I'm sorry if anything I said offended him."

"I don't think an apology is what he wants from you," I mutter.

"Oh. What do you think he wants?" Paige stares up at me, eyes innocent, mouth parted slightly as if to entice me.

I clear my throat before answering, "Nothing. I just...you don't need to apologize. For anything. Everything you did tonight was perfect."

The only light on the street is what shines out from behind people's curtains, but even in that muted glow, I think I make out a blush stealing over Paige's pale skin.

"Good to know. Well, everything you did tonight was perfect too."

Then, because, apparently, she wasn't tempting me enough, Paige steps into my space and wraps her arms around my torso.

The hug is soft, supportive, comforting, and yet sensual. The curves of her body mold to mine so well that I'm sure I could create a diagram of them. I know I'll map them out later tonight when I'm in bed. As I return the gesture and press my nose into her loose hair, the earthy scent of coffee floods my lungs. When her arms begin to retract, I pull in another deep breath, trying to hold on to every last bit of her for as long as I can.

"Damn."

Her quiet curse has me searching her face for anything that might've gone wrong. That I did wrong.

"Pumpkin is going to be so bummed."

"Why's that?"

Paige gives me a rueful grin. "Now, I smell like you." She lifts the white fabric of her shirt, showing off more of her midriff with the move. After holding the shirt to her nose for a moment, she lets it drop back into place. "She's going to sniff me and wonder where you are. That dog loves you." She sighs and flicks my chest playfully. "But who can blame her? You're a lovable guy."

Leaving me standing on the cracked, weed-covered sidewalk, Paige slides behind the wheel of her Chevy.

"Have good dreams, Dash!"

As the Impala disappears around the corner, I'm still dealing with a dangerous tailspin of emotions.

CHAPTER 14

"So, I may have gone just a tiny little bit overboard." I try not to cringe as Dash scans my parents' backyard.

What used to be a decent-sized grassy expanse is now a fully equipped doggy agility course. I've got tunnels. I've got ramps. I've got poles. I've got hurdles.

I've got an insane amount of free time and an intense obsession with making my dog happy.

I could probably host a competition here.

Should I have spent a hefty chunk of my savings on all these materials?

I've yet to reach a conclusion on that score.

"I guess that's a yes to training Pumpkin on agility." Dash turns to me with a smirk and an eyebrow raised, and I know my weirdness has been acknowledged and accepted.

This guy keeps surprising me.

When I texted him about Pumpkin's next training session, I, again, fully expected him to find an excuse to cancel on me. I know there were a few times during our hangout session that I made him uncomfortable with my awkward behavior. I'm not obtuse. What I can't figure out is when he'll reach his *Paige is super annoying* threshold. I thought it might be the forcing him to let me use his bathroom move, but apparently not.

"We still have some things to get comfortable with before moving on to obstacles." Dash's voice brings me back to the present tense.

I agree and call Pumpkin over so we can get started.

Everything goes well for about twenty minutes. Our review of past skills breezes by, and when I hook Pumpkin up to her leash, she stays by my side while we trot around the yard.

We're in the middle of practicing the command *drop* when everything in the lesson and my life goes to shit.

The creak of the back gate has Pumpkin's ears perking and Dash and me turning to see who the visitor is.

A man walks toward us, and the sight of him sends a shot of icy shock racing through my body, followed quickly by a boil of heated anger.

"What are you doing here, Martin?" My voice comes out low, an almost-animalistic growl.

My dog tenses at my side, and I realize I need to rein in my distress.

"I wanted to see you." Martin can't seem to decide which one of us to look at. His eyes skip between me and Dash, then touch on Pumpkin before coming back to rest on me, only to flick over to Dash again.

"So?"

Martin's wants are no longer my concern.

"Who is this, Paige?" Dash comes to stand by my side, his face a blank mask.

"I'm her fiancé." Martin glares at the only guy I *actually* invited to my parents' home.

"You should be using the past tense. You *were* my fiancé. Go ahead, try it out. I admit that it sounds weird at first. But trust me, you get used to it. Real quick."

Dash snorts at my side, and Martin's scowl goes supernova.

"You moved on from me already, Paige?"

I want to slap him, point out that he moved on from me while we were still together. But getting into an argument with my ex in front of Dash is not going to help my image of a rational adult that I'm trying my best to exude. So, I push the pain and anger down.

"Martin, this is Dash, my friend, my dog trainer, and someone I like spending time with. Dash, this is my ex-fiancé, someone I don't like spending time with anymore, and I have no idea why he's here."

"I'm here because we need to talk. And when did you get a dog?" Martin's demeanor lost a slight amount of hostility at the clarification that Dash and I aren't an item.

That cocky, possessive body language makes me want to retaliate by climbing my friend and mauling his face.

With my face.

In a sexy way.

Better never say any of that out loud, I decide.

"If you wanted to talk, you could have texted."

"Would you have responded?" Martin asks.

"Probably not."

He smiles triumphantly as if he somehow made a point.

My exasperated sigh mixes with another growl. Pumpkin whines and paces in front of me.

Breathe in. Breathe out. I'm calm.

"Go wait on the patio. We have a lesson to finish. If you behave, I *might* talk to you."

I glare at Martin until he turns around and walks to the back porch, settling in one of the wrought iron chairs with its thick, comfy cushion. He doesn't deserve to be comfortable. He should be sitting in the dirt.

With a shake of my head, I do my best to ignore him and focus back on Dash and my dog. Unfortunately, my trainer seems distracted, his gaze locked on the man lounging like he owns the house.

"Ignore him. I'll deal with him later. We have more important things."

Dash moves his stare to me, silent for a moment before nodding.

"Now, just like with the other commands, firm voice and a hand gesture." Dash demonstrates a closed fist, then spreads his fingers as if he were dropping some invisible object.

I try to mimic him, but he reaches out for my hand after I try the motion.

"No. Your fingers should spread wider. When they're closed, it looks like you're making the sign for sit." His fingers press into the spaces between mine to spread them out.

A loud cough echoes from the patio.

We both ignore it.

I try again, and Dash gives a nod of approval.

For the next ten minutes, we work on getting Pumpkin to understand the command, with varied success. Just when she seems to be getting it, a loud noise will distract her. Maybe it's another cough, or the scrape of a chair being adjusted, or even a quick, called-out comment.

In any other situation, I don't think these things would throw my puppy off so much. But she's clearly picking up on my discomfort. The past lessons have been fun and playful. This one is all stress.

There comes a point when both Dash and I realize today is going to be a bust.

"It's okay, Paige. Some days are good; some days are bad. We'll work on this again next week. When everyone is more relaxed." One of Dash's large hands smooths over my shoulder, then rubs a reassuring circle on my back.

"I'm sorry." I shove the toe of my sneaker into the dirt after tossing a ball across the yard for Pumpkin, letting her run off her tension. I'm going to need the same outlet once everyone leaves me alone. "I'll just grab my purse."

Disappointment that my brief time with Dash got interrupted wars with relief that once he's gone, I can confront my ex for showing up unannounced.

"Don't worry about it. Today was a bust. No need to pay me."

I glare up at Dash. "Your time is valuable. You gave some of it to me and my dog. We're going to pay you."

For a moment, he stares down at me, strange emotions flickering through his eyes before he settles on one of his not smiles.

"Nothing about me is valuable."

The breath gets knocked from me at the amount of self-loathing conveyed in that statement. But I don't have time to form a coherent response because there's an asshole nearby.

"Your lesson all done now? Gotta say, didn't look too productive. You know my aunt raises show dogs, Paige. I'll give her a call and set you up with a professional trainer." My ex saunters over to us, a smirk heavy on his face.

I move to stand in front of Dash as if I can protect him from the cruel words. Then, out of nowhere, another level of defense presents itself. Pumpkin places herself just in front of me, hackles raised, a low growl rumbling from her barrel chest.

I let the satisfaction of seeing fear on Martin's face roll over me for just a moment before crouching down and hugging my dog, whispering sweet, soothing words in her ears. After a moment, she calms down enough to lick my face and trot back to Dash. As she snuffles his pockets for treats, I stand up to face my ex.

"Damn, Paige. If you wanted a dog, you should've talked to me about it. We could've found you something small and cute, like a Pomeranian. It's not safe for you to have a violent dog." Martin glares at my sweet, loving Pumpkin.

The combination of his words and expression breaks a dam inside me. Fury rises in a steady pressure, like a flash flood about to drown everything in the surrounding area. I have moments before the destruction begins.

"Dash, watch Pumpkin. Martin, follow me." My voice sounds strange to my ears, and something in it wipes the confidence from my ex's face.

I head for the gate in the fence, my rage increasing even more because I can't keep from limping slightly as I stalk over the grass.

Once we're in the front yard, I turn on him, letting all the heated disgust burn bright in my eyes.

"Paige—"

"How dare you? How dare you show up here without an invite? My home. At least as much of a home that I can have after you took mine from me!"

"No, Paige, calm down. I want you to come back. Live with—"

I cut him off, ignoring his words, "And on top of your unwelcome visit, you think it's okay to insult my dog? And my friend?"

"I'm sorry." Martin steps closer, unaware of the danger he's putting himself in. "I guess I saw that guy and I got jealous." He gives a self-deprecating smile like we're going to laugh about his behavior together.

I want to dig my thumbs into his eye sockets and pop the offending orbs out, so they can't look at me anymore.

"I don't care if you walk in on me *fucking* another man. You can't say anything about it. We. Are. Over." My words ride out on a furious whisper.

And somehow, they seem to penetrate Martin's thick skull.

His face loses all color, and he stares down at me with lost eyes.

Finally, I think he gets it.

After a moment, he clears his throat and glares off to the side. "A lot of your things are at the house. I'm assuming you want them."

I want to say *no* and be done with this man forever. But I've collected more things in my twenty-five years than can fit into my Impala, which means a lot came to New Orleans in the moving truck Martin hired.

"Text me a day and time you won't be at the house. I'll come by to grab it all then." With nothing else to say to him, I turn on my heel and stomp back to the yard. Before unlatching the gate and slipping in, I drag in a few calming breaths.

If I'm lucky, that'll be the last I see of Martin for a long while.

CHAPTER 15

DASH

fold down the corner of my magazine to save my place when my phone starts vibrating. Even though I know it's useless, I try to make out a name on the cracked front screen.

Nothing.

When I finally get out from under some of my debts, a new phone is first on my shopping list.

I'm tempted not to answer. The people who call me tend to be the ones I don't want to talk to. My brother, preceded by that automated message from the prison, asking if I'd like to accept his call. My dad, reminding me to bring the monthly check by the house. Teresa, looking to hook up.

Still, there's the chance it might be Luna, my sister, so I flip the phone open and brace myself.

"Hello?"

"Dash! This is Paige. Of Pumpkin and Paige." Through the phone speaker, I hear a happy hum. "Ah, see, the alliteration sounds so good out loud."

A grin practically breaks my jaw. She's almost too fucking adorable to handle.

"Hi, Paige, of Pumpkin and Paige. What can I do for you?"

"Halloween is this Thursday. My parents—well, my mom—love Halloween, so there's going to be a big party going on at our house. Lots of people. Are you free?"

I can only imagine what that party will look like. Probably something from out of a movie with the amount of money the Herberts make. That house will likely be decorated top to bottom with shit you can't buy at Party City. I bet the whole thing will cost more than my rent for the year.

And all their guests? Bet they'll be equally decked out. Wonder if the crowd will lean more toward outrageous or elegant. I'm betting the latter, but in New Orleans, you never know. Rich people can go all out too.

I can see why Paige called me.

"You want me to watch Pumpkin?"

"Umm, I mean, if you want to say hi to her, I'm sure she'd like that."

Paige's response was not what I was expecting, so I try to get on her wavelength.

"You called me because you're worried about her at the party, right?"

"What? No. Pumpkin isn't the driving force behind this conversation. You are. You being at this party."

Me at the party?

Now, she's not making any sense. Sure, Paige being okay with spending time with me at a bar tracks, but at her parents' fancy holiday party?

That can't be what she means.

"I'm not sure what you're asking, Paige."

Her frustrated groan leaks through the phone.

"I'm shit at this. Phone talking is even worse than normal talking. Do you have an email account? If I type this out, I can make more sense. I promise."

I grimace, knowing she can't see me.

"I do, but I'd have to go to the library to use a computer to check it. Can you text me? My phone does that at least."

"Oh hell, and have my thumbs cramp up from typing all the words? No. I can do this. Just give me a second." She sounds slightly desperate, which makes me want to reach through the speaker and soothe her. Instead, I give her what she asked for. At one point, she starts talking, but it's soft, like a mutter, and she's clearly speaking to herself. "I can do this. Talking is like writing with my mouth."

I hold back a snort of laughter.

She starts again, the formalness of her tone somehow charming. "Dear Dash. On Thursday, October 31st, my parents, Mrs. and Mr. Herbert, will be hosting a party at their house, where I also reside. As you know." Her deep breath is audible through the phone. "I would like to extend an invitation to you to attend the party as my guest. I find my parents' friends to be tedious and dull, for the most part, while I find your company to be pleasant and engaging. Therefore, I would like to spend the night talking to you rather than them. Costumes are recommended, but not required."

It takes me a moment to realize she's done and then another moment to rein in my shock.

Paige didn't call because she needs me to do something for her. Nothing other than showing up at a party and being her friend.

It's been a while since someone asked me to do something with no ulterior motive. At least, I don't think she has one.

"You called to invite me to their party? You don't need me there for anything?"

"Well, for company. But if you have other plans, it's no issue if you turn me down. I know this invite is a little last minute, but I've been trying to avoid thinking about the social gathering."

Is Paige really that uncomfortable around people?

"Yeah. I'll come."

"Oh, Dash. You are a fantastic human being. Food and drinks are provided, so just bring yourself and show up anytime after six. Pumpkin is going to be so happy! And I'm happy, too, of course. Bye."

Paige hangs up before I can respond, which just makes me smile all the more.

Then, my expression falls when I realize that I, the ex-con car thief, may have just agreed to meet the classic Chevy mechanic and a judge.

Shit.

CHAPTER 16

DASH

The house looks different at night. The place went through a Halloween makeover. Orange lights line the gutters, and carved pumpkins sit along the walkway leading up to the front door. Tombstones litter the front yard, and skeletons dangle from the trees. From over the high fence, back in the yard I've become familiar with these past few weeks, I can hear music and laughter.

I still don't fully believe I was meant to be invited.

Instead of heading for the gate like I normally do, I walk up to the front entrance.

The ring of the doorbell results in some happy barking, and soon, I'm met with the sight of an exuberant pit bull, dressed in a bedazzled T-shirt. Seeing someone she recognizes, Pumpkin lets out an excited yip and tries to put her paws on my shoulders.

"Pumpkin! Sit." The command comes out in a firm, confident voice.

The dog drops to all fours, then plops her butt on the ground, even as her body continues to wiggle with the strength of her wagging tail.

"Dash! I swear you're the first person she's jumped on." Paige trots up beside her dog, clutching a giant bowl of candy to her chest. "I can't believe you made me look bad, Pumpkin!" Despite her grumpy exclamation, Paige pats her puppy's head affectionately. When she turns her gaze on me, all evidence of disgruntlement immediately disappears, replaced with an enchanting smile. "You dressed up!"

I smirk down at the sweater I'm wearing—a knitted monstrosity covered in bats with a full moon on the right shoulder.

"I borrowed it from Cole. He has a surprising number of ugly holiday sweaters."

"It's not ugly! It's gorgeous." Paige steps forward and brushes a hand over my shoulder as if to smooth down the material. At least with the long sleeves, she can't see how goose bumps race across my arms at the contact.

"It's not really a costume. Now, yours…that's something."

Paige is wearing a full-body black leotard with skeleton bones printed on the tight fabric. Showing an extra bit of modesty, she's pulled on a short black skirt over top, which sways with each of her movements.

Most women out partying tonight wouldn't have bothered with the extra piece of clothing, and they probably would have paired the outfit with a sky-high set of heels. Paige went with sensible flats, and she's piled her blonde hair on top of her head in a sleek bun. She's like an undead ballerina.

"To be honest, I didn't have much of a choice. My mom insisted on dressing up as David S. Pumpkins and demanded that my dad and I be her skeleton backup dancers."

"Am I supposed to know who that is?"

Paige stares up at me, speechless for a moment. "My God, Dash. *David S. Pumpkins*. Tom Hanks. *SNL*. You haven't seen this?"

Maybe now would be a good time to point out that I don't have cable. Or a TV. Or internet. Instead, I just shrug and enjoy the way Paige clutches my arm as if I'm on the verge of dying from lack of pop culture references.

"Well, by the end of the night, you will know who David S Pumpkins is. Even if you don't think he's hilarious, please pretend for my mom's sake. Doesn't matter that she's seen the sketch fifty times. Every time, it kills her. She worships the ground Tom Hanks walks on. If she ever met the man, my father would find himself without a wife."

Paige shakes her head sadly, even as a smile plays at her mouth, and then her eyes pop wide as she glances around us. "I'm a horrible host. Please come inside."

As I follow Paige, I get a better look at the decorated shirt Pumpkin is wearing. It's a simple orange T-shirt with a mathematical sign punched into the side.

"Is that…" I trail off and wait for Paige to explain so I don't sound ridiculous if I'm wrong.

"Her shirt? It's pi. Do you get it?" The grinning woman places the bowl of candy on a side table before crouching down to wrap her arms around the squirming pup.

"She's…pumpkin pie?"

At Paige's energetic nod, I can't help chuckling. This girl is sweeter than the bowl of Kit Kats she was about to hand out to trick-or-treaters.

The smartly dressed dog wiggles out of her owner's embrace and snuffles at my pants pockets.

"Pumpkin, stop. Dash doesn't have—" She pauses mid-sentence when I pull out half a dog biscuit.

I make Pumpkin lie down before I give her the treat. When I glance up at Paige, she has a curious smile hiding at the corner of her mouth.

"Do you constantly carry those around with you? Or do you have magical pockets that produce dog treats whenever you need them?"

I stand up, brushing the crumbs and dog drool off on my pants. "A bit of both."

I wink at Paige, and she blushes.

A shout of laughter sounds from the backyard.

Paige glances over her shoulder, then back at me, some of her enthusiasm fading. "I guess we should go back there. Trick-or-treaters have lessened from a flood to a trickle. No more excuses to hide out as the candy distributer."

Her reluctance confuses me.

Does she not want to be at this party?

Or maybe she doesn't want to be seen with *me* at this party.

I try to convince myself that the second option is wrong. If she didn't want to be seen with me, she didn't have to invite me.

After leaving the candy bowl out on the front stoop for the stragglers and scavengers, Paige returns to my side and loops her arm through mine.

"So, game plan. Food is on the far side of the yard. A lot of bobbing and weaving will be necessary, but I still think we can make it there with little pointless small talk. Still, I figure even if we get held up a time or two, this food is worth the risk. I'm talking high-quality snacks." She turns to face me just as we reach the glass doors that let out on the back patio. "My mom does not mess around on Halloween. I expect to roll you out of here, Dash."

Her hand pats my flat stomach, and at the contact, I feel a stirring in two areas.

One results in a growl that has Paige grinning. The second is a thickening that has me shoving my hand in my pocket to subtly adjust myself.

"Now, the biggest holdup will be if we encounter my parents. I'll introduce you at some point, but they're better dealt with when you have a full stomach. Hopefully, Mom is distracted with karaoke."

Paige misses my expression of horror upon finding out this night might require a sing-along and instead carefully opens the back door. Clearly, she's taking the sneak-attack tactic.

When we step outside, noise surrounds us. Apparently, the Herberts throw a big bash. At least I don't have to worry about sticking out awkwardly. Everyone here is dressed up—some costumes subtle, some outrageous, but all meant in a happy spirit of Halloween.

"This way." Paige tugs my arm, and we head toward a break in the crowd.

The mass of people is surprisingly thick, and she lets go of my arm, only to slide her hand into mine, tugging me along behind her. The yard that I've gotten familiar with over the past few weeks suddenly morphs into new terrain. A distance I was able to sprint across with Pumpkin in a matter of seconds has now become a distance requiring a full-scale expedition. In fact, I've lost track of the dog in the melee.

"Paige!"

She turns toward me when I call her name, eyebrows raised in question.

"I think we lost Pumpkin."

She glances around, then shrugs. "Don't worry. She's around here somewhere. And I put a sign up on the gate, warning people not to let her out of the yard."

"Is she okay with all these people?" A sense of protection swells in my chest, and I worry about how this group of upper-crust people will handle being around a pit bull.

Paige steps closer, sliding her hand around to my lower back in what seems to be an unconscious gesture. "I asked my parents to let everyone know she'd be here, and they all met her when they arrived. She's been really good. Like I said, you're the only one she jumped on. Everyone else she sniffs, then ignores. She's a good dog. Your training is working well."

I have trouble focusing on Paige's reassurances with her standing so close to me, holding on to me like we're close friends…or something more. I nod, she smiles, and we go back to navigating to the food.

When we locate the long table of offerings, saliva floods my mouth.

Paige's mom may be my new favorite person.

Because of a few new parts I had to buy to get my car up and running again, I've been living off ramen this week, which means my stomach has been cursing me in an endless stream of creative profanity.

But tonight, I feast.

"You fill a plate, and I'll grab us drinks. Do you want the punch? There's no booze in it unless you want to add it yourself."

"Virgin punch works for me."

Paige practically skips away, her black skirt swishing around her thighs with each step she takes. For a moment, I stand still, watching her leave and simply enjoying the view.

Then, my stomach gives an audible demand that I can't ignore any longer.

"Yeah, yeah. Food time," I mutter to myself, giving up watching Paige, knowing I shouldn't let myself do it in the first place.

She belongs to a different world than I do, and if I want to be part of this world too much, I'll end up doing something reckless to get here.

Just like my parents.

To get my mind off the out-of-reach woman and away from the dark parts of my life, I pick up a plate and view the spread. It's everything you could want at a party and more. Crab cakes piled high on a platter, surrounded by bowl after bowl of chips. There's enough dirty rice to serve a football team, along with crawfish, boiled and ready to eat. As I move along, I discover crispy fried chicken, po' boy sliders, creamy grits, and desserts in all sorts of Halloween shapes. One plate could never accommodate a sampling from each.

Well, Paige did say she wanted to see me roll out of here. I guess that means seconds and possibly even thirds are allowed.

My plate is almost filled to capacity when a throat clears meaningfully beside me.

I turn toward the noise and almost drop all my preciously collected food.

The man in front of me has taken the horror part of Halloween seriously. Some people might go for gore or gaping wounds for shock value, but this guy chose another route and achieved a greater effect. His entire face is covered in black-and-white makeup, skillfully executed, transforming him into a living skeleton. From the dark sockets, eyes stare unblinking at me.

Not many people can meet my eyes with me standing at over six feet. This man has no issue there, as he's as tall as I am, and his assured presence seems to add a few extra inches. If he had gone with a spandex skeleton suit, maybe the effect would have been more humorous than intimidating. Instead, he has on a sleekly tailored black suit, paired with a black silk shirt, and a slim black tie.

On the day I die, this will be the image before me. The Grim Reaper serenely adjusting his skull cuff links before dragging me to hell.

The embodiment of death speaks.

"You're here with my daughter, it would seem."

CHAPTER 17

DASH

This demon of a man is Paige's father.

"Yes, sir. That is, I mean, I'm her friend."

"Her friend."

Mr. Herbert continues to stare at me, and I do not doubt this man is a judge. I bet if he dressed like this when sitting on the bench, there would be a hell of a lot more guilty confessions.

"And I help train Pumpkin."

Normally, my reaction to authority figures is an unconscious urge to flip them the finger and break something in their vicinity. But I've been working to stifle that reaction, and for some reason, with Paige's father, I don't want him to see me as just another delinquent.

I wonder if Paige told him about my trouble with the law.

Would he have let me into his house if he knew?

"Dad! Don't scare him!" Paige appears from the crowd, my skeletal savior. She steps between her father and me, clutching two plastic cups full of colorful liquid.

"I'm not scaring him. I'm greeting him."

Paige rolls her eyes, and I can't help smiling down at her doubting face.

Healthy family interactions used to fill me with envy, but now, I view them like I might a sitcom. Enjoyable to watch, but with the knowledge that they'll never be my reality.

"Dash, this is my dad. People tend to find him intimidating. Dad, this is Dash. He's friends with me and Pumpkin, so you have to be nice to him."

Mr. Herbert's mouth gives a twitch, and I can tell he finds his daughter's command amusing. If my sister had ever talked that way to my father, she would've been locked in her room until morning.

"I don't *have* to do anything, baby girl." The indulgent way the man speaks makes me think he's just trying to rile his daughter up.

"You do if you don't want me to tell Mom about those cigars I saw delivered a couple of days ago."

Mr. Herbert frowns, but his eyes still hold a smile. The exchange fascinates me.

"Blackmail is beneath you."

"And being rude to my friends is beneath you. So, we've reached an understanding?"

Thinking it best not to let Paige fight all my battles for me, I transfer my plate to my left hand and reach my right around her, offering it to her father.

"Nice to meet you, sir."

He accepts my hand, gripping it firmly, but not attempting to crush any bones.

"Good. Now, we're all friends. Here's your punch."

Paige hands me my cup, turning her back on her father to do so. Without her focus on him, I watch as some of the amusement fades from his expression, and he keeps his sights locked on me.

"What is it you do, Dash?" He keeps his tone neutral.

"I'm an adoption coordinator at the NOLA Animal Rescue."

"And on the side, he's a dog trainer. You've seen how well behaved Pumpkin is. That's all because of Dash."

Paige's defense of me is sweet, but despite my unease toward her father, I don't need her protection. I've handled myself around much scarier individuals, ones who wouldn't hesitate to inflict creative methods of torture on me if I crossed them.

Besides, Paige is making it sound like she hasn't done any of the training herself. "Not just me. You're the one working with her every day."

"Yes, but you showed me *how* to work with her. Try the punch; it's delicious. And stop acting like you aren't awesome at your job." Paige stares up at me until I take a sip.

Only when I make an appreciative noise does she smile in a blinding way that almost makes me swallow my tongue. Or lean down to kiss her.

I doubt Mr. Herbert would take that very well.

Paige twirls back to face her father, and I wish I were wearing shorts, so I could feel the light brush of her skirt as it swishes against my legs.

Mr. Herbert has kept his face void of expression during our back-and-forth, and I'm having trouble reading what exactly he thinks of me. But I could make an educated guess. The guy probably wouldn't mind if I had a sudden emergency that took me far away from his house and his daughter.

I don't blame him. I wouldn't be any parent's first choice.

"Mom wants us to dance. You're not going to, are you?"

It's almost comical, the look of horror that crosses the man's face at such an innocent statement.

"Good God. No. We agreed to costumes. No performances."

"Then, you'd better hide the microphone. And the bourbon. That's a bad combination for her," Paige says.

Her father opens his mouth to respond when a man dressed as the Devil calls out to him and waves. He grimaces at his daughter good-naturedly, sweeps me with an arctic stare, then strides away.

"Here, I'll hold that, so you can eat." Paige retrieves the cup of punch from my hand.

"What about you?"

She shrugs. "I was snacking on it all when they set it up. Plus, I was sneaking pieces of candy while I was handing it out. I'm good for now. Eat. Please."

I oblige, biting into a crab cake and somehow stifling my moan as the deliciously flavored meat hits my tongue. As I chow down, I observe Paige.

Her eyes flit around the crowd of people, a frown tugging at the corner of her mouth, although when she looks back at me, the disquiet temporarily disappears.

A few partygoers approach the food offerings, and her shoulders get rigid.

"Let's find somewhere else to stand. Don't want to be a human barricade in front of the food." She cups my elbow, guiding me away from the large group of mingling people, and settles us by the fence.

I don't mind hovering on the outskirts of the party as I eat my food. I'm just not sure why Paige wants to be so far away from everyone.

Aren't any of these people her friends? Does she dislike everyone that her parents associate with?

Although thinking of the company my parents keep, I'm not really one to throw stones.

Despite her efforts to separate us, even keeping to the edges doesn't mean we're invisible. It seems like each time Paige opens her mouth to say something to me, a different middle-aged woman in a costume appears out of nowhere to make cryptic remarks.

"Oh, Paige! So good to see you out and about! We weren't sure if you'd want to make an appearance."

"You're looking adorable this evening. Glad you're not letting anything get you down!"

"Sad to hear what happened, but you're better off—I'm sure of it."

These comments come from multiple guests, each one sidling up to us and patting Paige on the shoulder with sympathy clear in their eyes. My companion keeps a brittle smile on her face through all the attention and avoids meeting my gaze after the well-wisher wanders off.

"I'm sorry. I hoped they would ignore me." Paige stares down at Pumpkin, who wandered over to us a moment ago. She maintains a laser focus on the dog's ears, ignoring my searching look.

Worry rattles through me.

Why is everyone so concerned for Paige? My stomach clenches, and I'm no longer interested in the contents of my plate.

"Is everything okay?"

Paige fiddles with the edge of her skirt, watching Pumpkin sniff my sneakers.

I want nothing more than to slide my fingers under her chin and tilt her head up until she has to look me in the eyes. Then, I'd use my thumb to smooth the anxious creases in her face before leaning down to press a reassuring kiss on her sweet mouth.

My hand lifts, only to drop almost immediately when we're approached again by a woman dressed as Jessica Rabbit.

"Paige! You brave girl! I never liked that boy anyway. Glad to see you're already back in the game." The woman leans in close to whisper that last bit, but it's still loud enough for me to hear. She winks at me, and Paige's cheeks light up brighter than brake lights.

"Oh! No. Please. That's not…Dash is my friend. We're just friends. He's not a Martin stand-in or anything." Paige shuts her mouth quick and grimaces as her cheeks go red.

Something begins to clarify, and the party food in my stomach suddenly isn't sitting so well.

"Of course not, dear. I just meant to say, I'm happy you're not moping around, letting him ruin your life. He was never good enough for you, and I bet he knew it. Probably why he did it too."

I don't know if this woman is cruel or just an idiot, but every word that comes out of her mouth hits Paige like an expertly sharpened dagger. My friend—because that's what we are now—closes her eyes, even as she attempts a smile.

I'm overwhelmed with the urge to save her.

"I'm sorry. I didn't catch your name."

Her eyes latch on to me, taking a leisurely perusal of my form as if I'm an offering that belongs on the food table. My opinion of her drops lower.

"Well, Dash"—she breathes my name out in a sultry manner that makes my skin crawl—"I'm Charity Emerson."

"Nice to meet you, Ms. Emerson. I'm sure we'll see you around, but Paige and I need to head inside to feed Pumpkin." I place my hand on Paige's lower back, and her eyes spring open, staring up at me in surprise. I lean down until my mouth hovers just next to her ear. "Call your dog."

"Pumpkin. Come." She slaps a hand against the side of her thigh, and the three of us retreat from the party into the relative privacy of the house.

I set my half-eaten plate of food on the kitchen counter before turning to observe Paige as she pulls a dog biscuit from one of the cabinets and feeds it to her eager puppy.

"Paige—"

"Do you want to see something cool? I think you'll like it."

I guess she's not ready to talk about what just went down outside. For now, I'll let her avoid the subject, but I can't help but wonder if more went on between her and Martin than a broken engagement.

"Sure. Show me something cool."

Paige grins in relief and waves for me to follow her. Together, we navigate down a long hallway, heading toward the opposite side of the house from where the fenced-in yard is. I've never been this way before, and I try not to stare too longingly at all the happy family photos hanging on the wall.

"You an only child?"

She turns back at my question, glancing at the picture frame I'm tapping. It's a shot of her sitting in a beach chair, a friendlier-looking version of the man I met earlier on her left and a beautiful blonde woman with the same nose as Paige on her right.

"Yep. Just me, Mom, and Dad. And Pumpkin now, of course." She makes as if to walk farther down the hall, but then stops suddenly and looks back at me. "Do you have siblings?"

I should've known the question would be returned. I debate telling her only about the person in my family I'm proud to be associated with. But she already knows about my criminal history. What's the point in hiding my family's?

"I have a sister and a brother. Twins, older than me. My sister lives in Nashville. My brother got sent upstate the same time I did, but his sentence is longer than mine, so he's still there."

Not for much longer though.

"Sorry to hear that."

I shrug. "You shouldn't be. He deserved it. So did I."

Paige frowns at her family photo, but I don't think the image is what's got her upset.

"It's okay, Paige. No reason to worry about things you can't change." I step in the direction she was leading me. "Now, what did you want to show me?"

She sighs, then passes by me to stop in front of a door at the end of the hall. Only then do I notice the key code attached to the wall. Paige types in a combination too quickly for me to follow, then pushes the door open.

"Thought you might like a Halloween treat." Paige grins over her shoulder before flipping on a switch.

CHAPTER 18

DASH

I approach the doorway, stumbling to a stop when Paige moves to the side, revealing the contents of the room.

We've entered what looks to be a fully functional mechanic's shop. The open space is large enough to accommodate at least six cars, with four currently parked inside. They're in a range of states—from shoddy and rusted to shiny enough to be straight off the production line.

Paige faces me as she backs into the room, a satisfied smile playing at the edges of her lips. I can't decide if she's an angel leading me into heaven or a demon enticing me toward hell.

This room is my addiction personified.

I ache to climb behind the wheels of these cars—all classic Chevys, I now realize.

Paige solidifies my guess. "This is my mom's workshop." She wanders over to a royal-blue muscle car, likely a Camaro, and trails her hand across the gorgeous body.

I don't know if I'm more jealous of Paige or the car.

"Come here. She's almost done with the '63 Corvette."

Like a drunk, I stumble farther into the garage on shaky legs.

Paige moves to the other side of the blue, where a golden Corvette sits prettily.

"Do you know much about classic cars?"

I shake my head. "Only what I've read. Never got to work with any."

Uncle Mike had clear ideas about who handled what, and he did not take it well when people deviated from his rules.

"Well, living with my mom, it's hard not to pick up on random facts. See here…" Paige glances over at me and rolls her eyes when she notices how far away I'm standing from the beautiful pieces of machinery. "They're not going to bite, Dash. Come here." She strolls up to me, grabs my hand, and drags me right up beside the golden Corvette. "Fun fact: the designers of the '63 had some debate over body style. There's this ridge here"—she reaches to the middle of the low roof, where there is a ridge smoothly rising like the car has a spine—"and one of the designers demanded that it run the entire length of the car. Which means"—she traces her finger along the ridge toward the back of the car, and when she reaches the rear window, I realize the peculiarity—"the back window is split right down the middle."

Paige lets her hand drop and steps away, running her eyes over the entire car.

"It's beautiful," I mutter my appreciation, barely able to get the words past the lustful fog in my brain after watching the stunning woman at my side stroke a car while reciting facts about it.

Has she been studying up on my wet dreams?

"Beautiful, yes. Practical? Not exactly. Here, sit in the driver's seat."

Oh fuck.

When Paige moves to open the driver's-side door for me, it's like being fondled through my jeans. I wonder if she has any idea how sweet a torture this is. From the innocent excitement in her eyes, my guess is no.

Unable to deny the invitation, I slide into the low car. Surprisingly, I don't need to adjust the seat to accommodate my long legs. Like this sweet girl was waiting just for me.

I almost groan out loud at the feel of the smooth leather steering wheel beneath my palms.

"Nice, right?" Paige slips into the shotgun seat, grinning at what I'm sure is an expression of pure ecstasy on my face. "But take a look in the rearview."

I reach up, gently tilting the mirror until it hits my eyeline just right. That's when I realize what the issue is with the '63 Corvette.

"Blind spot."

She chuckles, low and happy, the sound a caress against my ears. "Exactly. Needless to say, the '64 doesn't have a split rear window. But because of this design, collectors love it. Mom can make a nice chunk of change off each one she restores. A few of these helped put me through college, so I am immensely grateful for that beautiful blind spot."

Paige trails her fingers over the stitching in the seat, which is also covered in supple brand-new leather.

I find myself leaning closer to her side of the car, just to keep my eyes on the paths her fingers are taking. I can almost imagine we're out on the road, the engine roaring to life. I'd keep one hand on the wheel and rest the other on the gearshift, except for when I'd reach over to capture Paige's soft palm and lay it to rest on my inner thigh. She wouldn't need to do anything more than keep it there, but if she wanted to stroke my leg the way she is the upholstery, I'd never complain.

When my dick stirs at the fantasy, I clear my throat and try to distract myself.

"So, your mom taught you all she knows about fixing up Chevys?"

Shit, that's not the best distraction. The image of Paige dressed in a tank top and grease-stained jeans, bending over the engine of a car, pops into my mind, and suddenly, I'm rock hard.

"She wishes. Mom would've loved if I'd been interested in cars the way she is. But even though I like driving them and I find the history of them interesting, fixing them up has never been appealing to me."

A strange mixture of relief and regret fills my chest.

"When I was younger, Mom would insist I come out to the garage, so she could teach me. But more often than not, I ended up sprawled in the back seat of whatever car she was working on, reading my book. Eventually, she just accepted my disinterest, but I guess she still liked me hanging out with her, so she'd always make sure to have a pillow and green pens, so I'd keep reading out here."

The content smile curving Paige's lips is mesmerizing. She has a kind of distracted magnetism that pulls me closer.

"Why a pillow and green pens?"

Paige shifts in her seat, so she's facing me head-on, a silly grin plumping her cheeks. "A pillow for my head, so my neck didn't get tired while I was reading. And green pens because I would always write notes in the margins of the books I was reading."

"Book editor even back then?" I imagine a young Paige, chewing on a green pen, brow furrowed as she reads, the sounds of her mom rebuilding an engine in the background.

My childhood is like a darker reflection of hers. There were lots of days I snuck over to my uncle Mike's chop shop, trying to watch the men work from my hiding spots, fascinated with all the parts and components required to make a car run. Whenever I was discovered, I was more likely to get slapped than receive an invite closer. Luckily, I was too fast to get caught often. Hence the beginning of my nickname. Only right that my speed continued once I got behind the wheel.

I stole my first car at the age of fifteen.

Not liking the route my memories are driving down, I focus back on our conversation.

"Why not a red pen? I thought that was classic for you editors."

Paige sighs, tilting her head to the side to lean on the headrest. "Red always seemed so judgy. Who was I to tell them what was right or wrong? I just wanted to make suggestions. Green is a softer color. It's up for discussion."

The weird, logical way her brain works fascinates me. "Still, it's pretty ballsy to write all over a published book."

She chuckles. "That's only half of it. Sometimes, when I thought I had really good commentary, I would actually mail the book back to the publisher with all my notes in it!" Her cheeks start to glow with warmth, and she presses her hands to them. "A couple actually responded." She groans out this last sentence, clearly embarrassed by her childhood confidence.

"Really? What'd they say?"

She waves a hand as if to dismiss the past. "Oh, just something about thanking me for my passion about the stories. And appreciating my comments. I bet they laughed themselves silly, reading all my ramblings, if they even bothered with them."

I smile, enjoying her embarrassment and the way her flush still creeps down her neck, spreading over her collarbone to disappear beneath her skeleton leotard.

"You put yourself out there. That's pretty brave, Paige."

She's back to stroking the stitching on the leather seat, her eyes locked on her fingers. "Yeah. I used to be brave."

"Don't think there's any *used to be* about it."

Paige glances up at me, a frown dipping the corners of her mouth. "No. It's definitely a *used to be*. Somewhere along the way, I think I lost it. Now, I'm a ball of worries. All the time. And I'm back living in my parents' house. Like a child."

I let go of the gearshift to reach for her hand, partly to make sure her attention is fully on me, but also because the way she's fondling the seat is making this sweater feel way too hot.

"You're the girl who runs through shitty neighborhoods, looking for abandoned animals. The one who got my roommate, who normally sends people walking in the opposite direction, to smile and tell you about his writing. When you saw a dog most people categorize as terrifying, you decided to adopt it and give it a home. Now, some of those choices were not necessarily smart, but I don't think anyone could say they weren't brave."

That's one of the longest speeches I've given, but the cresting smile and shine in her eyes make every word I said worth it.

"I want to do something else. I don't think it's smart." Paige stares at me, nervous energy vibrating from her.

The look she gives me, full of burning heat, dries up any more long-winded responses.

"Go for it," I choke out, wondering if she's braver than I am.

When she leans across the few inches separating us, I know she is.

———

PAIGE

He thinks I'm brave.

All the sweet, strong words he just spoke fill the tiny car and press against my skin like an encouraging caress.

Dash stares into my eyes, seeing past them, into places even hidden from me. All that separates us is our breath, and even that feels like too much at the moment.

I want to be brave again, and he told me to go for it.

So, I do.

My aim is for his plush mouth, the one I've been daydreaming about when I should be applying for jobs. All I've wanted is to discover if his lips are as soft as they seem.

They're not. The first bit of contact has a bit of giving, but then I meet a firm pressure. And I realize this is what I want. He doesn't need to be a cushioned bed I sink into. He should be a steady force I can brace myself against.

When I press my mouth to his, I'm close enough to be overwhelmed by his fresh linen scent. With my eyes closed, I can drown myself in the crisp smell of his skin. I want to reach up and comb my hands through his messy hair, but I hold back. For now, we stay connected only with the gentle brush of my lips against his.

At first, I'm still, wanting to memorize what it's like to fulfill a fantasy. But when he opens to drag in a deep breath, like he wants to fill his lungs with me, I press in closer. What could have been a simple peck forms into an exploration of Dash's taste.

He can't be compared to a food or a drink. All I can think is, he tastes of man. A dark, full-bodied flavor that sits heavy on my tongue and loosens the muscles in my body until I want to drape myself over him.

My decision to keep my hands to myself seems impossible to uphold. My palms crave the touch of his face, the scrape of his beard along my sensitive palms. The coarse hairs tease my upper lip, daring me to give in.

I would, if it wasn't for a loud, metallic clang that crashes through the garage.

Ripping myself away from Dash's mouth, I stare around wildly, only to cringe when my eyes land on the image straight out in front of the windshield.

Standing in a pumpkin-patterned suit with a wild, curly wig, sporting an enthusiastic grin brought on by spiked punch and catching her daughter in a compromising position, is my mother.

"You can't hide from David S. Pumpkins!" She shouts and triumphantly holds up the two wrenches I'm betting she just smashed together to get our attention.

I collapse back to my side of the car, barely suppressing a groan. When I glance at Dash, he's wide-eyed, giving my mom and me a look like we're insane.

Guilt sweeps over me.

Not only did I practically jump his bones, but now, he has to deal with my off-the-wall mother.

I'm a horrible friend.

I can't believe I just went ahead and kissed him.

That's not brave. That's selfish.

I pretended like our conversation was foreplay when, really, Dash had just been asking about my childhood. That's not an invitation to maul his face.

My stomach aches as I slouch out of the car.

"Well, my naughty little skeleton, looks like you've decided to use my cars for something other than their intended purposes!" Mom doesn't slur a single word, but I can still tell by her overly bright eyes that she's more than a few drinks in.

"Sorry, Mom. I just wanted to show them to Dash." I wave at my friend, potentially ex-friend now that I've tried getting all sexy with him without asking. "He's a fan of cars. We didn't mess with them, I promise."

"It's nice to meet you, Mrs. Herbert." With more manners than I've shown, Dash climbs out of the driver's seat and holds his hand out to shake my mom's.

She takes it with a curious smile. "A fan of cars, huh? Does that extend to knowing how they run?"

He shoves his fists in his pockets and tilts his head to the side, as if considering her question carefully. "I know the basics. Never worked with anything like these though. They're gorgeous."

"These three are." Mom waves at the shiny, newly painted machines before turning to the fourth, whose better days were decades ago. "This one is a mess. Going to take me a while to get it sellable." She stares at Dash, suddenly appearing completely sober. After a moment, she walks over to the aged '67 Impala, propping up the hood. "I was struggling to get a few bits dislodged earlier. They're rusted over pretty bad." Mom massages her knuckles. "Don't have the grip I used to." She peers at Dash silently for one more moment. "Maybe you could give it a try for me?"

The floor tilts under me, which is strange because I only had one beer, back when I was handing out candy. No, my sudden disorientation isn't from alcohol. It's from the offer Mom just made to a practical stranger.

I mentioned to my parents I might have a friend come to the party. The two of them shared a look that clearly said, *Now, who could this be?*

Most of the people still in town from my childhood were more acquaintances that tended to be closer with Martin than me. My best friend, Charlie, they know is still over in Germany, and I hadn't mentioned any of my New York friends traveling south. Honestly, a lot of those NYC friends were also acquired through association with Martin, so I haven't even reached out to any since my move and the breakup.

Therefore, I didn't bother getting offended over my parents' poorly hidden disbelief.

Before today, neither of them even knew of Dash's existence other than the fact they were aware Pumpkin and I were working with a trainer.

Now, when it comes to these cars, Mom loves to show them off. But she turns into Gollum with her precious if anyone attempts to fiddle with what's going on under the hoods. A lot of her income comes from local customers whose cars Mom maintains. I remember one day, lying in the back seat of a Camaro, listening to her devise creative torture methods for an incompetent mechanic that had messed up the wiring when the car owner thought he could get some work done at a discounted price. He was lucky Mom was willing to take him back on, and it required a decent amount of groveling on his part.

So, for her to invite Dash not only to look under the hood of one of her babies, but to also touch something…my mind can't comprehend it.

I'm about to ask my mom if she has a fever when I notice the excited gleam in my friend's eye. He's staring at the exposed engine like a pirate who just stumbled upon a rotten chest full of golden treasure. Gone is the shock and discomfort from a moment ago. My mom's invitation has eclipsed the horrible blunder of me forcing a kiss on him.

The knowledge is a strange combination of relief and disappointment.

Obviously, being out of the dating world for eight years has destroyed my ability to interact with men in a romantic sense. I just hope my mom's friendliness will work toward earning Dash's forgiveness.

"I'm not sure I sh—"

"Oh, please do!" I interrupt his reluctant refusal, even going so far as to give him a gentle push toward the car. "If you don't, she'll make me. And then I'll mess it up, and we'll get in a big fight, and there will be shouting and threats of bodily harm. Really, you'll be saving this house from descending into World War III."

A smile tugs at the corner of his mouth, and I think I might be forgiven.

"I need to go find Pumpkin anyway," I say.

"Oh, honey, Rosa Keller wanted to say hello to you."

Excited tingles sparkle in my chest. "Mama Keller is here? I thought she was out of town!"

Rosa Keller—accomplished jazz singer and mother of my best friend, Charlie—was practically a second mother to me, growing up. She's gorgeous and has a voice that can make even the most cold-hearted sociopath bawl his eyes out. Even though her and Mr.

Keller's home is in New Orleans, her gigs take them all over the country and the world. Last we talked, the two of them were in Europe.

"Got back yesterday. Go give her a hug while I take advantage of your car-loving friend."

I want to sprint out of the room, but I'm also wary about leaving Dash alone with my mother. As Mom rummages around her tool bench, looking for a doohickey I'd never be able to figure out how to use, I move in close to Dash.

"You okay helping her for a minute? You can say no, and we can go get more food."

When he stares down at me, there seems to be a lot of thoughts flickering behind his dark eyes, none of which I can interpret.

"I don't mind helping. I'll find you when we're done." Dash's voice comes out low and sultry, and I can't remember if he's always spoken that way or if my ears are just filled with lust-soaked cotton.

Some space apart might be good. I need breathing room, and then I'll be able to give myself a firm talking-to and figure out the proper way to behave.

As I leave the garage, I try not to move so fast that it looks like I'm fleeing.

I'm relaxed. Super casual.

Outside, the party has reached a new volume level, likely fueled by the open bar. Doesn't matter that the majority of the guests are over forty; they still know how to get wild. I'm just hoping that they're all done telling me how sorry they are for me.

You'd think I built my entire life around Martin.

Well…I guess I kind of did.

I shake off that depressing thought and scan the crowd, hoping the Kellers aren't wearing some elaborate masks. But I'm lucky. Over by the live band, I see the two of them dancing together. The sight has me grinning.

Mrs. Keller is dressed in a flapper-style dress, the little strings flipping and swaying with each of her movements. The silver shines bright against her dark skin, and her normal tight curls have been covered with a wig of smooth, slick ringlets, adorned with a glittering headband and one lone feather. Mr. Keller has on a pinstriped suit and a fedora, matching his style with his wife's '20s look.

They are elegant and yet still playful as they swing each other around the dance floor.

I weave through the crowd until I'm close enough to catch their eyes and wave. Mrs. Keller immediately breaks away to sweep me up in a hug.

"Baby girl. We've missed you." Her whisper is soft against my cheek, and suddenly, I get the urge to cry.

"I missed you too, Mama Keller."

I press my face into her neck and breathe in deep. She smells like the coconut oil she uses to keep her skin soft and smooth. For a moment, I'm a kid again, sleeping over at my best friend's house and getting a kiss good night right before I slip into my sleeping bag.

"Paige." Mr. Keller's voice brings me back to the present, and I return his gentle smile. He leans down to press a kiss on my forehead, even as his wife keeps her arms wrapped around my waist. "I'll go find your father." He wanders off, likely to smoke one of those forbidden cigars.

The thought has me chuckling.

"Come talk to me, baby girl. You never stay long enough on the phone for me to learn anything."

I wince at the slight chiding in her voice as she pulls me toward the patio and settles us on a love seat next to each other.

It only takes certain well-aimed questions to have me spilling everything that happened between me and Martin. And not just the cheating discovery. I tell her about the distance in our relationship the year leading up to moving to NOLA. And the confusing hurt and relief of not being in a relationship with him anymore. When I detail the surprise brunch with his mother, she gives me a horrified look that does a good job justifying my anger. Just like her son did.

I love the Kellers.

As I'm nearing the end of my depressing story, Pumpkin wanders up to us and places her heavy head in my lap.

"Now, who's this sweet pup?"

That story is happier, and I find myself smiling again as I detail how the two of us found each other.

"I've been training her. With the help of my friend Dash. Watch." I stand up and put Pumpkin through her paces.

My dog performs like an actress made for the stage, and Mrs. Keller plays the appreciative audience, clapping and praising our demonstration.

I sit back down with a dramatic sigh, feeling just a bit lighter, having talked about everything. There's something about Charlie's mom, an easiness I have around her, that enables me to drag out every embarrassing detail of my failed relationship without drowning in shame.

"Now, I'm just trying to figure out where I go. What is my life without Martin? I spent so long with him that I'm not sure I know how to live on my own."

Her warm, coconut-scented hands cup my face, forcing my gaze to pair with hers.

"You are a strong woman. That boy meant something to you, but he didn't define you. It might take some time, but you'll be all right. I know it."

I have to blink fast to push back the tears. She lets her hands fall away, only to clasp mine and drag them to her chest with a silly, hopeful stare.

"Will you fall in love with my son now?"

A watery chuckle escapes my chest at the old joke. "I fell in love with Charlie a long time ago. It's just not the kind of love you're hoping for."

Mrs. Keller gives me a rueful smile as she tucks a stray hair behind my ear. "As long as he has you in his life in some way, I'll count myself a lucky mama."

In that moment, I wish more than almost anything that I could kindle a lustful flame for Charlie. Isn't that how all the romance novels go? Childhood friends grow up to realize they belonged together all along, and they live happily ever after.

Then, the patio door opens to reveal a slightly disheveled Dash. My lips pulse with the memory of his mouth, and my bones seem to tingle and expand, pressing at the confines of my skin.

Charlie never had this effect on me.

Mrs. Keller follows my gaze, her stare taking in the tall, lithe form of my friend. She probably sees all the harsh angles of him. High cheekbones, straight nose, jagged eyebrows. You need to look past that to realize how soft the curve of his mouth is and how a smile can liquefy the hardness in his eyes. And I'm sure with a few more healthy meals, that adorable sweater wouldn't dangle from his square shoulders, but instead hug his tempting body.

As he moves toward us, Mrs. Keller turns back to me with a smirk.

"Seems Charlie has some competition anyway."

CHAPTER 19

DASH

When I have a second to sit down at my desk, I pull out my phone and read Paige's text.

Paige: *Are we still on for a training session tomorrow?*

This isn't the first time. I got her message near the start of my shift. Not knowing how to respond, I left it and tried to use a full morning of meetings with potential adopters to push away thoughts of her.

But that was near impossible.

She kissed me.

In a badass car, a gorgeous woman I've been fantasizing about kissed me. If I let my mind relax, I can still smell her earthy scent and feel the lush, silky texture of her lips hesitantly brushing against mine. The memory is delicious torture because I know it should never happen again.

It won't happen again.

If her mom hadn't interrupted us, I'm not sure what I would've done, but it likely would've involved a lot fewer clothes and me getting to stroke and grab her pale skin until I left fingerprints.

I want to mark her. Make her mine. Take her from that mansion of a house, buckle her into that glorious car, race through the streets of this town, and finally drag her to my bedroom, where I'd make her scream and moan.

Even as I play out the fantasy in my mind, I berate myself for it.

I'm sick. Paige is turning into one of my addictions.

The only way to deal with those is avoidance.

Dash: *Not sure.*

I meant to type *no*, but my thumbs added a few extra letters without my permission. As my out-of-date computer takes the couple of minutes it needs to wake up after being asleep all morning, I wander off to the break room for a cup of coffee.

A generous donor gifted us with a Keurig last year, so the brew isn't half bad. My main issue is that the moment I get a whiff of the dark black liquid, another image of Paige fills my mind.

When Paige left me alone in the garage with her mother, I expected the wackily dressed woman to scold me about corrupting her daughter and inform me I was no longer welcome in her house. Instead, she handed me a wrench and began pointing out the rusty bolts giving her trouble. As I tugged them loose, she talked.

"I had a helper over the summer, but he left for college last month. Been slow-going on this beauty since then. When I'm done, she's going to look like the queen of the night. Onyx black. A character in a popular TV show drives this model, which means there's a group of diehard fans clamoring for their own. Not that I'm complaining. I love Impalas. Gave one to Paige for her college graduation. That girl got a 4.0. Can you believe it? Her dad and I couldn't. Not that she's not smart, mind you. Just, in high school, she was more often reading than doing her homework. But she went off to college and figured it out. You've seen her car?"

It took me a moment to realize she'd paused long enough to hear my answer.

"Yeah."

"Gorgeous, isn't it? Not the original color, but for Paige, I just had to get that candy-apple green. You know she loves green. Only uses green pens with her editing. She used to hang out in the shop with me, and I'd always have to check all the seats and the floors of the cars for green pens before delivering them." The woman chuckled, then grinned happily when I presented a handful of rusty bolts.

"You're a lifesaver. Dash, was it? Dash…" She trailed off, leaving room for my answer.

"Lamont. Dash Lamont."

"Well, Dash Lamont. You keep hanging around my daughter, and I'm going to keep taking advantage of you. Lord knows Paige refuses to help."

Mrs. Herbert didn't sound put off, just mildly exasperated with her daughter's lack of interest in cars. I could understand the disbelief. How could anyone have access to these vehicles and not want to spend all day tinkering on them?

I was about to ask if she needed help with anything else when a dark figure loomed tall in the door.

"Ginny, I thought we agreed that if you wanted to throw a party, you actually had to attend it." The skeleton man, aka Mr. Herbert, scolded his wife, even as he stared at me.

"I've only been gone for a moment." She waved her hand, as unaffected by her husband's intimidating presence as her daughter had been. "Besides, I'm getting to know Paige's friend. Have you met Dash?"

"I have." He left it at that, clearly not interested in knowing anything more about me.

All I could hope was it would stay that way. As a judge, Mr. Herbert could easily pull up my record and learn every dirty detail of my past. The minute that happened, there was no way he'd ever let me around his daughter again.

Which would probably be for the best.

Standing in that garage, flanked by two upstanding citizens who clearly doted on their daughter—the girl who had just snuck a kiss from me in a car I couldn't afford even if I sold all the organs in my body—I was overwhelmed with the knowledge that I didn't belong.

So, I left. With a stiff nod to both of them, I slid past Mr. Herbert and navigated back to the party. I found Paige sitting with a lovely woman dressed like she should have been attending a party a century ago. As I approached, I heard her murmured words.

"Seems like Charlie has some competition anyway."

I didn't know who Charlie was, but at that moment, I wanted to tell the woman he could keep his hands off Paige if he wanted to keep them.

That surge of possessiveness made it even more clear that I needed to leave.

Paige's smile dropped away when I told her, and she followed me to the front door.

I was ready to head out with only a wave, but just like at my house, Paige swooped in quick for a hug. Her coffee-scented hair pressed to my nose, and my whole body stiffened in immediate painful arousal.

She didn't linger. After stepping back, Paige gave me a smile that had a sad tilt to the edge. When I got to my car, just a short way down the street, I told myself not to look back.

But my self-control was pretty much used up at that point, so I gave the house one last glance, only to catch Paige still on the front stoop, watching my departure. She raised her hand in a final wave before retreating inside.

When I got back to my house, I realized my pockets were full of Kit Kats.

Apparently, her hug had had a purpose.

The image of her waving goodbye sits clear in my mind now, close to a week later. My plan is for that to be the last one I have of her.

Paige and I are from different worlds, and if I spend more time around her, I'll be tempted to scheme my way into hers. If I start using the methods I know for getting money fast, I'll likely end up back in prison. And Paige won't think of me as the nice guy who helped her out with her dog; she'll know what I really am. A degenerate.

I settle at my desk, letting the faint sound of barking lull me into a meditative state as I read over applications.

My concentration breaks with the vibration of my phone on the metal desk.

I stifle a groan. I know it's her. Deep in my bones, I'm aware that if I flip my phone open, I'll have more of her precisely typed words to read.

Why does she have to keep tempting me?

I snatch the phone off the desk, storm over to a filing cabinet in the corner, pull open the bottom drawer, and stuff the phone in a file before slamming the drawer shut.

Out of sight, out of mind.

Yeah, fucking right.

There's never been a day at work where I've been so completely aware of a particular piece of office furniture. All afternoon, I hear phantom vibrations, taunting me, telling me to retrieve my phone from its exile. Eventually, I give up on desk work and spend the last bit of my shift walking dogs.

The exercise helps, and a playful mutt gets me to smile with his insanely good fetch skills. The mangy dog catches everything I throw before the toy even hits the ground.

With only five minutes left in my workday, I finally head back to my office. Only when I have everything else I need do I open up the bottom drawer and pull out my phone from its hiding spot. With the broken screen, I have no idea how many messages and calls I potentially missed.

I wait until I'm in my car to flip it open. Three missed texts.

One from my dad, reminding me about payment he expects me to drop off.

"Fuck you too," I mutter, deleting the message.

One from my sister, asking when the last time was that I went to see the dentist. Even all the way up in Nashville, she's still trying to mother me. At least her nagging comes from a place of affection, so I respond that I went a month ago. No cavities.

And the last is from *her.*

Paige: *If tomorrow doesn't work, we can do pretty much any other day of the week. My schedule is wide open. Also, Pumpkin misses you.*

Attached to the text is a close-up image of Pumpkin's nose and pleading eyes. This girl knows how to cut into my chest and rip my heart out.

With fingers that almost ache from reluctance, I type a quick response.

Dash: *Think you can handle training on your own.*

Guilt makes me nauseous as I toss my phone into the passenger seat and pull out of the parking lot. I know leaving Paige alone is the right thing to do, but it feels a lot more like I'm abandoning her.

I'm halfway home when my phone lets out a continuous vibration, indicating a call rather than a text. Since I'm at a stoplight, I reach for it.

It could be Luna, I tell myself.

If I really thought that, I'd just let it go to voice mail and call my sister back later.

But I know who it is, and the temptation to hear her voice is too much. I don't have a filing cabinet in my car to hide my phone, and after a long day of work, I'm suddenly too tired to deny myself this one last taste of her.

"Hey—"

"Dash, I'm so sorry that I kissed you. I messed everything up, didn't I? I'm a horrible friend. You don't ever want to see me again. I totally understand. But I just needed you to know how sorry I am for making you uncomfortable." Paige's sweet, worried voice rambles at me through the phone.

I'm almost too busy soaking up the sound to register her words, but when I do, they shock me worse than grabbing a car battery with my bare hands.

"Paige, no. You're okay. We're okay."

"No, we're not. I messed up our friendship, and now, you don't want to train Pumpkin and me anymore." Even through my shitty phone speaker, I pick up on the catch in her voice, and it guts me.

Whatever plan I had to keep away from Paige crumbles to dust at the idea of her crying. I can't handle the image.

"Paige, calm down. You misunderstood." I scramble for another explanation for my dismissive texts while I navigate the end-of-workday traffic. "I just thought we could do something other than training tomorrow. Like, more NOLA stuff." It's a lame excuse, but I do my best to sell it.

"Really?"

"Yeah. Definitely. Let's…" I search my mind for something we can do other than roll around in my bed together, which is what my dick is voting for. "Let's go to the French Quarter. Pretend to be tourists or some shit."

"You'd want to do that? Wouldn't it be boring for you?" Despite her hesitant questions, I can pick up the excitement in her voice. The breathy way she asks her questions brushes over my skin, teasing me. Tempting me.

"It won't be boring. You make things fun." I bring my car to a stop in the dirt strip Cole and I use as a driveway.

"So do you. Make things fun, I mean. You're fun. But in a weird way." She gasps. "No! Sorry! You're not weird. I'm weird. You're…different."

I rest my forehead on my steering wheel, holding back laughter.

"Dash?"

"Yeah, Paige?"

"Your phone just cut out, right? You didn't hear any of that, did you?"

"Do you want me to pretend I didn't?"

"I think that would be best."

I cover the receiver, so she can't hear me chuckling.

"Also, I know we're getting better working on our own, but I still think I need your help with Pumpkin. She's developed a bad habit."

The seriousness in her tone sobers me up, and I get a twisting in my chest. "What is she doing?"

The pit bull seemed fine at the party, but if she's begun to display aggression toward people, then that could mean trouble.

"She's a thief."

For a moment, I'm sure communication did fail between our phones, thinking I must've misheard her. But this is Paige, so maybe not.

"A thief?"

"Yes. A sneaky one too. For weeks, I thought I was losing it, but then I saw her do it. Caught her red-handed. Or red-pawed, I guess."

"You're going to need to clarify because I'm lost."

"Towels. She keeps stealing my towels!"

"Your towels?"

A huff sounds through the phone. "Yes. I didn't know what was happening at first. I kept thinking I'd forgotten to bring one into the bathroom with me. But then I caught her in the act yesterday. I was in the shower"—*oh fuck*—"and I thought I heard a noise, so I pulled the curtain back a bit, and there she was, towel in her mouth, tail wagging like she was proud or something. Then, she sprinted out of the bathroom. So, for, like, the tenth time, I had to get out of my shower, soaking wet, with no towel."

Paige is trying to kill me. I'm sure of it. She cannot keep talking about her wet, naked body and expect me to live through the experience. I'll be lucky if I can stand up out of my car with my dick so hard.

"Apparently, she's been hoarding them under my bed. She's got a whole towel nest built up. So, what should I do? Is that something we could work on next time you come over? Like, maybe I'll get in the shower, and when she goes for the towel, you tell her no? Sorry. I'm not the dog trainer. I don't want to tell you how to do your job."

"I'll think on that. Text you tomorrow." I rush through the words and hang up without waiting for her to say goodbye, then throw my phone in the back seat like it's on fire.

Fucking hell. Did Paige just ask me to hang out in her bathroom while she showers?

Maybe if more of my blood was up north, I'd be able to figure out if she was flirting, or joking, or just oblivious. Unfortunately, I've lost all ability to reason, and I don't think it'll return until I take care of the misbehaving animal in my pants.

Time for a nice long shower.

CHAPTER 20

DASH

"You have powdered sugar…well, everywhere." Paige laughs as she uses a napkin to wipe my face.

I let her take care of me, enjoying the way her eyes focus on my mouth as she works to clear away the sweet white powder.

We've snagged a table outside at Cafe Du Monde, one of the go-to places for tourists. I can't fault out-of-towners for flocking here in search of beignets—squares of fluffy, fried dough drowned in the powdered sugar that now covers my face.

"I'm sorry, but you still kind of look like a coke addict."

I snort at her comparison, reaching for my napkin. If I don't take care of it, I'll be tempted to ask her to lick me clean.

Can't have that.

Dirty thoughts have been popping up in my head all day, ever since we met up in front of the aquarium. I'd decided that looking at fish would be a good way to stifle my sexual urges. Instead, the two of us wandered around in the perfect mood lighting for an hour, and I couldn't stop picturing what Paige would look like soaking wet.

Plus, she kept grabbing my arm as she pointed out all the creatures she liked. One time, I must have stiffened under her touch because Paige snatched her hand back and crossed her arms over her chest, effectively tucking them away.

"I'm sorry, Dash." She murmured the apology, staring up into my face with pleading eyes that reminded me of Pumpkin. "I know I said it on the phone, but I want you to know, I meant it. I promise I'll *never* kiss you again. I swear. And I'll keep my hands to myself."

That's what I should've wanted to hear. I told myself to go along with it.

Instead, a surge of loss and denial rose in my chest, so strong that I reached out for her without thinking about it. Prying one of her hands free, I laced our fingers together.

"I was just surprised. You can touch me."

Touch me everywhere, I wanted to beg.

We watched sharks circle, gliding smoothly past the glass, all with our hands clasped like a couple.

I'm surprised Paige isn't dizzy from the insane amount of mixed signals I'm sending her. It's like there's a tiny corner of my brain that knows what the right thing to do is and can shout about it pretty loud but has absolutely no control over my limbs or my mouth.

This is driven home when I reach up, using my thumb to wipe away a nonexistent bit of sugar on her cheek. "There. You're good to go."

Paige grins at me, then moves to stand. "You need to be anywhere, or you still okay to wander?"

An easy out, but I have no interest in taking it. "I could wander."

We walk by street artists and musicians, pausing ever so often to listen or watch them work. At some point, our hands twine together again, but I couldn't say who made the first move. The weather is perfect, mid-seventies and sunny.

It's like the world is telling me to relax and enjoy this. To let my guard down.

At one point, Paige's steps slow, and I realize she's staring into a shop window. Just behind the glass is a short green dress that's captured her attention.

"You want to go try it on?"

She jumps at my question, then gives me a sheepish look. "Oh, no. That's okay."

"I don't mind. Let's go in." I try to move to the front door, but Paige tugs on my hand to stop me.

"Dash, no. I was just looking. It's cute, but it's not for me."

The comment doesn't make sense because I've already pictured what she'd look like, wearing the dress, and I have a strong urge to see my imagination made a reality.

"What do you mean, it's not for you?"

"It's too short," she mutters.

"Paige, you took your shirt off in front of me the first time I came over to your house."

Her sudden onset of modesty fuels my curiosity flame.

"I don't care if you see my stomach." She snaps her mouth shut as if she just revealed too much.

I should let it go, but I want to know everything there is to discover about this odd, sweet woman.

Knowing it's manipulative but doing it anyway, I move in close, so she has to tilt her head up to meet my eyes. Then, I hold her chin pinched between my forefinger and thumb and speak low, so it's only the two of us that can hear. "Why don't you want me to see your legs?"

"It's not just you; it's everyone."

I might believe her if she didn't avoid my eyes while making the claim.

I decide not to push her on that particular detail. "Okay, then why don't you want *everyone* to see your legs?"

She keeps staring off to the side, but doesn't back away from me. I'd let her go if she did. At least, I think I would.

"In high school, I got into a car accident. It was...pretty bad. My leg got a bit messed up. They fixed it with screws and everything, but now, I've got this thick, ugly scar." Her teeth tug on her bottom lip, sparkling white against petal pink.

"That's impossible."

She scowls up at me. "It's my leg. I think I'd know whether or not there's a scar on it."

"I don't doubt there's a scar. But I do challenge you calling it ugly."

Her mouth pops open, but I continue talking over her. "You're going to have an extremely difficult time trying to convince me that anything about you is ugly. It's an impossible task, really."

With my fingers touching her face, I can feel the heat of her blush as it spreads over her skin.

"That was sweet, Dash. Wrong. But sweet."

"Come on, Paige. Try on the dress. You don't like it, then we'll leave, and I'll never say anything about it again."

Her hazel eyes delve into mine. Whatever she sees is enough.

"Okay. But if I don't like it, I'm not even coming out of the dressing room."

"Deal."

A small bell rings when we enter the shop. The place is colorful, and a helpful shop girl finds the dress in Paige's size. I sit on a purple chair, trying not to think too hard on the fact that Paige is undressing with just a curtain between us.

I expect her to either pull back the curtain and be wearing the dress or step out and have her jeans and tank top back on. Instead, just her head peeks out, and she smiles hesitantly at me even though there's uncertainty in her eyes.

"What's the verdict?" I ask.

"The dress is everything I could ever want a dress to be." She pauses, and I keep quiet, sensing she's got more to say. "But I still hate my scar."

"Will you let me see it?"

With a last wide-eyed glance past me out to the relatively empty store, Paige pushes the curtain fully open and moves to stand in front of me, hands nervously smoothing down the silky green skirt.

My breathing stutters, and I have to blink a few times to make sure this isn't just a mirage. Paige stands barefoot with her toned legs seeming to go on for miles before they reach the bottom of the dress. And what a dress. It's short. So fucking short that I want to find the designer and shake their hand. Maybe on other girls, it would fall lower, but with Paige's height, the fabric ends just a few inches below her pert ass. I get to drool over the curve of that ass as she rotates in a slow circle to display every inch of the dress.

When she turns her back to me, I have to sit on my hands to keep from reaching out. The front isn't low-cut; it could almost be considered modest, but the back is a set of crisscrossing strings that show off even more of her glorious skin.

"I know; it's gross."

The defeat in Paige's voice drags me out of thoughts involving bending her over and pushing that swaying skirt up the last little bit.

"What the fuck are you talking about, Paige? That dress is amazing on you."

She turns around so fast that the material balloons up, almost giving me a peek underneath. I stifle a moan of disappointment when it settles back into place.

"Of course the dress is beautiful. That's not what's up for discussion." Her face is red as her eyes dart around and her hand spreads flat on the side of her thigh.

Oh yeah. Her scar.

"Let me see. I forgot to look."

"Forgot to look? It's like a flashing neon sign," she mutters while turning again, putting her side on display.

When her hand slips away, I finally get a view of the offending bit of skin.

To be honest, I thought she was likely exaggerating. I figured it wouldn't be too far off from the little slash in her eyebrow. Odd but quirky.

However, when Paige claimed her scar was big, she wasn't lying.

The damaged tissue is a thick pink line beginning just above her knee and disappearing somewhere under the skirt. The healthy skin around it puckers slightly where it meets the mark. It's not delicate. It's not elegant or romantic.

But it's just a scar.

"Does it hurt?" Somehow, one of my hands got free, and I find myself cupping the back of her thigh, my thumb resting just next to the damaged area, not quite touching it.

"I use lotion to keep the skin from getting stiff." She talks in a hushed voice, making this moment intimate. "Sometimes, my leg aches. Like, the bone and the muscles. Exercise helps with that. Running."

I nod, eyes focused on where my fingers circle her leg. That skin is smooth, soft against my palm. With just a slight movement, I could slip my hand up higher to disappear under her skirt like her scar does. Better yet, if I tighten my grip and tug her closer, I could kiss my way up under the fabric until I find the center of her.

"Dash?"

When I glance up, her eyes are full of confused curiosity.

"Get the dress."

A smile tugs at the corner of her mouth, even as she bites her bottom lip.

"You think I should?"

I nod. "Anyone who'd judge you for your scar isn't worth knowing anyway. Get the dress. Wear the dress. You look great in it." I take my hand away, letting it fall to my lap and trying to stifle how empty it feels without being able to hold on to her.

"Okay," Paige says hesitantly. Then, she squares her shoulders and turns to admire herself in the three-way mirror. "Okay." This second one rings with conviction, and she practically marches back into the dressing room.

I've just finished readjusting myself when she tugs the curtain back open, still wearing the dress but now in her sandals too.

"Do you think they'll let me wear it straight out of the store?"

A determined fire burns in her eyes, and it's all I can do not to push her back into the privacy of the dressing room and have my way with her.

CHAPTER 21

PAIGE

don't know the last time I've gone farther than my parents' backyard with bare legs. In New York, I always made sure my skirts at least fell as far as my knees, if not all the way to the ground. My scar has haunted me for eight years, but today, I'm not letting it rule my outfit choices anymore.

The breeze brushes against my skin, and the sensation is so foreign that it's almost erotic. Or maybe that's just because a sexy man is holding my hand again.

I guess Dash doesn't mind touching. It's just the kissing I need to stop myself from doing. I never really thought friends held hands, but maybe it's just that friends in relationships don't. Or maybe I haven't had a lot of physically affectionate friends. Whatever the case, Dash has told me this is okay.

Problem is, if I'm so dense that I don't know what friends can do with each other, how the hell am I going to figure out the right way to date someone? I've never had to do it before. Martin has been the only guy in my life since I was seventeen.

I feel like a newbie. An amateur. If I don't start learning the rules,

I'm bound to make another huge, embarrassing blunder. And who knows if the next guy will be as forgiving as Dash?

"Thank you. Again. For help with the dress. And for being friends with me."

Dash stares down at me with a raised eyebrow. "You don't have to thank me for being your friend. It's not a chore."

Well, that's good to know. Hopefully, he'll still feel that way a few minutes from now.

"Do you mind helping me out with something then? As a friend?"

His mouth thins, but he nods, watching me instead of the sidewalk in front of him. I have to tug on his hand to navigate him around a large puddle.

"So, you know that I just got out of a long relationship. Martin. You met him. He's a dick."

Again, Dash nods, so I continue talking.

"When I say long, I mean, *long*. We were together since high school. And I realize this makes me seem like a complete moron for staying with a guy like that for so long, but I'm hoping, as my friend, you'll accept that, sometimes, I can be a moron."

This actually gets a smile out of him. "You're not a moron."

"Oh, just you wait. There's more." I pinch the edge of my skirt, keeping it down as a breeze brushes past us. "I, having only been with the one guy, am now realizing I have absolutely no idea what dating is even like today."

Dash glances away from me then, lifting his free hand to run his fingers through his messy black hair. "Can't see how I'll be any help. Haven't dated much since I got out."

I'm on the verge of asking what he means by *got out*, but then I remember. Oh, right. Dash was in prison. Doubt he did a lot of dating in there. Unless he did…

No, Cole made it pretty clear Dash hooked up with girls. Recalling that exchange, I'm certain that Dash isn't being totally honest with me. Or maybe he doesn't consider one-night stands the same as dating. Whatever is the case, he can still be useful.

"That's fine. I think I could figure out how to behave *on* a date, as long as I knew it was a date. I guess my biggest problem is how to approach men. Like, for romance. And sex."

Dash makes a funny noise, and I worry for a second he might be choking. On what though?

He coughs a couple of times before answering me, "I think you'll be plenty busy with men approaching *you*."

This has me snorting. It's not that I think I'm unattractive, but I can't imagine a scenario where some guy approaches me to ask me out. Where would that even happen? Am I supposed to just go sit at bars every night until I luck out?

No, better to figure out a way to be proactive.

"That's sweet. But really, what should I say to a guy I think is hot? Do people still get coffee together? Or do I suggest something sexier, like alcohol? But do I have to specify the type of alcohol I'm asking him to drink with me? Because I like beer best. But wouldn't wine or cocktails be sexier?" Oh no, my brain is on a runaway train, and my mouth is along for the ride. "And what if he doesn't drink, like you? Would I blow my shot by suggesting it? Like, for example, if I asked Cole to get a beer—"

"You are *not* asking Cole out." Dash pulls me down a side street with fewer pedestrians to dodge.

"But you said he's on parole too." One of the few scant details I've been able to learn about Dash during our training sessions was that he met his roommate in prison. "So, he's sober. Would I be better just walking up to him and saying, *Hey, I think we'd be really good together. In bed*?"

Hot palms cup my face and stop the babbling storm I've swept myself up in. Dash tilts my head up until I'm staring straight into his angry eyes. He holds me still, and when he speaks, I can't help but notice how deep and growly his voice has gone.

"You are not doing anything in a bed with him or anyone else."

"Why not?" I whisper, just like I did earlier when he had his hand on my thigh, hoping if I keep my voice soft enough, I won't scare away the hunger in his gaze.

His dark eyes flash as his jaw clenches, but he doesn't back away.

Instead, he leans in closer, until his words brush over my lips. "Because you belong in mine."

Before I can respond, he crashes down on me, fusing our mouths together.

———

DASH

Sweet and earthy, the taste of Paige on my tongue is enough to solidify my addiction. I'm going to need this every day, multiple times, just so I don't go insane.

And that little gasp she gave me when I finally took her mouth? Priceless. I need more of her. I want to hear every sound she makes. But not right now because her mouth is busy.

One of my hands tangles in her silky hair while the other moves around to her back, so I can press her soft body into mine. She's all curves against my hard angles. The heat of her skin burns under my palm, almost her entire back exposed because of this fucking perfect dress. To tease her or myself, I slide a finger under one of the slim silk straps and simply sweep back and forth, enjoying the shivers that shake through her in time with my movement.

But it's hard to focus on my hands when the tip of her tongue peeks out to trace over the seam of my lips.

She wants more? Who am I to deny her?

I open, letting in her hesitant caress. As her tongue delves past my lips, the pads of her fingers push under the edge of my shirt.

Fuck yes, I want to moan. *Take what you want from me.*

Our tongues dance together before it's my turn to push into the wet heat of her mouth, plundering, demanding. She needs to know what I can do. How well I'll take care of that little spot of pleasure between her legs when I finally push up her skirt.

A hoot and a whistle send a stiffening shock down my spine.

"Yeah! Give it to her!"

We break apart, and I search for the catcallers. Seems a group of frat guys decided to go day drinking. They loiter across the street from us, laughing and calling out like they're some kind of comedic geniuses.

I'm ready for Paige to pull away, expecting that when she does, I won't be able to stop myself from stalking over to their group and teaching them some manners.

But she doesn't step back from me. Instead, Paige buries her face in my neck, her shoulders shaking.

For a second, my rage spikes higher. Those fuckers made her cry.

They're going to die.

Then, Paige snorts, and I realize giggles spill out of her rather than tears.

"Hey." I pull my hand out of the tangle of her hair and smooth it over the buttery strands, enjoying the soft texture as I stroke her. "They're assholes."

She nods against my neck before lifting her head to gaze up at me with her hazel eyes wide, full of a mixture of humor and wonder. "You kissed me, Dash. That was definitely you this time."

"That was me."

Paige's smile blooms bright and quick, like the sun suddenly bursting over the horizon. "Will you do it again?"

"If you want me to."

"I do." She nods vigorously. Then, her eyes drop to my mouth, and she licks her lips. "Right now, please."

"We have an audience."

"Don't care." Her arms move to wrap around my neck, pressing her breasts even more firmly into my chest as she draws herself up until our breaths mingle, just on the verge of touching. And she waits for me.

A growl rumbles out of my chest before I loop my arms around her waist, crushing her to me and turning us so the group of idiots can only see my back as I indulge in another one of her decadent kisses.

This one I only let last for a moment before I move my hands to her hips and gently separate us. Paige loosens her arms reluctantly, pouting as I put a good foot of space between us.

"We do any more of that here, I'll do something that'll get me arrested for indecent exposure." Before she can tempt me again, I snag her hand and pull her back out onto the sidewalk. I figure constant movement is the best course of action if I want to keep from pressing her against a wall and pushing up the skirt of that flirty little dress.

Why did I convince her to buy it? The thing is a fucking torture device.

Paige doesn't say anything for a while, and when I glance down at her, she has the fingers of her free hand pressed against her lips. She seems confused, and I'm not sure I have a good explanation for what I just did other than I wanted to.

I keep quiet.

When we end up at the pay-to-park lot where Paige left her car, she finally breaks the silence, though not in the way I was expecting.

"Oh shit. Mom's going to be pissed."

I try not to flinch. Of course, I realize no parent wants their daughter making out with an ex-con who's only out on parole and can barely pay his bills. Still, for a moment, I convinced myself that maybe Paige wouldn't care what her parents thought. At least long enough for me to get a few more tastes of her.

When she tugs her hand out of mine, it's like someone tearing duct tape off my bare skin. A ripping sensation that leaves behind a persistent ache.

"I need to find a changing room." Frustration laces her voice.

I try not to snap when I respond, "I don't think wearing a dress is going to out you."

"What?" Paige's eyebrows dip low as she stares up at me in confusion.

I sigh. "I don't see why you need to change."

I don't see why she needs to worry about her parents at all. She could just pretend like today never happened.

"I'm not about to change a tire in my new dress. I love it, and I don't ruin things I love."

"Change a tire? What are you talking about?"

She rolls her eyes and gestures dramatically. "Just look at Penelope!"

"Penelope?" I try to run through the last bit of our conversation to pick up what I'm missing.

"My car. That's her name. Look at her."

I glance around until I spot the green Impala, then give the car a thorough once-over. That's when I spot the problem. A flat tire.

"I have a spare in the trunk, but I know I'll get all sweaty and dirty." Paige turns as if she's about to head back to the clothing store.

"Hold up." I wrap my arm around her waist, halting her steps. "I'll change it."

"You don't have to, Dash." She tilts a half smile up at me. "I know how. Done it a few times before."

"Let me handle it, Paige. That way, you won't have to change."

Her eyes flick between me and her car, and I wait for her to give me an opportunity to prove my worth.

"You don't mind?"

"No. I'm doing it." I've already started walking us toward her poor, off-balanced beauty.

With Paige pulling out all the necessary tools, it doesn't take long for me to have the Chevy jacked up, so I can start unscrewing lug nuts. Paige stands at my side, holding out her hand to accept each of the bolts as I remove them.

"Does your car have a name? The white Saturn?" she asks.

"I call it Jack," I grunt as I loosen another lug nut.

"Hmm. I thought most people named their cars after women. Why'd you go with Jack?"

"He was my cellmate."

"Oh."

I glance up to find Paige sucking on her bottom lip. From this angle, she towers over me, looking like my dream girl as she stands there in her silky green dress, cupping the lug nuts in her palms. At some point, maybe when I accidentally brushed against her, a little smear of grease appeared on her shin.

I imagine what she'd look like naked, covered in smears of motor oil left by my hands roaming over her pale skin. In the fantasy, I'm working at a mechanic shop, my own garage, and she wanders in at the end of the day and lets me strip her down and lift her onto my workbench, where I can easily slide between her legs.

"Did you like your cellmate?"

Her question is a cold bucket of water on my brain.

I would rather be thinking about her gasping my name than some prick I used to know.

"No. He was an untrustworthy piece of shit. Just like the Saturn."

Paige frowns. "I'm sorry. That must've sucked. I mean, I'm sure all of it sucked, in a big way. But to have to share what little space you had with someone you didn't like must've just been a rotten cherry on top of a shit sundae."

She's not wrong. Prison was hell. Every day locked in a cage, surrounded by violent psychopaths. Stress and fear were constant companions. And I didn't even have the worst of it compared to some guys. You want to stay alive and relatively whole in there, you need to have connections. Protection. I got that, but at a high cost I'm not done paying.

Paige doesn't need to know any of that.

"Got through it. And I met Cole. We watched out for each other."

I have the flat off and set it to the side before rolling and lifting the spare into place. The tire slides easily onto the screws, and Paige hands me back each of the individual bolts when I ask for them. After a little extra pressure applied, I've got the tire on as tight as it'll go, and she's set to drive at least as far as that beautiful garage setup her mom has.

Paige follows me around to her trunk, where I stow the ruined tire. "Thank you. I mean, I could've done it, but then I'd be all sweaty, like you." She grins up at me as she plucks at my now-damp T-shirt.

I'm tempted to pull her against me for another deep kiss, but I don't want to ruin her new dress with my sweat. "I don't mind. I like working on cars." That's been the truth since I was fifteen and my uncle finally let me help in the shop. Right around the time he recruited me to start bringing him cars.

Seems like today, I'm giving in to a lot of my baser urges. But when Paige hooks a finger through one of my belt loops, just fiddling with the material, I can't think of a good reason to stop myself.

"I want to thank you for helping me out. A fair exchange for your services."

Fuck. The idea of Paige giving me money makes me feel dirtier than my now-grimy T-shirt. I don't want to be her employee. On the walk to her car, I already decided that I wouldn't accept any more payment for helping her with Pumpkin. Not when I'm planning on having her straddling me soon.

"I think dinner would suffice. Do you have a free night this week? I'll come to your place and cook."

For a moment, I just blink down at her.

Come to my place? And cook?

"You know I still live in the same house." *The same shithole*, is what I mean to say. Who would want to spend any time there when they don't have to?

"Well, that makes getting there easy, seeing as how I know where it is." She perks up one eyebrow. "So, dinner? Will you be around on Tuesday?"

"Yeah, I'll be around." I sound like a douche, but I'm still having trouble processing the fact that she wants to voluntarily come to my place.

"And do you have a working stove?"

"I do."

"Good." Her grin tightens my chest and sends blood flooding south. "That's all I need."

CHAPTER 22

PAIGE

"You are acceptable cookies. Don't let anyone tell you different. Looks aren't everything." I comfort my misshapen blobs of dough and chocolate as I gently slide them off the baking sheet onto a cooling rack. When it comes to cookies, taste is my priority. Presentation be damned.

Also, fat content is high on my list. The amount of butter in this batch is enough to grease an entire pig. I'm guessing. I have no frame of reference.

Tilting my head, I glance over at Pumpkin, curled in her plush doggy bed. Every so often, she lets out a gentle snore. I measure her with my eyes.

"Enough to grease Pumpkin at least."

Her ear twitches, but she doesn't open her eyes.

Most people these days are looking for ways to turn their desserts into kale chips that somehow magically taste like chocolate. If anyone ever perfects that recipe, I'd be happy to try it, but those wouldn't serve my current goal.

Dash and Cole are too skinny. They both look like they've fallen behind on a few meals.

A lot of meals.

My guess is, it's something to do with money.

I feel an unfortunate mixture of relief and guilt that I've never truly had to worry about my finances. I'm not a trust-fund baby or anything, and all the money in my savings account I earned on my own. But I've always had Mom and Dad as a safety net. One I've fallen into more times than I'd like to admit.

So, here's me, comfortable, financially stable, and well fed.

I want that for Dash and his roommate. The only solution I've brainstormed so far is to make them a feast of high-fat food.

"Paige, honey. I need to talk to you about something." My mom's voice, low and serious, clears away all thoughts of cooking. She strolls into the kitchen, my dad as close as her shadow, his face grim.

"What is it?"

"I've just finished putting a new tire on the Impala. And I got a good look at the flat. Honey, did you see anyone hanging around your car? As you were walking up to it?"

I set down my spatula and wipe my hands on a dish towel. "No. I mean, there could've been. Parking was packed, and there were a whole lot of tourists around. Why?"

Mom glances over her shoulder at my dad, the two of them sharing a grimace. "The puncture in your tire doesn't seem to be from wear or a stray nail. There's a cut. On the side. As if someone slashed it."

Slashed my tire?

"That's ridiculous. Why would someone do that? Makes much more sense to smash my window and steal whatever I've got in the glove compartment. If someone slashed my tire, they're an idiot." I turn to place the baking sheet in the sink and check to make sure the oven is off.

"What cases are you sitting on? Have you gotten any threats lately?" my mom asks my dad.

"None for at least a year now, but they don't have to make a threat to do something dangerous."

"I think we should call Jerry. Have him stop by."

My parents converse with each other, effectively leaving me out of the exchange. The minute they mention the US Marshal who used to be tasked with my safety, I know I can't let them spiral any further.

"Stop it. The two of you. So, maybe my tire got slashed. We live in New Orleans. This stuff happens sometimes. If you haven't realized, Penelope kind of stands out. If an immature kid is looking to cause some mischief, they'd probably lock onto my car like they've got a laser-targeting system. You need to stop seeing murders around every corner."

"Paige, you know your father has a dangerous profession."

"Of course I know! It's why I barely had a social life, growing up."

"That's not true." My mother frowns. "We let you invite friends over."

"Only after doing a full background check on their entire families," I groan, pressing my fingers into my eyes to stave off a threatening headache.

"We just want you to be safe," she says.

"You may not always use the best judgment when picking friends." Up until this point, my dad has let Mom spearhead their side of the argument. But his comment pinches the end of my nerves, and I throw him a questioning glance. "How much do you know about that boy you brought to the party?"

He knows.

Why should I be surprised? My father is the king of background checks. I wonder if he even waited for the party to end before he was on his laptop, scanning every bit of Dash's criminal history.

"I know *plenty* about him." My strategic emphasis has him narrowing his eyes.

"Stop it, Richard. I'm not talking about Dash. Seems like a sweet boy. And he likes cars."

At my mother's offhand comment, my dad's mouth tightens.

Her response surprises me, and I glance from her open, honest expression to Dad's disapproving stare.

She doesn't know.

For some reason, my dad hasn't shared his findings with her. And despite his obvious dislike of my friendship with Dash, I experience a stray bit of hope. Maybe Dad hasn't completely signed off on him.

"You know what? If it makes you two feel comfortable, call Jerry. It's been a while since I've seen him anyway."

Jerry was my first self-defense instructor, teaching me all the vulnerable spots on a man I could dig my nails and teeth into.

It was an interesting relationship, to say the least.

"Thank you, Paige. You know we're just worried about you." My mom's voice has gotten tight, and I think I see a sheen across her eyes. My heart swells, and I am suddenly grateful for her overprotective love. Because it's still love.

"I know, Mom." I step around the kitchen island and wrap my arms around her shoulders. Taking my height from my dad, I stand a few inches taller than her, making me feel more like the protector in this embrace.

With my mom in my arms, I hit my dad with a loving but stern expression.

"And you don't need to worry about Dash. He's an *honest* guy."

Dad doesn't give me any kind of response. Not accepting or denying. Just blank intensity.

Another reason he's so good in a courtroom.

I step back, taking in the two of them. My parents don't necessarily look like a matching set, with my father tall and imposing and my mother short, full-figured, and upbeat. Somehow, they work, and despite how often we get into our verbal sparring matches, I realize I've missed them. A lot.

When I lived in New York, they would come up to visit a few times a year, and it would be pleasant but always over too soon. These last couple of months, I've felt a new connection develop between the three of us. A different kind of relationship than what we had when I was in high school and relied on them for everything.

I still want to move out from under their roof, but the idea of going back to those rare visits makes my throat tighten.

Maybe I could scan job ads a little closer to NOLA.

I try not to linger on how that would also keep me closer to a certain dog trainer too.

"I'm going over to Dash's house tomorrow night to make him dinner. I doubt he'd mind if I brought Pumpkin with me."

Every time I leave my dog here with my parents, I feel like I'm taking advantage of their hospitality.

"Oh no. Don't worry about that." My mom strolls across the kitchen and sits down on the tiled floor beside my dog, scratching a little bit of exposed stomach until Pumpkin stretches and rolls over for a full belly rub. "I'll feed her dinner and take her out. You don't need to worry about us."

I watch the two of them, and a tiny candle flame worth of hope lights in my chest.

Maybe if Mom can get over her distrust of pit bulls, she could also find a way to be around Dash when Dad eventually reveals my friend's less than respectable past.

I'm careful not to breathe too deep, worried the flame will go out.

CHAPTER 23

DASH

Paige shows up, and now, my piece-of-shit house is filled with a savory scent I hope seeps into the walls and never leaves.

When she texted me earlier, I couldn't help wondering how this night would go.

Paige: *Do you have any allergies? Specifically, I'm wondering about shellfish.*

Dash: *Nope. What are you making?*

Paige: *A surprise. Will Cole be around?*

Dash: *Not sure.*

Paige: *Does he have allergies to anything?*

Dash: *I don't know.*

Paige: *Could you ask him? I would rather not manslaughter your roommate.*

Dash: *He says pineapple. And I think you meant murder.*

Paige: *Murder is intentional. I would never murder Cole.*

Paige: *Scratch that. I don't like using absolutes. I, at this time, have no plans to murder Cole.*

Her questions about my roommate brought on a wave of jealousy.

Does she want to be cooking for him instead? Is he the guy she wishes would ravish her mouth on a busy street?

With a great bout of self-control, I tamp the dark emotions down.

It helped that immediately after entering my house and laying her bags of groceries on the table, Paige slid her arms around my neck and smiled up at me, eyes on my mouth, waiting expectantly until I bent down to kiss her.

She let out a happy hum before releasing me and taking over my kitchen.

The amount of food she unloaded was more than I buy in a week.

"This is insane, Paige. Changing your tire took less than ten minutes."

She waves me off, then goes back to rinsing shrimp in my shallow kitchen sink.

"And this will also take an amount of time that might be considered in the realm of ten minutes. Comparatively. Now, sit down and eat a cookie."

Paige slides a Tupperware container across the counter toward me. I eye the lumpy masses she claims are cookies.

"Shouldn't dessert come at the end of the meal?" Despite my question, I open the container, releasing the scent of chocolate and vanilla.

"Food is food. When you're hungry, you should eat. So, eat." Paige waves a wooden spoon at me.

That utensil was definitely not in my kitchen before she arrived. This woman came prepared.

I pick out one of the doughy creations that most resembles a cookie. The second I bite down, my tongue gets bombarded with dessert nirvana, and I'm unable to suppress a moan of ecstasy.

"They taste okay? I know they're ugly. My food never looks good." She watches me with worried eyes.

I want to assure her that these are the most delicious cookies I've ever consumed, but I'm too busy shoving a second in my mouth. So, instead, I stand up from the table and move to enfold her from behind.

The gesture was unplanned, but there's rarely a moment I'm around Paige that I don't want to touch her in some way. That kiss in the car felt like permission. And the public make-out session was me finally giving in to what I want.

As Paige rests her head back on my chest for a moment, I let go of all the reasons why I convinced myself pursuing her was a bad idea.

For once in a long time, I choose the course that makes me happy.

Letting the newfound freedom take full control, I press my lips against her neck. "Delicious."

"Are you talking about the cookies? Or me?" Paige's voice squeaks out in a way that has me smiling against her silky skin.

Instead of answering, I trail open-mouthed kisses down to her shoulder as I spread my hands wide across her soft stomach, pulling her body fully into mine.

"Dash." She gasps out my name.

I growl happily and bite the strap of her tank top, wishing I could tear through the fabric and watch it slide down to reveal all the treasures contained underneath.

The wooden spoon clatters into the heavy-bottomed pot a moment before Paige twists in my embrace. Now that we're facing each other, the heat between us sears hotter, and I swoop down, intent on her cushiony lips.

At the last moment, she turns her head, and I end up with her cheek.

"If your sexy face and lustful kisses keep distracting me, I'm going to have to ban you from the kitchen until dinner is done." Even in the chastisement, I can hear the smile in her voice.

"Sorry, Ms. Herbert. I'll behave." I make sure to pinch her butt as my arms fall away.

Paige gasps and swats my stomach before turning back to her ingredients. "Talk to me. I want to know about all the dogs you work with."

"All the dogs? That's a lot."

She grins over her shoulder. "We have time."

We do have time. Maybe even all night if things go my way.

I regale her with stories of rescued animals and the different characters that come in to adopt them. Each one has a happy ending because

I can't handle the idea of breaking Paige's heart with depressing situations.

Working in a dog shelter, I've had to learn how to compartmentalize the good and the bad.

She shouldn't have to deal with that kind of shit.

At one point, after Paige has added all her ingredients to the pot and is simply stirring the mixture, Cole wanders into the kitchen. I hold still as he leans around her to sniff the concoction. His expression remains shuttered, not displaying an ounce of approval. Or attraction.

I don't know what I would do if the two of them started flirting again.

"I'm going to need another half hour, but you should have a cookie." Paige glances over just in time to catch me shoving another sugary wonder in my mouth. "That is, if Dash hasn't finished them off." She doesn't seem put out by the thought.

And anyway, there's still plenty left. I've only eaten a few.

Maybe half.

My roommate picks one out, examining it closely, while Paige watches him covertly out of the corner of her eye. Clearly, she wants to see his response to her baking.

I vow that if Cole says one shitty thing, I'm going to smother him in his sleep.

Without warning, he pops the entire cookie into his mouth. After less than five seconds of chewing, he grabs two handfuls and gifts Paige with a nod before retreating from the kitchen.

I'm on the verge of apologizing for his rude behavior when I notice her beaming grin.

"He likes them." Her simple statement brims with satisfaction.

Again, that sick, dark feeling churns in my chest. *What exactly is Paige's fascination with my roommate?*

Tired of letting my fear of her answer stop me, I try broaching the topic as I brace myself for the sting of her words.

"So, you like Cole?" The strain in my voice doesn't throw her off in the slightest.

"Of course. He seems like an interesting guy." With her eyes focused on the bottle of Tabasco sauce she's dumping into the pot, she doesn't catch my grimace.

"Are you…" *Shit. How do I even ask this?*

Picking up on my pause, Paige brings her attention back to me. "Am I…" Her hazel eyes hold curiosity, but not an ounce of guilt.

"Interested in him?"

Her eyebrows draw downward as she mouths my question back to herself. It's like I've given her a riddle she's attempting to decipher.

After a moment, she takes a guess, hitting the nail on the head. "You want to know if I want Cole? In a romantic sense?"

A shrug is all I can give her because, honestly, no. I don't want to know that.

Paige's eyes widen. "Oh. Gosh. Is that…I mean…I'm not one to judge. But I just…" She crosses her arms. Then uncrosses them. Then shakes her head. Then rubs the back of her neck while avoiding my gaze. "If you and Cole…the two of you…with me…I know people do that. Polyamorous, right?" Bits of her red cheeks are visible through her fingers as her palms cup her face. "That's okay. You do you. But I'm going to…politely decline." Paige lets out a sigh and returns to stirring her gumbo.

Now, I'm the one struggling to figure out what her jumbled words mean. I've almost got it when my thoughts get cut off.

"I just wanted you." Her murmur barely reaches me, but when it hits my eardrums, the rest of my body flares to life.

Partly with excited heat, but also, more prominently in the moment, with hilarity.

"Threesome? You think I want"—I choke on my next words before forcing them out between chuckles—"a threesome?"

"I don't know what you want, Dash. You're being kind of vague."

She frowns at me, and my humor trickles off.

"Sorry. It's just…you seem like you might like Cole. I wondered if it was him you'd like to go on a date with. Him you want to be cooking for." *Damn, I sound so pathetic.*

Paige sets her spoon off to the side and turns down the burner before leaning back on the counter and meeting my eyes. "Is that what dating is like these days? Games? People dating the wrong person to make the right person jealous?"

Every word out of her mouth makes it even more clear how ridiculous my jealousy was.

"No. I'm sorry. I'm an idiot." I rise from my chair and bracket Paige in with my arms, hoping that she won't be searching for the closest exit when she understands I'm a fool.

"You're not an idiot. Don't say that."

She glares up at me, and I keep my mouth shut. Her hands cup my waist. I'm ready for her to shove me out of her way. Instead, she wraps her arms around me, hugging me close.

This embrace is different than before. Earlier was flirtatious and sexual. Now, she holds me like she's offering comfort.

I bask in it.

The hold of her arms is strong and secure. The warmth of her body fills mine. I never want to leave.

"I do want to cook for Cole. I want to cook for both of you. Food is important, and I want to feed you. But when it comes to dating, that's all about you. Cole isn't invited."

"Well, cut me with a knife, why don't you?" My roommate's dry voice sounds from the doorway to the kitchen.

I glare over at him, but he just smirks.

"You're still invited to eat dinner. Which should be ready, by the way." Paige's hand rubs a reassuring circle on my back before she releases me and gives the two of us guys a grin.

While she returns to her bag of foodstuff, I pull out our mismatched plastic bowls and some dingy cutlery. Paige doesn't blink an eye at any of it, serving her fragrant rice dish without hesitation.

The three of us settle around our kitchen table, silent as we dig in. Cole and I devour the spicy gumbo. My tongue burns in delicious torture, and I cool it down with a slice of crusty bread Paige handed me. Mouth too full of food, the only way I can thank her is by reaching under the table to squeeze her knee.

She jumps but gifts me with a self-satisfied smile. I want nothing more than to tug her out of her chair and settle her on my lap, so I can keep one arm around her waist while I gorge on her delicious meal.

Instead, I keep my palm on her thigh and shovel the food into my mouth one-handed.

For the life of me, I can't think of what I've done to deserve this night.

Life seems to agree because I'm about to grab myself a second helping when a loud knock pounds at the front door.

Cole and I share a look, and it's clear from his flash of confusion that he's not expecting anyone either. My roommate lays down his spoon and exits the kitchen.

Paige gives me an eyebrow raise, displaying mild curiosity that I don't know how to respond to yet. But I get my answer seconds later, when Cole stalks back into the room, not even trying to suppress a scowl.

"Delaney is here."

Shit. Our parole officer.

CHAPTER 24

PAIGE

Delaney must not be Dash's friend from the way his entire body tightens up at the sound of the name. I don't think Cole likes the person too much either from the extra-surly tilt to his mouth.

Behind Dash's roommate enters a tall, dark-skinned woman with a thick waterfall of braids, dressed in a worn pantsuit.

The woman's expression is hard for me to read, and I wonder why Cole would invite her into their house if both men dislike her so much.

Is Delaney their landlady? Boss?

"Mr. Lamont, I am here to conduct a random home search."

It takes me a second to realize she's addressing Dash. He mentioned Lamont was his last name, but I've never really thought of him in such a formal sense.

Then, the second half of her sentence registers, and that's when I remember that both Dash and Cole are on parole.

They make it easy to forget. I don't even know what Cole was arrested for.

This woman must be their parole officer, and from Dash's frown, he was not expecting her visit tonight.

Guess that's why they call the visits random.

"Fine. Nothing has changed since last time." Dash's words come out clipped, bordering on harsh.

My nerves spike. Whether or not he wants this woman to be here doesn't matter. She has the power to send both of them back to jail as far as I know.

"Who's this?" Delaney nods my way.

Dash stands from his seat and steps as if to block me from view. The tension in the room becomes a tangible thing, and my mind jumps around, trying to land on the right words to defuse the situation.

This woman is the law, just like my dad. How would I talk to him if I wanted to make clear nothing is amiss?

Honesty. He appreciates honesty and clarity. That's worth a shot.

"Hello. I'm Paige Herbert. I'm a friend of Dash's, and I'm just here making him and Cole dinner. There's plenty, if you want some. Gumbo." As I speak, I stand and move around Dash.

The woman stares at me with guarded eyes. I stop myself from offering a hand to shake because I get the sense she wouldn't accept it. Instead, I muster a friendly smile.

Delaney continues to watch me for another moment, as if judging me. Is this what Dash and Cole have to deal with every day of their lives?

Dash steps forward and wraps his hand around my wrist. "Can Paige wait in my bedroom?" His voice comes out strained as if he's attempting to sound cordial.

The woman's slim eyebrow rises just a touch, and she doesn't respond.

"Dash, it's okay. I'll just sit on the porch." I tug at my arm, but he doesn't let me go.

"If you search my room first, can she wait there?" The words push through clenched teeth, and his discomfort is so pronounced that I don't try to get away again. Instead, I rub my palm over his knuckles, hoping to soothe him.

Delaney's sharp eyes drop to watch my movement, but no expression changes her face. "All three of you will need to stay in the room as I search."

Tension radiates off of Dash, and when he opens his mouth, I can see that the next words are going to be some kind of argument.

"That works!" I cut him off and wrap my arms around his waist, trying to tell him with my firm embrace to let the subject drop.

From the pronounced muscle in his jaw, he's clenching his teeth painfully hard. But he nods, and I stifle a sigh of relief.

Our strange party moves into Dash's sparse bedroom. I'm excited to get a better glimpse into his personal space, which I missed out on during my mad rush to the bathroom last time I was here. However, if I thought Dash was tense before, he turns into granite when Delaney begins pulling open his dresser drawers.

Suddenly, I'm not so interested in looking around. The search seems like an invasion of privacy, which I guess is the point. Dash gave up his right to privacy when he broke the law. Still, I don't want to learn about him like this.

Instead of watching the woman pull out each of his belongings, I turn my head into Dash's firm chest and try to lose myself in the tart, fresh scent of clean laundry that clings to his shirt. The pressure of his hand gently cups the back of my neck, as if encouraging me to keep hiding my face.

The sounds of rummaging and items being shifted around fade away as I focus solely on my hands playing over the slope of his back. The cotton of his T-shirt holds the warmth of his skin and adds a layer of softness to him. I wonder how different the texture of his skin would feel. My fingers fiddle with the edge of his shirt, at first just tracing along the seam, then twisting the fabric experimentally around the tip of my pointer finger. I tease myself, brushing against the stiff belt loop of his jeans, envisioning the small separation between my curious touch and his bare skin.

Then, with a deep breath, Dash's back seems to expand, pushing backward just enough to give me what I want.

Something like a static shock emphasizes the contact. I revel in how hot he is against the tip of my thumb. My finger plays back and forth, claiming that small inch of skin resting just above his waistband.

"Seems to be clear. She can wait here." Delaney's curt voice breaks the spell Dash's skin held over me.

I step out of his embrace, crossing my arms over my chest to keep my searching hands to myself. I can't believe I just did that. Dash was in the midst of having his life manhandled, and I couldn't keep from fondling him.

What is wrong with me?

"You don't have to stay, Paige. You can head home if you want." Dash's soft voice has me jerking my head up toward him. Wrinkles mar the normally smooth area between his brows, and a pinched quality lingers on his lips.

I can't tell if he actually wants me to leave or if he's just being polite. But at this point, I'm not ready to walk out. If Dash is done with me, he's going to have to come out and say it.

"I'll wait here." I straighten the sheets on his bed before sitting down, wondering if the fabric was untidy because Dash didn't bother to make his bed or because the parole officer expected to find something hidden there.

"Fine. The bathroom next." The woman strides out of the room.

Cole follows after her with an insolent slouch curving his shoulders.

Dash hesitates a moment, throwing me a look full of regret. "This shouldn't take long."

I nod, and he leaves. Then, I'm alone.

In his room.

There's not much to the place. Simple furnishings, bare walls. It could be anyone's room. Except that when I lie down, the pillow holds Dash's clean scent. For a moment, I strain to hear if the group is approaching. Nothing. Good. I don't have to feel self-conscious when I flip over and breathe in a lusty breath of the pillow.

Letting my body relax into the mattress, I trail my arm over the side of the bed. Absentmindedly, I trace the wood patterns on the floorboards.

How often does Dash have to put up with these visits?

She obviously never finds anything, seeing as how both guys are still out of jail and employed.

My finger catches on something. A corner. Nothing sharp. I lean farther over the edge of the mattress and realize the corner belongs to a magazine poking out from under the bed. If this magazine was anything illegal, Dash would be in cuffs by now.

Still, that doesn't mean it's exactly innocent.

I'm torn by curiosity and shame at the fact that I'm following in the parole officer's footsteps. It's his private stuff. I should leave it alone.

Leave it alone, Paige.

But if he was really worried about the magazine, wouldn't he have hidden it somewhere harder to stumble upon? In reality, he probably just tossed it here when he was done reading it. Really, this magazine is trash. I'd be doing him a favor by picking it up off the ground. Just imagine if Dash were to step out of bed and slip on it. He could fall and break his neck!

Picking up this magazine could be saving his life.

I reflect on how well I might have done as a lawyer while I tug the curious reading material out from under the bed. I expect to get an eyeful of glorious fake tits, barely covered by some artfully placed wording.

But those are not the parts I see strewn across the cover.

"She's done her search. You're good to…" Dash's words trail off as he comes to a stop at the foot of his bed.

I don't even bother to try stashing the magazine back where I found it. I'm caught, so I might as well ask my questions.

"Why do you have a classic car magazine hanging out under your bed? I thought that's where guys normally kept their porn. That's where Charlie kept his."

"Who's Charlie?" There's a growly note to Dash's voice, and I wonder if my argument about saving his life will work as well as it did in my mind.

"A friend. Sorry. I didn't plan on snooping. But it was a tripping hazard, and I was concerned for your head."

"My head?"

One eyebrow curves up sharply as he sits down next to me. The mattress bows downward, and my body rolls into his. In particular, the front of my pelvis rests against his lower back. No naughty parts are touching, but suddenly, a whole lot of heat is boiling in my lower belly.

"Yes. Your head. You have a very nice one. I enjoy looking at it. Probably more than I should, but I figure since you kissed me, I'm allowed to now." Oh no. The dreaded babbling cliff approaches. I try to focus on the magazine, tracing my eyes over the cherry-red hood of a Mustang to distract myself from the way said handsome head is staring at me.

But I find that's impossible to do when a set of long fingers plucks the reading material from my hands and tosses it to the side.

"You kissed me too." Dash hovers over me, his arms braced on either side of my torso as I lie reclined on his bed.

"I did." *Is that husky voice mine?*

"I'm allowed some things too."

"What kind of things?"

Dash doesn't answer with words. Instead, he leans down to trace his nose up my neck before placing a kiss in that perfect spot between the corner of my jaw and the bottom of my ear.

Shivers rack through me like I'm suddenly standing on the street in NYC in the middle of winter without my coat. Only here, it's not the icy bite of wind, but the gentle bite of a sexy man bringing on the reaction.

Dash continues to kiss me there as he brings his hand to rest on my rib cage. From the curve of his mouth, which I can feel on my skin, I get the impression he's enjoying his effect on me.

Tired of being passive, I reach up to find the bottom of his shirt, only this time, I don't fiddle with it like a shy girl. Instead, I delve my hands underneath the fabric, spreading my fingers over his taut back.

"Paige," he groans, his hot breath caressing my ear.

"Yes?" I stroke him hard enough to feel the tense rolling of his muscles.

"Don't start something unless you want me to finish it." He whispers the warning just before his teeth pinch my earlobe.

My back bows upward, pressing me fully into him.

"Finish me. It. Whatever. Yes. Consent given." Babbling. I'm rambling like a loon, but Dash doesn't run away.

The man rests his forehead against mine as groaning laughter spills out of him. Our eyes clash, and I find myself hypnotized by the dark intensity of his gaze.

"You asked for it." Dash presses a hard kiss to my mouth.

Before I can recover my senses enough to respond, he's gone, dragging more of those lovely open-mouthed kisses down my neck.

Pleasure courses through my body. *Is this what it would feel like if I grabbed a car battery with my bare hands?* The way my body tingles and heats, I have to be conducting some kind of current. I'm surprised there aren't any blue sparks ricocheting between Dash's lips and the exposed skin on my chest.

What's more, I haven't felt this way in years. Maybe ever. If the chemistry between Martin and me was ever like this, it's been so long that time has dampened the memory. Or maybe Dash's steady downward path is successfully destroying my long-term memory.

Nothing matters other than him continuing on his journey.

The coarse brush of his fingers on my shoulder brings about another shudder. He slides the strap of my tank top down until my nipple peeks out over my neckline. The tank top has built-in padding, so I nixed the bra.

"Pink. So fucking sweet." Dash's lips brush the hard bud as he talks, and before I can formulate an answer, he tongues the sensitive tip.

All I can manage is a moan as I squirm underneath him.

Just like with my ear, he gives a firm pinch with his teeth before retreating. I work to drag in deep, steadying breaths, attempting to calm the shaking of my body. But, like my nipple is the power button on a vibrator, I can't seem to shut myself off.

Dash doesn't seem to mind. He's too intent on dragging up the hem of my long skirt.

When the material reaches my knees, the shaking freezes. All of me freezes.

He's going to see my scar.

Of course, he's already seen it. Didn't seem to mind it either.

So, I shouldn't mind it.

Right?

The fabric brushes against the tough patch of skin, and I bolt upright, grabbing for the green cotton skirt to hold it in place.

"Wait."

CHAPTER 25

DASH

wait. Even though I'm so close, dying to reach the hidden center of her, Paige's worried voice leaves no room for argument.

"Here. You can..." She removes the fabric from my hands, gripping one side tight against her thigh, while she inches the other up farther. Offering me what I want but in an odd maneuver.

"What's wrong, Paige?"

She blinks at me. "Nothing. Just...you don't need to push the whole thing up. The skirt is pretty loose and flowing. This works just fine. Feel free to continue." She grimaces, probably realizing just how oddly formal her words came out.

I sit up, staring down at her as I try to figure out where I veered off course. My eyes draw back to her fisted hand, pressing into her covered thigh.

That's when I remember the scene in the dressing room. Funny, I completely forgot about the scar.

"Paige, I've already seen your leg. And FYI, I like your leg. Every inch of it."

She huffs out a sigh. "Come on, Dash. You don't have to lie to me. I'm already in your bed."

I glare at her, determination fueling my hand as I push aside her fist and delve my hand under her skirt.

She gasps and moves to pull her leg away, but I keep a firm grip, the beginning of her scar tickling my palm.

"I'm not lying. Your scar is a part of you, so I like it. I want to feel it. You know why?" Slowly, I start to slide my hand farther under her skirt, my thumb tracing the tough skin deliberately.

"Why?" Her voice comes out on a whisper, her stare baffled.

"Because when I'm touching it, that means I'm touching you. And when I'm tracing it"—my fingers continue to creep upward—"I know I'm approaching a fucking fantastic destination."

The rough skin ends, turning smooth just as I settle on her hip, gripping the cushion of one of her luscious curves.

"Now, will you lie back down and let me have what I want?"

Paige plops back on the bed dramatically, and I can't help chuckling. But the laughter leaves me when I slide my hand to the apex of her thighs and stroke my fingers over the heat of her.

She's damp. For me.

"Fuck me," I whisper to myself, lost in the sensation of her arousal coating my skin.

"Maybe. If you're good at this next bit."

Her breathy comment makes me laugh again, and I hide my evil smile by kissing my way up her inner thigh. The skin is soft and silky like a pillow. If I wasn't so turned on, I'd be tempted to lay my head down and take a nap right here. Maybe afterward, once we're both spent, I can convince her to let me use her lap as a cushion.

For now, I'm happy to focus on her center. She has on a simple pair of white cotton underwear, made sexy by the lace edges. Before tugging them down, I press my mouth against the damp fabric, grinning even broader at the way she shifts and fidgets under my exploration.

Needing to see her, I hook my fingers in her waistband and pull the panties off. One edge catches on her toe, so I take a moment to untangle them. Paige deserves care and attention, not a mad dash to the finish line. She's a country road, not a racetrack.

And there she is, pink folds, slick with arousal, framed in blonde curls the same buttery yellow as her hair.

My skin gets tight and feverish, the need to lick and suck making lust a suffocating haze over my brain.

"God, Dash, please."

I don't need anything more than those raw words.

As I drag my tongue up the seam of her, the salty, musky tang of her fills my mouth. I hear a muffled moan and take a break long enough to glance up and see Paige smothering her noises with my pillow. I'm torn between humor and disappointment. I want to hear her.

Well, pillows aren't completely soundproof. I just need to push her to levels that cotton can't cut off.

That means paying special attention to her clit.

I start with my tongue, tracing circles, then suck on her hard nub until she's writhing underneath me. I blow on her before returning my mouth to her hot center. Over and over, I repeat this action, and then I slip a finger inside her glorious, wet pussy.

A whimper sounds, so I add another. One more slow lick, and the walls of her tense and pulse as Paige gasps out her orgasm. I leave my fingers inside to enjoy the sensation until she goes completely limp, my pillow slipping to the side.

A red flush blooms on her cheeks and across her chest, which rises and falls as she pants. I pull myself up against her prone body until I can rest my cheek over her frantically beating heart, enjoying the rapid rhythm, paired with the scalding heat of her flushed skin.

"Are you two—oh shit. My bad." Cole's voice has me grabbing for a sheet to throw over Paige's exposed body.

He retreats down the hall to his bedroom, and I curse our shotgun floor plan.

"Paige, I'm sorry. I should've warned him." I expect her to glare at me, maybe storm out of the house.

Instead, she begins to shake again. Only this time, it's with barely suppressed laughter that eventually spills out.

"Oh no!" Despite the exclamation, she doesn't sound worried. "We scared Cole!" Paige snorts and covers her face with the pillow again, barely muffling her giggles.

All the while, I stare down at her, trying to figure out what I did to deserve such a sweet, sexy, amazing woman.

CHAPTER 26

PAIGE

love watching Dash walk toward me. He pushes his hair out of his eyes as he trots down the front steps of his house. Leaving the engine running, I climb out of the driver's seat.

"You know, one of these days, you're going to have to let me plan the date." Dash pretends to scold me, even as he approaches.

I can't help grinning as I lean back on my car, getting the sense he likes looking at both me and my beautiful piece of machinery. "You planned the first two. Besides, you work all day. I've got nothing to do but plan how I want to spend my time with you." I finish speaking just as he reaches me and reaches for me. His tender hands cup my cheeks as he rubs his nose against mine.

The gesture is silly and affectionate, doing a good job of turning my heart to goo.

Then, Dash kisses me, and a lot more of me starts to melt. A few minutes later, when he lets me up for air, I realize I enjoy being sandwiched between the warm metal of my car and the hot hard body of my...

My what exactly?

Does licking a girl's pussy equate to commitment?

Probably not.

Cole's words from our first meeting come to mind.

Am I just another one of the women Dash is interested in fucking, but nothing more?

The thought steals some of the happy warmth from my chest, but I try not to let the disappointment show on my face.

Anyway, it's not like I'm making any long-term plans with Dash as my anchor point. The last job I sent my résumé to was in Chicago.

Cold, windy Chicago. Much different from New Orleans.

"So, where are you taking me?" Dash asks from the passenger seat as I slide behind the wheel.

"It's a surprise." I wink over at him before putting the car in drive.

As I navigate away from the city, I ask about Dash's childhood.

If I wanted him open and laughing, I picked the wrong subject.

"My parents live in town, but I don't see them much. Usually stop by once a month to say hi to my mom."

Once a month? The idea seems ludicrous to me for a moment, until I realize that while living in NYC, I often went that long or more without even talking to my parents on the phone. But now, after being back here for a few months, the thought of not speaking to my mom regularly or asking my dad his opinions about the goings-on in the world seems so depressing.

I guess I'm bumming us both out.

Time for another subject change.

"Tell me about your dream car."

"My dream car?"

"Yeah." I throw a quick grin at him before focusing back on the road. Not that I'm in any real danger of hitting someone. The other drivers have begun to disappear as we get farther away from the metropolis. "A guy with a pile of car magazines under his bed has to have a dream car."

Dash sits silently for a moment, but I let him think, enjoying the view of mangroves rising on either side of the road. An indication that we do actually live in the middle of a swamp. I have a particular stretch of road in mind as we head west.

"Used to be a 1969 Mustang Boss 302." He shifts in his seat, turning to face me.

I notice a strange smile on his lips. Almost sad or disappointed. I can't quite place it, but the expression doesn't scream happy to me.

What is it with my ability to pick out topics that make Dash uncomfortable?

My very own superpower. Or curse.

"My uncle had one, one time. Not for long. He sold it. But one night, I crept into his garage and jimmied the lock so I could see what it felt like in the front seat. Sat there for hours, just pretending that I was a street racer, tearing up the road, leaving everyone in the dust." An energy fills his voice, and I wonder if I was too quick to berate myself. "That car was cherry. Lust on wheels."

When I risk another glance, Dash is staring out the windshield, eyes glazed over in memory. I'm loath to break his trance, but something he said is tickling at me.

"Used to be?"

"Hmm?"

"You said *used to be*. Do you have a new favorite?"

His long fingers tap on his jean-clad leg as I wait impatiently for his answer. When a whole minute goes by, I glance to the side, curious to realize a streak of red colors the tops of his sharp cheekbones.

He clears his throat. "Maybe."

Keeping my eyes on the road, I reach past the gearshift. My fingers grip Dash's thigh, just a little bit higher than what is acceptable in polite society. He gives the slightest grunt when I squeeze.

"And what am I going to have to do to get you to tell me?"

"Paige." I think he meant for his tone to sound scolding, but that's hard when it's pretty much a groan.

I slide my hand an inch higher as I keep my stare forward and my foot on the pedal.

"For someone looking for flirting pointers, you're pretty fucking good at turning a guy on," Dash growls as he clasps my hand, keeping it from moving any farther. "A '63 Chevy Corvette. Happy now?"

I ease my foot off the gas, risking a longer look at Dash as I pull over to the dirt shoulder of the road.

"Really?"

Even as the charming blush remains in his cheeks, Dash stares me down, fire in his eyes. "It's a beautiful car. Plus, I've got some pretty good memories in one."

Now, I'm the one blushing. I tug my hand free and shift the car into neutral, so I can take my foot off the clutch and pull the parking brake to keep us from rolling anywhere while I climb out.

"Paige?" Dash's confused stare follows me as I cross in front of the hood, only to reach his side and pull the door open.

"It's not a Corvette, but the Impala is still a dream to drive. I think it's time you took a turn behind the wheel."

His eyes go wide the same moment his mouth drops open. For a moment, we just stay there—him magnetically adhered to his seat, me standing with the one hand on my hip, the other on the open door.

"I shouldn't, Paige." His mouth says no, but his flexing hands say they want to grip that steering wheel.

"Why not? Something in your parole say you can't drive? We're not leaving the state. Just cruising down this practically deserted road." I gesture to the two lanes that appear to be empty for miles—or at least as far as we can see into the distance.

"Not my parole. Just...I don't deserve to drive a car like this." He glares out the front window, his mouth going hard after his confession. His self-proclaimed punishment.

I want him happy. Joyous. Laughing from his stomach and reveling in the glory that is Penelope.

So, I push.

"Dash," I murmur, sliding into his lap and wrapping my arms around his neck.

His expression softens as he meets my gaze. I lean forward to press my lips against the strong line of his jaw, loving the scrape of his stubble against my skin as I trace the lines of his face.

"I'm *so* tired of driving." I put an element of whine to my voice, like I'm a petulant child on the verge of a temper tantrum.

My wheedling is rewarded with a twitch at the corner of his mouth, so I lay it on thicker.

"I *want* you to drive. Sometimes, at night, when I'm alone in my bed, I…" I trail off.

Dash shifts, the muscles of his legs tensing beneath my butt. "You…" he prompts, and I hide my triumphant grin by pressing my mouth against the strong pulse on his neck.

"I imagine us," I whisper against his skin, "speeding down a road like this one. The windows rolled down. My hair blowing everywhere. And you, in the driver's seat, one hand on the wheel, one hand on the gearshift, showing me just how fast we can go."

A moan tears out of his throat, and his rough fingers clasp my face to tilt me up for a searing kiss. Our mouths meld, tongues clashing. Heat rises between us, and a rushing noise fills my ears, louder than any revving engine.

He's consuming me, and I'm letting him. Gladly. Passion has been gone from my life for years, long before Martin betrayed me. But I've found it here, again. But with a man, not a boy. Someone who has experienced life and is stronger for it. Someone who needs a little help remembering that there's more to life than just surviving it.

I shove my hands against his chest, breaking us apart, panting and cursing myself even as I do.

"Drive my car. Please." You wouldn't think I'd have to beg him to do something that he wants, but I'm beginning to discover that Dash doesn't give in to his impulses without a little help. I'm happy to act as the devil on his shoulder.

"Okay." His voice comes out hoarse, sending delicious shivers prickling over my skin.

Before he can change his mind, I reach down to unclip his seat belt, and then I slide off his lap. Dash lets out a growl-groan combo as his hand cups my ass. To help me balance, I'm sure.

Having given in, he doesn't hesitate any longer. He's around the hood and sliding into the driver's seat before I'm even buckled in.

After adjusting the position of the seat to suit his longer legs, Dash grins over at me. "You ready for this?"

"Show me how fast we can go."

CHAPTER 27

DASH

knew it was a bad idea, but I did it anyway.

My mind is so fucked up; I don't even know what the final straw was. Was it the idea of sitting behind the wheel of a gorgeous machine that runs like it's brand-new, or was it the beautiful woman describing her fantasy to me?

Whatever the reason, I'm giving in and shifting into first to pull us back onto smooth pavement. The Impala rumbles and purrs like a lioness ready to sprint. Out on the hunt.

With the empty road stretching before me, the sun setting on the horizon, I forget all my misgivings and let my body work from muscle memory.

It's been years since I let myself go, enjoyed a set of tires eating up pavement, gloried in the scenery whipping by so fast that it blurs into a muddle of browns and greens. The engine roars in a happy celebration that encourages me to join in.

I am connected to the car in this moment. We're one powerful machine, unstoppable. Despite the sheer weight of the vehicle, I'm light as air as we hurtle down the road, seconds away from losing touch with the earth.

There's just one part of me that maintains a firm grip on the world. As the rest of my body takes on a weightless quality, my cock grows hard and heavy, anchoring me to the present and the woman at my side.

A glance Paige's way reveals she's living out the fantasy she so breathily described moments ago. With the window rolled down, her golden hair twists and dances around her flushed cheeks. She beams at me, smiling wide. I want to tug her sunglasses off, so I can experience the full joy in her hazel eyes.

Instead, I release my grip on the gearshift to push my hand under the edge of her billowing skirt, thanking the universe she opted not to wear pants today. Over the rush of the wind, I can't hear her gasp, but I can see it in the O-shape her pretty pink lips take.

Suddenly, the rush of flying down a country road in a classic Chevy is not enough for me. When I rub the damp fabric barely covering the center of her, I'm ready for a whole different kind of ride.

A turnoff approaches, and I slow just enough to take it, gravel and dirt flying in the rearview. We go maybe another mile as the light in the sky dims, and I turn down another random road. An abandoned barn, rotting and half caved in appears ahead. I pull into the weed-choked drive leading up to it. Once we're well off the road and fully obscured by the building, I shut off the engine.

"Get in the back seat. Now."

Paige visibly shivers at my command and practically kicks open her door. I climb out of my seat at a more sedate pace, trying to rein in my raging need so as not to scare her. When I circle around the car, I find Paige perched on the edge of the generously-sized bench seat, sunglasses gone, teeth pinching her bottom lip.

"Do you want me naked? Because I want you naked." Her words tumble out, breathy and eager.

My dick twitches in anticipation.

"You're not too cold?"

With the sun down, the temperature has started to drop.

"You'll warm me up. Right?" She gazes up at me, and I have to grip the roof of the car to keep from attacking her.

"Fuck yeah, I will. Take your top off." I rip my shirt off, ready to feel her skin against mine.

Like a good girl, Paige follows my order, tugging the blouse out from where it was tucked into her skirt and pulling the fabric over her head before tossing it into the front seat.

And there she sits, like a piece of art, lacy white bra cupping her round tits, flowery skirt teasing at what's underneath.

Suddenly, I feel like I'm back in high school. The screwup who somehow convinced the straight-A class president to give him a shot, and I only get her until her father realizes she's snuck out her bedroom window and calls the cops to find us.

As much as I want her completely bare before me, I also want to play out my fantasy. The dream that, instead of ruining my life when I was sixteen, I found a young Paige, a girl who would push me to walk a respectable path and love me, even when I fucked up.

Wait. Shit. Love?

Paige doesn't love me. And she shouldn't.

And if I let myself love her, that'll only lead to ruin.

I shake my head to get all the ridiculous thoughts of love out of my mind.

"Dash." My name on her lips pulls me back to the present. "What should I take off next? And choose fast because I'm feeling very animalistic. I may just maul you if you don't get in this car soon."

Paige's impatience kicks my lust back into full gear, and I find myself leaning forward to shove my hands under her skirt.

"Once these panties are off, we're going to fuck like teenagers in this back seat. Only I'm not some fumbling idiot who doesn't know how to make you come." I don't bother pulling the underwear down her legs, choosing instead to rip it at the seams. That way, she won't have the option of putting them on again for the rest of the night.

"Condom. I put some in the glove compartment before picking you up," Paige gasps out as her nails delve into my hair, raking against my skull in an erotic, teasing sensation.

Grinning, I shove the scraps of her underwear in my back pocket as

I stand up. Quickly rummaging through the compartment, I find the small box, only containing three condoms. I make a note to swing by the store to grab more because there's no way I'm stopping after three times with the goddess in the back seat.

With the car doors open, a small light stays on, bathing Paige in a golden glow. I drink in the sight of her as I unzip my fly, pulling out my hard dick. Her gaze rakes over me, and the tip of her pink tongue sweeps along her bottom lip as I roll the latex on.

"I need you inside me—yesterday." Paige fists her skirt, pulling it up to fully expose herself, offering her pussy to me as if she thinks I'm worthy.

But I'm too far gone to point out she should leave me here, drive off, and never give me the time of day again. No, I'm a selfish bastard that's going to take every little bit of her while I can.

She lies back as I stretch out above her, lining up my hips with hers, bracing my weight with one arm as I reach down to finger her clit with my other hand. Her light-blonde lashes flutter, and suddenly, the car is heady with the scent of coffee and arousal.

I let the head of my cock rest just at her entrance as I roll and press her little nub of pleasure. Once I'm inside her, I'm not sure how long I'll last, the aftereffects of driving a fast car still thrumming through my veins, mixing with the aching need to watch her fall to pieces under me.

Paige needs to come first because no way am I finishing without getting her off at least once.

"Dash! Inside me!" She gasps out the demand as her flushed chest presses into mine with her rapid breaths.

"Not yet. Come for me first."

She groans, and I chuckle. That is, until she slides a hand past the loose waistband of my jeans to dig her nails into my ass, trying to urge me forward. Commanding me to bury myself in her tight, wet heat. I clench my teeth and hold firm, maneuvering my thumb to massage her clit as I delve my fingers into her folds.

Paige moans, and I think I've got her. Just one more push.

"After you come, I'm going to slide deep into you and fuck you hard. You'll be feeling my cock tomorrow. Begging me to drive you back out here and take you over and over. And I'll do it, Paige. Because this is my sweet little pussy." I curl a finger inside her to emphasize my point.

"Oh!"

I smile at the shocked ecstasy on her face as she falls apart underneath me. Her fingers claw into my back, and her face flushes an intense red, even in the dim car light, and it's the most glorious sight I've ever seen.

Plus, it means I can fulfill my promise.

With the walls of her still clenching, I pull my fingers out and push inside her, sliding in slow until I'm completely in her embrace.

"Dash." My name on her lips is more a moan than anything else.

I take it as permission, dragging myself out before slamming home again. Over and over. The friction of our bodies connecting threatens to roll my eyes back into my head. Her noises, whimpering and gasps interspersed with my name, make my blood pound harder.

With the tightening of my balls, I know I'm close.

And that's when she lets out a yelp, her core pulsing around me again.

I made her come a second time, and the knowledge is the last bit I need.

"Hell, Paige!" With my head buried in her shoulder, my shout comes out muffled, and then I lose all ability to speak as pleasure rolls down my spine.

I finish, sitting deep inside her.

When my brain reboots after its temporary short-circuit, my first thought has me wrapping my arms possessively around Paige's waist.

If she tries to leave me, I don't think I'll be able to let her go.

———

PAIGE

Dash's panting breaths against my neck slow to a normal rhythm, but instead of moving to slide off me, he chooses to hug me tight to his chest instead.

Not that I'm complaining.

The feeling of his hot, slick skin against mine is enough to get me drunk, and I don't like the idea of being left cold without him. So, I circle my arms around his neck, returning the embrace.

After a moment of holding still, Dash turns his head enough to press warm, open-mouthed kisses against my neck. Goose bumps chase down my skin, a pleasant reaction to his affectionate display. He moves lower, sliding out of me, but still keeping his lips against my skin.

"Two times." Disbelief colors my voice, and Dash raises his head to grin up at me.

"Wanna go for three?"

"You can't be serious."

"When it comes to getting you off? Fuck yeah, I am." Dash stands up, sliding off the condom and tucking himself back into his jeans, but not bothering to put his shirt on. Instead, he grips me around the hips and drags me along the smooth leather seat of my Impala until my ass sits at the edge.

Then, the magnificent man crouches down and dives in to lick me.

I buck and groan, pressing the heel of my hand to my forehead as if that will somehow keep my mind from liquefying and spilling out my ears.

I love the way he plays with my body, finding every little pleasure spot.

I love the way his eyes go wicked and dark.

I love hearing him curse when he comes.

I love listening to him growl my name.

I love the way he smells of clean sheets when he's pressed up against me.

I love…him.

That last thought almost cuts off my rising orgasm.

It's just the sex. That's why I'm feeling this way.

I'm not in love with Dash. I can't be.

With another strong stroke of his tongue, the worried thoughts drift away, and I let the pleasure overwhelm my anxious mind.

CHAPTER 28

DASH

The minute I open the door, the scent of spiced beef cooking teases my nose. The few happy memories I have from childhood with my mom bombard me, all tied to the familiar smell of her cooking. Like a mouse being led into a trap with the promise of cheese, I follow the trail toward the kitchen.

Another one of the shotguns so popular here in NOLA, the house requires me to navigate through a series of rooms first. The shell of this place is familiar, seeing as it's where I grew up. I'm pretty sure the only reason my parents were able to hold on to the place is because my grandparents had willed it to my dad. If they were renting, things would've gone a lot differently.

At a glance, someone might think the occupants of this house are doing well for themselves. A fat leather couch takes up half the room with high-quality speakers tucked in the corners, and the latest, largest TV hangs mounted on the wall. But behind the shiny electronics and plush furniture lurks ratty wallpaper, scuffed floors, leaking pipes, and plenty of other code violations.

I step over the spot in the area rug that has nothing but a hole beneath it. You learn the tricks of this house after living in it for close to two decades.

It's not that my parents don't make money. Well, my dad does. Uncle Mike makes sure to include his little brother in all his under-the-table activities. At least, all the ones I know about.

But the second either of my parents has cash in their pocket, they're out spending it. Dad wants all the latest gadgets; Mom wants manicures and designer clothes. I'd be surprised to find out they even had a savings account.

The TV shakes just slightly with each of my footsteps across the living room. I wonder if, one day, the weight of all their purchases will cave in the old walls of this house. Then, they'll be trapped, finally buried under a pile of their bad decisions.

When I come upon my mom in the kitchen, she has her back to me, busy stirring a pot at the stove. The sight, mixed with the hearty smells, twists a combination of happiness and depression in my chest. When I was a kid, the scent of beef noodles meant that Vivian Lamont was home and acting like a normal mother.

The situation was rarer than Christmas.

"Mom."

She jumps, whipping around, only to gift me with one of her eye-shattering smiles. I've never had to wonder why my dad fell in love with her. Vivian Lamont is a beautiful woman. She's dressed in clothes normally reserved for girls half her age, but seeing as how she looks half her age, there's not really a problem. The only hint she's passed the forty-year mark is a set of light wrinkles hovering at the corner of her eyes. But ask any passerby on the street, and they'd guess she was my sister.

Staying young and wild is the only life plan Vivian Lamont ever made.

"My little prince!" She glides across the kitchen, a spatula in one hand, short glass with clear liquid in the other. When her lips press against my cheek, I pick up the pine scent of gin on her breath. "Oh, I'm so sorry. You don't like to be called that, do you?" She feigns disappointment, blinking up at me like an innocent kitten.

"You can call me whatever you want, Mom." I rub her shoulder before pulling out a chair at the tiny kitchen table and settling in it. "Why're you cooking?"

Throughout grade school, kids never let me or my siblings forget that we were the minority. Over half my classmates were Black, most of the rest were white, and then there existed a small amount of Hispanic and Asian kids.

That tiny slice was where Luna, Leo, and I existed. None of us inherited our father's blond hair or anything more than a hint of his Anglo features. And for some reason, that made us targets. The vicious teasing only stopped when Leo got big enough to fight back and Luna grew cunning enough to enact creative revenge on our tormentors.

There were times I hated the way I looked. Other times, I wondered if I wouldn't mind so much if I knew even a little bit about where that side of my family had come from.

Mom never spoke about her parents or anything to do with her life before she met our father. The time might as well be a blank slate. I don't even know what type of Asian I am. If I had money to throw around, I might think about doing one of those DNA tests where you spit in a tube.

The only hint I have at my ancestry is the generic beef noodle dish. The one that my mom makes when she's in a really good mood. The one that she offhandedly mentioned her mother taught her to make. The one she's gone back to stirring right now.

"Your father bought me a gift last night." She places down her drink before extending her arm toward me. Dangling from her wrist is a bracelet, sparkling with some sort of indigo jewels. "Those are real sapphires. Can you believe it? And you know how I love blue." A sigh of pure happiness drifts out as she admires the stones, turning them side to side so they catch the light. My mother is a simple woman to please. Simple but expensive.

Although I'm not sure *bought* is the best word to describe how my father acquires gifts for her.

"You're cooking for him?"

She nods. "Nothing says thank-you like a full stomach. Well, that and a special dessert."

My mother winks at me, and I'm no longer feeling so hungry. I do *not* need hints about my parents' bedroom activities.

For the next few minutes, she updates me on the neighborhood gossip in between sips of her drink, and I find myself enjoying her animated storytelling. When I was a kid, this was all I wanted—my mother spending her time talking to me rather than shooing me away. Now, apparently, I've reached an age where I'm not such a bother to have around. As long as I don't think about it too much, I can keep the memories from stinging.

"And your uncle is working on some big things. You really should talk to him about getting your old job back."

"I have a job."

This isn't the first time she's pushed me on my decision to work at the shelter.

"But it's such a good opportunity. Not like messing around with those dirty dogs all day. And you were the best he had." She gives me an indulgent smile over her shoulder. "No one is as fast as my little prince." One of her perfectly manicured hands covers her mouth as she feigns embarrassment over the slip. "Sorry. My little Dash."

Trying to change the subject, I blurt out the first topic I can think of. And of course, my mind is never far away from one thing.

"I met a girl."

Shit. Bad topic choice.

"Really?" My mom's eyes grow wide in actual interest. "Tell me everything about her. What makes this girl good enough for my boy?"

I grimace. "If anyone isn't good enough, it's me for her. I met her at the shelter. She was adopting one of the dogs. She's sweet. And beautiful. Like gold." I'm waxing poetic, but I don't have a lot of people willing to listen to me obsess over Paige. "She's smart, but doesn't hold it over you. And weird, but in this adorable, sexy way."

Fuck. I sound like a lovesick fool.

And even my mom, one of the most self-centered people I know, easily picks up on it. "You sound like your father when he first met me."

She grins and preens at the memory while I experience a dark, sick feeling in my gut.

I don't want to be anything like my father.

"Where's she from?"

I avoid her gaze. "She's local. Grew up here."

"What neighborhood?"

"Don't think you'd know it."

Her eyes get hard, drilling into me, and I try not to fidget.

"She's not from around here, huh? Lives in a big house? Parents making big bucks?"

I keep my mouth shut, fiddling with the peeling plastic of the kitchen table.

"Don't do this to her." My mom's command shocks me into meeting her eyes.

"Do what?"

"You know. This." She waves her spatula around to indicate the dilapidated house, filled with its temporary treasures.

"I don't know what you mean," I lie.

"Rich girls want to stay rich. This is how rich you're gonna get, and that's only *if* you start working for Mike again. Do you think this is what she wants?" Her once-happy voice has taken on a scathing quality.

For the first time in my life, I'm getting a glimpse of my mom's true feelings. The disdain she hides toward her own life. And again, I wonder who she was before my father.

"I don't plan to live like this."

"Neither did your father. But this is where he is. This is where I am." She stirs the beef noodles.

This might be my only chance for an honest answer, so I push for more than I ever have before. "What was your life like when you were growing up? Before Dad?"

She doesn't answer for a long time, her entire focus on the stovetop. When she does talk, it's as if I never asked the question. "You talked to your brother lately?"

I shouldn't let the disappointment fill me, but it does.

"Leo and I don't see eye to eye anymore."

Last we talked, he was adamant about getting behind the wheel of another hot car to get back in Uncle Mike's good graces. Like it was the only thing he could think about.

I don't need to gain my uncle's approval. I've got a debt, and when that's paid off, I'm done with that branch of the family. For good. So far, it seems like Leo plans on keeping his ties strong, which means I need to cut myself off from him.

"He misses you. And I miss you. I just want our family back together again." Mom reaches for a small box on the counter, rapping it against her palm and sliding out a fresh cigarette. When she lights it up, the stench of the smoke begins to overwhelm the delicious cooking smells. Just like the toxic memories from my childhood always overwhelm the good ones, eventually.

Suddenly, I'm not enjoying the mother-son bonding time anymore.

She wants her family back together? Wonder if that includes everyone.

"You talked to Luna lately?" I throw her question back at her, feeling no satisfaction at the tensing of her spine.

"Luna who?"

This is the part where I'm supposed to take the hint and leave it alone. But I'm not feeling too charitable.

"My sister. You know, your daughter?" The sarcasm is heavy in my voice as I play along with her game.

Mom stands quiet, one hand stirring the food, the other bringing a cigarette to her red-painted lips. Eventually, she whispers, barely loud enough for me to hear, "I don't have a daughter."

The statement breaks my heart. But it also makes me cold.

This is the hard part of my mother. The sharp part. The aspect of her personality that allows her to sit comfortably in a life of crime.

But in a strange way, I have to agree with her.

Luna was rarely ever in the *daughter* role. More often, she played the babysitter, cleaning lady, cook, chauffeur, plumber, electrician, and all the other things parents normally took care of so their kids could enjoy childhood.

I love the beautiful, selfish woman that gave birth to me. But when I think back on the woman who raised me, the one who tried her hardest to mold me into a man, that's always been Luna.

And I broke her heart the day I started driving for my uncle.

The smoke and the memories are making my head ache.

"When's Dad getting back?"

My mother softens, smiling over her shoulder again. "A little later. But I told him to make it home in time for dinner."

I slip my fingers into my back pocket, pulling out the reason I stopped by in the first place.

"Can you make sure he gets this?" Standing up, I hold the check for her to see, then place it in the middle of the table.

The smile drifts from her face. "You're leaving? But there's plenty of food! And you can give him the money yourself. Don't you want to see your father?" She has her sad-kitten eyes again, but the guilt washes around me without leaving a mark.

I have no interest in seeing my father any more than I have to. We'd just end up arguing, and depending on how many drinks he has, he might even try to re-create another childhood memory of him using the back of his hand to put me in my place. Luckily, those were rare occurrences. Being the oldest boy, Leo got the brunt of our father's anger when we were growing up.

"That's okay. I've got somewhere to be." I don't really, but that doesn't matter.

"But I never see you! Please just stay a little longer."

Those words bring up more memories, ones where I spoke almost exactly the same thing as she strolled toward the door. So many nights when I wanted my mother, but she had no time for me. All I got was a smile and a pat on the head before she and my father left for a night of partying, not worrying that their three young children had to fend for themselves.

"Can't. I'll see you some other time."

I leave her and the twisted vortex of my childhood memories behind, focused on a future where the people I care about don't hurt me and don't leave me.

CHAPTER 29

PAIGE

The boring front of the house mocks me and my past pain. You'd think it would have flames painted on the side or caution tape pasted over the door. Something to indicate that one of the most embarrassing moments in my life happened here.

But it's as plain as steel-cut oats. A bran-cereal house. Living in it probably helps lower your cholesterol.

"Screw you, you healthy, sensible house," I mutter under my breath as I climb the front stairs.

At least this time, I don't have to knock. A plastic rock that isn't fooling anyone sits off to the side of the porch. It only takes me a second to find the little latch needed to pop the hiding spot open and release the spare key Martin texted me about.

After three weeks and no word from my ex, I thought I might never get my stuff back. But then, last night, my phone finally lit up with a message from him, letting me know tonight was a good time to swing by.

Martin is out on a Friday evening. Probably with Miss Petite and Pretty.

I pause in the act of sliding the key into the door, revisiting my assumption.

Martin, on a date, with another woman.

I search every corner of my brain with a megawatt flashlight, but I don't find what I was expecting to feel—jealousy, hurt, anger.

None of those ugly, dark emotions burn in my chest.

There's still discomfort. I know I don't want to run into Martin when he's out with another woman. But it's not the *other woman* part that's causing my skin to tighten. It's Martin himself.

He was a man I loved and a man I started to fall out of love with. Then, instead of trying to work out his feelings with me, he jumped into bed with someone else.

I'm not angry anymore. I just...don't like him. As a person. Martin is a different man from the boy I fell in love with. Or maybe I'm a different girl. Either way, one or both of us changed, and we don't work anymore.

Sucks that cheating had to be the catalyst to realize that, but I'm better off now.

When I push the front door open, I find a dark house. After flipping a switch to illuminate the hallway, I experience a moment of panic.

Scattered across the floor is a sparse collection of rose petals.

Shit, did I get the day wrong? Am I about to walk in on Martin and his new lady? Again?

My racing heart calms when I notice the vase of red roses on a table in the hall. That's when I recall the greenhouse in Mrs. Blanche's backyard. Roses are her specialty. That, paired with Martin's complete incompetence when it comes to vacuuming, explains away the sight.

I exhale a sigh of relief, reassured I'm not going to walk in on him pounding away into the robe stealer.

Avoiding the petals so I don't crush them into more of a mess than they already are, I veer to the left and enter a living room. Navy, white, and gold are the colors of choice for the place. The setup is nice, in the same way a picture in *Good Housekeeping* is nice. But it's not real life. Martin clearly hired someone to decorate.

I maneuver around a glass coffee table and a white couch. *White?*

Hell, that thing would be covered in muddy paw prints and fur if Pumpkin got anywhere near it. This is not a house for a dog.

Next is a dining room with a table big enough to seat eight, and it looks like it can extend to hold more. *Would Martin have expected me to host dinner parties here?* Our New York apartment was too small for more than a handful of friends, but I remember him mentioning larger get-togethers in the future. I shudder.

Bullet dodged.

My eyes scan the walls, and a creeping unease tightens my shoulders when I realize there are framed photos artfully placed around the room.

Of us.

Me and Martin.

"What the hell?" I try to think of a reason for their existence as I step through another doorway into a massive kitchen.

The room is dark with black cabinets, onyx countertops, and oak hardwood floors. One bright spot stands out, illuminated by a handful of candles placed on the kitchen island.

Martin. Or at least Martin's pale-as-hell back. I get a full view of the white expanse and his pasty legs because my ex-fiancé is standing in the middle of the room in nothing but a pair of Scooby-Doo boxers I bought him as an April Fools' joke earlier this year. I always said he looked like Fred from the cartoon, but he would never dress up like the character for Halloween, no matter how much I begged.

Who isn't willing to put on a white sweater and orange ascot for the woman they love?

I'm getting off track. *Brain, please focus on the calamity of weirdness in front of you.*

"What the hell?"

At the sound of my stunned question, he whirls around.

If I'd bet that Martin would say something to clarify the situation, I would've lost.

"Why did you come in that way? You were supposed to follow the rose petals." He sounds put out, as if *I'm* the one acting odd.

A lot of times, I get this tone from people, and I know I've made a misstep. But in this situation, I'm almost positive I'm not the weirdo.

"Why would I do that?"

Before Martin can answer, the creak of the front door opening echoes through the large house.

"Paige," Dash calls out from down the hallway, "any idea how many boxes you'll need?" His voice reaches us a second before he does.

Dash stops dead in the doorway Martin expected me to walk through, expression as shocked as I'm sure mine is.

The three of us stand silently for a moment.

Martin shatters the quiet by slamming down a wineglass I only now realize he was holding. The dark red liquid sloshes over the rim with his aggressive movement. "What the fuck is your dog walker doing here?"

A response doesn't even form in my mind before the squeak of the front door's hinges announces another cast member appearing in this comedic show.

"I brought four. More in the truck if you need 'em." Cole's dry voice precedes him as he appears just behind Dash's shoulder. The only sign of surprise he gives is a slight raise of his brows. "Who's the naked dude?"

A pause, then—

"It's her ex," Dash answers, as if it's just the two of them having a casual conversation.

"Thought he wasn't supposed to be here," Cole responds in a deadpan tone, which is somehow extremely hilarious in its emotionless delivery.

My throat tightens as I shove down a hysterical giggle.

"I think he's trying to win Paige back." Thankfully, Dash doesn't sound too concerned about this.

Cole's eyebrow quirks up again. "By stripping down? Don't think girls go for that."

Dash meets my eyes across the room, a smirk curling the corner of his mouth. "Sometimes, they do."

Tears push at the back of my eyes from the demands of holding back my laughter. I might die of it if I don't let it out soon.

As my two companions trade comments, Martin's face transforms from a bright red to a deep purple. He may also die from emotional overload, but I don't think it has anything to do with humor.

I still haven't made sense of the situation, but it looks like at least one new introduction needs to be made, and that gives me something to focus on other than Martin's exposed…everything.

I clear my throat. "First off, Dash has never been my dog walker. He is Pumpkin's dog trainer. He is also my boyfriend now." I gesture over Dash's shoulder. "This is Cole. He's my friend. Here to help me pack my stuff." I turn to said friend now to finish the intro. "This is Martin. My ex-fiancé. He was not supposed to be here."

When I face Martin again, I consider Dash's interpretation of the situation. Maybe this *is* a ploy to win me back. If it is, once again, my ex has proven he no longer knows me.

The urge to laugh fades momentarily.

I'm done with this. I'm done with him.

"This is your house," I say to him, "so if you want to hang out in the kitchen in your underwear and drink wine while we pack up my stuff, then go right ahead. But I am not coming back another day." I meet Martin's once-hypnotizing blue eyes, making sure he understands me. "When I leave this house today, it'll be for the last time."

———

DASH

After Paige dismisses her almost-naked ex, she leaves the kitchen and waves for Cole and me to follow her. We share raised eyebrows and amused smirks before following her imperious command.

I catch sight of her sneakers jogging up the staircase.

When I reach the top step, I stop in surprise. Hanging on the wall in front of me is a picture of Paige and Martin standing side by side on a beach, wearing giant flower necklaces, a fat diamond ring on her finger.

I guess the guy really did think he could win her back.

My feet start moving again as I try not to think about the two of them jetting off on some fancy vacation together. Somewhere I'll probably never be able to afford to go.

I locate Paige in the master bedroom, standing in front of a closet door with her hands on her hips.

She doesn't look at me but seems to realize I'm in the room because she starts talking, her voice high-pitched and hysterical. "He's insane. Completely mad. I mean, what did he think would happen?"

When I come up behind her, I get a glimpse inside the walk-in closet. One side is taken up with an array of men's clothes. The other side though has a more feminine air. Colorful sweaters, a handful of dresses, and neatly lined-up heels and flats on the floor.

"It's like he thought I'd come in here, see all my stuff unpacked, and say, *Oh well. Guess it's just easier to stick around.*" She storms into the space and starts tugging all the clothing off their hangers, tossing them into haphazard piles on the ground. "But that's Martin for you. Arranges everything according to his plan and expects you to go along with it. I wonder if he wrote *seduce Paige by standing naked in the kitchen* on his calendar."

I can't help a snort that escapes. Paige glares over her shoulder at me, but only for a moment. A smile pushes at the corner of her mouth, clearing the annoyance from her eyes. Cole enters the bedroom with the boxes and sets to unfolding them.

When I turn back to Paige, she's moved in close to me, uncertainty clouding her eyes.

"I just realized…I'm just as bad as him."

My body immediately rejects the statement, and I pull her into my arms. "No, you're not. Why would you even say that?"

She turns her head so her lips rest against my neck. The hot puff of her breath almost distracts me from her answer. "Because I didn't ask you about us. What we are. I just blurted out that you're my boyfriend." Paige pulls back enough to stare up into my eyes. "I'm not trying to control you."

"I didn't think you were. And I want to be your boyfriend."

Joy splits across her face in a wide grin. "You do?"

"Fuck yeah, I do."

Just as I'm leaning down to taste her bubblegum-colored lips, a slam of the front door practically shakes the house. My roommate abandons the boxes, sauntering over to the window to peer down at the lawn.

"Did he leave in his underwear?" Paige asks, mild curiosity coloring her voice.

"No," comes Cole's disinterested drawl. "Seems like he found a shirt and some pants somewhere."

I don't know if it was his words, or his delivery, or just the craziness of the whole situation, but something causes Paige to crack.

She slides to the ground, out of my arms, burying her face in her hands as she dissolves into uncontrollable giggles. Actual tears slide through her fingers, and her whole body shakes with her reaction.

The sight of her at my feet, overwhelmed with laughter, brings an unfamiliar but still welcome warmth to my chest.

When I meet Cole's eyes, we share a shrug, and just before he turns back to the boxes, I think I catch a hint of an approving smile.

CHAPTER 30

PAIGE

"Damn, I'm going to need a new one." I fiddle with my pen, lamenting the fact that its ink has run dry. I'm only halfway through the book, but I guess I've been reading more lately.

After the unfortunate cheater and robe-theft incident, I lost interest in books for a little while. I'd go to pick one up, try reading a page or two, but I'd lose focus almost immediately.

It was like Martin broke more than just my heart. He also crushed my ability to sink into a good story.

But the past few weeks, more and more, I've been longing to slide back into the old, comforting pages.

Part of it was that night I sat on the scuffed-up floor of Cole's bedroom as he hinted at his own tale. My curiosity ran rampant, and I had to read something else to keep from bugging him.

But that was just a small spark, and I think Dash is the one who's been fanning the flames. There's the fact that he constantly asks me about my past work, and I've spent long periods detailing my favorite stories I edited. But there's also the fact that being around him reminds me that just because something I relied on got blown up doesn't mean that there aren't good, hopeful things in my future.

I stick my dry pen in the pages of the book, using it to mark my place. The timing works out because as I place the paperback down and reach for my glass of cider, Dash pushes through the patio doors.

He saunters toward me with a happy tilt to his lips as he wipes his hands on a damp rag. I'm betting moments ago, his fingers had a generous coating of motor oil.

"My mom finally giving you back to me?" I smile up at him as he looms over me.

I like his height. In middle school, I had a growth spurt, and I was the tallest girl in class. None of the boys wanted to be near the giant. None except for Charlie. Best friends don't care when you're suddenly eye level with them.

"She just needed a quick hand. You know how her grip is getting." Dash leans down to press a kiss on my forehead before settling beside me on the porch swing.

I try not to frown at his comment. The idea that my mom might not be invincible isn't something I want to contemplate. So what if I left home for eight years? Mom and Dad should've stayed exactly the same.

Who gave them permission to age?

"This for work or pleasure?"

Dash's question distracts me from my anxiety, and I push the worries to the side. He's holding up the book I was just reading, flipping through the pages slow enough to reveal the occasional green note.

I shrug. "Both, I guess. I'm reading the book because it's interesting, but it doesn't hurt to stay in the habit of writing down the comments I have." Practice is important, especially now. "I've been meaning to tell you…I have a job interview with a publisher in town."

"Really? Paige, that's awesome!" Dash's face takes on a level of excitement I wish I could match.

Unfortunately, the local job isn't anything like the position I had in NYC. The publisher works on textbooks. Much drier material than I'm used to.

And there's the fact that I got a mysterious email from my former senior editor, asking for a moment of my time to talk on the phone.

"So, is this one of the publisher's books?"

"Nope. Just in the mood for a crime thriller." I pluck the book from his grasp and open it to a random page. "And I try not to get too technical when I'm reading for fun. That would take me too far out of the story. These are just some random thoughts." I tilt the page, so he can see.

"*This guy is definitely going to die*. Wow, Paige. Way to go dark." Dash grins at me.

I chuckle. "Well, all the clues are there. I mean, he's practically begging—"

The sound of the patio doors swinging open cut me off. I expect my mom to walk out or maybe my dad, seeing as how it's a Sunday.

Instead, my heart stutters to a stop, then revs into a rapid pace when I realize who the newcomer is.

"Charlie!"

―――――

DASH

I watch as my girlfriend launches out of her seat to jump into the arms of another man. When he returns the embrace, a huge grin on his face, I have to clench my hands into fists to keep from dragging her away from him.

Through the onslaught of jealousy, I try to remind myself that I'm not my brother. I have self-control. And Paige isn't the type of girl to be hooking up with a string of guys.

Charlie.

My mind catches on the name Paige shouted out, and I'm transported back to that muttered comment on Halloween. Charlie is my competition. The man who's swinging Paige around like he has some claim to her is the one that woman at the party was talking about. The guy who has a stash of dirty magazines Paige knows about.

Who the hell is he?

"Dash, this is Charlie!" My girlfriend has finally let go of the man, but she still has her hand in his as she drags him over to me.

Yeah, no shit. I want to mutter the words out of pure pettiness, but I don't want Paige to realize how immature I am.

Charlie would probably never say something so rude.

I swallow down my worried anger as I stand and strive for cool detachment.

"Hey." That, paired with a nod, is the best I can do.

Paige's happy grin loses a bit of its sparkle as she stares up at me, and even though I'm not the one who brought the joy to her face, I'm sorry to see it go.

Good job, idiot.

With a deep inhale, I smother the jealousy until it's little more than a tickle at the back of my neck. I even manage something that could be considered a smile as I offer my hand to the newcomer.

"Nice to meet you, Charlie."

He lets go of Paige and accepts my hand, his friendly eyes morphing into something more calculating as he studies me. I return his inspection.

Yet another guy in Paige's life that's tall enough to meet me eye to eye. Charlie still gives off a relaxed air despite his size. He's all wide smiles with white teeth. I hate to admit that the two of them look good, standing next to each other. Where Paige is pale and blonde, Charlie is dark and ebony. They're like yin and yang.

And I don't belong anywhere near them.

"Charlie, this is Dash. He's the hot guy I refused to tell you about." She steps into me, wrapping a possessive arm around my waist, settling my feet on firm ground. Suddenly, I don't have to force a smile anymore. From her spot at my side, Paige grins up at the guy. "I took your advice."

"Paige?" I ask. She returns her gaze to me. "Not to be rude, but who exactly *is* Charlie?"

She frowns. "*Charlie.* Come on. I told you about Charlie."

I shake my head, and a guilty blush pools over her cheeks as the guy gives a scoff.

"Really, Paige? I leave the country, and you just forget about me?

I'm wounded. Deeply." Charlie clutches his chest, but humor flashes in his eyes.

"I'm a dunce. I can't believe it. Charlie is my best friend. We've known each other since we were five. His parents live a few houses down. He's been living in Germany, but now, he's back!" Paige does a little happy jig, her body pressing up against mine in the process.

"Speaking of my parents, they're inside," Charlie says.

"Inside?" Paige sounds just as confused as I am.

"Yeah. It's a Keller-Herbert reunion."

And apparently, I'm crashing it.

"My mom is probably already at work, mixing up cocktails." Charlie takes a step toward the doors that lead back inside, only to be met by a furry blockade.

At some point during introductions, Pumpkin wandered her way up to the porch.

Charlie holds out his hand for the dog to sniff. She does, briefly, but then brushes past him to push her head against my thigh until I scratch behind her ears. Another burst of satisfaction streaks through me. Seems I'm petty enough to want Paige's dog to dismiss everyone but her and me.

It almost feels like I won something.

Then, Charlie has to open his goddamn friendly mouth again.

"You two coming? Papa Herbert's been on me about sharing travel stories, and I doubt you'll want to miss them."

Papa Herbert?

I don't know whether to be jealous or demand a sit-down with Charlie, so he can explain how he won over the Grim Reaper.

———

PAIGE

On a scale of one to them realizing they're long-lost brothers, I think the first meeting between my boyfriend and my best friend hits somewhere in the middle.

As we stand in my parents' kitchen, I only half listen to Charlie's flight horror story, something about two drunk girls that needed a cold shower. My concentration is too focused on trying to decipher how Dash is fitting in with the group.

The Kellers are some of the most loving people I've ever met. They travel the world and collect friends in each country they visit. My only worry comes from Mama Keller's futile hope that I'll still fall in romantic love with her son. But she and Mr. Keller gave Dash smiles and handshakes, so I try not to stress over it.

Then, there are my parents, two people who can get a little prickly. I'm pretty positive that Dash's love of cars has fully solidified him as acceptable in my mom's eyes. My dad though still puts on his icy-judge face whenever he looks at my boyfriend. Luckily, I don't need his approval when it comes to the men I sleep with.

Or fall in love with.

Not that I'm in love with Dash. But if I was, that's my choice.

Currently, Charlie holds the majority of the attention, gesturing wildly with his hands as he gets to a high-tension part of his story. The display from my friend is funny because when we're not with family, he tends to sink into silent, observant mode. My hope is that his energetic display is a point in Dash's favor. I want Dash to have all the points.

Charlie was never a Martin fan. He only told me once, in high school, when he got back from a trip to find out the two of us were dating.

"He's too bland for you. And I bet you he'll figure that out eventually if he doesn't already know it," Charlie said to me the night of prom as I waited for Martin to show up.

My date didn't ditch me. Martin was exactly on time. Charlie rolled his eyes behind my mom as she took pictures.

But after that day, my best friend never said a word against him. Not even when I called to tell him about the engagement.

I knew though. When you grew up with someone, you pick up on the way they don't say things. And Charlie didn't say a lot of things concerning Martin. Specifically, he barely ever said my ex's name.

Suddenly, I have a strong urge to hear everyone in this room say my boyfriend's name. Next to mine.

I want to hear *Paige and Dash.*
Paige and Dash are on their way over.
Paige and Dash brought an appetizer.
Paige and Dash left to walk Pumpkin.
Paige and Dash look so cute together.
Paige and Dash…Paige and Dash…Paige and Dash…

"Paige?" Dash murmurs my name close to my ear, making me shiver in delight at the hot puff of his breath.

"Dash?" I respond, creating the pairing as best I can.

He stares down at me, one eyebrow curving up in that perfect arch. Well, not exactly perfect. There's just a bit of a point at the bridge, like it's too rigid to fully bend and instead threatens to snap. "Mrs. Keller asked you a question."

"Oh!" I scan the room for her, finding everyone staring at me with a mixture of expressions, none of which I can interpret. Aren't these the people I've known most of my life? Shouldn't I be able to read them as easily as the books on my shelves? Although I guess those I have to study in-depth and take detailed notes on. Maybe if I could stare at their faces for a good ten minutes, I'd figure out what they're all thinking. "Sorry. I wasn't listening."

"Great. I was gone for a year, and suddenly, I've become boring."

Charlie's sarcastic voice clarifies his thoughts, and I smirk at him. He's not offended, and if my guess is right, I'd say he's intrigued. By what? I don't know.

"I asked if you'd like a drink, dear. I'm mixing sangria." Mama Keller wears a tiny smile as her gaze flits between me and Dash.

"Sangria? Isn't that a summer drink?"

She shrugs. "My home is in the South for a reason. It is summer, no matter the time of year." Her teeth shine beautifully white against a plump set of lips I've always envied.

Sometimes, I'll watch a music competition show, and a contestant will walk on the stage, looking like the minute they open their mouth, nothing will come out but a scratchy off-key note, but then they shock the crowd with a gorgeous set of pipes.

No one has ever been deceived by Rosa Keller's looks. Whenever a new person learns that she is a jazz singer, nine times out of ten, their first response is, "Of course." Because Rosa Keller is the embodiment of jazz. If the music became a corporeal being, gifted with skin and bone, it would solidify into Mama Keller. She's that glorious, and every word she speaks hides a hint of melody.

"Well, I can't say no to that." I reach for a glass.

"And what about you, Dash? Or are you a beer drinker like my son?"

"No—"

"He doesn't drink." My father's curt answer overpowers Dash's before he could even get it out.

I glare across the room at the man who raised me, suddenly ashamed of him. Of course, he knows Dash doesn't drink, what with him being on parole. Or he knows Dash shouldn't drink, which may have been why he was so fast to answer for him. But if Dad had just given him two seconds to speak, he would have known that Dash follows that rule. He follows *all* of the rules. Probably better than the majority of people on parole.

I want to rage at my father at that moment, suddenly able to read his expression too.

Disdain.

How dare he? He, who was so accepting of Martin, the guy who ended up betraying me and breaking my heart.

And what's more, he knows exactly why Dash went to jail. That, more than anything, should encourage him to give the guy a second chance. Unlike me, I doubt Dash has had many of those in his life.

Suddenly, my leg aches, and I reach down surreptitiously to rub my old scar.

My dad knows nothing about our relationship, and I'm almost overwhelmed with the urge to start listing off all the reasons this parolee has so easily slipped into my heart.

How he smiles when I say something weird rather than rolling his eyes. How he has the calmest demeanor with Pumpkin. How he encourages me to use a firm tone when I have something important to say. How he wore goofy clothes for me and showed me all the reasons to fall in love with this city. How he looked at my scar with mild curiosity rather than pity. How he touches me and sets every inch of my skin on fire.

That last bit might be a little too much for my dad, but that doesn't mean he shouldn't hear it.

Again, the room is quiet, and discomfort has started to creep its way in. I glance up at Dash, the man who makes me feel like I could conquer the world, and I notice a redness hovering at the tops of his gorgeously sharp cheekbones. For some reason, I can read him without hesitation. He's embarrassed, and it's my family's doing.

Shame sits heavy in my chest, next to angry defiance. I want to use my body as a shield between him and society's judgment. There's no doubt in my mind that more people than my father would hear the word *parole* and pass judgment on Dash before getting to know him.

Those people would never discover how gentle a hand he has when it comes to an abused dog. They would probably sneer at his dilapidated house and bare bedroom. When they found the magazines under his bed, they'd immediately assume there was some nefarious purpose. Their eyes would gloss over his unhealthy weight, only to sharply focus on the past he works so hard to make up for.

None of those people deserve Dash.

"Do you want some sweet tea? I promise I won't spill it this time." I stroke my boyfriend's back and beam up at him, trying to eradicate the tension in his shoulders.

When he glances down at me, a ghost of a smile haunts his mouth.

So close.

"Sit down. I'll grab you a glass." I push Dash into one of the seats at the kitchen table before navigating to the fridge. As I pass Charlie, I give his side a friendly pinch. "You have any more stories?"

His grin appears with ease. "Loads." Then, he's off again, and the thick air in the room begins to dissipate.

With precision I wasn't able to master the first time Dash was in this kitchen, I pour him a full cup of tea. While the fridge door blocks me off from almost everyone in the kitchen, I toss a quick warning glare at my father, where he leans against the counter. He meets my heated eyes with an expressionless glance that only boils my blood more. I use the coolness of the fridge to calm myself down before returning to Dash.

My boyfriend sits stiffly in the chair, discomfort an almost-physical layer coating him. I'm surprised the tea makes it past his pinched lips.

Working on instinct, I lean down until my lips brush his ear.

"If I sit on your lap, do you think I'll squish you?" I whisper.

Dash snorts and turns his head to meet my eyes. He has a real smile now.

Happy bubbles pop in my chest.

"If you do, I'd die happy." His murmured response comes as he wraps a long arm around my waist and guides my butt down onto his legs.

More bubbles fill me, so much so that I can almost believe I'm weightless.

The two of us settle, twined together, my arm resting across his shoulders, his arm circling my hips. I lean my head against his, breathing in a lungful of fresh sheets with a tinge of motor oil, for a moment feeling as if everything is right and good in the world.

"So, my neighbors are interesting, to say the least, but the walls are thick, and my place is a decent size. It's actually a pretty nice setup." Charlie finishes whatever story I forgot to listen to again.

I push aside the twinge of guilt about being a bad friend. Charlie loves to tell stories. I doubt he'd mind repeating them for me some other time.

"It's been too long since we visited. Germany will have to be our next trip," Mr. Keller declares, holding a beer out to his son, who clinks his in cheers.

"I'd love to have you. Really, the place is almost too big for one person." The jovial quality is gone from Charlie's voice, drawing me to examine his face.

My friend stares at me, a hint of determination lurking behind his dark eyes. "You should come to Germany, Paige."

"What?" I use the exclamation as a filler word because I heard what he said loud and clear.

"Come to Germany with me."

Dash shifts underneath me, and I try to make it easy for him to move, worried I might be cutting off circulation in his legs.

Germany. I had planned to visit Charlie, back before Martin told me we were using our vacation for Hawaii instead. Now that I think about it, I should've bought a ticket to Europe months ago. Between jobs, while not the best financial situation, is a good time to schedule an impromptu international trip.

But if I'd run off to see Charlie, I wouldn't have found Pumpkin. And if I'd never found Pumpkin, I wouldn't have met Dash.

I don't regret how things worked out, but a trip in the near future might be a possibility.

"That's not the worst idea. Until I get hired somewhere, I'll have a lot of free time, so visiting you for a week would be easy-peasy."

"No, Paige. Not to visit." Charlie holds my eyes from across the room, his expression more serious than I've seen it in years. "Come live with me in Germany."

CHAPTER 31

DASH

She doesn't say no.

Paige could have laughed and brushed him off.

Instead, she sits stone-still in my lap, gazing, slack-jawed, at the guy she claims is her best friend.

Seems like someone doesn't want to be in the friend zone anymore.

I fight the urge to scoop her up in my arms and sprint out of the house. Most states consider that kidnapping. But the idea of letting this Charlie guy woo her away to some foreign country hits me like a Mack truck plowing into the side of my car.

Maybe I can't steal her away, but purely on instinct—or maybe self-preservation—I tighten my hold around her waist. As if that'll somehow keep her here with me.

"What do you mean, come live with you in Germany? I can't live in Germany."

I wish her voice sounded less confused and more resolute.

"Sure you can. I'm doing it. And it'll be easier for you because you've already got a place lined up to live." The guy steps closer, focusing solely on the woman in my arms. I might as well be a piece of furniture. "Imagine it. The two of us exploring Europe. Every day would be an adventure."

Even I have to admit, that sounds tempting, which makes me hate Charlie all the more for saying it.

Paige glances wildly around the room. "I have Pumpkin. I can't just put her in a carry-on." She waves at the brindle pit bull, currently snoring in a plush dog bed in the corner of the kitchen.

"We can take the dog," Mr. Herbert says, momentarily silencing the room with his offer.

"The fact that you just referred to Pumpkin as *the dog* makes it clear that you cannot, in fact, take *the dog*." Paige has lost her befuddled tone, scowling at her father.

In my hold, she quivers, and I stroke her back because I have nothing I can add to this conversation other than comfort. My mind reels, and my chest aches, and I beg the universe for this discussion to be a bad dream. Maybe I fell asleep out on the patio couch next to Paige, and I'll wake up to find her reading her book while her fingers fiddle with a green pen.

No Charlie. No glaring father. No Germany.

"Come on, Paige. All through high school, all you ever wanted was to leave. Now, you're back, living with your parents. No offense." Charlie throws a conciliatory smile at the Herberts before pushing on. "I'm giving you a chance to get out of here."

I try not to wince at his words.

"I don't need you to give me anything, Charlie. I can make my own chances. Besides"—she shifts back, leaning just a bit into me—"I don't hate New Orleans like I used to. There's a lot to love here."

At this, Charlie's eyes finally acknowledge me, and he lets out a sigh.

I want to punch him.

"It's a very sweet offer, Charlie. But Paige has things going for her here. She's got a job interview, you know." Mrs. Herbert jumps into the conversation, a hopeful tilt to the woman's voice. In her, I get the sense I have an ally. Someone who wants Paige to stay in NOLA too.

The Kellers' feelings are a mystery, the couple choosing to stand off to the side and sip their drinks as the situation unfolds.

"Ginny, jobs come and go. Paige might not have another chance like this." Mr. Herbert moves to place a hand on his wife's shoulder, but she shrugs him off with a glare that makes her look remarkably like her daughter. Paige's father lets his hand drop but keeps speaking. "Besides, isn't it time she and Charlie figure things out between them?"

Again, silence descends upon the room, and I battle the heat rising in my head.

Charlie clears his throat. "Papa Herbert, that's not—"

"You think if I went to Germany with Charlie, we'd start dating?"

I've never heard Paige's voice so shrill.

Her mother matches her in pitch. "I don't want her dating Charlie! Then, she'd never come home!"

"At least he's a good man." The rough sentence carries a whole truckload of meaning, and Paige's father drove it directly at me.

Mr. Herbert knows. Or maybe I should say, Judge Herbert knows. Of course he does. I'm surprised he even let me in his house once he found out.

Paige's fingers dig into my shoulder. Someone else might find the grasping hold uncomfortable, but with the knowledge that this fantasy is soon going to fall to ruin around me, I welcome any connection with her I can get.

"Stop being rude, Richard. Just because you don't know Dash doesn't mean that he's not good enough for our daughter." Mrs. Herbert smiles apologetically my way.

I get the morbid urge to laugh.

Paige's dad glares at me across the room. "How about it, Dash? Should we all get to know you better?"

CHAPTER 32

PAIGE

am going to murder my father. I'll have Pumpkin help me dig a hole in the backyard to hide his body.

No one will miss a judge, right?

"Ask me whatever you'd like." Dash's deep, smooth voice comes out calm.

He's a still water pond while I'm a raging ocean storm.

"No. We're not interrogating you." I comb my fingers into the hair at the nape of his neck, more to soothe myself than him.

My dad, never one to let something go, shifts his focus to me. "Do you even know his real name?"

I try not to growl out my answer. "It's Lamont. Dash Lamont."

But the minute I say it, I'm suddenly not so sure. My dad wouldn't bring it up if the answer was that easy.

My father doesn't smile or crow in triumph. Richard Herbert isn't the type to lord over others. He simply shakes his head, eyes cold.

My boyfriend nudges my side until I look at him. He's got a twist to his mouth that worries me something bad is coming. "No, actually. Dash is a nickname." He sighs, dragging his hand through his hair, leaving it messy in the way that I love. "Sorry, I just kind of hate my first name."

"What is it?" I watch him shift under my curious stare.

"Prince."

"Your name is Prince?" I choke on the word, but not because I'm angry.

Dash, aka Prince, grimaces. "My mom was a fan of Prince. The singer. She thought it would make for a good name. FYI, it didn't."

We stare at each other, and I try not to react. But when the pressure in my throat can't escape my mouth, it comes out my nose in an inelegant snort, which I immediately regret.

"I'm sorry! I'm not laughing at you, I swear! It's just...Prince Lamont? You sound like royalty." Pressing my hand over my mouth, I think I can keep all further inappropriate reactions at bay.

Dash smiles, but it's one of those fake ones, where his eyes stay sad. "Don't worry. I've heard it all before. Can't go to public school with a name like that and expect to make it through unscathed."

Shame at my silly response stabs through my ribs, straight into my heart.

How could I be so clueless?

Dash's scruff tickles my palms as I cup his cheeks and force him to meet my stare. "I don't care if your name is Mr. Darcy William Shakespeare Sunzi Lamont. I would still l—" In an unprecedented feat of self-control, I hold back from blurting out that revealing four-letter word. "*Like* you. I like everything about you."

Letting our audience fade to the back of my mind, I pretend it's just Dash and me. I sink into his gaze, as dark as the ink of a brand-new ballpoint. People hurt him in the past. I don't know the number or how exactly, but behind his stare is a pain that I never want to contribute to.

I lean in and place a gentle kiss on the tip of his nose.

Dash blinks, and then the false smile stretches into the real thing.

"Are you done tormenting the boy, Richard?" My mom seems almost as put off by my dad's display as I am.

"Not quite."

And just like that, Dash's smile is gone, and I'm contemplating patricide once again.

"Dad"—I turn my head to glare at him—"don't—"

"He's on parole."

I've lost count of how many times my father's words have sent the kitchen into shocked silence, but I am goddamn tired of him acting like a drama queen.

The Kellers are clearly trying to sink into the walls and disappear from this awkward situation. Charlie stands still, narrowed gaze fixed just over my shoulder on Dash. My mom's hand hovers in front of her mouth as if she's trying to stop herself from speaking.

I wish she'd put that effort toward shutting her husband up.

"Yeah, I know. He told me before I even asked him to help me with Pumpkin."

"Parole? What are you saying?" Mom's voice trails off on the question.

"He was in prison, Ginny. Should probably still be serving his sentence if there wasn't such an issue with overcrowding." At some point, my father stopped leaning against the counter, rising to his full height, giving the sense of him looming over the entire room.

Cold skitters over my skin as Dash lets his arms drop from my sides.

"Prison? But...for what?" my mom asks before I can figure out a way to defuse this situation.

"Grand theft auto. Prince here is a fair hand at stealing cars."

"Cars?" The horror in my mom's voice echoes through the kitchen.

Out of the corner of my eye, I catch the almost-imperceptible sag of Dash's sharp shoulders.

Fuck defusing. I'm the bomb.

And here comes the explosion.

"Yes! Cars!" I shove off Dash's lap and stand in front of my boyfriend, fists against my hips, legs spread wide, shielding him from whatever my father plans to say next. "He stole cars. He was found guilty. He went to jail. He *served* his *sentence*." If glares could burn, my father would be trapped in an inferno. "You'd think a judge would respect the legal system, wouldn't you? But I guess Dad doesn't believe in reform. He thinks Dash should be punished for the rest of his life!"

I take a menacing step forward, and my father's cold exterior cracks just slightly.

"Now, Paige—"

"So, go ahead. Judge him. Deny him your acceptance. Withhold your respect."

Somehow, I've ended up directly in front of the man I've held up as a moral standard for my entire life. And my rage is all the fiercer because he just shattered that illusion for me. Today, my father revealed himself for what he truly is. A judgmental, closed-minded hypocrite.

My voice shakes, and I jab a finger into his chest. "And remember, everything you think about him, everything you say about him"—I glare straight up into my father's frowning face—"applies to me."

"No—"

"You hate someone because they stole a car?"

"Paige—"

"No. This is good to know." I retreat, arms raised, holding back tears of rage or sorrow. Likely both. "I guess my father hates me."

CHAPTER 33

DASH

Paige's declaration rings through the kitchen.

I try to figure out what her words mean and come to the conclusion that I'm missing something.

It almost sounds like…but, no, I've got to be wrong.

Just as I'm rewinding the argument, Paige turns to me, her face an uncomfortable mixture of anger and guilt.

"Come on, Dash. Let's go."

"Baby girl—"

"Paige—"

Mrs. Keller and Charlie try to talk to her, stop her, at the same time, but Paige backs away from them, her arms held up almost as if she's defending herself.

"No. I'm sorry, Mama Keller. Papa Keller. If I'd known tonight was an ambush, I wouldn't have agreed to it. And, Charlie—" Her voice cracks, and I'm on my feet at the devastated sound. Thankfully, she doesn't ward me off like everyone else, letting me support her with my palm against her back. "I know you think I'm naïve when it comes to men. But he's not Martin."

Her friend's eyes go wide, and he steps toward her, which only drives Paige stumbling back into my chest. "I don't think—"

"Bullshit. You've had *months* to bring up Germany again. But you waited until now?" She shakes her head and grabs my hand. "We're going to pass on dinner."

I let her drag me from the kitchen, throwing an apologetic look at the Kellers while I avoid Mrs. Herbert's searching gaze.

To be honest, I never really expected to get Paige's dad's approval. But her mom? I guess after getting invited into her garage again, I let myself hope.

Now, that's all gone to shit. I heard the horror in Mrs. Herbert's voice when my past got dragged out into the open.

When Paige swings open the front door, I hear the distinct clicking of claws on the hardwood floor. The two of us glance back to see a certain pit bull, liquid brown eyes staring up at us expectantly.

"Pumpkin, car." Gone is the uncertainty in Paige's voice. The command comes out distinct, leaving no room for question.

Pumpkin gives a happy puppy grin, completely unaware of the tension overflowing in the house. She trots out the front door to sit meekly beside the Impala.

"You okay with going for a drive?" The confidence Paige just demonstrated with her dog seeps away as she stares at my chin, not meeting my eyes.

It's like she's already slipping away from me, and on pure reflex, I tighten my hold on her hand.

"Wherever you want to go, I'm there."

Apparently, *wherever* is the drive-through of a fried chicken joint.

Paige's face drips in guilt as she glances down at the gearshift between us. "Since we're missing dinner."

"I wouldn't say no to some food." I only have five bucks in my wallet, but I'd give up a whole paycheck just to see her smile again.

Paige orders a family meal and resolutely ignores my attempt to hand her my cash. With the tantalizing scent of extra-crispy chicken filling the car, I think Pumpkin and I are drooling equal amounts. After cruising around, Paige pulls off into the empty parking lot of a strip mall.

The three of us share the food, eating in silence. I don't think she's trying to ignore the drama from earlier. Just sift through it.

"I told you my parents were overprotective." Her murmur fills the silence of the car.

"Yeah. I can't say I'm surprised about their concern." Every day, I wish I had made better choices. And now, more than ever, I just want to be a decent guy who deserves a girl like Paige.

"I'm not talking about that shit show." She chews her lip. "Well, maybe I am a little. But I'm trying to confess something here."

What in the world would Paige have to confess to me?

Suddenly, my stomach isn't so happy about the chicken and biscuits.

"When I was in high school, they finally trusted me to stay home alone. It was their anniversary, and they wanted to go away together for the weekend. I was so excited because there was going to be a party that Saturday night and I could finally go. No parents around to stop me. My first party." Her voice holds a hint of the excitement a younger version of her must have been feeling. "So, I went, and it was wild. Loud music. Lots of people were dancing and drinking. I didn't drink." She grips my arm as if scared I would judge her.

Wonder how she'd feel, knowing I had my first beer when I was fourteen. Stole it from my dad and got my ass beat for the trouble.

She continues with her confession, not knowing the dark memory lane I started to head down. "But just being in that house with all that energy, it was a different type of intoxicating. Plus, guys were finally starting to talk to me. Maybe it was because they were drunk, but they didn't seem to think I was weird anymore. One in particular I'd had a crush on for a while paid me attention."

"Martin." I speak the name before she can, knowing on some instinctive level.

Paige nods. "Yeah, Martin. We were hanging out together all night, and at one point, a group of us were in the kitchen, and someone mentioned what my mom did for work. All the guys got stars in their eyes when I talked about her cars. They really liked the sound of the '68 Camaro a local sports agent had just asked her to tune up. She'd finished the work and was set to deliver it back to him that Monday."

Paige lets go of my arm to twist her hands in her lap. "At school, I was a bit of a loner. I had Charlie as my best friend and some girls I hung out with at lunch and in between classes. But other than that, I kinda flew under the radar. I wasn't used to the rabid amount of attention these guys were paying me. It made me want to impress them."

I wish I could travel back in time, take young Paige in my arms, and glare at those idiot boys that thought they deserved any of her time or attention. The idiots didn't know what they had.

"When Martin said he'd love to see the car, I had a ridiculous idea. Of course, at the time, I thought it was genius, and Charlie was traveling with his parents, so he wasn't there to keep me grounded." Her smile looks more like a grimace. "See, my mom had always asked me to help her out in the garage. Sometimes, that meant driving a car, so she could listen to how it ran from the outside. I knew exactly where she kept the keys. I got my friends to drop me off at my house, and then I drove the Camaro back to the party." Paige laughs in a hollow, self-deprecating way. "When I rolled up, all the guys were practically shitting their pants. I even let Martin sit in the driver's seat."

As Paige continues with her story, a shadow envelops her voice. "Then, he asked if he could drive it. And when he said that, all the guys crowded around the car and started begging me for a turn. That's when I realized just how reckless I was. Somehow, I'd convinced myself that taking that car, someone else's property, was fine. That messing around with my mom's business was fine. That because I was a good girl, that any decision I made somehow wasn't a big deal. But thinking about all those strangers in that Camaro shocked my brain back onto the right track. I told Martin to get out of the car and ignored all of them as I peeled out toward home."

Paige wraps her hands around the steering wheel as if she's back in that car again. "I was panicked, frantic to get back. Worried that my parents would return from their trip a day early to find not only me gone, but the car with me. I started speeding. Then, something jumped out in front of the car. A dog maybe. I don't remember. When I think back to that moment, there's the memory of jerking the wheel. And then nothing."

We sit in silence, and it takes more effort than I expected to keep from begging for the end of the story. What helps is having her here, next to me, safe and sound.

"A week later, I woke up in the hospital. Broken bones, aching head, and two parents staring down at me like I was some kind of miracle." She rubs her thigh, and I remember her telling me the cause of her massive scar was a car accident. "Even though I was awake, my brain was a mess, and I kept asking about the Camaro and telling them I was sorry. They said not to worry about it, that everything would be fine, but I was sure I was going to jail the minute I got out of that hospital bed. I mean, it was a sixty-thousand-dollar car that I'd stolen and destroyed. You don't just walk away from that."

Her voice cracks, and my heart hurts to hear her still so upset about something that happened close to a decade ago. I reach over to run a soothing hand down her thigh. She flinches in response and leans away from my hand, drawing her knees up and curling into her chest, glaring over at me.

"I don't deserve your comfort, Dash. Don't you understand? It took me a while to get it out of him, but my dad eventually copped to everything. How they paid Mom's client off with money and a promise of a new Camaro. And they lied to the cops, telling them I was supposed to be driving the car. A final test run. After everything, I just got a ticket for reckless driving. Didn't even lose my license."

If she expects me to be surprised by the outcome, I'm not. "That's good."

"Good? What the hell, Dash?" Paige rakes her fingers through her buttery-yellow hair as her wild eyes flick over my face. "I stole a car. I did exactly what you did, but the only consequences I got were a fine and a few scars. You went to jail. How do you not hate me?"

Understanding dawns, and with it, I feel a frown tugging at my mouth. "I could never hate you, Paige. Did you really think I'd wish you'd gone to jail?" I lean across the console to cup her despairing face in my hands, pressing my forehead to hers. "I want to drop to my knees and thank your dad that he didn't let you end up in that hellhole. Fuck," I mutter, my gaze catching on the delicate slash through her eyebrow. "You don't know what it's like in there. How hard you need to be to get by. And the daughter of a judge? I can't imagine what would've happened to you."

Just the thought has panicked anger heating my neck and face. Sweet, quirky Paige would've lost herself under the pressure of being incarcerated.

"But it was *my* mistake. I should've paid for it," she whispers, the soft puff of her breath brushing over my lips like a kiss as tears collect on her lower lashes.

"You paid for it in the hospital. Now, you're healed, and you know better. You can move on." I let my thumbs trail over the crests of her cheeks, catching the moisture before it can fall.

"Why am I supposed to move on, but you have to keep paying? When do you get to move on from your mistakes?"

Her words sneak past my rib cage and pummel my chest.

I don't have an answer. Instead, I lean the last few inches to fuse our mouths together, letting the taste of perfection drown out the knowledge that I still don't deserve a flavor this sweet.

CHAPTER 34

PAIGE

"And this is Betsy. She works in the office just beside yours. Well, yours if we hire you, of course." Mr. Stanford lets out a chuckle and gives me a friendly wink as I wave at the smiling Betsy.

Betsy looks nice. Mr. Stanford is nice. Everyone I've met so far has been...nice.

And I get the same sense that *nice* is the exact word I'd use to describe this job.

Nothing spectacularly good or bad about it.

Stanford Publishing deals primarily with textbooks. Definitely important pieces of work that require talented editors. So, I would be editing. The material might be slightly drier than I'm used to. But it's a job, in my field, in New Orleans.

And who knows? This might broaden my horizons in new and interesting ways. Maybe I just think the material will be dry when, in actuality, I'll find it fascinating.

Plus, money. My savings have taken a hit over these past few months. Not the massive hit that I would've been dealt if my parents had refused to take me in. But still, I've got bills.

With a steady paycheck, I can pay those bills and move into my own place. Pumpkin and me, taking over New Orleans. Dash as our helpful, sexy guide.

My own place means privacy.

Just the memory of our excursions in Penelope has my thighs tingling and my nipples tightening. But rolling around with him in a bed all night has a different sort of appeal.

A serious, committed one.

"Here's the break room. We sprang for a Keurig earlier this year."

I push away inappropriate thoughts of alone time with my boyfriend as my potential boss ushers me into a small room with a kitchenette. I fake a smile at his mention of the coffee maker, hiding the disappointment at the realization that when I move out, I won't be able to craft my regular morning latte on my grandfather's cappuccino machine anymore. I guess there are a few perks to living with my parents that I've overlooked.

"And that's the end of our tour."

"Your office is nice." There's that word again, but Mr. Stanford beams like I just said his business should appear on the cover of a design magazine.

"I'm glad you like it. I'm sure you'll fit in here splendidly. Your résumé was everything your father said, and you seem like a good fit. Of course, we need to go through all the formal channels, but, as the boss, I think it's safe to say you should be getting a good call from us soon."

His reassurances have the opposite effect. Blood thunders in my ears, and I'm sure it pools heavily in my cheeks.

"My father?"

"He was singing your praises. Well, maybe not singing. You know how your father is. Relatively quiet man. But that's why when he talked about you, I paid attention. And I'm glad I did. Of course, I was also in a good mood after having soundly beaten him on that final hole. Poor man got caught in a sand trap." Mr. Stanford clucks his tongue.

All the while, my ears ring like the building caught on fire, and I'm holding all the alarms.

Mr. Stanford and Judge Herbert are golfing buddies.

And I was the last to know.

I wonder if he's the first person my dad asked to give me a job. Or just the first one who agreed. For all I know, my parents have been peddling my woes around town, trying to drum up sympathy and a career for their incompetent daughter who can't hold down a job. Or a man.

Poor girl can barely stand on her own two feet.

"Thank you, Mr. Stanford. For your time and your consideration."

He smiles at me, and the expression comes off as indulgent.

I want to vomit.

Luckily, I make it out to my car before the frustrated tears begin to fall.

CHAPTER 35

DASH

fold down the corner of my magazine when I hear the back door open. Ever since I licked her pussy in my bed, I told Paige not to worry about knocking.

After sliding the issue of *Car and Driver* back to its hiding spot, I consider getting up and meeting her in the kitchen. But I stay put, wondering what might happen when she finds me here.

"Dash?" Paige strolls into my room, lighting the place up with her smile. "Is someone being lazy?"

When I stretch my arms over my head, I get a satisfying crack from most of my joints. "Just resting up."

"Ah, bracing yourself." My girlfriend toes her shoes off and crawls from the foot of the bed toward me. She has on a loose sweater, and from this angle, I can see a beautiful view straight past her neckline. "Well, I've given everyone a stern talking-to. My dad mainly, but also Charlie. He gets how the Germany offer was manipulative, and he apologized. So, this shouldn't be like last time. Besides"—she sprawls next to me, hooking one of her legs over mine and settling her head in my chest—"it's a holiday. We're all supposed to be focusing on what we're thankful for. Still, we'll leave if they step out of line. You shouldn't have to deal with that."

Her body is heavy and warm in my arms as I tug her closer to me. For a little while, we just lie, wrapped up together in my bed. Even though I often can't stop thinking about getting Paige naked and underneath me, right now, all I'm focused on is the contentment seeping into every inch of my muscles.

In a little bit, we'll leave for Thanksgiving dinner at the Herberts' house. But for right now, it's just the two of us. With Paige in my room, the place doesn't seem so bland and lifeless. Part of that is her presence, but there are also the few changes I've made.

A neighbor had some leftover paint, enough for me to coat one of my walls in a deep forest green. An accent wall, Paige called it, running her fingers over the surface before grinning over her shoulder at me. Then, there's the weirdly colorful blanket Cole's grandmother knitted for me, folded and hanging over the back of the chair in the corner. But my favorite addition is the simple wooden frame sitting on my bedside table that holds a photograph of Paige, smiling big, her arms wrapped around Pumpkin, who has on her trademark doggy grin.

When I told Paige I wouldn't accept her money for training anymore, the next session I showed up for, she handed me the picture.

"So you know how much this means to us. How much *you* mean to us." My girlfriend scratched her dog behind the ears, looking down long enough for me to swallow the lump clogging my throat.

In the present, Paige sighs and props herself up on her elbows to meet my eyes.

"Probably should head over soon. Turkey time and all that. Also, before we go, I wanted to let you know about something."

Her fingers pinch and fiddle with a button on my dress shirt. The only one I own. I made sure it was clean, so I could look presentable for her parents. Not like a convict.

"What's that?" I stroke my fingers through her hair because she suddenly seems agitated, in need of soothing.

"The publishing company I worked for in New York—you know,

the one with all my amazing writers? The one that let me go right before I moved here?"

I nod.

"Well, they called me a couple of weeks ago. Left a message, saying they wanted to talk."

Something like a rubber band wraps around my rib cage. Only this one is a big fat motherfucker, more likely to crush me than snap from any tension.

"I didn't know if I wanted to talk to them. But I thought maybe it was important. Or maybe one of my authors was hoping to get in touch. Or…I don't know. I just couldn't ignore it. Like fire ants burrowing into my brain."

I know the feeling. It's happening as she speaks.

"I called them back on Monday. They're interested in re-hiring me. They want me to go to New York to talk in person."

"What did you say?"

Fuck off. Please tell me you told them to fuck off.

"I told them I'd think about it." She doesn't give me enough time to relax before she pushes on. "But I'm going to go."

I sit up, suddenly feeling too vulnerable, sprawled out on my bed with her hovering over me, able to see every emotion that bleeds onto my face. Paige sits back, crossing her legs and arms as she watches me.

"You want to go to New York?"

She shrugs. "New York is where the job interview is."

"What about that local job?" The one that wouldn't take her away from me.

"I found out my dad had set it up."

"So?" The only job my dad ever arranged for me landed me in jail.

"So, I don't want him to keep fixing my life for me! I screw up, and Daddy is there to kiss the boo-boo and make everything better. I'm tired of it." Paige slides off the bed so she can pace across the creaky wooden floor.

Even annoyed, she's beautiful. Her golden hair sways around her flushed cheeks. With every step, her toned legs flex beneath her skinny jeans, barely any limp today, which means she probably ran this morning. She's curvy perfection, filling my room with her energy and that subtle scent of fresh-ground coffee beans.

If she goes to New York, I'll lose her.

My desperate mind rejects that conclusion, forming another plan.

My car is out of commission again, but a week of work and some extra parts will have Jack up and running. Question is, will he make it all the way to NYC?

Doesn't matter. If my car dies, I can always boost another. I'll just avoid toll roads. No photographic evidence of where I've been or where I'm heading.

Somehow, someway, I'll make it to New York City.

And when I'm there, I'll…

This is where my brain restarts, and I realize how close I am to skidding off the road of sanity.

Skip out on parole? Steal a car? Stalk the woman I'm falling in love with?

I'm a piece of shit.

What would I even do when I got to the city? What kind of job could I hope to get with a warrant out for my arrest? I'd be lucky if Mr. Herbert didn't call the NYPD and tell them exactly where to find me. And if by some miracle he didn't, I'd end up as a bum on Paige's couch. On top of that, I'd be making her an accomplice to my crime.

How long would it take her to realize how worthless I was and kick me to the curb?

Why hasn't she done it already?

"You should go to New York." Even though I know the words are right, they come out of my mouth, sounding like a dead man learned how to speak.

Paige doesn't seem to notice, her tense shoulders relaxing as she gifts me with a relieved smile. "I really want to. I've missed my old job. It was everything I ever wanted to do."

Her words ring loud and clear. New York is her place. Not New Orleans. This town will only ever be the city she grew up in, not the place she fell in love with.

And I won't be the man she falls in love with.

"It's better this way." *No, it's not,* my gut screams. But I suffocate the protest with the strength of my self-disgust. "We both knew this thing with us never really had a future."

Paige rears back like I tried to hit her. "What?"

I push on, even though it feels like forcing my body through a fence made of barbed wire. "We had fun. But come on, Paige. Did you really think this was serious?"

"You're my boyfriend." She whispers the words like they're a question as she stares at me from across the room.

I don't deserve to be her boyfriend. Sooner or later, I'm going to fuck up again and probably land back in jail. That's the kind of person I am. A screwup.

A girl like her will find something better. Someone better.

"Yeah. We were dating. Now, we're not. No reason to make a big deal out of it." I'm being a dick on purpose because I know if I let myself soften, I won't be able to walk away from her.

"I don't get it. You want to end things just because I'm interviewing for a job?"

She needs to leave. I need her gone before I beg her to stay.

Standing up from the bed, I cross my arms and glare down at her. "Job, no job, I don't care. I'm tired of being another risk you're taking for the hell of it."

Paige plunges her fingers into her hair as if she's going to pull the silky strands from their roots. "You're not making any sense."

"Stealing cars. Running in dangerous neighborhoods. Adopting a pit bull. Dating an ex-con. See the pattern? I'm done with being the deadbeat boyfriend you rub in your parents' faces. Find another way to piss them off." I growl out the words, tasting them like poison on my tongue.

If I were to bet that Paige would burst into tears and run out of the house, I would've lost my money.

She doesn't break down. She just freezes, wide eyes locked on me. Her sweet bubblegum lips have popped open, forming a delicate O that makes me want to swoop in and kiss her until she forgets all the hurtful things I just said.

But I hold myself back. Because I'm bad for her. And she's too much of a temptation for me.

"You're an idiot." The words fall from her mouth like she's had an epiphany.

I try not to flinch, knowing the end has come.

Her blank expression morphs, not into sadness, but into anger. "I'm sorry my affection is so abhorrent to you, but if you think I'm using you as some kind of *screw you* to my parents, then you need to get your head out of your ass."

Paige stalks toward me, and I stumble back out of pure self-preservation.

Still, she gets in close, scowling up at me. "You know what I think, Dash?"

Her saying my name almost breaks me, but I tighten my lips and shake my head.

"I think you're a coward." She leans to the side, reaching behind me. When she straightens up, the framed picture of her and Pumpkin is clutched in her hand.

"No—" The word is out before I can stop it. But the idea of her leaving with every trace of her hurts worse than a head-on collision.

Paige frowns at me, then down at the picture. Without warning, she chucks the frame to the ground, angling her throw enough that the gift slides partway under my bed.

"There." She turns away, grabbing her shoes as she heads for the exit. "Now, it's with everything else you pretend not to care about."

I'm left standing there, still and miserable. Only when I hear Penelope roar to life do I crouch down to retrieve the picture. On impact, the glass cracked in a spiderweb formation, obscuring Paige's face.

When I brush my thumb over the mess, a sharp sting pierces my skin, the fractured glass slicing me open.

I welcome the pain.

CHAPTER 36

PAIGE

"I should've brought a thicker coat. I forgot how cold it gets up here!" I feel the need to shout with a scarf half obscuring my face.

Charlie grins down at me. "Wimp. The South has made you soft! Good thing you turned me down. You'd never survive in Germany."

I give him a playful shove with my elbow and experience a small spark of warmth, solely from happiness that the two of us can joke about his ridiculous invitation.

Thanksgiving dinner, I was a barely contained mess, and after the pie was passed around, Charlie pulled me from the table and got me to fess up about everything that had happened. He held me while I cried, calling Dash all range of names until I felt the need to defend my recent ex.

"I think he was pushing me away on purpose," I said. "Like he was being harder on himself than on me."

"Paige—"

"No, I know it sounds like I'm reaching. That I sound naive."

"You don't sound naive. You sound like you love the guy."

"Fuck." I buried my head in my best friend's chest as Pumpkin nosed my leg. "Why can't we just fall in love with each other?"

His chuckle surfaced from deep in his chest, vibrating through me like a massage to my tense muscles. "Love isn't easy like that. For what it's worth, I think you're right."

When I peered up at him, Charlie grimaced, as if the words pained him to say. "He's not Martin."

"What do you mean?" I rubbed my eyes, fingers coming away black from the mascara I'd put on for the special occasion. I left little dark streaks on my dog's fur when I reached down to scratch her head.

Charlie sighed and rubbed my shoulders. "Martin looked at you like you were his. Like he owned you. Had an unquestionable right to you."

"And Dash?"

My friend didn't answer right away, frowning as he stared at me. When he spoke, the words hit me in my already-bruised chest. "The guy looked at you like he wanted to be yours."

I had to stifle another sob, shaking my head. "Let's stop talking about this. I want to talk about New York."

When I told Charlie about the interview, he suggested making it into a whole trip. The two of us exploring a place, like we hadn't gotten to do in years. I mapped out all my favorite spots that I wanted to take him to, some of them tourist traps and others little gems I'd only come to discover after living in the city for years.

Then, my old publisher shocked the hell out of me by offering to cover not only my airfare, but my hotel for the entire two-week trip. Going from getting fired to having all my expenses paid for was messing with my head.

So, in my normal fashion, I distract myself with food.

"This is the best pizza. Well, the best that was within easy walking distance of my old apartment." I tug Charlie into a small shop that's warm and smells of melted cheese.

We each order, cradling the massive slices that practically drip off the sides of the paper plates. Structural integrity be damned, the important element is taste, and these deliver.

Even as I consume the glorious slice of pie, I can't help remembering all the delicious food offerings I just started to explore in NOLA. New York City has everything, so somewhere on these grid streets, there's likely a shop selling po'boys. But would they compare or just be sad shadows of the real thing?

"How can you frown when your mouth is full of this heavenly pizza?" Charlie gives me a mock glare across the tall metal table we claimed.

I shrug because I don't know how to explain the little empty spot in my chest. Or I do, but I'm not sure I want to say the word out loud.

Homesick.

Since when did New Orleans start to feel like home?

Was it all Dash?

I play around with that idea but dismiss it. He does keep shoving his way back into my thoughts, pricking at my heart like a handful of splinters. But when I envision New Orleans, he's not all I see. There's Pumpkin, romping around in my parents' backyard. There's Mom, smeared in oil, brewing herself a cappuccino with my granddad's old machine. There's Dad, his ingrained frown lines clearing into a smile as he listens to the women in his life bicker.

And I envision the city too. Heavy, damp heat, always embracing me. Music a constant, drifting from street corners and bars. Color—so much color—everywhere. New York has ever-present energy, like a perpetual moving machine. But New Orleans has a rhythm, and at some point, that melody started singing to my soul.

But I can't figure out words for it. And even though Charlie is used to my less than sensical way of talking, I'm not sure even he would understand me if I tried.

Dash would though.

I shake that off and focus on the man I'm with.

"It's weird, being back here. With the interview. I just don't get it. Why go through all of this—the calling, the plane ticket, the hotel —for me?"

"They want you, Paige." Charlie finishes off his crust and wipes the grease from his hands with a napkin.

"They had me. And they fired me."

"Obviously, they realized they're a bunch of idiots. The real question is, do you want them?"

I barely have to think about my answer. "I want my authors. I miss them. Working with them. Talking with them. Maybe we weren't friends, but it always felt like it."

Charlie nods. "My advice? Keep that to yourself. I don't think this is going to be the normal kind of interview with you trying to sell yourself to them. They know what you can do, and they want you back. It's your turn to make them sweat."

I grimace. "That's not my style."

"You've gotta be kidding me, Pancake." His use of my childhood nickname has me grinning. "I was in that kitchen when you gave your dad, one of the scariest men I know, a verbal beatdown."

"He's not that scary," I mumble, suddenly embarrassed.

"Maybe not to you. But he's more than that. He's someone you love." Charlie loops his arm through mine and pulls me back out into the cold. "Being honest with someone you love can be harder than it is with a stranger. Because you actually care about their opinion. These interviewers? Who cares what they think?"

"Well, me."

Charlie tugs me to a stop at a crosswalk. "You shouldn't. They should care about what *you* think of them."

I mull over his words as we walk the last few blocks before arriving at the skyscraper my old employer has offices in. We're early, so Charlie pulls out his phone, taking a picture of me by the front entrance and sending it off to our parents.

"Are you sure you're good on your own while I do this?" Even though my friend is a world traveler, I feel bad, abandoning him in the big city.

Charlie smirks and grasps my shoulders. "Don't worry about me. I want you focused and ready for battle."

I roll my eyes, but he gives me a gentle shake.

"Remember, you're a badass."

After a quick kiss on the cheek, Charlie turns me toward the doors and gives me an encouraging push forward.

Determined to live up to his idea of me, I don't look back, facing forward, and brace for whatever this meeting might hold.

———

"You would have your position back with a salary increase of two percent, and we would cover all relocation expenses." Mr. Shoemaker, my old boss, sits across the boardroom table from me. He has his hands clasped on his stomach as he reclines in his chair and offers me a congratulatory smile. On his left is a guy from HR who introduced himself as Tom, and on Mr. Shoemaker's right is Francine Walters, who, if I remember correctly, ranks a bit higher than my ex-boss.

The three of them sit silently, waiting for my answer.

Giving myself time to think, I smooth my hands over the silky green material of my skirt. The dress I bought all those weeks ago with Dash probably isn't the most common interview attire, but I don't care. Even pairing it with a set of thick black tights and a well-fitted blazer, I get the same shot of confidence I felt the day I marched out of the store, wearing it.

I knew I'd need that memory today.

My old job, a raise, and help to move back up north. I could live in New York, on my own this time. The place I rented, the food I ate, the bills I paid—everything would fall on me. Finally, I would be living in the world as a fully functioning adult.

For years, this is what I've been saying I wanted.

My answer should be obvious.

"No."

"No?" Mr. Shoemaker clears his throat and glances to the woman beside him. "You mean, you won't accept our offer?"

"I haven't decided about the offer yet." I wave my hand as if the idea of the job is of no concern to me. "I'm saying no to this." I gesture between the two of us, him and me. "This farce. This idea that we're going to sit here and pretend you didn't fire me after agreeing to let me work remotely. If you want me to even consider working with this company in the future, you'll need to explain why we are in this situation in the first place."

With a confidence I'm just starting to get comfortable with, I nod my head, indicating it's his turn to talk.

My old boss sits forward in his chair, his easy posture gone as he fiddles with the papers in front of him. "Well, Ms. Herbert, you see... when running a business, it's important—"

"Oh, just stop." Ms. Walters glares at her colleague before turning to me. "I apologize for the way you've been treated in the past. You are familiar, I'm sure, with Marianna Tweep?"

"I'm the reason she's a client of this publishing house." This whole confidence thing is kick-ass.

"Yes. A fact we are extremely grateful for."

I'm sure they are. Marianna publishing a book means the company is making millions.

"It seems when she was informed that you were going to work remotely, she expressed dissatisfaction in communicating with an editor electronically."

I hide my wince, barely. Apparently, my worries that Marianna wasn't as attached to me as I was to her weren't unfounded.

But Ms. Walters continues, "My colleague here"—she gestures at a red-faced Mr. Shoemaker—"took that to mean your services were not vital to the company and could therefore be done away with."

"At the time, it made sense," he mutters, the man I used to have a level of respect for now sounding more like a sulky child.

If Ms. Walter's glare is any indication, she holds an equal level of disdain toward him. "Upon further, more detailed communication with Ms. Tweep, she explained that she finds your one-on-one in-person meetings to be a vital part of her creative process. Her original comments were meant as a demand for us to offer you incentives to stay within the city. When she found out you had been fired...well, let's just say, she was not pleased."

"I don't think it's out of the question to ask an author to work with a different editor." Mr. Shoemaker's comment seems more directed at Ms. Walters than me, and I wonder if I'm the only one under consideration in this meeting.

The woman in charge ignores him, her focus solely on me. "Ms. Tweep is under contract with our publishing agency for her next five books. However, she claims that without your assistance, anything she sends us would be, and I quote, 'utter shit.' And it seems she meant that literally. These are the last pages she sent in for editing."

Ms. Walters opens a folder and slides a stack of papers across the table. When I lean closer to read the type, I can't help letting out an involuntary snort.

Over and over, almost like the printer had a glitch, one word marches across the page.

Shit.

SHIT. SHIT. SHIT. SHIT.

Just to satisfy my curiosity, I flip through the rest. Every so often, there's an *UTTER SHIT* thrown in. To mix things up, I guess. If I were alone, I'd be curled up on the floor, driven to the fetal position by laughter. But in this meeting, I only let a half smile grace my face.

"Seems like a very Marianna thing to do."

The HR guy chuckles but tries to cover it with a cough. Mr. Shoemaker scowls at the offending pages. Ms. Walters meets my eyes with a firm stare of her own.

"She wants you back. Back with our company and back in the city. We never should have let you go. I'm hoping my honesty about the situation will help smooth over some of the hurt from the way you were treated in the past. Now, if we could discuss you potentially rejoining the team?"

I barely register her words, too focused on how happy I am at the loyalty Marianna showed me. This woman wants me so badly that she'd piss off her publisher.

That's the kind of badass I hope to be one day, and it sets off little happy bubbles in my chest that I still have a friend here in the city.

"Thank you for inviting me to meet with you all and explaining the situation. I'll have to consider your offer. I'll be in touch."

As I stand to leave, I gather up Marianna's beautiful prose, slipping the pages into my bag before I stroll out of the room.

CHAPTER 37

DASH

The flames heat my skin as the smoke burns my eyes.

Good. This is meant to be a punishment. A lesson. A warning.

I pull another magazine from the stack and almost laugh at the way fate mocks me. The title flows across the top in curving yellow letters.

Corvette.

On the cover is a canary-yellow '63 with its telltale split rear window. That gaping blind spot. Just as dangerous as the girl who sat me down on the leather seats and kissed me in that car.

I don't remember buying this magazine, but I've picked it up so many times since getting out that I could've bought it a week ago or a year ago. Mrs. Herbert works on a quality brand that caught my attention even before I met her daughter.

Before I loved her daughter.

I let out a growl and throw the offending magazine into the flames, the force of its landing sending up sparks. Good thing I live in New Orleans, where humidity reigns supreme.

Still, I tried not to be too reckless about my ceremonial burning of all things tempting. Borrowed a cheap firepit from the couple across the street. They've got an energetic pit-bull mix I helped train and sometimes walk for them when they work late, so they were happy to lend it to me.

Cole sat on the back stairs while I set everything up, but when I brought out my armful of contraband reading material and started tossing them in, he scowled and retreated inside the house.

Not that I cared. He can think I'm an idiot all he wants.

In fact, fuck him.

I grab another magazine and feed it to the hungry flames.

He should be happy I'm doing this. Fucking overjoyed. It was absurd for me to have bought these in the first place. Just more temptation. One day, I probably wouldn't have been content with just looking at the cars on glossy pages. I would've gone out and stolen one just for the love of it.

Better to cut myself off from them completely.

Just like with Paige.

My pile of kindling runs out, but I know I have at least one more load. The back stairs creak under my feet as I mount them. I don't linger in the kitchen, worried the memory of Paige stirring her gumbo at the stove and laughing at my work stories will drive me insane. But my bedroom isn't any better. The sheets are rumpled, just like they were when I pushed up her skirt and feasted on her until she clutched my hair and called out my name.

I press my fingers into my eyes and drop to the floor. When I reach under the bed, I locate an untidy pile of offending magazines. I bundle them into my arms and hurry back outside, to a place where Paige hasn't left her mark. A place she never will.

In my hurry to be free of the images of beautiful cars, I add too many to the fire at once, almost snuffing out the flames.

"Calm down," I mutter.

Talking to myself now? That's just great.

While the flames slowly recover from the influx of fuel, I straighten the remaining ones, so the smooth, shiny covers aren't sliding out of my arms. But for some reason, I can't get them exactly aligned. There's a bulge in the middle of the pile, throwing the whole thing off.

Thinking one of the magazines has just been folded in half, I sift through the pages until I reach the obstruction. The item slips out of my hold and lands with a light thump on the damp grass.

Realizing what it is, I swoop down to save it from possible damage, reminding myself a moment later that my instinct is ridiculous.

The novel Paige first wrote her phone number in belongs in the fire more than anything else I've burned today.

But the flames are still too low, I reason. I'll get rid of it in a minute.

My fingers, acting completely on their own, flip to the first page.

Above a familiar phone number, the letters sit, small and precise.

And green, of course.

Please teach me your magical dog-whispering ways. I want to know all the spells.

—Paige

A reluctant laugh sneaks out of my chest. Some people would've read this and thought she was out of her mind.

To be honest, Paige *is* a little out of her mind. But in the perfect way. A wonderful, rambling way. I love the odd way she talks and her unconscious need to touch me. The way she realizes she said or did something unconventional, but she's never really sure what exactly it was. And the ridiculous fact that she refers to her dog as her life partner with complete sincerity. I do not doubt that Pumpkin will have Paige's devotion until the last breath she takes.

To be loved like that, it's something people could go wild for.

Something I'd break every law for.

Someone I'd destroy my carefully arranged life for.

The fire is roaring again, ready to take whatever I feed it.

The book should be next. It's light in my hands, and I bet the dry pages will crisp and blacken faster than anything I've thrown in so far. The paper has little more pressure than feathers when I fan through the pages.

A hint of green catches my eye, and I stop with my thumb on the page.

Just let her love you, you idiot!

The note is written in Paige's signature green ink, the letters running up the side of the page, taking up the small amount of free space in the margin.

And it's like she's standing next to me, murmuring the words in my ear.

I drop the rest of the magazines in my arms and flip through more of the pages at a slower rate than before. A lot of them are exactly as they were originally printed, but every so often, I hit on gold. Well, I hit on green. Scattered throughout the book, Paige has left commentary.

He sounds dangerous and handsome. Swoon.

Love the play of dark and light.

She is a badass. I want to be her when I grow up.

None of the words make sense to me because I have no idea what's going on in the story. It's like hearing half of a phone conversation. I want the whole picture.

I settle on the back steps, the same spot Cole occupied not too long ago.

And I read.

I start at the beginning, immersing myself in the historical story, discovering the characters Paige called dangerous, handsome, and badass. Every page I come across with her writing, I devour. My hunger for her thoughts grows exponentially stronger than the ever-present emptiness in my stomach.

About halfway through, I realize I'm holding the book an inch from my face, trying to make out the words, only to realize I'm struggling so much because the sun set and the fire died.

I pause long enough to check for stray embers before heading into my bedroom and clicking on the thrift-shop lamp. The bulb flickers for a moment, as if deciding whether or not it wants to wake up, then finally flares to life.

With my pillow balled up enough to elevate my head, I continue reading.

———

I don't remember falling asleep, but I realize I'm waking up. My eyes are still closed as my mind pushes through a comfortable fog. Fingers brush against my forehead, teasing my hair.

Paige. Paige is here.

She's come back to me. She'll stay here, close. When I wake up, I'll see her face. The curve of her lips, the round button of her nose, and that slim scar cutting through her pale eyebrow.

She'll say something strange, and I'll kiss her mouth. Drink in her coffee scent.

Coffee.

Why don't I smell coffee?

I breathe in deep as my eyes crack open.

Citrus.

Luna.

"Hey, little prince." My sister sits on the side of my bed, staring down at me with concern etching deep lines into her forehead.

Disappointment spears through me. Then shame because I should be happy to see her.

And I am. But it's not enough to completely overshadow the crush of dark loneliness.

"Luna?" I sit up and pull her into a hug, hoping she didn't notice my initial reaction. "When did you get here? What'd I do to deserve a surprise visit?"

"Cole called me when you started burning things."

She returns my embrace for just a moment before pushing me away, far enough to search my shifty eyes. I know if I meet her gaze, I'll have trouble holding back the turmoil in my head.

"Tell me what's wrong." Her voice, gentle but demanding, makes me feel like I'm ten again. Those days when I'd come home from school with bruises hidden under my clothes.

Bullies were good at hurting me where teachers couldn't see. But Luna would know. She'd see the pain in my face, and she'd drag the names of my tormentors from me.

And Luna would exact revenge in the way only she could.

But I don't need my big sister to act as the avenging angel. Paige hasn't hurt me intentionally. This pain is all self-inflicted.

She can't defend me from myself.

"Dash, talk to me."

In her eyes, I realize there's more than just concern. I see fear.

Probably afraid I'll do something reckless. Something illegal.

No need for that. I've gotten rid of all temptation. There's nothing left to make my life anything more than just existing. I'm back on the straight and narrow.

But why does doing the right thing have to hurt so much?

I lean my forehead against hers, closing my eyes and stifling the ache in my chest.

"Have you ever had a broken heart?"

CHAPTER 38

PAIGE

A New York City hotel room is not good for pacing, but that doesn't stop me from circling the tiny space I have. My limbs hum with raw, excited energy that's hung around for days. A few times, I've tossed up a random fist pump. Usually when I'm alone in the bathroom, so as not to scare random people on the street.

I'm a badass.

I didn't let them push me around. I kept my cool, accepted my worth, and left that office with my spine straight. If only I'd been wearing a cape or something to add to the dramatic effect.

The high of that moment hasn't worn off.

But every time I'm about to reach the pinnacle of happiness, one thought enters my mind.

I want to talk to Dash.

If we were on speaking terms, I'd call to give him a play-by-play. Tell him how firm my voice was, just like he'd taught me. How the green dress he'd convinced me to buy was a suit of armor I wore into corporate battle. Then, I'd tell him all about New York and how much fun it is to be back, but that I miss him and just want to crawl into his bed and fall asleep in his arms. Or maybe do something else before we go to sleep…

I groan and collapse on my hotel bed. It's a nice cushy mattress. The softness mocks me.

When Charlie and I were booking hotel rooms, we decided to go separate. He's an early riser, and sometimes, he talks in his sleep.

But tonight, my room seems overly quiet. I'm too high up to hear the busy streets of NYC without opening a window. And hotels don't give you that option.

For a while, I just stare up at the textured ceiling, and then I let my eyes roam around the room until they land on a jackpot.

Hello, minibar.

Hell, I'm not paying for it.

I crack open a tiny bottle of wine and cheers myself in the mirror before downing it in a few swallows.

Classy.

The next one I open lasts longer as I sip the dry red, but the beverage still disappears rather quickly. As I open a ten-dollar bag of peanuts, I enjoy the warm alcohol fog my brain begins to drift through.

And in that fog, I make a decision that seems completely reasonable.

If I call Dash, he can always decide not to pick up. But maybe he *will* pick up because he's been waiting for *me* to call.

The opportunity needs to be presented.

My normal distaste of conversing on the phone barely registers. When it comes to Dash, I'll settle for any type of communication.

My thumb slides across the glass screen of my phone, and when I find the right number, I press Send and hold the device to my ear.

He doesn't pick up on the first ring. My heart thuds heavily in my chest.

He doesn't pick up on the second. Sweat gathers on my lower back.

He doesn't pick up on the third.

Because someone else picks up on the third.

"Dash's shitty-ass phone. Who's this?"

Peanuts bounce around on the floor, the bag having slipped from my slack grasp. The surprise at hearing a woman's voice steals the strength from my muscles.

"Hellooooo?"

"Who's this?" I don't recognize the raspy voice that comes out of my throat.

"Not how this works. You called me. You tell me who you are."

"I didn't call you. I called Dash."

"Who called Dash?"

"Me."

"And who is me?" The woman on the other end of the line sounds like she's having a fun time, jerking me around.

"Me is Paige. I'm Paige."

"Paige." Whatever amusement existed in her voice a moment ago is gone now, leaving behind a cold so strong that I shiver.

"Yes. And you are?"

"Luna."

Luna.

I try to remember the name of the girl we met briefly in the bar, but I come up blank. For a second, I convince myself she's just a friend, but then I recall my first encounter with Cole.

If a girl is in their house, it's because she's fucking Dash.

I shake my head, trying to dislodge the thought.

Maybe she's fucking Cole?

"Um, hello, Luna. Could I please speak to Dash?"

The other end of the line is silent for a moment, and I pull my phone away from my ear to check if she's hung up on me.

She hasn't.

"He's busy."

"He's busy?"

"That's right. He's in the shower."

"In the shower?" Oh no. I've started parroting the girl.

"Yep. He's in the shower. I'm in his bed. And Cole has made himself scarce to give us some privacy. Anything else you need to know, Piper?"

My mouth opens, ready to run through her words just so I have them right.

But then the meaning of them hits me, and I choke.

"I'm in his bed."

I still don't know who this Luna girl is, but I suddenly have a very clear picture of her in my mind. She's small, petite some might say, with long, dark hair, probably slightly damp from having just stepped out of the shower. A shower that Dash joined her in. And now, she's sprawled out across his clean sheets that smell like him. She's not naked though. No. She's wrapped in a green cotton robe.

"It's Paige," is all I'm able to mutter through my frozen lips after a full minute of silent suffering.

"Sure it is. Well, Dash'll probably be busy for the rest of the night. Try back some other time. Or don't."

I'm not sure if she hangs up or if I do. But at some point, my phone screen goes black as I sit on the edge of the mattress, staring down at the offensive device.

Slowly, I lie back on the bed, then roll over until my face is fully pressed into the cushy comforter.

If I stay like this all night, would I suffocate?

My stomach growls, wanting more than half a bag of overpriced peanuts to fill the grief hole left in my abdomen. For some reason, this gaping chasm feels bigger than the one left by my fiancé.

How could a man I've known for three months dig deeper into my soul than one who I was with for eight years?

Am I just getting more gullible with age?

With a reluctant push, I heave myself up and open the Maps app on my phone, searching for the closest fried chicken joint.

500 feet away. Gotta love NYC.

My jacket is halfway on when the reality of the situation hits me.

I'm in a loop. A rut. If I leave my room now to binge-eat my pain away, I'll probably end up running back to Mommy and Daddy the minute I wake up from my food coma.

The realization brings on a wave of anger that burns away some of my hurt. My head clears enough for me to toss aside my coat and sit down in front of my laptop.

When the browser opens, I navigate to a real estate website.

No more excuses. Time to get my shit together.

Maybe Dash helped me learn how to stand firm, but my ability to function in the world is not solely dependent on him—or any man for that matter. I'm my own woman, and I can figure this out by myself.

I've saved the information for five different homes when my stomach lets out another growl. Maybe I've pushed my hurt to the side temporarily, but no amount of willpower can tamp down my hunger.

Barely taking my eyes off the next listing, I dial Charlie's number.

"Hmm?" my friend answers, clearly half asleep.

"I need you to wake up, get dressed, and bring me some pizza. Major life decisions are being made, and I require the presence of my best friend."

"Okay." His voice sounds less sleepy, which miraculously makes me want to smile. I may not have hordes of friends, but the few I have are good ones. "Why do you need me to bring you pizza?"

"Because fried chicken is for misery. And pizza is for badasses."

CHAPTER 39

DASH

"Hey, Luna. Have you seen my phone?" I set a cup of coffee down on the table in front of my sister.

"I plugged it in to charge over there." She shoves her nose in the mug while waving toward the counter.

With the smell of coffee strong in the air, thoughts of Paige push into my mind. I'm tempted to snatch up my battered phone and flip it open to check for a call or text from her.

Instead, I sit down across from Luna and wrap my hands around my mug. Even if there is a message from her, I shouldn't respond. Nothing has changed other than the amount I miss her, which only grows the longer she's gone.

Who the fuck am I kidding?

The second I hear my phone ring, I'll be lunging for it like a drowning man reaching for a flotation device. I've lost track of the number of times I've navigated to her name in my Contacts and just stared at those five letters, willing her to call me and tell me I haven't ruined everything.

"Okay, so next on the agenda for getting you over this chick is leaving this house." My sister's stern voice snaps me back to the kitchen.

"She's not just a *chick*. And I've left the house."

"Going to work doesn't count. We need to do something fun. Camilla told me about a new band. You love live music."

The last live show I went to was with Paige, where we danced, pressed up against each other.

I shrug. "Maybe. So, you and Camilla patched things up?"

My sister and her childhood best friend had a falling-out I never really understood. Of course, I was two years younger than them and completely self-absorbed at the time, as is the way with teenagers.

"You think she'd be letting me crash at her place if we hadn't?"

"You know you're welcome to stay here."

Last night, after Luna listened to me spill my guts, she shoved me in the shower to, quote, "wash away the stink" of my misery, then left to spend the night in her friend's guest room.

Luna smirks. "I love you, little brother, but I'm not about to spoon with you. Invest in a full-size couch, and I'll consider crashing at your place next time."

As my sister reaches for the cereal box in the middle of the table, the sound of our half-hearted doorbell sputters through the house. With Cole at work, I'm left to answer it. Luna gives me a curious look as I move to stand. I just shrug and make my way to the front of the house.

When I open the door, I stutter back a step in shock.

"Really, Dash, I'm not *that* scary." Paige's mom grins at me as she stands on my crumbling front stoop.

"Sorry." I move to open the door wide. "I was just surprised. Would you like to come in?"

My silent begging that she'll refuse does nothing, as Mrs. Herbert crosses the threshold into my shithole house.

For a moment, we stand awkwardly in the small front room. Well, I'm awkward. Paige's mom still has a gentle smile as she peers around. There's not much to look at, just a worn love seat Cole's grandma gifted him and a rickety card table I've piled random car parts on.

Occasionally, I tinker with them to pass the time, the way someone else might work on a crossword puzzle.

"Do I get a tour?"

Mrs. Herbert's question makes me want to groan, but I stiffen my spine and offer a small nod.

"There's not much to it," I offer as I lead her deeper into the house.

We pass through Cole's room without stopping, but she lingers in mine.

"Green." Her hand brushes the wall, just like her daughter's did. "She must've loved that."

And just like that, I'm stabbed in the chest. I actually glance down at myself to check if there's a red stain spreading over my shirt.

Nothing. Must all be internal.

Either unaware of or ignoring how her comment gutted me, Paige's mom keeps exploring. She picks up the broken picture frame, another memento that somehow escaped the fire.

I harden my heart, trying to brace for another casual attack, but nothing comes. Mrs. Herbert stares down at the picture for a moment, then places it back on the chair where she found it.

"Is there any more?" It takes me a second to realize she's asking about the house.

I nod, directing her into the kitchen. Completely forgetting about my other guest.

"Hello." The older woman's word sounds friendly, but her smile has gone tight as she runs her eyes over the pretty woman in my kitchen.

"Uh, hi." Luna glances at me, clearly confused, and I hurry to clear things up before Paige's mom adds *playboy* to my list of sins.

"Luna, this is Mrs. Herbert. Mrs. Herbert, this is Luna. My sister." I step fully into the kitchen, making sure both women can see me as I make introductions.

The hint of tension in Mrs. Herbert's shoulders relaxes at my explanation, but my sister still looks lost. I consider explaining exactly how I know the new arrival.

Instead, I keep my mouth shut.

Partly because thinking and talking about Paige hurts. But also, after I gave a brief summary of what happened between me and my ex, I got the sense Luna had decided she disliked the girl I love.

Ever the protector, ready to destroy anyone who hurts her younger brother. Even if I'm the one who brought the pain on myself, I don't think Luna sees it that way. And I don't want my sister to have any reason to be rude to Mrs. Herbert.

So, I let Luna stew in her confusion.

"It's nice to meet you, Luna." The older woman turns back to me. "I was hoping to speak with you for a moment, Dash. Do you mind taking a walk with me?"

"I…uh…sure. Of course."

She gives me another genuine smile, and in the happy expression, I catch some of the resemblance between her and her daughter. Paige is taller, and her face has a few more straight lines than her mother's round one, but their cheeks plump up in just the same way. And their button noses are almost identical.

Apparently, more than just Mrs. Herbert's words can carve painfully into me.

The two of us head out the back door, circling to the front of the house. We pass my beat-up Saturn on the way, and the mechanic clicks her tongue in obvious disappointment.

My cheeks flush hot, ashamed of Jack in all his obvious disrepair. The vehicle pairs nicely with my life. Shitty car for a shitty person. And it's all on display for the mother of the woman I love.

"You deserve better than that, Dash. You belong in a…" She trails off, looking me over with searching eyes. "A Stingray. Yeah. I could see you in a '65 Corvette Stingray."

Mrs. Herbert gives a satisfied nod and heads off down the sidewalk. Her words shock me into a frozen statue, and I have to shake myself before jogging to catch up.

"Mrs. Herbert, I'm sorry—"

"Stop, please. Don't apologize to me for anything. My husband treated you horribly, and I just stood by and let it happen. *I'm* sorry."

She shoves her hands into a set of large pockets. Only then do I realize she's dressed in some loose overalls with a simple black T-shirt underneath. I bet Mrs. Herbert makes more money in a month than I do in a year, but no one would guess it by looking at her.

That's probably why I tricked myself into believing Paige's mom might approve of me.

"It's okay. I understand." Even though it hurts.

Mrs. Herbert steps in front of me, bringing us both to a halt on the cracked sidewalk. She gazes up into my face, concern etching deep lines into hers. Carefully, as if she's worried I might run, the woman lifts her hands to cup my cheeks in a gentle embrace.

"It's not okay."

Suddenly, my eyes feel dry and scratchy. I have to blink rapidly, and I thank the universe when Mrs. Herbert lets her hands drop. She starts walking again, and I follow along beside her.

"Paige is in New York right now. She and Charlie left a few days ago. She has that interview, and then they're making it into a vacation."

I grunt in answer, unable to form words. Half of me is starved for information while the other part wishes I never had to hear Paige's name again.

"Every day, she's demanding I send pictures of Pumpkin. I'm chasing the dog around the house, trying to get a shot of her." Mrs. Herbert chuckles, and something like amusement tugs at the corner of my mouth. "You know, when she brought that dog home, I nearly had a heart attack."

I frown but keep my mouth shut.

"We never had a dog when Paige was growing up. I was too scared of them. Got bit by a dog when I was a young girl. Never told Paige that. Maybe she would've thought twice about bringing Pumpkin home if I had." The woman shrugs as she steps off the curb to cross an empty street. "But she didn't know, and so she brings home this huge, scary-looking animal. Well, you know."

Despite the fact that I'm sure beyond a doubt that Pumpkin is as sweet as they come, I still sympathize with Mrs. Herbert.

"I tried to tell Paige to take it back. She refused. I told her it's dangerous. She quoted studies and facts at me. Still, I was sure the dog wasn't safe."

As we meander through my neighborhood, I listen to her story, trying to figure out why she needed to drive over to my shitty side of town to tell it to me.

Mrs. Herbert looks up, meeting my eyes.

"But I only needed to be around Pumpkin for maybe a week to realize something. I was wrong." She sighs out a chuckle. "Paige was right. She saw that dog and realized it just needed love. She wasn't scared of something most other people were terrified of. She wasn't blinded by prejudice. Paige has always been good at that. Looking past the surface and finding the good underneath. Just like with her job, she pulls out the best in everything around her."

My chest squeezes tight, so much so that I have trouble dragging in my next breath. Still, Mrs. Herbert stares at me.

"Sometimes, you think one way for so long that it becomes comfortable, and you need someone to give you a good shove to realize how off track you are. How closed-minded. Mr. Herbert and I jumped to conclusions, judged you, and for that, I am sorry." She sighs, then offers a rueful smile. "My husband is slower to admit when he's wrong, but Paige really laid into him. I think, if you're ever willing to give us another chance, you'll find the older Herberts have learned the error of their ways."

A thick lump in my throat makes it hard to swallow, but Mrs. Herbert doesn't seem to be waiting for a response.

"Now that that's said, on to what I really want to talk to you about."

I swallow a couple of times before I can speak. "What do you want to talk about?"

Her lips split into a wide grin.

"Cars."

———

"Who is that young man sitting in my car?" Mrs. Herbert's question comes out with only mild curiosity as we return to my house.

When I follow her line of sight, dread pulses through my veins.

"That's"—I don't want to give voice to the image, but keeping quiet won't make him disappear—"my brother."

When did Leo get out?

He sits in the driver's seat of Mrs. Herbert's Camaro, running his hands over the steering wheel like he owns the thing.

"Leo!" I bark out his name, trying to keep the angry bite from it.

For some reason, Paige's mom has decided not to condemn me for my past transgressions. That doesn't mean I suddenly get a free pass to be a scary asshole in front of her.

At the sound of his name, Leo's head pops up. Our eyes meet through the windshield, and while I'm doing my best to keep all expression off my face, my older brother breaks out his shit-eating grin.

He slides out of the driver's seat, movements casual as if he didn't get caught with his hand in the cookie jar.

"Baby brother! I was just waiting for you to get back." Leo's voice is jovial.

I wonder how he knew I was even gone. Most likely, he saw me walk off with Mrs. Herbert because if he'd actually knocked on the door and been met with Luna, there'd be a lot more shouting going on right now. Probably a few things on fire. Maybe some broken bones or openly bleeding wounds.

"I'm back."

Paige's mom is a smart lady, and she clearly picks up on the tension pulsing across the air like a sonic beam between my brother and me. "I should be heading home. Still have a full day's work to put in." She turns to face me, wrapping a reassuring grip around my forearm and waiting until I give her my attention. "Consider what I said."

I nod, my neck suddenly creaky and stiff. Her smile is gentle as she lets me go and walks to where my brother lounges against the hood of the Camaro.

Unlike most well-off women, she doesn't shy away from Leo, scared of his dark stare, tatted-up arms, and a general air of menace. Instead, she stops right in front of him, dragging her eyes from his boots to his smirking gaze.

"You any good with cars?"

My brother's *don't give a fuck* persona wavers slightly at her question, surprise curving his eyebrows. After a moment, he nods.

She reaches out to pat him on the shoulder, then moves him to the side with a firm hand. "There's hope for you yet."

Leo's left standing, wide-eyed, as Paige's mom climbs behind the wheel, revs the engine, and slides away from the curb. The purr of the Chevy hangs in the air, even as she disappears around the corner.

Then, we're alone.

"So, you're out."

Leo blinks a couple of times before reasserting his air of cocky disinterest.

"Would've known that if you'd kept in touch, baby brother."

"I've been busy."

How did I not know he was out? Someone should've told me. Did my mom know?

Of course she did. Guess she didn't feel the need to share.

Leo laughs, but there's no real humor in it. "Yeah. Busy. I'm sure." He moves out of the street, sauntering over to a battered yellow Mustang. "Get in the car, Dash. Enough fucking around here. Uncle Mike wants us back, and he's offering some real cash. Not whatever half-ass paycheck that dog place gives you."

Before I have time to respond, a tiny figure ghosts in front of me, so fast and smooth that I'd be surprised to learn her feet touched the ground.

"He's not going anywhere with you." Luna stands with her arms outstretched, acting like a wall between me and Leo.

"You still letting our sister boss you around, huh? Acting like she's your mom? It's pathetic." My brother sneers at me over Luna's shoulder.

She shifts as if his expression is a projectile she can keep from piercing my skin by using the blockage of her body.

"I'm not bossing him. I'm protecting him. You only care about Dash when he can help make you money. You're not going to keep him safe. You're not going to keep him from getting sent back to jail. Hell, I'm pretty sure you're happy the two of you got arrested. Think it's some weird badge of honor," she scoffs as he glares at her.

Suddenly, I'm worried for my sister. There was a time when I thought Leo could do no wrong, but at some point, my brother flipped a switch. A darkness overtook him, and I'm not sure what that shadow might drive him to do.

"Back the fuck off, Loony." The childhood nickname doesn't faze her like it used to.

"No way in hell. I didn't do anything last time. I just let you have him. But never again. I'll fight you, Leo. Physically if I have to. But you're not taking him anywhere." She growls the words, her chest heaving.

"Luna—" My words get cut off when she glares at me over her shoulder.

"No, Dash. You're better than what they'll give you. You're worth fighting for."

"And I'm worth shit? That's what you're saying?" Leo barks his accusation, taking a menacing step toward our sister.

She whips her head around, matching his step forward with one of her own—all the while, her hand reaches under the back of the loose shirt she's wearing.

And that's when I see the holster.

Fuck.

"Prove to me you're something different, Leo." Despite the fact that she's clearly ready to use lethal force or maybe because of it, a pleading note has entered my sister's voice. "Dash is out. You could be too. We never needed to be like them. I thought for a long time, it was something we had done, some wrong we'd committed, and that's why Mom and Dad kept walking out on us. But it wasn't my fault, and it wasn't yours, and it wasn't Dash's." She breathes in deep, and I hear a catch. "They don't deserve our love or our loyalty. Just walk away, Leo."

Luna still has her hand on the hidden piece, but the desperation in my sister's speech reveals how broken she'll be if she has to hurt our brother.

I can't let her do it.

"Leo." The tone I use is one I developed in prison. That place wasn't made for hesitating. The command in it, a new addition neither of my older siblings seems to have expected, garners me all the attention. "I'm done driving. Uncle Mike and I have an understanding."

A fucking twenty-thousand-dollar understanding. Payment for the protection I got behind bars. But when I'm done paying, I'm done with the family business. And when that man makes an agreement, he sticks to it. Honor among thieves.

"Luna's right. When we were kids, it seemed like it was the only way. And it was fun. Until it wasn't. So, I'm out."

"He'd clear your debt if you came back." Behind Leo's angry eyes, I think I catch a glimmer of loss. The same bit that flashed the day in the court when our guilty sentence was read out.

"I don't want to come back." I step forward, placing my palm on Luna's lower back, gripping her hand to keep her from drawing on our brother.

When we were kids, I would have done anything for Leo. He was my hero. But now, as I stand next to the woman who did everything in her power to raise me right and keep me happy and healthy, I realize how twisted that relationship always was. Love isn't dangerous acts and risking your life and freedom to prove yourself to someone. Love is keeping someone safe. It's making sure you're around every day to support and encourage them. It's working hard rather than taking the easy way, so you build a solid, unshakable life.

Luna showed me what love was when we were kids.

"You think that pretty blonde is going to hang around with some broke dog walker?"

My heart freezes.

"What did you say?"

Triumph shines in my brother's face like he thinks he just won something.

"I've been out for a while now. Didn't think I'd check up on you? Saw you in the Quarter. She's a hot piece of ass. Nice car too."

"Shut your mouth."

"Thought she'd cry though." He continues like he can't hear me. "When she saw how I slashed her tire. But no. You stepped in and saved the day. Her little helper boy. How long you gonna be her bitch? Girls like that take money to keep, and you sure as shit don't have much of that." Leo flicks his eyes over my run-down house before smirking at me, thinking he made a point.

Idiot. If anything, he's just killed any chance of me having a decent relationship with him.

"Get the fuck off my lawn and out of my sight. We're done."

"To hell with that. I say when we're done."

"That girl whose car you fucked with? Her dad's a judge. You mess with her, the law is going to come down on you hard. You think Uncle Mike is gonna give you another pass?"

My brother's face loses color as he comes to the same realization as me. Leo showed up here, trying to get me to take my old job back, not realizing he might not even have one himself.

"Leave me alone, leave Luna alone, and leave that girl alone, or I'll tell Uncle Mike you're fixin' to bring the law down on his operation."

That man's loyalty only lasts as long as his business isn't at risk. One of the reasons no one bailed us out or paid for a decent lawyer when we got pinched.

For a moment, Leo's dark eyes glare into mine, but he eventually turns his head. "Fuck you both. You're dead to me." The declaration comes out on a heated mutter as he storms to his car.

After slamming into the vehicle and revving the engine to life, my older brother peels down the street, flipping us the bird out the window.

To my surprise, Luna snorts.

"You think that's funny?"

"No. I think it's sad." She shakes her head and finally loosens her grip on the gun.

The gun.

"What the hell, Luna? You have a piece? And you brought it here? I'm on parole!" I back away to scowl down at her.

"Yeah. But I'm not. And I wasn't sure who I'd run into in town." Her hand waves down the street where our brother disappeared. "I have a concealed carry permit in Tennessee that's also valid here. As long as you're not the one handling the gun, there's no issue. So, don't go grabbing for it, you idiot." She glares right back at me, never one to back down even though I've got a good foot on her.

The fire in her eyes burns bright, and it's clear to me at that moment that she doesn't carry the weapon around for shits and giggles. My sister is too smart for that. If she has a gun, she knows how and when to use it.

"When did you get so scary?"

Luna scoffs as she brushes past me, heading back into the house. "I've always been scary. You were just too dense to notice."

CHAPTER 40

PAIGE

The second I open the door, I'm attacked.

"Pumpkin! Oh, baby girl! I missed you too!" I crow the words in my ultimate baby-talk voice, sitting on the ground in my parents' entryway so I can embrace my happily squirming puppy.

She wriggles and writhes in ecstasy.

I'm not embarrassed to admit a few tears slip out the corners of my eyes. Who knew I would come to love an animal so much? Every day in New York, even when I was having a great time with Charlie, there was a hole in my chest that ached for my puppy.

Right next to it was another hole, but I've decided not to acknowledge that one. Maybe if I spend enough time ignoring it, the pain will eventually go away.

When Pumpkin finally lets me stand back up, I set my suitcase by the stairs and go searching for my parents. My mom stands at the kitchen sink, using a bar of strong-smelling soap to scrub the grease off her fingers.

"Paige! You're back! I'd hug you, but…" She holds up her sudsy hands and reveals the oil smears down the front of her overalls.

I circle the kitchen island and press a kiss to her cheek, one of the few clean spots on her person. "Where's Dad? I want to talk to the two of you."

Mom shuts off the water to give me an intense stare. "Are we going to like this talk?"

I shrug. "How do I know until I give you the talk? I'm not some future-telling mind reader."

"Well, it sounds like I've failed as a mother. I bet all the other kids can see into the future and read all the minds."

I snort. "Yep. I have been thoroughly neglected. My brain is forever stunted. Now, where's Dad?"

"Upstairs, last I checked. Grab him and meet me in the garage. I've got a few things to put away."

With a quick pat on her short head—occasionally, I like to remind my mom of her miniature status—I bound up the stairs with Pumpkin following closer than a shadow.

At least I know someone I love missed me.

After pulling my dad away from his laptop, the two of us enter my mom's dominion. Hip-hop fills the space, spilling out of the speakers she mounted in each corner of the shop. The music isn't her usual choice, but she cycles through phases, and I like the beat.

The clang of metal on metal sounds out as she arranges her tools on the big, beautiful workbench just inside the door. Seeing us approach, Mom grabs a remote and lowers the volume on the music until it's just background noise. Pumpkin wanders off, probably searching for the dog bed my mom set up for her.

"So, what's this talk, Paige?" she asks over her shoulder, continuing to sort her tools.

Dad moves to stand next to her, eyes wandering around the garage.

Before I can respond, he starts to ask, "Isn't d—"

"Dinner can wait, dear. Paige wants to talk to us." Mom stops her fiddling to grab my dad's arm, and she nods for me to start.

I steel my spine and meet my dad's confused gaze. "I know you arranged the job interview with the local publisher."

He has the grace to grimace. "Paige—"

"No, Dad. It's okay. I know why you did it. You love me."

"Of course I love you."

I nod. "And I love you too. But I need you to stop loving me like that."

The two of them share baffled stares, and I breathe in deep, trying to figure out how to explain it. The words came so much easier when I was talking to Dash.

No. I will not think about Dash.

"I mess up in life. Pretty regularly. And I think you see those messes and want to clean them up. When I was a kid, that's what I needed. But now that I'm older, I need to clean up my own messes." I watch them process my words. "Does that make sense?"

Slowly, my dad nods. "I think so."

Relief washes through me. "Good. Because me losing my job and my fiancé, those are my messes."

"Martin is a mess. You're not a mess." My mom's declaration comes out so fierce that I can't help smiling at her.

"You're right, and you're wrong. But this isn't about him. It's about me. So, I'm not taking that job." When my dad goes to open his mouth, I hold up a hand. "Not just because you arranged it, even though that's a big part, but also because it's not what I want to do. I'm not passionate about that type of editing, and I have an opportunity to do what I'm passionate about."

My mom's eyes tighten, even as she attempts a smile. "They offered you the New York job then?"

"They did."

"And you're going to take it?"

"I am."

Her sigh comes from a deep place in her chest, and I watch my mom's small figure deflate slightly. "I don't blame you. But I sure will miss you." My parents exchange another look. "It's a more complicated route, but I think it'll all work out."

A lead weight that has been hanging around my heart since I made my final decision drops away, and I tear up for the second time since coming home. After Mom's blowup at Charlie's Germany invitation, I expected a lot more fight from her at the idea of me moving back to New York. The fact that she's so accepting of my decision makes my next announcement taste all the sweeter on my tongue.

"I certainly won't miss you." She flinches like I struck her, and I hurry to explain. "Because I'm not leaving. Well, I'm leaving your house. Sorry, but if I stay here much longer, I may end up murdering you. A quick, loving murder. But a murder all the same."

"Wha—what are you saying? And for the sake of my heart, please try to make it comprehensible." Mom clutches her chest dramatically and watches me with hopeful eyes.

"They offered me my old job and money to move back to New York. But I'm a bigger asset to the company than they or I realized. People like me there."

My last night in New York, I met up with Marianna at her favorite speakeasy bar and received a rib-cracking hug when I told her my decision.

"So, I made a counteroffer. A raise, working remotely as I had originally agreed to, and every other month, I'll fly to New York for a week to meet with my authors in person, like a few have requested. The hiring committee agreed."

Silence reigns in the garage, except for the pulsing beat of background hip-hop. Then, my mom practically shatters my eardrums with a happy squeal. Without warning, she wraps me in a hug that rivals Marianna's in pure strength. Good thing I opted for casual traveling clothes because there's no way I'm coming out of this embrace without a healthy amount of grease.

"You're staying! She's staying, Richard! Did you hear?" Mom sings and hops and claps as my dad fights a growing smile.

"Yes, dear, I heard."

"Then, react, you boar!"

As she continues to celebrate, my dad's gaze connects with mine.

"Does your decision have anything to do with Dash?"

Mom's dancing comes to an abrupt halt, and silence once more falls over the garage.

All the joy that filled me at telling my parents I wasn't leaving them drains out through my toes. What's left is a toxic mixture of anger, betrayal, and soul-pulverizing sadness.

"This has *nothing* to do with Dash." The venom in my voice shocks my parents.

At my dad's skeptical eyebrow raise, I feel a teaspoon amount of my anger redirect toward him. "Stop it, Dad. Don't you say another word about him being an ex-con. I've made my stance clear on that, and I haven't changed my mind. Disliking Dash because he committed a crime and paid for it is ridiculous. Now, disliking him because he's an asshole is a much more viable option."

"I could've sworn you cared for the boy." Mom's voice comes out breathy, laced with bafflement.

I snort. "I more than cared for him. That bastard got me to fall in love with him! That shithead had me opening up after Martin, and then he turns out to be just as bad. I mean"—an embarrassing hitch mars my words—"can any guy keep it in their pants? He waited a *week*"—I blink rapidly at the sudden pressure of tears behind my eyes—"or maybe not even that long—to jump into bed with another girl."

If I had told my parents I intentionally mowed down an old lady with Penelope, I doubt they would've looked more shocked and upset. My father's stern face creases deeply with his frown as his hands clench into white-knuckled fists. A fire smolders behind my mother's eyes as she glares off to the side at the poor Corvette like it was the man hurting me.

Her once-bubbly voice goes eerily quiet. "What happened?"

I swipe at my eyes and clear my throat a couple of times. "When I was in New York, I called him. Some random girl with a sexy voice named Luna picked up."

"Oh," they say, almost in unison.

At the immediate relaxing of my parents' stances, I get the sense I'm missing something important.

"*Oh*? That's all you've got?"

My mom shakes her head. "You think Dash is sleeping with Luna?" she asks as if she somehow knows Dash's newest fuck buddy.

"Well, yeah. That's what she told me."

A loud clatter sounds from the opposite side of the garage, and I worry something heavy may have fallen on Pumpkin. That thought skitters away immediately when I glance over to find a tall figure rising from between two of the cars.

All ability to think abruptly ceases when I come face-to-face with the man who most recently broke my heart.

CHAPTER 41

DASH

Luna's foot bounces along to the beat of the music pounding through the garage. From my spot under the Corvette, I can see her from the chest down. She leans against the wheel of an Impala parked next to the vehicle I'm working on.

When my sister demanded she come with me today, I didn't put up much of a fight. I figured Luna wouldn't be happy until she saw the garage and what I was doing in it. Good thing I slipped a book in my bag for her to read or else she'd be bugging me, bored out of her mind.

As she lifts the reading material from her lap to flip a page, I catch sight of the bright pink cover. The idea of her reading the book and Paige's scribbled notes makes me grin. Maybe Luna will start to see what I love so much about that awkward, amazing woman.

The music suddenly drops low enough that I can hear Mrs. Herbert moving around at her workbench. Pumpkin wanders into view, sniffing my pants, then nuzzling Luna's arm, demanding attention. My sister scratches the pit bull at the base of her thick square skull.

I pause, waiting to hear if Mrs. Herbert will call out a question or comment. She doesn't speak to me, but still, her words garner all of my attention.

"So, what's this talk, Paige?"

A shock wave quakes through my body, the wrench in my hand trembling with the force of it.

She's here.

After over two weeks of silence, I'm mere feet away from Paige.

As I try to come to terms with this fact, Luna leans down enough to meet my stunned gaze, her eyes just as wide with shock.

Her mouth moves in one silent word. *Paige?*

I may not have clarified exactly how I knew the Herberts.

I disregard my sister's disbelief as I listen to the conversation between the tiny family. Briefly, I consider making my presence known. But both Mrs. and Mr. Herbert know I'm here. For some reason, they don't feel the need to share that info with their daughter.

Quiet as I can, I roll out from under the car, listening.

I burst with pride as I hear her finally be honest with her parents about her need to stand on her own. My chest clenches when I think she'll be moving to NYC, then loosens in relief at her declaring she'll stay in NOLA. Shame heats my face when she says my name in obvious anger.

But none of those emotions compare to the level of shock that rockets through me when I hear exactly where her anger is rooted.

"He waited a week—or maybe not even that long—to jump into bed with another girl."

What the hell?

"What happened?" Mrs. Herbert's voice might as well be ice, and I wouldn't blame her sudden rage if what Paige said was true.

"When I was in New York, I called him. Some random girl with a sexy voice named Luna picked up."

My gaze locks on my sister, who suddenly finds it necessary to glare at her shoes. As my brain tries to catch up with this insane exchange, I miss a few words, but then Mrs. Herbert's question, the same one shouting in my mind, rings loud and clear.

"You think Dash is sleeping with Luna?"

"Well, yeah. That's what she told me." Paige's answer comes out in such a confused, devastated tone that it finally flushes energy back into my limbs.

I drop my wrench and lurch into a standing position.

When I catch sight of Paige, every bit of me tightens and pulls toward her. Just her presence is magnetic, and when I notice the stray tear tracking down her cheek, I can't handle even a car between us.

"You're here. Why are you here?" Paige's voice comes out panicked, and she backs away from me with her arms raised as I approach.

I try not to let the reaction break me.

"I'm helping your mom out with some cars. Paige, what did Luna say to you?"

Saying my sister's name was a mistake. Paige's frantic eyes harden to stone, and she crosses her arms over her chest, shielding herself from me.

"I called to talk to you and got her instead. She made it clear you were indisposed. I guess I really am naïve when it comes to men."

As I watch some of the hatred in her eyes turn self-directed, I get the urge to wrap my hands around my sister's throat.

"Luna! Get your ass out here!" I growl.

Paige stumbles back another step. "You brought your fuck buddy to my parents' house?"

"No! God, no. Just let me explain." I stalk over to where Luna is taking her sweet time standing up. Wrapping a firm grip around her arm, I drag her into the awkward confrontation. "Paige, this is Luna. My *sister*."

Paige's wild eyes flit between the two of us, probably taking in the family resemblance. Leo may be her twin, but we still look a hell of a lot alike.

"Your sister? But she…"

Instead of apologizing, like a decent human being would do, Luna goes on the defensive. "To be fair, I never actually said that we were sleeping together. You came to that conclusion on your own."

"You said Dash was in the shower, you were in his bed, and Cole left to give you privacy!" Paige rushes through the words, but I pick them all up just the same.

"What the fuck, Luna?" If I wanted to strangle her before, now, I want to take my time and then bury her in a shallow grave.

But my sister doesn't pay me any attention. She squares off with Paige, fists on her hips, brows drawn low in a dark scowl. "You broke my brother's heart! I wasn't just going to pass off the phone so you could do it again!"

Paige scoffs. "Broke his heart? *He's* the one who ended things with *me*!"

Luna's mouth bobs a couple of times before snapping shut. Then, she shifts her angry glare to me. "Then, Dash should've been clearer about the details. All I know is that I show up at his house, and he's a full-blown puddle of misery, asking me how to deal with a broken heart. I didn't realize he had done it to himself."

"Can you give us a minute?" I scowl at my sister, torn between fury at her interference and a twisted burst of love, knowing she was just trying to protect me. Seems like Paige isn't the only one with family members attempting to clean up messes for them.

"Fine. But if this ends badly, you'd better not start burning shit again." Luna stomps out of the garage, and Paige's parents make as if to follow her.

"No." Paige holds out a hand to stop them. "You're not going anywhere until you explain why my ex is helping you out with cars."

Her use of the word *ex* guts me, but I don't give up hope.

"You know I've been needing a strong set of hands." Mrs. Herbert massages her fingers as if they pain her. "And I knew Dash was going to need to earn some extra money."

"What?" Paige stares between the two of us, suspicion clear on her face.

"New York City is expensive." Once again, I've shocked her. This time, I hope she doesn't yell at me.

"We'll leave you two to figure things out." Mr. Herbert wraps his arm around his wife's shoulders, starting to lead her out of the garage. But he pauses by his daughter, resting a hand on her shoulder. "I admit, I may have misjudged the boy."

His intense eyes land on me for a moment, holding a weight I'm not afraid to shoulder. Mr. Herbert nods once, then exits with his wife.

Finally, the two of us are alone.

"I don't understand." As Paige gazes at me, she no longer holds anger or distrust in her eyes. She just looks lost.

The separation is too much for me to handle, so I approach cautiously, speaking in a soothing tone as if I can keep her from startling and backing away from me again. "I realized you were right. I was shoving away the things I loved. I thought they would tempt me into doing something rash, and I'd go back to jail." I shake my head at myself, just inches away from Paige now. "Except that's not exactly right. I was more scared I would get to have the things I loved, and then I'd lose them. That I'd lose *you*. I thought love made people do wild, reckless things."

She's within my reach, and this time, she doesn't flinch from my touch. My hands settle on her upper arms, smoothing over the soft cotton of her sweater, absorbing the heat of her skin as it seeps through the fabric.

"But that's not what love is." We're so close; my voice lowers to a hushed murmur, and Paige leans in close to catch the sound, her gaze focused on my mouth.

The sight of her entrancement fills me with satisfaction. I haven't lost her.

"What is love?" she whispers.

"Love is being there for someone. Being strong for them. Caring about their happiness. Supporting their hopes and dreams. Love isn't selfish. Love isn't fear." I swallow, the words heavy in my throat. "I haven't had much experience with it, and that's why I think I fucked it all up. But I want to show you how much I love you. The way you've been showing me."

I hope my guess isn't wrong. I'm rewarded with a grin brighter than high beams.

"You figured out I love you, huh?"

I wrap an arm around Paige's waist, pulling her flush against me. My other hand goes to cup the back of her head, tilting it at just the right angle for my mouth to tease hers.

Hell, I missed the heady taste of her lips against mine. But I don't sink into oblivion with her. A few more words need to be said.

"I'm sorry for hurting you. I only want to love you."

Paige blinks up at me. "You were planning on moving to New York?"

My nod brushes our noses, and she smiles so sweetly that my teeth ache.

"I can petition my parole officer to leave the state. But even if I was denied, parole doesn't last forever. When I'm a free man, nothing can stop me from being where you are."

Paige sighs and loops her arms around my neck. "Don't worry, Dash. I won't make you chase me. I fell in love with New Orleans almost as fast as I fell for you."

I have her. Not for just a moment. We belong to each other now.

Paige gives out a surprised squeak as I swoop down to kiss her neck, jaw, ear, and everywhere else I can reach without separating us. Every breathy laugh she lets out fuels the electricity pulsing through my veins.

My affectionate mauling of the woman I love is only interrupted when we're set off-balance by a heavy pair of paws landing on my back.

We pitch to the side, the two of us scrambling to keep upright. Then, Paige lets loose a happy peal of giggles as she crouches down.

"Seems like someone else wants to make sure she's not forgotten." I watch the two of them on the floor, my heart light and my jaw cracking from my grin.

Pumpkin huffs and wags her tail as she snuffles Paige's hair. My woman wraps her arms around the pit bull's neck, beaming up at me.

And in the two of them, I know I've found my family.

EPILOGUE

PAIGE

EIGHT MONTHS LATER

My lower back aches from sitting in one of those uncomfortable plane seats, and I pause halfway to my front door to press the heel of my hand into the offending vertebra.

What I need is my mattress.

And a shower. Hot water sounds like a sinful experience at the moment.

My keys jingle as I slide them into the door. I expect my arrival to set off a round of barking. Instead, I walk into an empty front hall. A blue glow filters from the back of the house.

Following the light, I come upon an adorable scene. Dash lounging on the couch, feet propped up on the coffee table, head lolling backward with his mouth slack and emitting gentle snores. Curled up at his side is my traitor of a dog. She barely acknowledges me, cracking an eye open for a moment, then falling right back to sleep. Reruns of *Top Gear* play at a low volume on the TV.

Leaving the two of them be, I sneak upstairs with my suitcase and head straight for the shower. Just as I expected, the steaming water is a glorious treat that eases most of the tension from my sore muscles.

With my clean hair wrapped in a towel, I go searching for some pajamas, almost tripping over a duffel bag on the floor of my bedroom. Inside is a haphazard collection of Dash's clothes. I grab one of his T-shirts, taking a deep sniff of the clean-laundry smell that usually mixes with the scent of motor oil after a day of him working in the shop.

I love that smell.

The fabric doesn't fully cover my ass, but I just grin at myself in the full-length mirror. Dash likes the way his shirts fit me.

Not bothering to blow-dry my hair, I comb it out and let it sit clean and damp on my shoulders as I make my way back downstairs.

The pair are still asleep. Copying my dog, I settle on Dash's other side, curling into him.

He starts awake, blinking sleep from his eyes as he gazes down at me.

"Paige?"

"That's me." I snuggle under his arm as he shifts to face me.

"Shit, when did you get here?" He rubs a rough hand over his face. "I was supposed to pick you up at the airport. What the hell is wrong with me?"

"Shh." I rub a soothing hand over his stomach, enjoying the way his muscles twitch under my touch. "You're fine. My last meeting got canceled, so I caught an early flight home."

Dash relaxes. "Tomorrow. I was supposed to pick you up tomor-row. Still, why didn't you call me?"

I smile up at him. "Because I thought you'd be asleep at your place. Did you stay here every night I was gone?"

He shrugs, his fingers fiddling with the ends of my hair. "I sleep better when I'm surrounded by your smell." Leaning in closer, he buries his nose in my damp hair, making me giggle and squirm.

"I sleep better next to you," I admit, which has him raising his head enough to grin down at me. "Move in with me." The words come out of my mouth on their own, but that doesn't mean I haven't been thinking them for months.

Dash's expression falters, and he searches my face with intensity. "I want to, but it's going to take a while for me to save up."

"Save up for what?"

Dash is a month into his new job as manager of a local mechanic shop. The decision to leave the rescue had been a hard one that we talked about for weeks, but he eventually decided to apply for the position. He still helps my mom out on weekends and swings by the rescue to volunteer a couple of times a week.

But now, he's getting paid for work that he's passionate about. And he's finally stopped referring to his love of cars as an addiction.

"To get us a bigger place," he says while his thumb brushes over my bottom lip.

"You want a bigger place?" I glance around the living room, taking in the green-painted walls and the street art I hung up randomly. Multiple pieces Dash took down, adjusted the nails, then rehung them so they sat straight.

Dash tilts his head as he stares down at me. "I don't care actually. But your parents' place..." He trails off, and clearly, we're both picturing that mansion Mom and Dad decided to make their home.

I shake my head, holding on to him with a firm grip. "I love this house. It's the first one I moved into all on my own."

This little place is maybe half the size of the clone house Martin picked out, but the minute I visited it, I fell in love. Doesn't hurt that there's a fenced-in backyard, perfect for Pumpkin.

"I don't want a new place. I just want you in this place. With me. All the time."

Dash's smile returns, and I enjoy watching it grow. "To be honest, it doesn't sound a lot different from what we have going on now."

I finger the edge of the shirt I'm wearing, and his eyes drop to my hands, apparently just realizing how exposed I am. "But all your clothes would be here. Which means I can steal more of them."

The chuckle Dash lets out is full of dark satisfaction. "How can I argue with that?"

"You can't." Finally, I tug his face toward mine to get a taste of him, what I've been craving for a week while in New York. There're thousands of restaurants in that city, but none of them have a dish as delicious as Dash.

He shifts to rise over me.

Behind him, I hear an annoyed huff, and the couch creaks as Pumpkin hops off. My dog glares at us before stalking out of the room.

"Oh no." I laugh. "Looks like you're going to have to make some apologies before you're allowed to move in."

Dash lays his body down on top of mine, tracing his hand up my thigh, only to plunge it under the loose fabric of my stolen shirt.

"Tomorrow. Tonight, I need to take care of my woman."

I relax under the heavy weight of him. Finally, I'm ready to let someone take care of me.

The End

***

Thank you so much for reading RESCUE ME. I hope you enjoyed Paige and Dash's love story! If you did, please consider leaving a review to help other readers find this book. Reviews mean so much to independent authors like me, and your kind words are an important part of the bookselling process. Thank you for being one of my readers!

Want more romance? Check out the next book in the Forget the Past series!

READ ME

Forget the Past book 2

Cole Allemand visits the library for the books, but he stays for the librarian. Summer Pierce is as bright and warm as her name, and he's been crushing on her for months. Cole is determined to get Summer to fall for him before she finds out the secrets of his past. The ones that could drive her away.

Keep reading for a sneak peek of *Fall Back Into Me*, a steamy contemporary rom com between a stuntwoman and a bodyguard. Join Harper as she finally faces the guy who used to be her best friend until he ghosted her without a warning…

FALL BACK INTO ME

FRED

SEVENTEEN YEARS OLD

We linger at the foot of the escalator that will take Harper Walsh up to the airport security line and out of my life.

"Don't go," I beg.

"Come on, Fred. Don't do this." Harper stands still in front of me. Quiet. Subdued. Not her. She's been this way for the past month, and now, she's leaving before I can get her—the real her—back.

"Me? *I* shouldn't do this? I'm not the one leaving!" My voice rises with my panic, and a security officer gives me a closer look.

Harper digs her fingers into my arm and drags me to a corner, glaring at me all the while.

Good. This is the first sign of life I've seen from her in weeks.

"That's right. I'm leaving. Stop making this harder than it already is." The cracks in her calm allow anger and desperation to seep through.

Those I can grab on to. Use to change her mind.

"But you don't have to go. You can live with Mom and Phoebe and me. Finish high school here. Go to college here. Your whole life is *here*." And my whole life is her. She's taking my life on a plane to Ireland.

I can't lose someone else I love this soon. This will break me.

"You three have each other," Harper says, and I stifle a flinch at the reduced number. "My mom needs me. And I need my mom." All the fire from a second ago dims, snuffed out by the wetness gathering in her eyes.

Oh no. She can't cry.

I can't take it when Harper cries. I'll give her anything to stop the tears.

"Please, Freddy. Just hug me and tell me to have a safe flight." She slides the strap of her duffel off her shoulder before opening her arms, begging me with her damp eyes.

"Motherfucking goddamn shit!" I mutter the profanities while wrapping her in a crushing hold.

The glorious sound of her laughter brushes against my ear as her strong grip hugs my neck.

Normally, I complain when she uses that annoying Freddy nickname. But what I wouldn't give for her to stay here and call me that every second of every day.

"It's not forever," Harper whispers.

Not forever, but it is for an undetermined amount of time. Do I have to wait a whole year to see the girl I love again when she's old enough to come back for college?

What guarantee do I have that she'll come back at all?

I can't let Harper leave without her knowing how I feel. How much she means to me. That she's my best friend, but every part of me wants us to be more. I should've been telling her all this time. Every day. Starting from when we were five years old and she shoved me off the swings at the playground and I fell for her in every way possible.

"I love you," I growl into the soft skin of her neck.

There. I said it. Now, she can't go because I'm the person she's supposed to spend the rest of her life with, who's going to love her forever. You can't leave that person. You can't just take a plane across an ocean and go to live on the opposite side of the world from your soul mate.

Harper releases her hold on me to cup my face with her hands. Tears trickle in uneven tracks to pool and drip from her chin, and her normally ivory-colored cheeks have gone blotchy red. She's an ugly crier. That makes me love her more.

"I love you too." Her words don't sound the same as mine did. Hers sounds like a goodbye. "I'll call you as soon as I get to my nan's place. And I'll text you the minute I get a phone over there."

She drops her hands to my arms, only to grip my wrists and unwrap my hold from her waist, sliding away from me.

"Please—"

Harper covers my mouth. Her skin is warm and smells like her favorite peppermint hand lotion. She stares me down, determined, even in her sorrow.

"I'm going now. It might be a while, but I'll see you again. I promise."

Harper steps back, grabbing her bag off the floor as she uses the sleeve of her sweatshirt to wipe away her tears. But she doesn't leave. Not yet. Instead, my friend waits, arms crossed, cheeks damp, staring at me with expectation.

I glare back at her. "Soon. You'll see me again *soon*."

The side of her mouth curves right before she plants a kiss on my cheek.

"Goodbye, Freddy."

I catch her hand as she goes to walk past me.

"Not goodbye." The words hurt and are harsh as they leave my throat.

Harper smiles and shrugs one shoulder. "See you soon then."

Her fingers slip from mine. My hand fists, grasping at the bit of warmth that was hers, hoping I can hang on to that small part of her at least.

The escalator carries Harper up and away from me. Just as she reaches the top, my friend turns at her waist to give a final wave. The last sight I have is of her silky crimson ponytail swinging when she turns and disappears from my view.

I wait.

Maybe she'll change her mind. Maybe I'll see her bright yellow

Converse sneakers sprinting down to me. Maybe she'll fling herself into my arms, declaring that leaving me is too painful to bear. Maybe her heart is breaking as much as mine.

But Harper doesn't come back.

She said she'd see me soon.

Apparently, soon means ten years.

To find out what happens next, read Fall Back Into Me…

Sign up for my newsletter for book news and freebies! All subscribers get a FREE copy of LOVE AND THE LIBRARY.

Get my free book:
https://www.laurenconnollyromance.com/free-book

ABOUT THE AUTHOR

Lauren Connolly is an award-wining author of contemporary and paranormal romance stories. She has lived among mountains, next to lakes, and in imaginary worlds. Lauren can never seem to stay in one place for too long, but trust that wherever she's residing there is a dog who thinks he's a troll, twin cats hiding in the couch, and bookshelves bursting with the stories written by the authors she loves.

www.ingramcontent.com/pod-product-compliance
Lightning Source LLC
Chambersburg PA
CBHW061642190726
48289CB00006B/1702